WHERE SHADOWS LIE

KATIE-LOUISE MERRITT

Katie-Louise Merritt

Where Shadows Lie

© Katie-Louise Merritt

Cover design © Sean Croft

First Edition June 2009
Second Edition Dec. 2009

Published by:
Palores Publications,
11a Penryn Street, Redruth, Kernow, TR15 2SP, UK.

Designed & Printed by:
The St Ives Printing & Publishing Company,
High Street, St Ives, Cornwall TR26 1RS, UK.

ISBN 978 1 906845 04 9

DEDICATION

For my sons, Mark and Jeremy with love

ACKNOWLEDGEMENTS

A very big thank you to my family and friends, and in particular, Enid Mavor and Wendy and John Carter, for their suggestions, advice and encouragement in the writing of this book.

My appreciation to the staff of Redruth Cornish Studies Library for their friendly assistance in tracking down details of local events, and references to the 2nd World War in Malaysia.

My gratitude to Richard Andrews for proof-reading and guidance on the initial draft, Michael Nicolinakos for his memories of the German occupation of Greece, and to Armina Ivey for her wonderful gesture of faith in me.

I would like to acknowledge the use of an amusing anecdote by Rex Ryder who, after several avenues of enquiry, I have been unable to trace.

Chapter One

January 1941

I CAME WITH the snow. Circumstance and the weather had conspired against her and Octavia, waiting and watching the thick flakes drifting down could take no pleasure from its crystal-iced beauty. In the grip of the first pains of childbirth, she knew there would be no chance now of her reaching one of the few beds allocated to civilians in the local hospital, for the snow lay deep with cars slewed across the road unable to negotiate the steep hill to the house. It was iron cold and the lifeblood of the land had slowed and was silenced beneath a sky bled to whiteness that obliterated the hedges and bowed down the branches of the elms that stood behind high walls at the foot of the field before her, beyond which, through the tree's frozen limbs was the stark outline of the old manor house of Nancarrow. It looked bleak and forbidding and she shivered, pulling her cardigan protectively around the swell of her unborn infant as she looked anxiously along the terrace for a sign of the district nurse. Turning from the window, she made her way from the iciness of the front room into the passage and down into the warmth of the kitchen of Greenview. It was a house that she had loved from the moment she saw it with its sweeping views that took the eye out over the fields from Marazion and along a thin blue line of sea, abruptly cut from vision by the trees of Nancarrow. Granite built in a terrace of seven with large bays and small arched attic windows below fretted gables and decorative finials, it had appealed to her senses as she stepped into its air of stability and permanence that fulfilled a deep and unconscious desire for constancy in a world of uncertainty.

Summoned by her neighbour, Mrs. Retallack, a District Nurse pushed her way purposefully through the drifts and fell panting and crimson cheeked through the back door into the kitchen. At the sight of her familiar and reassuring face, Octavia felt unexpectedly close to tears.

'Oh, thank God, you're here! I was so worried you wouldn't make it in time with all this snow. I've never been so glad to see anyone, in my life. I had nightmare visions, I'd be having this baby on my own!' she admitted with a strangulated laugh of relief.

'No fear of that, my dear,' Nurse Richards replied calmly. Where there's a will, there's always a way. Yesterday, it was on a tractor! It was quite an experience,' she said, as she took off her snow covered boots, dived into her black bag and produced a pair of regulation shoes.

Octavia had a sudden mental picture of the nurse's stout frame sitting atop a tractor, and smiled to herself as she hooked open the doors of the old range. There was a blast of banked up heat. 'Your feet must be frozen. Come and warm up by the fire,' she said.

Nurse Richards sat down heavily into the kitchen chair and pulling on her shoes then held her hands like a fan to the glow and rubbed them vigorously together. 'What a winter! This snow is becoming a nightmare for essential services and people having to get to work.'

'I know. Mr. Retallack, next door, is finding it very difficult to walk the hill with his gammy leg. He had polio as a boy, you know. His wife has been very kind keeping an eye on me. She offered to be of help if you needed her, but she has a little boy who is poorly with a chesty cough. I told her . . .' Octavia began, and then, caught in a spasm of pain, she doubled over, holding onto the table, her head dropping and breathing rapidly.

Nurse Richards moving from the chair with surprising agility gave Octavia a comforting clasp around the shoulders. 'How often are the contractions?'

'Every ten minutes,' she gasped. 'Does this mean it won't be long before the baby comes?' she asked, with a tremulous smile of ease as the pain subsided.

'It could do, but close contractions can go on for quite a while. It's not unusual. First babies have a way of taking their time.'

'Is that a fact! What bliss!' Octavia said in a weak attempt at humour.

'I know it's hard, my dear, but try and relax. Come and sit down and take deep breaths each time you feel the pain coming. I will make us both a nice cup of tea and then it's down to business.'

The thought of tea churned Octavia's stomach as she sank into the comforting familiarity of the wooden armchair with its soft cushioned back and seat, that stood in the corner by the range.

'There's plenty of hot water in the kettle, nurse, and the tea caddy is in the cupboard.'

Nurse Richards bustled around. 'You're the second mum for me in two days. It was Mrs. Bray at Trevarran Farm yesterday, where I trundled in on the tractor. She had a lovely baby boy. Image of his dad,' she said, as she located the cups and poured the tea. She glanced up at the window as the snow began to fall again, adding a further layer of white blanket to the window panes, and laughed. 'You young mothers certainly pick your times to have a baby!'

Late that afternoon, and wrong footing them both, Octavia panting from the final push and delivery of her baby, heard Nurse Richards give a sharp exclamation of surprise. 'My God! There's another on the way! You're having twins!'

Octavia gazed at her in astonishment from eyes framed with hair dishevelled and damp against her face. '*Twins*!' she cried. 'Are you sure?'

'I've never been more certain,' said Nurse Richards, hiding her dismay at this sudden unexpected delivery. Her voice was urgent. 'There's no time to waste. This baby is practically here, Octavia. Now, come on, my girl. A deep breath and one last push for king and country.'

'Bugger the king!' Octavia muttered as she hung onto the wooden bed rails. 'Never no more!' she avowed through gritted teeth and pain and with the last of her remaining strength she bore down and felt the quick slithering release.

Nurse Richards worked with a sureness born of experience, thinking of the number of times she had heard that vow, 'never again!' Always made and invariably broken. A woman who had not experienced childbirth herself, she found it a strange phenomenon, the pain that mothers could never recall. Nature was indeed a mystery and wonderful in its knowing.

There was a quiet in the room. I had not come lustily into the world. My entrance, as silent as the snow that covered this strange new kingdom of shapes and form. Octavia was instantly alert. Something was wrong. 'Are the babies alright, Nurse?' she asked, fearfully.

'You've had identical twin daughters, but I'm afraid, my dear, we've lost the first one. I'm so very sorry.'

'You mean . . .' Octavia's voice faltered . . .' she's died?'

'She was barely alive, and with no time for me to attend to her between the births . . .' her voice trailed away. Visibly distressed, she wrapped the second twin in a warm towel.

'I see,' said Octavia, struggling to digest the wild card thrown at her of life and death in an instant of time. 'Please don't blame yourself, Nurse,' she said, reaching out to touch her arm, as the nurse came to the side of the bed. 'It all happened so quickly. You couldn't have done any more. I can't believe I was carrying twins,' she half-spoke to herself. 'I could barely feel the movement of one, let alone two.'

'It sometimes happens that one baby lies behind the other and it's virtually impossible to detect two heartbeats,' Nurse Richards explained quietly, as she placed the infant in her arms. 'You have a lovely little daughter, Octavia, but be prepared. She's very, *very* small.'

Octavia was dumbfounded. The joy and love she had thought to experience died on her lips. Is this the best I can do? she thought, staring down at her damp and floppy infant whose skin was suffused with a bluish tinge that was beginning to turn a dark pink. Her head was bald and large, out of all proportion to her minute body with its matchstick arms and legs. Her finger and toe nails were transparent and her eyes shut beneath the merest suggestion of eyebrows and hair. 'Merciful Heaven! She's like one of those skinned rabbits you see hanging in the butchers!'

Nurse Richards smiled in spite of herself at Octavia's self-deprecating sense of humour. It was an apt description. 'Not what you expected, I know, but in time she'll fill out and grow to look like a normal baby, although I realise it's hard to believe it, right now.' Infants of three and a half pounds, in truth, were not a pretty sight. She had known mothers anticipating a normal bouncing baby to reject them out of hand.

Octavia, wrapping the towel back around her parcel of skin and bones, was filled with a mixture of fear and apprehension. How could anything this small survive?

Nurse Richards was also worried, covering her unease with action as she cleared away the signs of birth. She took pride in the fact that she had never lost an infant, although there was little else she could have done under the circumstances with this unforeseen baby arriving on the heels of her sister. Quietly, without a fuss, the flickering spark of life had faded and was gone. She gave Octavia a comforting pat on the hand as she plumped up the pillows and lifted her voice to a reassuringly bright level. 'She's very small, there's no getting away from it, but there's one big factor in her favour. She's full term and fully developed. Baby's going to be just fine.' But she knew her hold on life was tenuous and that the baby would need every ounce of her spirit to survive. The next twenty-four hours would be critical. The temperature in the room was barely warm, despite the fire that Octavia had kindled in the small grate following the breaking of her waters. A bed would have to be brought downstairs and a coal fire kept burning there, night and day. The infant would need round the clock feeding and the care of another nurse as well as herself. Time was of the essence and she would be with them every step of the way. She was *not* going to lose this one. Wrapping the infant in soft layers of blankets and placing a hot-water bottle near the still form, she encouraged the fire and drew the cradle in front of the heat.

'Have a little sleep now, my dear, whilst yet you may! I must be off, there's a lot to arrange and people to contact, and in particular the doctor. We're going to need him.' With a lightness of foot, she was out of the room, down the stairs and, with a bang of the door was gone.

But although Octavia was weary she could not sleep. The arrival of twins had thrown her off balance, she needed to think and collect her thoughts. She looked over at the cradle where her infant lay still and silent and bearing no resemblance to the pink and white babies she had seen gurgling happily in their prams with their proud mothers. Her thoughts shied from taking her out in a pram. She was ugly. She could hardly bare to admit it, and felt immediate guilt to have harboured such a thought of her own flesh and blood. She lay thinking of the other tiny form in her shroud of a cot sheet that Nurse Richards had taken away with a quiet dignity. 'You poor little thing,' she murmured. Picking up a photo of James smiling at her from his silver frame at her bedside, she was suffused with a longing to see him, to comfort her in the loss of their infant daughter and to share the anxiety she felt for her twin whose life hung by a thread. *Why aren't you here, James? I need you beside me.*

She had had so little of him, just three short weeks following his return from his tour as a mining engineer in Malaya. Company policy did not permit wives to join their husbands on their first three year assignment and it had been a long and lonely wait for the start of their life together in Malaya. She had been eagerly looking forward to returning with him to the mining camp and then Hitler had thrown his terrifying spanner into their plans. She sighed, and picked up his photo. Those few days with him were as distant as a dream that she couldn't quite recall. She held it close, as if, by the holding, she could materialize his voice, the scent of his skin, his touch, but he was elusive and shadowed as the woods they had walked, when her joy to re-discover and recapture that first happiness with James had been marred with disappointment. He was distracted, distant. In the chilly evenings with the fire lit, they'd sat in its flickering warmth and Octavia listened and experienced through James's eyes the vibrant colours, the clamour and vitality of life in the Far East. And all the while he talked, she felt a disquiet and wondered. Is it fear that holds him back? A premonition he cannot voice? Or, she hardly dared the thought, could it be an entanglement? . . . No, surely not that . . . ? The unbidden suspicion was dismissed in nights of consuming love when she had clung to him with a desperation born of fear, and just as she was beginning to feel he was hers again, sharing the laughter at his flashes of wit and dry humour, he was gone to a war that took lives with impunity. She, too, must face the unthinkable. What if he never returned to see his daughter? Jonathon, his friend, so fired with life had been snatched out of the skies in this war that she knew would not end quickly, no matter what people were saying. Her eyes returned to the cot, to her scrap of life that on first sight seemed barely human. She slipped from her bed and bent close to the half hidden face muffled up with the blanket and felt a surge of pity and compassion. She gave the baby's cheek the softest stroke of her finger, almost afraid to touch her. Was there the faintest breath of air? She could not tell. She spoke softly to her. 'You are going to have to fight for life, Elizabeth, just as your father is doing, and together we shall win,' and in bed with tears threatening, she finally gave way to them. She wept for James and Jonathon, for the loss of her twin and for her infant, barely of the world. She cried for them all. Spent and exhausted, she slipped into the oblivion of sleep and into the silence of the room came a valedictory light that shone over me with her promise. *'I will always be with you.'*

Chapter Two

HER SISTER MAY summoned from work and crunching her way up the hill to look after Octavia was, on seeing the baby, struck dumb that anything so small could be born and survive. Concealing her shock, she expressed her delight to Octavia on becoming an aunt. Privately, she wondered how long she would be remaining one as she began to sort out the sheets and blankets before going downstairs to Mr. Retallack who, having assembled the single bed in the front room, was now, on particular instructions from Nurse Richards, banking up a fire, it seemed, halfway up the chimney.

'I'll say cheerio, then,' he said. 'Missus will be in to see the babe in a few days, I expect, once Terry is over his cold. I shan't be able to keep her away.'

'Of course, and thank you for all your help,' said May, gratefully.

With the fire burning brightly and the curtains drawn against the night, the room was warm and inviting and had taken on the air of a nursery. A teddy sat at the foot of the lace-edged cot by the fire, and towels and cot sheets stood draped over the clothes horse. In the alcove by the fire was a table covered by a white fluffy towel that held a much loved china wash basin and jug that had come from their mother's house; the hand painted flowers bringing a breath of summer to the room. To the uninitiated, there were surprising items: olive oil, packets of cotton wool, a premature baby's feeding bottle and a breast pump, discreetly covered. It would be many months before Octavia would enjoy that particular scent of a baby mingling with Johnson's soap and talcum powder that lay on the table, or to hear May's gift of a silver rattle shaken by a tiny hand. For now, it hung by a white ribbon inside the cradle.

'Have you thought of a name yet?' asked May, as she came into the room with cups of tea and slices of seed cake. Perching herself on the edge of the bed, she passed a cup to Octavia.

11

'I thought I would call her Elizabeth after our mother,' she answered, softly.

'I like that,' said May, her eyes glistening with sudden tears, and Octavia said no more, except to suggest that she sleep in the back bedroom away from the buffeting winds from the sea.

In the front room, Octavia and Elizabeth spent their days and nights, the snow outside cloaking any sounds and sign of movement. The birds too, were silent, conserving their energy for the fight for the scraps that Octavia threw out onto the snow of the courtyard at the back from which steps led up into the garden, before refilling the coal bucket from the wash house and returning into the warmth and life of the fire. Her teeth chattered as she threw on a shovelful to keep it burning brightly for Elizabeth who lay silent and motionless, her eyes the only sign of movement in her cradle. The intense brightness of the snow illuminated the walls and the white plasterwork frieze around the room, and the ceiling rose, so that each fern and flower was sharply defined within the encircling fretted plaster work. Octavia felt as if she were in a white cocoon. As if the clock had stopped and there had never been a time without her baby. Her love and amazement at her tenacity to live, grew, as her infant struggled for life, emitting an occasional death-gurgling rattle. To the unsuspecting ear, it was unnerving.

On first hearing the rattle, May, quietly curled up in the armchair reading a magazine, shot out of her chair, looking down at Elizabeth in horror. 'Oh my *Lord*, Octavia! She's gone!'

'It's alright, May, this is quite normal,' said Octavia, amused at her electrified reaction. 'She's just struggling for breath when drinking her milk.'

May, plump and sweet faced, sank back into her chair. 'I've never heard anything like it. Do all babies make such a ghastly noise?'

'I shouldn't think so.'

'It frightened the life out of me.'

'I know. It's awful isn't it? But at least I know she's still alive!'

The room settled down to a comfortable silence again and Octavia was thoughtful as she continued feeding Elizabeth.

'I've been thinking, May.'

May looked up from the Woolton recipe she was reading.

'This war could go on for years and with us both on our own, it would make sense if you were to stay on here with me. I remember you saying you were hoping to find somewhere better to rent or buy, once Ted returned. This could solve the problem for the time being. We could combine rations and share expenses and I'm sure . . .'

'What a marvellous idea,' interrupted May, her hazel eyes alight. 'I know Ted wouldn't mind. He'd be only too pleased for us to keep each other company.'

'That's just what I was about to say before you butted in,' smiled Octavia at her characteristic quick decision, an endearing, if at times, exasperating part of May. She had, on many occasions, smoothed feathers ruffled by her impetuous reaction to situations. The last being her whirlwind romance and marriage to Ted, that took place shortly before he was called up. On that particular decision, she had heartily approved of the rapid arrangements for she had known and liked Ted Curtis for many years as she went in and out of the bank, and exchanged pleasantries with him across the counter. A few years older than May at nineteen, and with a reassuringly solid build and easygoing manner, she felt he would be a stabilizing influence after the horrific death of their mother that had left them both traumatised.

It was getting dark, and with Octavia last on her list for a visit, Nurse Bowden, as thin and bony as Nurse Richards was rotund, and who shared the twice daily care of Elizabeth, was ready for a warm room and a gossip. She knocked on the door and entered the kitchen.

'H-e-l-l-o' she called out as she stamped the snow off her feet and taking off her boots and coat, put on her apron and shoes.

'I'm in the front room feeding Elizabeth,' Octavia called back, pleased to hear her voice that lifted Octavia's spirits with her fund of anecdotes and mimicry, from her round-the-clock daze of two hourly feeds that were long and tedious, for Elizabeth sucked only weakly and slowly from her bottle.

Octavia smiled up at her as she entered the room and looked down on her charge, before sitting in the chair opposite beside the fire. She chatted for a few minutes about Elizabeth and then proceeded to the latest goings-on in the village, which for Octavia, confined to the house, brought a sense of normality to her world shrunk to feeds and sleep and the constant vigil of her skinned rabbit.

'May not home yet from Holmans?'

'No, she's on afternoons this week. Last week she was on the graveyard shift. It's a killer. She told me she fell asleep at her machine. That really worried me. The girls put the safety barrier around it and let her kip for a while during their break.' Octavia frowned. 'She's very young to be doing such work, but there was no stopping her, and I think she enjoys being 'one of the girls.'

'What exactly does she do?'

'She makes aircraft parts. After the noise and racket of the machine shop and then walking the hill, she arrives home dead beat, but her first thought is always for Elizabeth. She dotes on her, although she's still nervous of picking her up and leaves that to me.'

'It's a common fear when handling a baby as small as Elizabeth,' Nurse Bowden replied, pushing her toes closer to the heat of the fire, her eyes steadfastly on the infant, her thoughts private. How strong the will to live. She would not have given her a whisper of a chance. She gave Octavia an old fashioned look, amusement in her eyes. 'I saw Denzil the other day.'

'Oh did you? What's he been up to now?' smiled Octavia, suspecting that Nurse Bowden was not a little sweet on him, for his name frequently crept into conversations. As the local postman and living a few doors away from her, he popped in from time to time, keeping her up to date on the welfare of the elderly and regaling her with yarns heard on his country rounds.

'He was telling me that before the snow came, he took the West Briton and a few letters out to Mr. Croker's farm on the back road there, between Troon and Falmouth. It was bitterly cold and Missus called him in for a cup of tea to warm up and in the course of chatting, said that their old gander had died and they'd just heard a replacement was in Camborne station waiting to be picked up. She wondered if Denzil could help them out and pick it up later that day in his post van. He agreed, and arrived back at the farm and let it loose in the yard, after which, Mrs. Croker invited him in and plied him with gallons of tea and a mountain of treacle and cream splits – she dearly love er belly – and home he went fit to bust. Next morning, he called to the farm as usual, went through the farm gate, and was just crossing the little bridge over the stream when Missus come hollering down the field. "AW! Postie, don't ee cum no further. That new gander is a heller! We've ad some time, widdin. He went let nobody cum near the plaice. He wouldn't let Percy cum home from work, or the cheel home from school, and this morning, ee chaised the baker away – I abben got no brade! – and I've ad to shut'n in. Don't ee ever cum no further if ee's about."

Nurse Bowden pressed her lips, holding in her amusement. 'The next time he went there, was the day of the newspapers and there was no sign of the gander or Missus, so he decided to risk it. "In a minute," he said, "that ole gander, he caught sight of me, and come flying out the yard and down the field like streak of lightning with his neck stretched out and his wings flappin and screechin like a banshee. So I rolled this great Guardian up, stepped to one side, and whack'n across the ear-ole, with this yer paper, an his head went all the way round, and ended up in the other direction! He *skittled* to a stop, and give me some look. Now, you just git on with that me ansome!" I said, and the gander made off down to the stream, and he's never had a bit a trouble with him ever since.'

'You ought to be on the stage,' Octavia said, laughing, as she placed Elizabeth in Nurse Bowden's arms. 'That yarn deserves a cup of tea and a piece of May's sponge cake. I wish I had his nerve when I visit the farm here for cracked eggs. They've got ganders, too, and I'm mortally afraid of them. Their peck can be vicious. They're better than any guard dog.'

'Denzil said, you have to stand up to them, but I've met a few on my rounds and that's easier said than done. One woman he knows, grabs them behind the head, swings them around and lets fly! Her daughter said, when she was a little maid, she thought that's why ganders had such long necks! Children say the funniest things.' Nurse Bowden chuckled away as Octavia went into the kitchen to put the kettle on and warm the oil for Elizabeth. On her return, Nurse Bowden unwrapped Elizabeth onto a soft folded blanket and towel on the table, and began with large, deft hands to stroke the oil soaked cotton wool onto her skin.

Octavia stood for a moment, watching. 'How you manage to keep hold of her, I shall never know. She's slippery as an eel with that oil. If I did it, she'd end up on the floor!'

15

'Practice makes perfect,' smiled Nurse Bowden as she continued oiling the baby's matchstick arms and legs, and every nook and cranny as Octavia disappeared back into the kitchen. She covered the infant with a tiny piece of flannelette that served as a nappy, and left it folded around and unpinned for there was never a flicker of movement to disturb the cloth and laying her in the white wicker cradle that stood directly in front of the fire, she whispered, 'Did you like my story Elizabeth? Do you think it cheered mummy up?' Two eyes stared steadily back at her. Noticing that the fire was getting low, she shook the scuttle and shovelled some coal over the murmuring flames. 'And there's a fortune going up the chimney keeping you warm, my girl, so don't imagine for one minute, you can fade away on us, because it isn't going to happen,' she added, with a determined look as Octavia returned with a pot of tea.

Chapter Three

THE SNOW HAD melted, gathering speed with the first rays of brittle sunshine and sliding away from the rooftops and dripping droplets under the trees where the snowdrops had stood with their promise of spring. May, damp and glowing from her trek up the hill, burst in through the kitchen door to find Octavia making pasties. 'Oooh lovely, pasties. I'm starving. I'm just going to have a quick look at Elizabeth, before I tell you the latest big news!' and before Octavia could say a word, she was up the passage and into the front room. Octavia continued crimping, listening to May's murmurings at Elizabeth. 'How's our little skinned rabbit, today? Have you been a good girl and taken all your milk? When you've grown a bit, and the weather bucks up, mummy and I will take you for a walk in the pram.' As if aware of May's voice though her sleep, there was the faintest stretch of movement from the cradle and she bent over and dropped a soft kiss on her forehead before returning to the kitchen, and hanging her mac on the back door, flopped down into the chair by the range.

'So, what's this big news, then?' asked Octavia.

'You'll never believe it. They told us today that the King and Queen are coming to Holmans!'

'Oh, when?'

'Sometime next year.'

'Next *year!* That's a bit of a way off, isn't it?'

'I suppose these things take time to arrange. We've been told they will be coming around the factory to see what we do, and everything will have to be spick and span. I said to my friend, Vi, if they stop by me, I shall just die! Our supervisor said that we have to call them mam and sir, and if asked a question about our work, to answer to the best of our ability, although I wouldn't put Dot past asking a question or two herself. Nothing fazes that one. Do you remember her? She used to be in my class.'

Octavia nodded. 'I seem to recall she was always a bit fast.'

May gave Octavia a knowing look. 'Yes, she was. Thought she was in the family way, once. Turned out she wasn't, which is probably just as well, as she hadn't a clue who the father was!'

Octavia chuckled at May's pithiness. 'A visit from King George will give the town a lift. One thing about our royal family, they don't do a runner when the going gets tough. They know where their priorities lie, which is more than one can say about his silly brother and that ghastly woman of his, if the rumours are to be believed,' she said, as she placed the pasties on the sheath and pushed them into the kitchen range. She took the pastry board to the sink and began washing it down. 'Dr. Lewis popped in today, and said that Elizabeth is progressing well, and unless something untoward happens, he will now leave everything to the nurses. I shall miss his visits. I've thought more than once, what providence it was having a consultant physician living nearby. I don't know how we would have coped without him when we were snowed in. He was so down-to-earth, I felt I could ask him anything. He had a calm way which was very reassuring.'

'Yes, he's a lovely man. It's good news about Elizabeth, but did he say when she will finally start to move around in her cot or to cry for her feeds?'

'He said, we just have to be patient. It will happen in its own good time, and then, like you told Elizabeth, we shall be able to show her there's a world outside.'

'I can't wait to show her to the girls at work. I'm sure I must bore them to death, but they are forever asking for progress reports. They think it's amazing that a baby so small, can survive.'

'Another month will tell a different tale, I expect, and you'll have your wish to take her out.'

And in that, Octavia was right; it was April and life was burgeoning as was Elizabeth who, clinging on with a tenacity at which she could only marvel, gathered strength and slowly grew. Weighed each day on the kitchen scales, and lying in them as easily as a bag of sugar, each small weight gain they celebrated with as much jubilation as news of a gain by the allies. Nurse Richards and Nurse Bowden continued to call and oil her, and still she lay silent and motionless.

'I think we're finally winning, my dear,' Nurse Richards said one blustery May morning, looking down fondly at Elizabeth who lay under her lace-edged coverlet. The faintest sheen of gold glinted on her head and two eyes stared back intently at her. 'It's time you stirred your stumps, my lady,' she said. Within the week, responding to her clarion call, Elizabeth began to move, mewing for her feeds like a kitten, and giving an imitation of a kick with her matchstick legs.

Although no longer needed, Nurse Richards continued to pop in to see Octavia for a strong bond had formed between the women from their shared experience and against all professional instincts, she had grown to love Elizabeth. At six months, their long wait was rewarded. Elizabeth weighed in at a comfortable seven pounds.

'At *last*, I can take her to the clinic, like other mothers do, and make arrangements to have her christened Elizabeth after my mother, God rest her soul,' said Octavia with a fleeting sadness in her eyes.

They drank a cup of celebratory tea, and clinked cups. 'To Elizabeth,' said Nurse Richards, her eyes bright with unspoken affection. 'May she always be happy and healthy and grow up to be a little bigger than she is now!'

Octavia lifted her doll of a child up in her arms. 'For a baby, so minute, she gave me such a fright the other day. I heard this noise coming from her cot. I raced to the room and found she had managed to slide down and her little feet were drumming away on the bottom cross bar.'

'She's making up for lost time,' replied Nurse Richards giving Elizabeth a tickle under her chin. 'How's my li'l luvver, then?' she said, affectionately.

'Come on Kitty, give Nurse one of those smiles of yours.'

'Kitty?'

'May's nickname for her after Elizabeth finally started to cry. Said she sounded just like a kitten. I'm not really one for nick names but I like this. It suits her.'

'Well, it's certainly an improvement on skinned rabbit!' said Nurse Richards dryly, and Elizabeth, her wispy hair brushed up into a shining quiff of a curl, yawned and blinked in the sunlight, and gave her a golden smile.

Chapter Four

IT WAS HOT and sultry, and May, weary from walking the hill and from hours of queuing in the town, was surprised to see as she entered the terrace, a platoon of men in the field in front of their house. She walked self-consciously along the terrace, feigning disinterest to their side-long glances, and looked up at Octavia who sat sewing in the bay of the front bedroom window, seemingly oblivious to the commotion in the field. May turned into the entry by the side of the house, and entering, dropped her groceries, and putting the kettle on, came up the stairs and dropped exhausted into the chair opposite Octavia. The room was warm and light from the sun streaming in and with its open views to the coast, they gravitated to it on long summer evenings and sat reading or chatting until the sun sank in a blaze of orange and gold over St. Ives.

May nodded in the direction of the men in the field. 'Where did they spring from?'

'I don't know. I suppose they must be billeted, nearby.'

'Gosh, they must be hot in those uniforms,' said May, watching the men marching up and down the field, their young faces fresh and open, as yet, unmarked by the reality of combat.

Octavia glanced up at them from the dress she was altering. 'Yes . . . they've been at it for a while now.'

'No news from James, I suppose?'

Octavia gave a little sigh, 'No, not yet.'

'I've been so lucky to have had letters from Ted in North Africa. I read them over and over again. Without them, I think I'd go insane.' She leaned over and gave Octavia a sympathetic touch on her arm. 'I'm sure you will hear soon. When you think about it, we seem to have heard very little as to what's going on in the Far East, and with the bombings around the country, I'm amazed we get any post at all.'

Octavia struggled to move her thoughts away from James. 'I hope Alice is alright.'

'She's fine. When I popped in to see dad today, he said, he'd finally had an official postcard from the Red Cross in Greece, but you should have heard him grumbling. "Your sister had her pick from the whole of Camborne, not to mention the Mining School, but *no*, she had to go and marry a *Greek* mining engineer! Now, she's stranded in an occupied country and why didn't she have sense enough to come home to the family at the start of the troubles where she would be safe?"

'He has a point, but he always did get het up over Alice. The anointed one.'

May grinned at her mutual understanding.

'The problem is, he knows only too well the horrors of war, but nobody's immune. Look at our Phoebe – already been bombed out in Plymouth. I think it's best for the moment if we keep quiet on that one. Dad's worked up enough as it is with the worry of Alice. I wonder what this hush-hush business is, that Phoebe's doing?'

'Heaven only knows. Even if she could tell us, she wouldn't. You know how close she can be, always was, even when we were children. I used to think it was because she was the eldest, and me being the baby of the family, I musn't be told anything. Now, I know, it's just the way she is,' said May, idly watching the men. A flicker of a smile crossed her face. Octavia gave her a questioning look. 'Just a silly idea,' she said, and with that went out of the bedroom and returned with a mop. The Drill Sergeant with a pace stick tucked neatly under his arm, stood square backed and crisp and could be clearly heard through the open window as he brought the men to a halt and barked out for them to present arms.

May, standing in the centre of the window followed suit, throwing her mop from shoulder to shoulder where it slipped from her hand and clattered to the floor. Recovering it, she beamed a flirtatious smile on a boyish soldier in the first row, who, straining to hide his amusement, turned beetroot.

'May, sit down. You're making that poor boy blush. If the sergeant turns around and sees you . . .' said Octavia, entertained in spite of herself at May's high jinks.

'Well, what can he *do* about it? Confine us to barracks? Come on, Octavia. Leave your sewing for once.' She playfully attempted to pull her out of the chair. 'Be a sport. Stand and salute, or something. It's only a bit of fun, the lads will love it.'

Infected with May's bubbling spirits, and in need of light-hearted diversion from her troubled thoughts, she threw caution to the wind and standing like a ramrod, saluted the squad standing to attention. A soldier gave a quick broad grin and winked, his face at once becoming devoid of expression on the sergeant's stare with a look of one who had seen it all before.

'Something amusing you, Foster?' he bellowed.

'No, SUH!' he roared back, his eyes glued to the head of his mate in front of him.

The drill continued, and May dissolved into giggles at Octavia, who by now thoroughly into the mood of the moment, marched on the spot, swinging high her arms and legs and mischievously laughing at the men's stifled smirks at the sight of two women in a window taking the Micky.

The sergeant was uneasy. Hairs had begun to prick at the back of his neck with the finely honed instinct of one being watched. Something behind him was unsettling the men who gazed straight ahead at his hard stare. He swung around.

Caught unawares, Octavia and May dived to the floor in a laughing tangle of arms and legs.

The sergeant's eyes ranging over the houses, caught a tale end glimpse of them. Damn and blast. Women! He might have known. This distraction had to stop. He turned and walked briskly out of the field.

A stir passed through the ranks as he began advancing along the terrace. 'What the hell is he doing?' muttered one of them under his breath. 'Flipping 'eck! He's marching towards the girl's house. He's never going to their door . . . ?' he exclaimed, echoing the thoughts of the squad. A breath of relief rippled through their ranks as he stopped and planted himself on top of the hedge.

'You are here,' he bellowed, 'to become soldiers. Lack of discipline, such as I have seen today, will not be tolerated under my command. There's a war on, in case you hadn't noticed, and I have the unfortunate task of making you sad and miserable specimens of manhood into a fighting machine. And by God! That's what I'm going to do. There will be times when you will hate my guts, and would like to kill me. That is good. That is the instinct you will need to win this war. You will drill at the double and all weekend's passes are cancelled.' There was a collective groaning sigh. 'By the left, double march,' he roared.

'Do you think he saw us?' May whispered.

'I think he must have,' Octavia whispered back, 'and I think we're to blame for the cancelled weekend passes.'

'Oh Lord. I feel awful. It's my fault.' May chortled suddenly at the absurdity of them on all fours. 'Honestly. We're like a couple of kids and why are we whispering to each other? He can't hear us.' She crawled to the curtain and hiding behind it, peered down. 'Octavia! The sergeant's moved. He's standing on our hedge.'

'Oh, he's *not*, is he?' she exclaimed, as she joined May and watched the men panting around the field in front of the sergeant who now had their undivided attention, standing with his feet planted firmly apart and whisking his pace stick up and down behind his back.

'He's running those poor lads into the ground,' said May, as he brought them to a near collapsing halt and gave the order to march out of the field. He jumped down and to their chagrin acknowledged his awareness of their presence with the briefest touch of his pace stick to his cap.

'Somehow, I have a feeling that will be the last we shall see of the drill sergeant and his men,' said a sobered-up Octavia. 'It's time we went downstairs, in any case. Kitty's feed is due.'

'Oh my giddy aunt! The kettle!' May cried out with alarm. 'I put the kettle on for tea.' Dashing out of the room, she flew down the stairs to the kitchen to find it bone dry and blackened.

May, hunting through the old hatbox of Christmas decorations, found a packet of balloons, and was relieved to find they had not perished. She began blowing them up as Octavia stood beating together the margarine, sugar, eggs and fruit that had been hoarded for weeks for Elizabeth's birthday cake.

'I'll make some sandwiches tomorrow with the eggs that are left. There should be just enough bread to make a round or two. Is Vi coming up with you from work?' she asked May, whose face was pink from the effort of blowing up the balloons.

'Yes.' she gasped. 'She wouldn't miss it for the world.'

'So there will be six of us, not counting Kitty. Just a nice number around the table,' said Octavia.

May continued blowing. 'Doing this always makes my ears hurt . . .'

'But for Kitty, you would do it even if your ears burst,' smiled Octavia.

May grinned back. 'I'm so glad I'm on early shift and can be home for her birthday tea. I was chatting to Mrs. Retallack yesterday, on our way up the hill, and she told me Terry is very excited to be invited and had been helping his daddy to make a little doll's cot for Elizabeth from wood in the shed. Isn't that kind of him?'

'Yes, it is. What a wonderful surprise for Kitty. She will love it for her teddy. Do you remember how it was bigger than she was, when she was born? And the teddy was small to begin with.'

'Yes, I do, only too well. I've never said this before Octavia, but when I first saw her, I had my doubts that she would survive. Looking at her now, it's still hard to believe she was only three and a half pounds at birth.'

'I know. Sometimes, I find it hard to believe, myself. She took some rearing!'

'Not half,' laughed May. 'And now, here she is, nearly two and having a birthday party and inviting a little friend around.' May gasped, in between sucks of air. 'Terry will be someone to play with when she's older. And right next door.' There was a pause as she pulled a face and her ears popped. 'I'm glad Nurse Richards will be able to come. She will certainly see a difference in Kitty. It's a shame though that Nurse Bowden won't be able to make it.'

'Yes it is. I don't know what I would have done without them both. Nurse Bowden *was* funny. She could mimic anyone and the yarns she used to tell with that mobile face of hers,' said Octavia as she spooned the mixture into the tin, hooked open the oven door and pushed it into the range. On the table stood dishes of red, orange and yellow jellies and rough chopping them up, she scooped them into a cut-glass bowl that made an appearance on such occasions, and stirred and mixed them together. Picking it up, the colours a shining rainbow through the facets, she took it to the front room, standing it on the marble mantelpiece that served as a cooler. May came into the passage, her hands full of balloons, as Octavia shut the front room door behind her, shivering. 'It's like a morgue in there.'

'Can you give me a hand with these, and do you know where the drawing pins are?'

'In the sideboard drawer, I think,' replied Octavia, as they went into the sitting room, and pushing the furniture back, began hanging up the balloons.

On the arrival of the dress for Kitty's birthday from James's parents in Canada, May had been ecstatic. 'Oooo! Octavia, isn't it beautiful? Kitty will look like one of those china dolls we used to see in boxes and wished we could have when we were children. Do you remember?' she said.

'Yes, I do. It certainly is lovely,' Octavia replied, turning the dress over and examining the needlework. 'It's machine-made but beautiful. James's mother wrote what a big selection of children's clothes they have out there. Mind you, they haven't got a war on their doorstep. It's a very tiny size. She's obviously taken note of my letter saying how small Kitty is. And just look at this coat and bonnet and these fine wool lacy leggings,' she said, holding them up. 'Have you ever seen anything so dainty, and warm?' She picked the dress up again, fingering its lace. 'I shall have to try and get a photo taken of Kitty wearing it and send it to them. They must wish they could see her. It's a pity they are so far away.'

'Yes, it is, but at least they're not having to endure this war with all its shortages.'

Kitty sat in her high chair, flushed with excitement, her eyes bright as the candles on the cake that Octavia brought into the room as they all began singing. May lifted her up and held her over the candles, smoothing down her gift of the blue smocked-velvet dress with delicate trimmings of white lace.

'Now Kitty, you must blow all your candles out, like this.' May pursed her lips and blew gently onto her face. Kitty smiled shyly, self-consciously lifting her shoulder and tilting her face away.

'We'll blow them together with mummy, shall we?' May dropped her gently back into the chair as everyone clapped and the doorbell rang.

'You answer the door, May, I'm just going to spoon up the jelly.' In the overcast gloom of a sky threatening rain, the telegram boy stood there. May felt life drain from her as she took the envelope. It was addressed to Octavia. She closed her eyes and swallowed with guilty relief. Composing herself, and full of foreboding, she slipped the envelope into her dress pocket and returned to the sitting room.

'Who was that?' asked Octavia.

'Tell you after tea,' May replied.

Octavia felt a shiver of fear run down her spine.

The party over, Octavia busied herself fetching coats from the hall and was unable to shake a feeling of dread as she saw everyone to the door. May was similarly fearful and conscious of the envelope in her pocket as she cleared the remains of the tea and took them into the kitchen where Octavia followed her with Kitty in her arms. 'It's time, Aunty May, for a little birthday girl to give you a kiss before going to bed,' she said, holding her out to May.

'Night, night sweetheart,' she said, kissing her. 'See you in the morning.'

Octavia returned as May was drying the dishes. 'I thought it went off very well, didn't you?'

'Yes, it was a lovely little party. Octavia, I have something for you.' She held out the telegram.

'Oh my God, May,' she said, her hands trembling as she ripped open the envelope.

The War Office regrets to inform you that your husband Captain James Treneer has been killed in action. Octavia's face drained of colour. 'I knew it. I felt as if someone had walked over my grave when you went to the door,' she said, handing it to May.

Chapter Five

OCTAVIA STOOD IN the butcher's queue, looking cold and pinched. Her navy coat fell softly around her, the padded shoulders accentuating her slim figure. A navy felt hat sat jauntily on her short bobbed hair with a small red feather in the encircling band, and her innate flair for colour and style was displayed with a silk scarf of bright red poppies, a statement of her rebellion to the weather and circumstance. The October air was raw and she bent with an anxious look to tuck the blanket more closely around Elizabeth sitting in the pushchair. She felt a touch on her shoulder.

'Hello, Octavia. How are you these days? Isn't it bitter?'

Octavia, drawing herself up from the pushchair was momentarily taken aback.

'Oh, *Hello, Jack,* how are you? Dad said you were home from Leicester. Yes, it is cold, isn't it, especially waiting here in the queue.' She nodded at the butcher behind the plate glass window. 'I hope the little he has will be worth the wait. How was army life?'

Jack gave a self-conscious chuckle with a shrugging up and down of his shoulders that Octavia remembered well. 'Hectic. I think the Pay Corps had had enough of me, so they sent me home!' His eyes were sympathetic. 'I was so sorry to hear about James.'

She briefly glanced away. 'Thank you Jack. Life has to go on, doesn't it, and this one keeps me on my toes,' she said, nodding at Elizabeth.

Jack could not bear the passing look of pain and made a show of Elizabeth sitting up under the hood of her pushchair. 'She's lovely Octavia. How old is she, now?'

'She'll be three next January. She's growing away so quickly. It's hard to believe how small she was when she was born.'

'Yes, I've heard a lot about her from her grandpa.'

Octavia's face lit with pleasure. 'He thinks the world of her. He was rather hoping for a boy, but girls seem to run in our family, don't they? I'm afraid she's going to be very spoilt,' she replied, smiling indulgently at Elizabeth.

'How's May these days? I hear she's living with you now. Still as scatterbrained as ever?'

Octavia laughed, 'Sometimes, but she has calmed down a bit since she married Ted. She keeps me going.'

'Yes, I'm sure she does. You're company for each other.' Jack cast around for something else to say, desperately wanting to prolong the conversation, but with the surprise of seeing her, after months of pushing away her memory, found his wit had deserted him. 'Well . . . I suppose I'd better get back to the office. I've just been up to Holmans and picked up some draft papers for your father. Look after yourself, won't you, and the little one.'

Octavia watched him as he walked along the pavement back to the School, short in stature, a man born and bred of the mines. He doesn't look well she thought. Standing in the queue, her feet numb with the waiting, her mind filtered back to the days before the war, remembering Jack sitting at his desk beneath the soaring windows as a junior clerk under her father William, the Secretary of the Camborne School of Mines. Such carefree days when she, May, Phoebe and Alice picked up William from his office on Friday afternoons. She remembered with a wistful smile, the pranks of the students during rag week, and in particular, the day of the bloomers. William's eyes, on arriving at work, had risen to meet the top of the flagpole which stood on the main school building. A pair of voluminous pink silk bloomers blew defiantly in the breeze.

'Built to repel,' William observed, shaking his head at a grinning Jack waiting on the doorstep and wondering who the culprit might be. William suspected James's hand in the matter. 'He's crazy enough to pull a stunt like that. He's bright but his inventiveness needs to be channelled into a job. It's a miracle he wasn't blown off the pole with last night's wind,' he said.

Their Friday arrangements had not gone unnoticed by a group of students, and as his daughters spilled through the heavy oak door into the office, dropping their shopping beside William's empty desk, for a staff meeting was still in progress, there was a scraping of feet outside on the tiled floor of the lobby. A quick tap on the door and they were in, a commotion of young men in high spirits and high hopes that with a little manoeuvring a weekend rendezvous with William's daughters, known in the hotbed of student circles as Slim's harem, was a delightful possibility. There were ribald comments on the bloomers snapping above them in the wind as they left the office and gathered outside the school walls.

'A masterstroke, Treneer. It was you, wasn't it?' asked Bailey, whose reputation for long-legged sprints to touchdown on the school rugby pitch were a byword.

'Not me, dear boy. Pray, where would I get such a *delectable* undergarment,' replied James in his familiar impersonation of Noel Coward, whenever discomfited. 'In any case, I've no head for heights.' He passed the buck, clapping Wilton on the shoulder. 'This is your man, climbs like a mountain goat and I've heard whispers that his landlady's voluptuous daughter secreted a certain garment of pink silk beneath his pillow!'

Amidst the general laughter, Alice raised questioning eyebrows at Wilton, her current conquest, from under a wing of golden hair as he blushingly protested his innocence.

Their names echoed through Octavia's mind. She wondered if they were still alive, those unsuspecting young men brimming with esprit de corps and eager to go forth and stamp their mark on the mining world as those that had gone before them. James keeping the incident close to his chest, and admitting nothing, had finally confided to her that it had been him. Octavia was horrified. 'You could have been killed!' she replied, and James laughing off her worried look, whirled her around and held her close. 'You must never worry about me. I'm tough as old boots and will live for ever,' but the war had mocked his youthful assumption, and extracted its revenge, and he was gone, like the bloomers that had stayed flying defiantly in the winds, until they had slowly disintegrated into tatters and blown away. Pensive as the queue slowly moved forward, Octavia reached the counter as frozen as the last two lamb chops she was offered.

William sat down heavily in his chair, an immense man troubled with the legacy of the great war. He handed his crutches to May and settled down to enjoy a Sunday roast cooked in his kitchen. Octavia came in and placed his dinner before him. How fortunate he was to have good girls, he thought. Some became such fly-by-nights, intent on their own needs, and playing fast and loose with their men away. They were a credit to their dear mother. What delight she would have taken in Kitty, who sitting propped on her cushions, looked as pretty as any Pearl's soap advertisement.

'How's Joan these days, dad?' asked May. Joan, a widow, and a close friend of their mother before she died, lived next door and had offered to cook and generally keep an eye on him since the loss of his leg which had left him unsteady on his feet. That he had any legs at all was due solely to his batman and to the sheer bloody-mindedness of William. He had shared the icy waters of the trenches with his men for weeks on end and finally lost all feeling in his legs. He had seen men disappear behind the lines for amputation from gangrenous frostbite, a risky and brutal affair from which many never recovered, and having survived the tough discipline of rising through the ranks, Regimental Quarter Master William Tremayne of the 5th Duke of Cornwall's Light Infantry, was damned at this late stage of the game if he was going to meekly lay down his life for a pair of frozen legs. Peeling off his puttees, he had urged his batman to constantly knead and massage them until the pain of life returned. He had won the day, but ultimately, lost the battle. Jack would see him in the office, seized with a searing pain, and in time, it became necessary to amputate one leg, and he was left with an artificial limb in harness to his waist.

'Her cooking isn't as good as your mother's, but I can't complain. She looks after me very well, really, and we have a laugh and a chat over a cup of tea, and sometimes we share something a little stronger. He chuckled. 'She's not adverse to a little medicinal brandy.'

May and Octavia exchanged amused surreptitious glances across the table.

'I saw Jack in town the other day.' said Octavia. 'I thought he was looking dreadful. He's lost weight.'

'Mmmm, I know. I'm not surprised,' said William. 'After two years of twelve hour stints of figure work followed by drills and guard duty, he was found slumped over his desk. It seems he has a bit of a dicky chest and his eyesight had deteriorated.'

'Oh gosh. Poor Jack,' said May.

'From a purely selfish point of view, I'm glad that he was released from the army and is back in the office. He's utterly reliable, and I missed his memory for facts and figures. It's exceptional. He will be the right man to take over from me when the time comes, which can't come soon enough. I've had enough of struggling to work on this old 'tin' leg of mine.' William laid down his knife and fork with a satisfied grunt, and chortled. 'He doesn't know one end of a gun from the other, for all his time away. He's lethal.' He reached for his pipe. 'Pass me the matches May,' he said, as he tamped down the tobacco, lit a match and drew the flame through. 'The School is Jack's life and he would defend it to the last if he had to, but watching him handle a gun makes me nervous. I'm thankful the use of bullets is restricted.'

The girls laughed.

If there was one thing with which William was familiar, it was a gun. As a crack shot on the National Roll of Marksmen, a fact that did not go unnoticed, he had been detailed as a sniper in the great war. It was a role he had loathed and was greatly relieved when that particular duty finished and he returned to sharing the hardship of the trenches with his men.

'I can't imagine Jack shooting anyone, not even the Germans,' said Octavia.

'I wouldn't go as far as that, but I told him he'd better watch what he's doing or he'll shoot himself and save the Huns the bother. He took it all in very good part. He's a decent chap, Jack, for a Camborne man.'

'Dad!' exclaimed May, smiling indulgently, 'Isn't there enough trouble in the world without Camborne and Redruth people still bandying names at each other.'

'It's tradition. In your grandfather's time, it was stones they would hurl at each other. You should have heard them in the pub after the rugby match, yesterday. They couldn't stomach the fact that we ran them into the ground. There was a wonderful last-minute try by young Knight in hellfire corner, and beautifully converted by Harris. The ball sailed through the posts, sweet and clean as a bird,' said William, his eyes alight at the memory. 'That set their tails on fire!'

'Perhaps you'd better cast me out of the family since I was born in Camborne,' teased May.

'That was an unfortunate blip on my part. I might live and work here, but I'm still a Redruth man at heart; always have been and always will be,' he said, looking at them both with a fanatical gleam to his eye.

33

Octavia shook her head at May. 'It's a tribal thing. You'll never change them,' she said as she got up from the table and started to clear the dishes. 'And I've just decided, I shall invite Jack to enjoy the sherry you put away for us for Christmas. As a *Camborne* man, he'll enjoy that!' she said, disappearing through the door.

After the pitch-black walk from the village of Beacon that lay beyond the top of the hill, Jack blinked in the sudden light of the porch as the front door was shut behind him by May.

'Hello Jack, come in, come in,' she said, leading him into the hall and smiling with pleasure at seeing him. May had a soft spot for Jack who over the years had made a point of chatting to her on their weekly visits to the office, sensing she was a little overshadowed by her sisters, and had been especially attentive to her after the death of their mother when she had appeared shocked into virtual silence. 'How are you? Let me take your coat,' she said hanging it on the hall stand, and ushering him in to a burst of laughter from William in the front room. 'Octavia will be here in a minute, she's just in the kitchen pouring the drinks.'

Jack stepped through into the room, feeling a little self conscious. 'Come over and warm yourself by the fire, Jack, and lend me some moral support. I'm surrounded by women,' said William, seated to one side of the fireplace, with Phoebe perched on the arm of his chair.

'Hello, Mr. Tremayne. Hello, Phoebe,' said Jack, as she looked up at him, and thankfully stayed put, for when standing, he felt like Jack and the beanstalk. 'How are you keeping these days?'

'Oh, quite well really, all things considered.'

'I heard you were bombed out, Phoebe. That must have been a terrible experience.'

Phoebe shot Jack a cryptic look with the familiar slant of her feline eyes. 'Not half as terrible, had I'd been there at the time! The centre is certainly looking dog-toothed and ragged. Very little left standing, but the dockyard thankfully escaped fairly lightly and is still working. I saw a bus on the roof of a building the other day. The driver took a wrong turn!' She grinned at him.

Jack grinned back at her wit, sharp as ever. 'Yes, Plymouth has had a pretty bad time of it,' he said.

'It was a weird sight, but the worst of it all is seeing thousands of people trekking out into the countryside, sleeping where they can - barns, cowsheds, even ditches. I've heard of one woman with two small children living in an old hen house. She has no light, heating, or water. It doesn't bear thinking about. This war is beastly in every sense of the word.'

Jack nodded in agreement. 'Where are you living now?'

'I moved in with a friend who lives on the outskirts of Plymouth, though I hardly ever see her. We work different hours, so we're like passing ships in the night.' A small secretive look flitted across her features, so fleeting, it barely registered until later, when he remembered it, and it occurred to him, she was no longer in Plymouth.

'Are you home for long?'

'Just a forty-eight hour pass. Lucky to get that. But it's good to be able to see everybody, if only for a short while. Especially dad,' giving him an affectionate squeeze of the arm.

William, absentmindedly smoothing his moustache down with the back of his fingers, and listening, covered Phoebe's hand with his own. 'And it's good to have you home, Phoebe. I worry about you working in Plymouth. Dockyards are always a target,' he said, looking up at her with a mingled look of concern and fondness. 'And I worry about Alice in Greece, too,' he added, 'and wonder how she is out there.' His head dropped at the thought.

'We all do,' replied Phoebe, knowing his closeness to Alice and hesitant to say anything further for fear of upsetting him.

There was an awkward pause and Jack stepped in. 'This is a beautiful room,' he murmured, casting his eyes along the frieze of Acanthus flower plasterwork, the ceiling rose of ferns and flowers, and coming to rest on the decorative architraves of the panelled door as Octavia entered with a tray of drinks, and began offering them around.

'Mining money built this,' said William. 'A chap called Jimmy Hocking left during the depression for South Africa, and was one of the few to make a fortune and return with it. He had the plans drawn up, no expense spared. It's a real one-off, quite unlike the rest of the houses on the terrace.' William touched the fireplace. 'Italian marble, beautiful isn't it?' He paused as Octavia came over.

'Hello Jack. I'm so glad you were able to come,' she said, handing him a sherry. 'I'll just finish giving everyone their drinks and then I'll introduce you to the ladies.' Jack's eyes followed her, thinking how lovely she looked, the folds of her woollen dress, recently updated and enhanced with her needle, falling seductively around her slim figure. The drinks dispensed, she returned and took his arm, the scent of her perfume heightening his awareness of the closeness of her body as she guided him past the tree glittering with baubles and tinsel in the bay of the window, to the settee where the women sat chatting. 'Jack, I'd like you to meet Nurse Richards who helped me to care for Elizabeth after she was born. I don't know what I would have done without her. And this is Mrs. Retallack, my neighbour, who's husband made the most beautiful little doll's cot for Elizabeth, Mrs. Carveth our neighbour on the other side and last, but not least, this is May's friend, Vi. She and May muddle around on small aircraft parts. They make it sound very technical but I'm sure they don't know one end of a twist bar from another.'

'How did you guess?' laughed Vi. 'May and I are known as the terrible twins, Jack.'

Acknowledging each in turn, Jack found himself laughing a lot with Vi and wrapped in the bonhomie of the Christmas spirit and the warmth of the room that held Octavia, the woman he had loved and desired for so long, he had never felt so alive. He could barely take his eyes off her as she moved around the room, aware of her voice as William discussed with him the recent capitulation of Italy, the tilt of her head as she sat on the settee exchanging ideas with the women on creating a new look from old clothes, and the ingenuity needed to conjure up a meal from rations, reduced, yet again.

There was a collective lull in conversation and William seizing the moment stirred from his chair by the fire. Struggling to his feet with the help of Phoebe, he held up his hand and the room fell silent.

'I'd like to wish you all a Happy Christmas in these difficult times. Let us hope and pray this war will soon be over. To King and Country.' Phoebe passed him his sherry and they raised their glasses.

They stood, each with their own thoughts, until Nurse Richards broke the silence. 'Well, I'm afraid I shall have to take my leave. It's been a lovely evening, my dears, thank you so much.'

Jack downed the last of his sherry and turned to Octavia, 'I think I ought to be making a move as well. Mother hasn't been too good lately, just getting over the flu.' Octavia gave him a wide smile and nod of understanding, as he wished them all a good Christmas and left the room with her, leaving Nurse Richards saying her good-byes to William and the ladies.

'Thanks again for coming Jack,' said Octavia, as he put his coat on. 'I'm hoping it will buck dad up, seeing Phoebe. He said how pleased he was that you were able to join us. He was glad of some male company. He missed you when you were away. We all did.'

Quite unaccountably, Jack's spirit surged and moving with a sureness born of the knowledge that fate would not deal him such a card again, said, 'I was wondering, Octavia. Would you like to come with me to the pictures next Saturday? Providing May can babysit, of course. It's a Bob Hope film.'

He waited.

Taken by surprise, Octavia hesitated, looking at Jack as if for the first time, suddenly aware of his inherently kind face and gentleness of manner. She thought of James, and conflicting emotions mingled within her.

'Tom from the lab went to see it in Redruth, and said it was very funny,' said Jack, anxious not to lose the initiative and sensing her confusion. 'Unless of course, you'd rather see something else? *The Little Foxes* is on at the Scala.'

'No, I'd like to see Bob Hope. He's always good for a laugh and we could all do with cheering up. I would love to come,' said Octavia, with a nod of her head, as May appeared in the passage to pick up Nurse Richard's coat from the stand, and gave Octavia a knowing smile which puzzled her. 'May, you're not doing anything next Saturday evening, are you? Only Jack has invited me to the pictures.'

'No, no, I'm not. After a week of night shift, all I shall want to do is catch up on my beauty sleep. You go out and enjoy yourself.' She looked at Jack, her pleasure obvious. 'It will do her the world of good, she hasn't been out for months.'

'I'll look forward to seeing you then, and will pick you up at about seven en route down the hill, if that's OK with you?' said Jack, the uplifting happiness he felt catching in his throat as he took his leave.

'What was that look in the hall all about?' Octavia asked when everyone had left.

'Oh! Octavia. Jack has been sweet on you for years. You must have known, surely?'

'No, I didn't, as it happens,' feeling a little irritated at herself for obviously missing cues.

'Well, I think he's lovely. Bags of intelligence, which is something you know you rate quite highly, and he's nice looking too, but not in an obvious way. So many men think they're the bee's knees with egos to match. I'm glad you're going out with him. It's time you came back into the land of the living.'

'Dear me! That was quite a speech. Well, we shall see.'

And so it was, in his quiet way, that Jack began his courtship of Octavia, taking long country walks, an activity they found they both enjoyed and as they walked, Jack recounted incidents of past students to her with sharp detail. He had a sense of the ridiculous and a keen intellectual mind coupled with a deep sense of the spiritual which she found intriguing. He read books of all persuasions, discussing them with her, and she discovered, like herself, he was a political animal, eager to embrace new ideas without compromising old and trusted ideals. Stimulated by his enquiring mind, and surprising her with his ability to sort out the wheat from the chaff of a situation, she found herself eagerly looking forward to his company, and without being consciously aware of it, his love and attention. Elizabeth too, fell under his spell. She was now a child of quicksilver movement and curiosity, sitting on his lap and listening with wide-eyed attention to his stories and touching his glasses with a fascination, and so it was in the Autumn of 1944 as the leaves of the elms surrounding the old manor of Nancarrow turned golden in the fulfilment of season, so his too, after years of loving Octavia from afar came to an astonishing fruition. Gathering Elizabeth up, they were married and his life began in earnest.

Chapter Six

April 1951

AN AIR OF gloom pervaded breakfast. Even Kitty's customary chatter had stilled. She stared dismally out of the window at the all encompassing dampness from a week of drizzle and a low ceiling of cloud that had lain like a blanket over Greenview. The familiar words of the cricket commentator on the wireless that Jack listened to in the summer months, popped into her head. 'Rain stopped play,' she thought as several interesting possibilities for the day slammed like a door in her face. She heaved a sigh.

'Do stop sighing Elizabeth, it's becoming a habit, and sit up,' Octavia said, raising her well-defined eyebrows at her.

She was Elizabeth again. Always a bad sign. She made a face, arched her back and dropped her shoulders. Lately, it seemed to her everything she did displeased her mother. Only that morning before getting up, she had promised herself she would turn over a new leaf, she would not talk too much, or quarrel with Grace, she would even go to the village and fetch the shopping without complaint. But now, it was all spoilt, she couldn't even breathe right. It was so unfair. She gave another involuntary sigh as the early morning post clattered through the letter box. 'I'll get it,' she said, skating off her chair and running up the passage to the porch before Octavia could make any further comment. She returned placing the square white envelope into her mother's outstretched hand, and keeping her eyes low, slid back onto her chair.

'It's from Roy,' Octavia said, as she ripped open the envelope. 'Something must be up to get a letter at this time of the year.'

Jack watching her from across the large wooden kitchen table, relaxed back into his chair and waited. A state of affairs to which he was not unfamiliar. Catching his look, Octavia gazed at him with eyes, which if asked, he could not have said if they were blue or grey for they were as mercurial as the sea and, like the sea, seemed to change with their every mood, and still had the capacity to seduce him.

She frowned as she began reading the letter. 'I was right, they've had big worries in Birmingham. Diane has been very ill with diphtheria.' Octavia exchanged a look of disquiet with Jack, and continued reading. 'She's through the worst of it and the doctor has said she must now have complete rest. Roy's wondering if he could bring John and Peter down with him to stay for a few days at Whitsun.'

'Who's John and Peter, mummy?' asked Kitty.

'Hush, Kitty, and get on with your breakfast. He thought if the boys were out of Winnie's hair, it would give her a break and give Diane a chance to recover.' Octavia's look turned to one of amusement. 'He says the boys are driving Winnie quite mad with their antics, the latest being, they let the hamsters out, who promptly headed at breakneck speed for the piano, disappeared underneath and have never been seen since. He goes on, he realises it would be a push for us for space, but with the use of the company car, he would be able to get out from under our feet and to take us all around.'

Kitty's knife that had been busy buttering her toast, stopped in mid-air at the mention of a car. 'Did you say Uncle Roy has a *car*, mummy?'

'Elizabeth! Will you just do as you're told and finish your breakfast. Take a leaf out of your sister's book and learn to keep your tongue quiet for once.'

Grace smiled smugly at her across the table as Octavia stood up and fetched the calendar hanging by the kitchen cabinet – a magnificent print of Land's End, the sea wild and white-capped, a courtesy Christmas gift from the local engineering firm of Holmans. 'That's barely a month away,' she exclaimed, flicking through it.

Kitty slid slightly down the chair, but Grace anticipating the move, was ahead of her.

'Mummy, Kitty's going to kick me!'

Kitty's jaw dropped at Grace's quick reaction and she exploded with guilty indignation. 'I wasn't. That's a lie.'

'Yes, you were,' Grace cried back at her.

'I was not. I wouldn't touch you with a bargepole,' Kitty shrieked back, an expression she had recently overheard in the school yard and thought rather splendid.

'Liar, liar, pants on fire,' Grace taunted.

Octavia banged the calendar down onto the table. 'That will do, you two. Elizabeth, keep your feet to yourself, or I will see to it that you do,' she warned, glaring at them both.

'But I didn't *do* anything. It isn't fair, you always blame me,' Kitty replied, with a murderous look at Grace, who stuck out her tongue. 'See! Did you see that? She stuck her tongue out at me.' Incensed with injustice and rage, Kitty pushed her chair back and stood up.

'Sit down,' hissed Octavia.

Thomas, affected with the rising tension, joined in the mêlée and began banging his spoon on the table.

'Jack, I can't stand much more of this, for heavens sake, do something before they kill each other or I do,' cried Octavia, snatching up Thomas's spoon and pushing a spoonful of cereal into his mouth in one swift, practised movement. Thomas recoiled in surprise and looked ready to cry.

'You both heard mummy, just behave yourselves, and Kitty, sit down and finish your toast,' said Jack mildly, giving the top of her head a gentle stroke as she sat down around the corner from him.

'Why do I bother?' Octavia sighed in irritation at him, raising her eyes to the ceiling in sheer exasperation.

Jack shrugged his shoulders up and down with a self-deprecating smile at Kitty and Grace that immediately placated them both. He returned to the matter of the letter in an attempt to restore the Saturday morning calm. 'I hope Diane will be alright. She's very young to have had diphtheria, but children are resilient and usually bounce back quickly.' He paused, thinking for a moment. 'It would be nice to see Roy again, and for the girls to get to know Peter and John, but Roy's right, darling, it would be a houseful with eight of us and a lot of extra work for you and where will you sleep them all?'

'Oh, I'm sure I'll think of a solution and rise to the occasion, like I always do,' replied Octavia with a bite of sarcasm.

The waters were ruffled, and at times like this, he was reminded of Phoebe. That same quick sparring retort. Choosing to ignore it, he continued. 'As Roy says, he would be able to take the children out in the car, and I will be here over the weekend to help out. I think a change of faces and scenery would do us all good.'

His cereal finished, Octavia plucked Thomas out of his chair, sat him on her lap and kissed the top of his curls, her mood softening with the pleasure of the last of his babyhood. How easy it all is when they're this small, she thought. She rocked him for a moment or two, mulling over Roy's letter and Jack's words, and half listening to Kitty, whose anger had evaporated as quickly as steam from a kettle, and was back to asking Jack about John and Peter.

'They're your cousins. John is twelve and Peter is ten, the same age as you Kitty, and from what I hear, you and Peter are not unalike. He won't do as he's told either.' She gave Jack a rueful look. 'Diane, their sister, who's very sick at the moment, is three years old and was a great surprise to the family!' He stifled a smile at his slip of the tongue and continued quickly at Kitty's puzzled and questioning look. 'Uncle Roy is your mother's first cousin. He used to live in Cornwall until his father died and then his mother re-married and they went to live in Birmingham.'

'Have they really got a car, daddy?' Kitty asked.

'Yes, they have but it belongs to the company that Uncle Roy works for. As he is a manager, he was provided with a car for business meetings with clients.' He decided to omit the fact that it was the chocolate firm of Kunzels, for with sweets still on ration, it would invite too many questions from Kitty that he really did not feel equal to, so early in the morning.

'The lucky stinkers! I wish we had a car. We could . . .' Kitty began.

Octavia broke in and Kitty looked at her with a frown for she had always been told it was rude to interrupt when someone else was talking. 'You're right Jack,' Octavia was saying. 'It will do us all good to see them. I shall write and tell Roy to come.'

'Oh goody!' Kitty said. 'Isn't it exciting Gee Gee? We've got new cousins and they're coming to *stay*.'

'They're not new cousins, Elizabeth, you just haven't met them before and how many times have I told you not to call your sister Gee Gee.'

'But you call me Kit . . .' Kitty began, lapsing into silence on receiving a warning shake of the head from Jack. Kitty turned her thoughts to the visit. No-one had ever stayed with them before. Even inviting friends to play and stop for tea was discouraged by Octavia. 'I have enough to do looking after you three without any more adding to the turmoil.' With pointed sighs of sufferance and muttering darkly, they bowed to the omnipotence of grown-ups. Her words were in part, truth, but there was an underlying reason for her reluctance and one common to all. Rationing. The continuing bane of life for every housewife in the country, although one which Octavia and Jack felt keenly was the only fair way to move forward from the aftermath of the war that had left the country on its knees.

The more Kitty thought about it, the more thrilling the idea became, and unable to contain herself any longer, her questions began to spill in a headlong stream of excitement. 'Mummy, will they sleep in my bed and Grace's?'

'I haven't decided, yet,' Octavia replied.

'Oh . . . Well, can I take Peter and John to see the horses on the farm, and to the American swing at the recreation ground? They'd really like that. It goes ever so high. And please can we go to the woods? I could show them the bird's nest that I found, and we could play French cricket in the garden. And then, a wonderful thought struck her. 'We could go to Gwithian in the *car!* All my friends would be pea-green with envy and . . .'

'Steady on, Kitty,' Jack laughed, 'All in good time. I expect we shall do everything you want and more. What do you think?' he asked Octavia with a raise of his unruly eyebrows. She returned his look and shook her head in one of humorous wonder at Kitty's non-stop deluge of words.

'Yes, I'm sure we will,' she agreed.

Jack pushed his chair back from the table and stood up, 'Well, that seems to be settled then. Now, it's time we went down to the library, and then I've got to pop into the office and sort out one or two papers for the board meeting on Monday.'

'Will we be staying in your office long, daddy?'

'Long enough for you to have a go on the typewriter, Kitty,' Jack replied, reading her thoughts.

'Yippee.'

Jack took their hats and coats from the peg on the back door, and helping Grace with hers gave her a special smile. 'Are you happy that your cousins are coming to stay?' Aware that she felt things deeply and took time to digest and accept situations. Kitty's exuberance could be overpowering. Grace nodded at him, her amber eyes serious beneath her thick mop of hair.

In penetrating drizzle they set off, huddling under Jack's large umbrella as they walked down the hill on their weekly visit to Camborne library.

'I hope the next Famous Five book is in. I've been waiting ages for it,' said Kitty, pressing close to Jack and placing her hand in his pocket. 'I wish our gang could have exciting adventures like they do. Nothing ever happens to us,' she sighed.

'All we do is have pretend adventures and say stupid passwords, and Kitty's always bossing me around,' came Grace's quiet voice from the other side of Jack.

Kitty poked her head around Jack, half skipping in front of him as they walked, in her attempt to look at Grace and make her point. 'I'm the leader and leaders tell their men what to do, for heavens sake,' said Kitty, quite unconsciously mirroring Octavia's tone and common phrase when annoyed. 'They didn't want you in our Secret Service, you know, because you're only six. They only let you join because you're my sister. I shall tell them now, what you said.'

'See if I care! I don't want to be in your silly Secret Service anyway.'

'That's enough, you two, I don't want a repetition of breakfast,' said Jack as they made their way down the hill to the squish of their feet on the wet pavement. On passing the house of Sandra, Kitty was struck with a thought, and Jack, his mind on the forthcoming visit was delivered with a bolt from the blue.

'Daddy, where do babies come from?' came Kitty's voice loud and clear and just as they were passing a couple walking up the hill, who having heard the question, shot him a tickled look.

Caught on the hop, Jack's equilibrium was knocked sideways, and he struggled to hide an involuntary smile of intense embarrassment. What on earth could he say? He decided to duck the issue. 'I think you'd better ask your mother the answer to that question.'

Kitty who had no notion or desire to learn the intricacy of nature, was taken aback. She looked up at Jack in astonishment. He always answered her questions. Why did she have to ask her mother? And why was he looking so . . . well . . . 'funny'? she decided. She beamed back innocently in response to Jack's self-conscious smile. 'Sandra has a new baby sister. She's so small. Like a doll, and Sandra helps to feed her with a bottle. Can't we have a new baby, too?'

So that's what the question was about, thought Jack, with relief. 'We've got Thomas,' he replied.

'He's not a baby. He's big. Mummy said, the time goes by so quickly that it won't be long before he's three years old,' replied Kitty.

'Will he have a birthday party like me?' asked Grace.

'Yes, I expect so,' Jack replied, by now heartily sick of questions. But Kitty was still wondering why she had to ask her mother about a baby and was on the point of asking Jack again, when Richard Trevithick's statue in front of the library, loomed up before them out of the drizzle, and before Kitty could form the question, as Jack knew she would from past experience, he quickly shut his umbrella, trotted them both up the steps and into the distraction of books.

Kitty was happy, her Famous Five book was in, and she was impatient to be away to Jack's office where she knew a typewriter waited. She idly looked around as Grace and Jack browsed the shelves and suddenly spotted her ballet school teacher, Miss Edwards, standing tall and elegant by the counter in her camel coat and a cinnamon coloured beret, set back at a carefree angle. She looks different, thought Kitty, younger and prettier. I know what it is. Her hair! It was down and fell in waves to her shoulders instead of her normal neat chignon. Jack and Grace finally decided on their books, and together they joined Miss Edwards at the end of the queue. Kitty, who had a crush on Miss Edwards was uncharacteristically shy when she turned to greet them.

'Good morning, Mr. Pengelly,' she smiled. 'Miserable weather, isn't it?'

'Yes, it's depressing,' replied Jack.

'Hello, Elizabeth. Hello, Grace.'

Grace replied with a whisper, and promptly took a slight step back behind Jack, as Kitty blushingly replied.

'And how are you Elizabeth?'

'Fine thank you, Miss Edwards.'

'Have you been practising your steps?' for Miss Edwards had chosen her to dance a solo at the forthcoming summer gala concert to raise money for the church organ restoration funds.

'Oh yes, Miss Edwards, and mummy has finished my Pierrette costume. It's in pink satin with black pom-poms. I made the pompons myself with milk tops. Mummy sewed them onto my hat and tutu.'

Miss Edwards was perplexed. Milk tops? And then understanding dawned, the children's latest craze of winding wool around two old milk top rings, and cutting between the thick bulk of wool to make fluffy balls.

'It sounds lovely Elizabeth, I'm sure you will look very pretty. I look forward to seeing it at the dress rehearsal.' Elizabeth had dance in her soul and Miss Edwards, recognizing that spark and delight of movement had encouraged her with a solo dance as a pierrette, requiring a considerable amount of miming as well as technique in her steps. She had wondered whether she had been over ambitious for Elizabeth having to display the emotions of unrequited love. She was, after all, only ten. Elizabeth, who would have willingly died for Miss Edwards, was embarrassed at the miming, but nevertheless, threw herself, body and spirit into the dance and, watching her, Miss Edwards had the feeling her performance would stir many a heart in village halls and fetes.

Kitty glowed. She did so like Miss Edwards, she always said the nicest things. Miss Drew would never call me pretty, she thought, remembering her last P.T. lesson at school, when it was decided they would all learn some new folk dances in preparation for the summer fetes. As Miss Edwards dropped her books on the counter to be stamped, Kitty cringed even now, just thinking about it. She had wanted so much to show Miss Drew how well she could dance, but found herself very quickly put in her place. Miss Drew, small and tight lipped, stopped the class. 'What have we here?' her voice rising an octave with sarcasm. 'A ballerina. This is not your ballet class, Elizabeth, this is folk dancing and in folk dancing you do not point your feet, you dance on the balls of them, like so. Set, set, turn two, three four,' she demonstrated. 'Do you see the difference Elizabeth?'

'Yes, Miss Drew,' replied Kitty, her eyes smarting with tears. She had wished the ground to swallow her up and then Miss Drew had delivered her coup de grace. 'You can partner Rosemary and copy her.' Rosemary! Her mortal enemy, who couldn't dance for nuts. Kitty with a barbed look took her place beside her and for the first time in her life had wished the P.T. to be over as fast as possible.

Miss Edward's books now stamped, she placed them into her shopping bag. 'Hope to see you too at the concert Mr. Pengelly? Your daughter's going to be one of the star turns.'

Kitty was speechless, as Jack smiled back at her favourite teacher. 'Yes, we shall all be there. We're looking forward to it.' He held up the books and nodded down at Kitty and Grace. 'Meanwhile these should help to keep them occupied until the weather improves.'

'Well, goodbye then, see you at class Elizabeth,' she said, and glided through the library doors.

Kitty was radiant with happiness. 'Did you hear what she said, daddy? I'm a star! No-one's ever called me that before.'

Jack smiling at her slight misunderstanding of the expression, let it pass as he put their books down in front of the librarian, and with the books stamped, he shook open his umbrella as they stepped out into the cold drizzle, and headed down into town and to Jack's office.

Miss Edwards, meanwhile, on walking home was deep in thought. That child had a quality and a look she could not define – her mouth was wide for her face that was long and thin although the hint of beauty to come was there with those high cheek bones and with the filling out of maturity. Her hair the colour of gold with glints of copper was striking when set free from the constricting plaits but it was her eyes that stayed with her, extraordinary in their colour. A crystal-like gaze of emerald-green that seemed to see far beyond the commonplace. They were eyes whose intuitive look pushed Elizabeth to the fringes of her peer group, fearful that she could read their secret thoughts, but Miss Edwards could only wonder at the beauty of them.

Camborne was bustling with life and the rain which was slowly beginning to dissipate with a rising wind, had not put a damper on the surge of shoppers who wandered up and down the long, wide main street. Despite post-war restrictions, it had an air of prosperity and was distinct from other hilly and twisting Cornish towns by its straight and well laid out roads radiating on slight gradients from the centre. The spiritual and material needs were supplied, side by side. At the head of the main street stood Centenary chapel, built in the eighteen hundreds from the great religious revival of John Wesley, when 'chapel' became the centre of life and was reflected in its enormous seating capacity for twelve hundred souls. Beside the chapel stood the solid granite frontage of the large engineering works and foundry of Holmans, spawned from the practical needs of the mines in Cornwall and around the world, making pneumatic drills, compressors, boilers, pumping engines, pithead gear, cages and all manner of subsidiary equipment. Camborne's time of day was regulated by the blast of the works' hooter, heard for miles, when a tide of men clocked in and out. Reminiscent of a Lowry painting, they poured through the foundry gates, and the shoppers were caught up and lost to sight in a surge of flat caps and oily clothing and the tramp of thousands of feet.

The School of Mines standing in the centre of the town was built of a more refined persuasion than that of Holmans. Dressed granite held soaring Corinthian-style pillared windows and entrances through which thrusting young men entered from around the world, hungry for the knowledge that had grown with the old mining town of Camborne that had survived the many booms and slumps of the mining industry. A town that hummed with a constant vitality and excitement that took the young men along with it, caught them up in its ancient quest for minerals, for it lay in an area exploding with mines and associated industry, that in turn, spawned men of invention and ingenuity - Trevithick, Davy and Bickford-Smith.

Opening the heavy framed door, Jack took Kitty and Grace through into his high and airy office and picking up one of the typewriters, carried it into the boardroom next door and placed it on an enormous table that stood on thick splayed legs and shone with the patina of use and years of polish. Kitty and Grace sat themselves down on the high back chairs, inset with studded leather, sinking low into the seats and at full stretch to reach the top of the table as Jack went back to his room and hunted through his trays for paper. He returned and thought how lost they looked in the room with its lofty ceiling and tall windows, and the length of golden elm stretching away from them. 'Right, these should keep you quiet whilst I sort out my papers,' he said, handing them a pile of old foolscap paper and an assortment of coloured pencils, rubbers and rulers that Jack kept for such occasions. 'Take care with the typewriter, Kitty, strike the keys gently, one at a time, or they will stick together.'

'I know, daddy, you told me that before,' replied Kitty, arching her eyebrows and giving him a wry look out of the corner of her eye.

'I'll leave you to it then,' said Jack and disappeared, smiling to himself at Kitty's sardonic look.

Kitty turned a piece of paper into the typewriter. She would type out the next plan for the Secret Service adventure – to climb over the fence at the back of the theatre in town and explore the dark room she had found after prising open a back door. Inside it was dark and creepy with shadowy shapes and the sound of water, dripping. Above her, voices echoed weirdly, and the sound of something being dragged over the floor sent shivers down her spine. Was it a body? She had turned tail and fled, and leaving the door ajar, raced to the fence. When her legs had stopped shaking, she had laughed at herself, and planned that with candles and the rest of the gang with her, it could turn out to be the biggest adventure they had ever had, and like the Famous Five, maybe they could solve the mystery of the voices and the dragging body. After her sarcastic outburst this morning, she was glad Grace had said she didn't want to be in the Secret Service any more, for it caused problems and irked the others, and she was tired of fighting Grace's corner for her to be with them.

Jack leaned back in his chair at the scroll topped desk. The minutes for Monday's board meeting were now in order and the figures finalized. The office which was a busy one seemed unnaturally quiet without the constant coming and going of staff and students. He could hear the echoing tap-tap of the typewriter keys from the boardroom, and the tick of the old gilt-edge hexagonal faced clock on the wall. He glanced at the time. Eleven forty-five. He would give Kitty a little longer on the typewriter before heading home for dinner.

'Oh fishhooks!' came a loud exclamation of annoyance from the boardroom.

Kitty had struck the wrong key again. He knew there would be frantic rubbings out and the word would dissolve into a hole in the paper, and out it would come and another sheet inserted with much sighing. Octavia was right, Kitty did sigh rather a lot. Jack absentmindedly twisted his fountain pen through his fingers, thinking of the days before the war. He could see the sisters now, spilling into the office. They had been as arresting in character as they were in their looks, and he had watched them flower from young girls into women, bright and captivating as butterflies and

Jack had eagerly looked forward to their Friday visits. Dear May, only fourteen when he had first met her – engaging and impulsive with a ready smile for Jack and solicitous of his well-being. He remembered his embarrassment when she had turned the spotlight upon him on enquiring as to how he was feeling after a bout of flu. Mrs. Bassett, the secretary and lynchpin for the smooth running of the office looked at him from under her fringe, aware of his discomfiture, as a hush descended in the office while they waited for his reply. And Alice, a replica of William as a youth, sweeping back with a graceful gesture of the hand her curtain of golden hair, and laughing at a joke with Phoebe whose tawny feline eyes missed little. They had brought life and gaiety to the office but from the moment of introduction, it was Octavia with hair like jet that filled his thoughts. She had an energy that swung her clothes around her slim figure, and watching her from the wings, he had daydreamed of making her his own. And then, one day, she had married James and his world had become as dark and cold as an eclipse of the sun. He smiled in amusement at the memory of the students, never straying far from the light of their passion with boyish manoeuvrings for a weekend rendezvous with William's daughters. They conversed with a confidence born of ease and position, but were naive in the ways of an old soldier like William. Aware and amused at the name given to himself and his daughters of Slim's harem, he kept them close and his ear to the ground and was way ahead of them when news of their ex-curricular activities came to light, as they invariably did with polite and regular enquiry from the local police.

'Have 'ee heard the latest? Some one's blown they concrete posts in the Mining School lane to smithereens. Made some 'ell of a bang. Hear it did 'ee?'

William, he remembered, had been hard put to deny the students responsibility for the annihilation of the posts. It had been a roaring success and the talk of the town. What they had learned in class had been used with spectacular effect. Constable Phillips, a fresh-faced young man, barely older than the students themselves had been obliged to call, once again, during rag week, and arrived as anticipated, at coffee time. He was, by now, almost part of the establishment and the atmosphere was relaxed and informal as they discussed the weather, the recent rugby matches and local news.

The conversation meandered back to the small matter of dynamite. It was agreed that the students were sillier than a pack of wagon horses, and with tactical omission on both sides to the question of who the culprit might be, the police were, as on previous occasions, 'accommodating,' and, providing the School funded the latest mayhem, no charges would be brought. Their faces were as clear in his mind as a snapshot: foolhardy young students who overnight became men and died for their country, as James had. He would never know the joy of fatherhood, and his death had changed Jack's life beyond anything he could have dreamed. He suddenly felt rather humble. There was a scraping of chairs and Grace came running through the door.

'Look what I've drawn, daddy. A vase of flowers for mummy. Do you think she'll like it?'

'It's lovely. I'm sure she will,' replied Jack studying it. It really was rather good. She had an eye for detail.

Kitty came in holding a piece of paper close to her chest.

'What have you been typing Kitty?'

'Nothing much,' replied Kitty, not wishing for Grace to know her ideas.

'Well, it's time we made tracks. We shall stop for our ration of sweets on our way home.' Jack picked up the heavy ring of office keys which Octavia grumbled made holes in his pockets faster than any money he might possess as Kitty threw herself on her grandfather's chair, spinning herself around and giggling.

'Now that's enough Kitty. Put your coat on. You too, Grace.

'But I want a turn, daddy.'

'Go on then, and hurry up,' Jack sighed.

Chapter Seven

THE HULLABALOO OF breakfast was over with the girls chasing each other down the stairs in an attempt to see who could reach the bottom first, and arguing all the way. Kitty's school coat needed a last minute button sewing on and it was followed by a frantic hunt for her homework which she stuffed into her satchel, and with a bang and a blast of air from the door, they were gone with Jack. The house settled itself like leaves after a whirlwind. It was blissfully quiet and Octavia sent up a prayer of thanks for the educational system as she began washing the dishes.

With the decision made for Roy to stay, Octavia had risen with the lark to begin her annual spring cleaning. She lit the fire in the 'fringle' and filled it with pails of water from the tap attached to the wall inside the wash house. It stood adjacent to the kitchen, a low stone building with small paned windows and a corrugated roof, and, amongst its many uses, served as headquarters for Kitty's Secret Service. By the door stood an elaborate iron mangle with large wooden rollers, under which were two pails and a dipper for emptying the brick-built 'fringle' encasing the copper boiler. On the adjacent wall lay a heap of coal, and opposite the mangle were the garden tools, the grass mower, and a galvanized bath hanging on the wall. Under the window was a small scuffed wooden table and deckchairs, which found their way into the garden for teas when the summer sun moved high in the sky.

The dishes washed, she chased Thomas up the stairs, playing the family game of banging each step behind him with her hands, and growling in a low voice, 'tiger bumps! tiger bumps!' He squealed and chuckled with the fun of it, scrambling out of her reach on hands and knees, and laughing with him at the top of the stairs, she playfully chased him into the bedrooms where she stripped the windows bare of curtains. She took them out to the wash house and pushed them down into the bubbling water with the wooden puncher, and replacing the lid, returned to the kitchen and filled the stone sink with hot water for the delicates and small clothes that accumulated unremittingly in the laundry basket. Again and again, her eyes returned to Thomas, as she rubbed the clothes with a bar of yellow Sunlight soap until she was elbow deep in suds. He sat amidst his picture building bricks, pushing around a small wooden train. The morning sun glinted on his mop of curls that were turning from baby gold to the warm chestnut of Jack and Grace. He was two years old, the son she had long awaited and her love for him was fierce and protective. Her hands stilled for a moment thinking how history repeated itself, first Kitty and then Thomas barely surviving birth from an attack of gastroenteritis that had raged around the nursing home after he was born. If he had died, Octavia would have died with him, and for the first time realised the desolation her mother must have felt on the loss of her infant son from meningitis. And then, Grace had caught Thomas's infection, and days had come and gone in a blur of sleepless nights and crying children, holding heads over enamel basins, coaxing Grace to take her medicine which she fought tooth and nail, and the endless washing of sheets. Kitty had mercifully stayed well, and unexpectedly proved to be a blessing, reading the tell-tale signs before anyone of Grace fetching to throw up. 'Mummy, Grace's going to be sick again,' she shrieked, dashing away for the basin and depositing it into Grace's lap. At night, Octavia would jerk awake to the sound of the squeaking handle of the pail, as Kitty raced back from the bathroom. On stumbling out of bed to attend to Grace, she would find Kitty back in her bed, her small face like paste at the sight of Grace urging, and seeing Octavia, shut her eyes in relief and turned to face the wall away from the whole stomach-churning sight. Finally, the crisis was over. Thomas began sleeping through the night and Grace's colour crept back into her cheeks and life took on a semblance of normality. With Grace's sickness, Kitty was compliant and offered help in every small way that she could, but once released from her vigil, returned to the Kitty of harebrained schemes and independent streak that reminded her so much of herself, although even she, in her wildest moments as a child, could not have dreamt up such a caper as Kitty had done with her friend Sandra.

She shook her head and tsk-tsked to herself at the memory of the uproar created the previous year. With the incident now safely behind her, she could smile at the thought of two daft children throwing macs over their heads and bleating away as they crawled up the back field towards the ewes. The sheep nervously eyeing the moving humps coming towards them, scattered in all directions at the sight of two faces peering at them from under their camouflage. Kitty and Sandra had stood up in dismay, and without further ado, several of them leapt onto the low hedge and dropped out of sight. Pandemonium had ensued with farm hands chasing sheep that dived and darted away from them, up and down the road. It had taken all afternoon to round them up, and how the sheep had never broken their legs on the long drop down onto the hill was a miracle. Kitty who attributed a great deal to the Almighty, said, it was divine intervention. God had nothing to do with it, my lady, it was sheer good luck, thought Octavia. What it would have cost them if the sheep had been killed or broken their legs, she dreaded to think. She continued with the washing and rinsing, and murmuring at Thomas, 'Who's my baby boy, then? You won't do such silly things as your scatterbrained sister, will you, Thomas?' He returned her gaze with limpid brown pools under a sweep of lashes. Fans, she called them. May said they were outrageous lashes for a boy and would be the envy of any girl he met. Considerably piqued at the description of his eyes, the girls had marched off and Octavia found them struggling to measure their own lashes with a ruler. They did the funniest things those two in their love-hate relationship with each other, ganging up when it suited them, whispering and giggling, or turning on each other and fighting like cat and dog. To see and hear Kitty now, who would have believed how lifeless and silent she had been, she thought, as she twisted the water out of the clothes and dropped them into an enamel bowl ready for mangling. That firey spirit of hers, still evident in battles of will, had fought and survived that iron cold January when events and the elements had conspired against them.

She slipped Thomas into his coat, for the air outside was cold, and with him at her heels, hurried to the wash house to fill the galvanized bath with water to rinse the curtains, and to mangle the clothes. Hanging them out in the courtyard she was chilled to the bone with the wind funnelling up the wide entry at the side of the house, and ran shivering back inside with Thomas. She warmed up a saucepan of milk for his drink before taking him up for his morning nap, and making herself a quick cup of Camp coffee, sweet and warming, she returned to the steam and damp of the wash house. Lifting the dripping hot curtains out of the 'fringle' with the tongs, she dropped them into the rinsing water, and turning the big iron handle of the mangle, she fed them through, and thought of the girls who liked to watch and wait for their bed sheets to appear on the other side like long, stiff boards.

With the curtains hung on the line running the length of the garden, the rising wind took them and they billowed and snapped. They would not be long in the drying and ready for the iron. She glanced at the sky which thankfully seemed set to stay clear of rain and returning to the kitchen, began peeling the potatoes for a quickly prepared meal of egg and chips. Jack and the girls would soon be home. With the school at the other end of town and with just over an hour for lunch, it was a race for Jack to pick them up and walk them at break-neck speed up the hill. On wet days, when they arrived bedraggled and soaked to the skin with rain, the kitchen became a Turkish bath as the steam rose from their coats hanging over the clothes horse in front of the range. Mealtimes were a concentration of eating, for there was little time or energy left for anything else, and once finished, coats were thrown back on, and they were gone like wind before a storm.

Kitty felt disorientated and irritable. Both rooms were shrouded and looking ghostly with old white sheets thrown over the furniture, as they awaited the chimney sweep the following morning and the house echoed footsteps and voices from the loss of the curtains and mats on the floor. Furniture upstairs and down had been pulled away from walls and brushed free of lurking cobwebs but the 'mountain' –an enormous mahogany sideboard – remained immovable. It had defeated her mother's enthusiasm for turning the whole house upside down thought Kitty as she went into the sitting room which had lost its friendly look without the familiarity of books, ornaments and the wireless sitting on the cupboard shelf at the side of the fireplace. It was there Kitty would sit with her ears glued to the dramatic opening music of *Dick Barton*, Special Agent; a thrilling serial which was discussed avidly the following day with her friends in school. Hunting for her plimsolls and book, she could find neither.

'Mummy. Where's my shoe bag with my plimsolls?' she shouted from the cupboard under the stairs where the bag usually hung, her head diving amongst an assortment of old coats, shoes, Wellingtons, the Ewbank and general cleaning paraphernalia and gas masks, that Kitty, if aggravated enough by Grace, would put on and chase her, terrified and crying around the house. Octavia's reaction was always sharp and threatening, and Kitty did not dare it often.

There was a clatter of broom and mop falling out onto the tiled floor and another cry of annoyance as she cracked her head on the shelf of bottled fruit, concentrated orange juice from the clinic, and cod liver oil and Virol that Kitty loathed in equal measure.

'Mummy, it's not *here*. Where've you put it? I have to have my plimsolls for P.T. tomorrow.'

Octavia sighed at her daughter as she came out from the front room and made her way along the hall with an armful of china.

'Stop shouting. I'm not deaf. Your plimsolls are where you left them, in the kitchen by the armchair. How many more times do I have to tell you to hang them up out of the way under the stairs.'

Kitty felt Octavia's barely contained annoyance in the set of her walk and made a face at her retreating back. She followed her. 'Have you seen my 'What Katy Did' book, mummy?' she asked, in a tone of placation.

'I found it upstairs under your bed.'

'Oh, yes. I was reading it before I fell asleep. I wondered where it went.'

'You really should be more careful with your things, Kitty. And pick up the broom and mop from off the floor, put them away and shut the cupboard door.'

Kitty bundled everything back and banging the door shut against the disorder she had created, and muttering loudly, stanked upstairs to her room. 'I *hate* spring cleaning and I hate everybody!

57

THE THOUGHT WAS with her the instant Kitty opened her eyes. Today, they would be here! She had awoken with the dawn and lay feeling squishy inside with excitement. The soft early morning light filtered through the faded and freshly laundered pale green curtains with their sprigs of yellow flowers. She stared at them. Where had the pink curtains gone? And then she remembered she was sleeping top to tail with Grace in Thomas's room at the front of the house. Their large room had been prepared for Roy and the boys. William's old army camp bed was finally located in the loft, half hidden amongst old trunks of army clothes and pre-war dresses, the black-out blinds, a battered tailor's dummy and nursing chair, the old cot, suitcases and the hatbox with the Christmas decorations. The camp bed was found rather the worst for wear, but once the cobwebs and dust were brushed away, it looked presentable enough, standing in front of the window between the girls' beds. Boys being boys, they will probably find it a novelty, thought Octavia, as she made it up. It would certainly have to do. Thomas was somewhat bewildered to find himself back in his cot, brought down from the loft, and was installed in their bedroom, and with the evacuation and swopping of rooms completed, the house now lay sleeping peacefully and awaiting the invasion.

Unable to return to sleep, Kitty jumped out of bed and drew back the green curtains. Her mother's love of green manifested itself in various ways throughout the house. Kitty and Grace, mightily tired of the colour, had taken up arms when paintbrushes had made their appearance in the previous year. Uniting, they issued their ultimatum. 'We're sick of green and we want our room painted pink or we're leaving home.'

   'I'll help pack your bags shall I?' said Octavia, amused at their outburst. 'Come on then, what are you waiting for?' Utterly taken aback at this unexpected reaction, they stood there non-plussed.

Octavia took pity. 'Well, we'll see.' Grace and Kitty exchanged glances of hope at the familiar reply to their pleadings and requests. The answer was a good omen. Returning home from school one bright April afternoon, any lingering doubts – for nothing was absolute with their mother – were replaced with gleeful jubilation. Their room was bathed in a pink glow and there was talk of Octavia making new pink curtains to match.

Kitty looked out towards St. Michael's Mount, the weather barometer for the family. It was hazy and indistinct. It was going to be a lovely day. The sky was bathed in pale pink, lifting to gold as the sun rose in the sky. It lit the scene before her with an incandescent light and was a picture of which she never tired, a kaleidoscope of colours, contours and textures. A playground of humpy green fields and apple-green woods blazed with bluebells in the Spring. At night, the coast became a glittering chain of lights around St. Ives that on clear frosty nights seemed to Kitty to merge with the stars. The rooks were already raucously cawing from the elms around the old manor house of Nancarrow, and she stood thinking about the children she had seen there the previous day by the old boathouse. She had fled there in a fit of despondency and a feeling of alienation from all around her. Tensions had been running high all week at home from the expectation of the visitors, and school had been no better. Kitty had fallen foul of Miss Martin, her favourite teacher who had said 'a three year old could write a better composition,' which had wounded her greatly. She had fallen out with her best friend Sandra, and she had been barred from taking her P.T. lesson for talking in assembly. The whole horrible week had culminated in Kitty wishing 'they were never coming,' following a pushing and shoving argument with Grace over who would sleep top and tail in Thomas's bed, and bringing a swingeing rebuke from Octavia. 'You two are beginning to get on my nerves. Just get out of my sight.' Kitty ran out to the terrace to hide admission of tears with Octavia's angry parting shot at her back. 'You'll sleep where I tell you to sleep.'

She threw herself over the terrace hedge into the field and raced to the small gap in the thorn hedge, slipped through into the lane, and keeping a wary eye out for the carthorse, went down through the farmer's fields adjacent to Nancarrow until she came to a door, slightly ajar, in the wall of the estate. She squeezed through into her own private kingdom: a magical garden of terraces leading down to a lake and where in sheltered nooks, she would sit on dilapidated seats and look out over the lake and the boathouse. It was here that she felt at home. It had been familiar to her from that first moment she had stepped through the doorway into its peace and tranquillity that never failed to assuage the tumult of her emotions and grievances. Making her way from the wooded area to the seat above a stepped cascade where water trickled beneath an overgrowth of ferns and greenery into the lake, she stopped dead at the sound of children's laughter. She slipped to the side of the path behind a rhododendron tree and watched them clambering into a boat in the open, gable-ended boathouse. She saw that their clothes were old fashioned, as the eldest boy on picking up the oars, began rowing to the island in the middle of the lake. Who were they and where had the boat come from? She had never noticed it moored anywhere on the water, or in the Victorian boathouse with its tiled bellcote spire and pretty trefoil shaped stained glass windows. As she poked her head around the crimson flowers, one of the girls on turning around, seemed to look directly at her. There was something about her that was familiar, and with a shock, Kitty realised that she could have been looking at herself. Goose bumps rose on her arms, and prickles ran up and down her spine. Had the girl seen her? She had thought to be well hidden. Should she declare herself and attempt to make friends? She made to move, but her limbs were as lead, and a call to them died in her throat, when on reaching the island, they jumped out and appeared to fade into thin air beneath the feathery shade of the swamp tree.

Although she could neither see nor hear the children any more, she decided to return home and take stock and as she retraced her steps, she wondered about them and the strange way they seemed to disappear. It was probably a trick of the light, but how did they get into the garden, which, now she thought about it, had looked quite different? She had the oddest sensation of having awoken from a dream where the terraces were attended with beds of cottage flowers and roses between neatly cut grass, the lake was clean and the cascade ran bright with tumbling water. The trees were not trailing branches into the lake and the shrubs were shaped and smaller. Her thoughts ran on to the children. They could not have scaled the wall around the estate as it was of sufficient height to make climbing difficult, and was very much on view as it ran parallel to the road with spiked iron gates at the entrance with an enormous padlock. The door in the field was well hidden with an elder flower bush and a rampant growth of ivy hanging like a curtain. A sudden, awful thought struck her. What if they had come to live in the manor house? It would mean the end of everything – making dens in the woods with Terry and Sandra and Michael, who were sworn to secrecy as they made campfires, and swung on the rope hanging from an old oak tree with the leaves and sky dizzily circling above them. Above all, she would mourn the loss of the garden, her space to be alone. It would be hers no longer. There was no one to ask who they might be or if they had come to live there, for that would admit to entering the grounds which were private property and strictly forbidden. 'Trespassers will be prosecuted,' the notices said, and her mother had warned her many times, 'Stay away from Nancarrow. I don't want you going anywhere near the place.' On asking her why, for there was no-one living there, Octavia had frowned and her reply had been vehement. 'Just *stay away*, Kitty. It has a bad history. If I find you've been there . . .' her eyes were wide with warning and something else, a fleeting look of fear. What could it be about Nancarrow that provoked in her mother such an alarmed reaction? She decided to branch off from the path and skirt the house to see if there were any signs of habitation. There was none. The house still had the same air of neglect. It was all very puzzling and now, she thought with annoyance, she would have to wait until her cousins had returned home before she could go back to see if the children were still there.

She turned back from the window as Grace stirred and turned her face away from the morning brightness, her mass of hair lay thick upon the pillow. With her elfin face and the amber eyes of their father, she was, to Kitty, a complete mystery. Quiet and shy, the complete antithesis to herself, who engaged anyone in conversation, Grace's lack of response to friendly enquiry would drive Kitty mad with exasperation. She toyed with the idea of whipping away her pillow, jangling her out of sleep as Grace had so often done to her, precipitating many a fight between them, but decided that today she would let sleeping dogs lie, as her father would say.

Breakfast was dispensed within minutes and they raced each other up the stairs to sit in the bay window of the bedroom to watch for the car.

'They won't be here for *hours*!' Octavia called after them. 'They live hundreds of miles away.'

The distance was meaningless. The farthest they had travelled was to the towns and beaches by bus or train, and no matter how far away it was, they were coming in a car. It had to be quicker than boring public transport. They sat there gazing out over the fields to the sea beyond, until Octavia appeared to make the beds. 'They won't arrive until this afternoon, so you might as well go out and play,' she said, as she stripped and re-made the bed and disappeared back down the stairs.

They debated what to do.

'I don't want to go out to play. I want to be here when they arrive,' said Kitty, watching the cows wander in from the next field.

'We could stay in the garden and make a tunnel with the clothes horse and play at escaping through it from a prisoner of war camp, like we did the other day,' said Grace.

Kitty mulled it over. 'Except, it would only be you and me, and not like when we had Terry and the others crawling through it again and again. That was fun, just like *The Wooden Horse* film when there were *hundreds* of men who went through a tunnel.'

'Yes, but we'd be able to hear a car coming if it's just you and me in the garden,' said Grace with quiet logic.

'I suppose you're right. OK then. We'll do that. You go and fetch the old blanket from under the stairs, and I'll carry out the clothes horse.'

The afternoon found them, once more, sitting in the upstairs window half-heartedly reading their library books.

'I'm fed up reading, let's dress up in mummy's jewellery,' said Kitty. She stood up and fingered the padded lid of Octavia's jewellery box covered in a turquoise flowered fabric. She pressed the catch and it sprang open to reveal glints of colour, a jumble of necklaces, brooches, bangles and beads lying on a bed of faded cream silk. She picked up a necklace and held it to the sunlight, turning it this way and that, entranced with the stones refracting light into flashes of colour onto the scalloped mirror. 'This is my favourite,' she said, opening the clasp and putting it around her neck. 'Mummy told me an old maiden aunt gave her this necklace for her twenty-first birthday.

Grace slipped a string of jet beads over her head and put on a chased silver bangle.

'Aunty May gave those beads to mummy, and the silver bangle was from daddy,' Kitty informed her. She lifted up the tray and picked out from amongst dress rings and strands of pearls and amber, a diamond brooch in a spray of flowers. '*This* was granny's, and very precious to her, mummy said, because she died a long time ago.'

'How did she die, Kitty?'

'I don't know. Daddy said it was an accident,' she replied vaguely, holding up a long gold necklace with a medallion of raised decoration, delicate and exquisite, in gold and jade with a matching bracelet. 'I wonder why mummy never wears these? They are so pretty. She said she couldn't remember who gave them to her. When I'm older, she told me they would be mine.' She examined the Chinese letters linked to the jade leaves. 'I wonder what they mean?'

'Did mummy say if she would give me any jewellery?' asked Grace, feeling put out.

'No.'

'That's not fair.'

'She's bound to give you some of her jewellery to wear, Grace. Well, she can't give them to Thomas, can she?' She giggled. 'Imagine him wearing bangles and beads! He'd look a right cissy.'

Grace looked back at her seriously. 'I think she would give Thomas anything he wanted,' she replied, 'because mummy loves him best.' She took off the jewellery and dropped it dismissively back into the box. 'I don't want it, anyway.'

'Oh, don't be upset, Grace. Sandra's mother is just the same with her baby sister. Having a baby seems to make their brains go soft. And anyway, mummy loves you much more than me. I'm forever in her bad books and she's always saying, "why can't you be more like your sister." I get fed up with that, too. When I get married and have children, I shall treat them all the same.' She reflected for a moment. 'But mummy does do nice things for us. Remember when she picked us up from school and took us to Gwithian, and we had a lovely picnic on the beach and stayed there until the very last bus home? And then there was that night we thought she was coming up the stairs to tell us off for not going to sleep, and instead, she came into our bedroom with chips from Beacon. You know we *never* have food in our beds unless we're sick.'

Grace gazed at Kitty with something akin to pity. 'And what about the time when she came flying up the stairs because you were jumping from bed to bed, and she smacked you with her slipper?'

'Yes, but she didn't hurt me because I dived under the blankets!'

Grace groaned in frustration. 'Thomas can do anything and he never gets told off, like when he climbed up onto the table and upset a jug of orange juice.'

Kitty, neither able nor willing to defend Octavia any longer changed the subject. 'I've just had an idea. Let's watch the cars coming up the hill and make bets as to which one will be Uncle Roy's. It will help to pass the time.'

With a look of resignation, Grace reluctantly agreed. Hidden by the hedge, they could just see the tops of them, and their mood lifted with the fun of betting against each other when a car slowed down as it changed gear, and hopes rose that it would enter the terrace, but time after time, it would sail past the entrance. Kitty's patience finally exploded. 'I'm sick of waiting. I'm going to see if Terry can play and I don't give a *bugger* whether they come or not! So there!'

Grace sucked in her breath, open-mouthed with shock, and gazed after her in wonder as she flounced out of the room and thumped her way down the stairs.

Octavia saw her through the open sitting room door. 'What's the matter with you? You look like a thundercloud.'

'I'm fed up!' she replied, entering the room. Octavia threw a white cloth over the table that billowed and fell into deep crocheted edges of peacocks. 'Why aren't we eating in the kitchen?' she asked.

'Now why do you think?'

'Because Uncle Roy and the boys are coming . . .'

'And we need the bigger table, of course,' said Octavia.

At that moment, Grace came flying down the stairs into the sitting room. 'They've come, they've come!' she cried. 'They're outside the house.'

With their bodies tingling in anticipation, they dashed to the front window and watched the three unfamiliar faces getting out of the car and walking up the path to their door.

Chapter Nine

ROUTINE VANISHED AND tea was late. With the arrival of
Jack, the front room overflowed with arms and legs, smoke, talk
and laughter. Leaving Octavia and Jack expressing their concern
for Diane and recalling old times, Kitty and Grace disappeared
upstairs and peeping into their normally tidy bedroom were aghast
to see a clutter of suitcases, clothes, books, comics, toiletries and
packets of cigarettes scattered over their beds and dressing table.
'Mummy will have a fit,' Kitty declared, as they ran back down
the stairs.

'Tea is ready,' Octavia was saying, as they re-entered the front
room. Thomas, bewildered by the influx of noise and people,
looked anxiously up at her and Jack sweeping him up, invited them
to all move into the sitting room. Octavia sat the boys on either
side of Kitty, who on pulling up her chair, was struck that the table
was laid with different cups, saucers and plates. 'I don't remember
seeing these before mummy. Are they new?' she asked innocently.

Octavia gave her a stony stare. 'They've been in the cupboard
for *years*, Kitty. Make yourself useful and pass Peter one of the
little pasties,' that were piled high on a plate.

Feeling silly, she flushed with embarrassment and handed the
plate to Peter. He took a pasty and gave her a look of commisera-
tion. 'I hope we can go out and play after tea,' he whispered.

'So do I,' Kitty whispered back, glad of his sympathetic response. Kitty appraised him, taking in his sharp features that
transformed with his cheeky grin and decided, there and then, she
would show him the manor house and garden. 'I will take you to
my secret hideaway, if you like? Nobody knows about it but me
and my friends.'

'Where is it?'

'I'll tell you later.' Mindful of her instructions to make her
cousins welcome, she turned to John, a tall and gangly youth with
a shock of black hair. 'Have you ever played French cricket, John?'

'No,' he replied abruptly, and continued eating.

Kitty persevered. 'It's ever so easy and not like English cricket at all,' she said, warming to her latest craze. 'You hold the bat in front of your legs, and we stand around you in a circle taking in turns to try and hit your feet or ankles with a tennis ball. Wherever the ball lands after you've hit it, the person has to throw the ball from there. It can be quite tricky protecting your legs when they are standing behind you. Would you like to play it?'

John gave a non-committal shrug and helped himself to another saffron bun. Kitty gave up.

Peter frowned at him. 'You could at least answer, John. I'd like to play, Kitty. It sounds fun.'

But Kitty, accustomed to the shyness of Grace, gave him a comical sideways look of understanding. 'We've got one like that,' she whispered, pointing a low finger from her lap at Grace.

'Oh, I see what you mean,' he grinned in understanding.

With tea over, Kitty went hopefully to Jack. 'Can I go outside with Peter, daddy. I want to show him something. P-l-e-a-s-e, can I?' but her plea failed to sway him.

'Not tonight, Kitty. Time is getting on. Why don't you all have a game of Ludo?'

With ill grace she mooched over to the games cupboard for the board and flopped it onto the dining room table with a woeful glance at Peter, who on getting the counters out from the box, said under his breath. 'Don't worry, we can see you–know–what tomorrow. Have you ever played Hangman's Noose?'

'I've never heard of it,' replied Kitty.

'All you need is paper and pencils and this dice.'

Kitty brightened at the thought of a new game.

'Is it difficult to play?' asked Grace.

'Nope. It's dead easy.'

'OK. But let's play Ludo first, Kitty,' said Grace, and on moving their counters around the board, they found no quarter was given. It was the first taste of Peter's competitive spirit. He liked to win.

Jack was already on his way out of the door to work as Kitty and Grace came into the kitchen the following morning, and having assessed the invasion, were cock-a-hoop at the prospect of riding in a car.

68

The weather was warm and bright, and after what seemed like hours of waiting for sandwiches to be prepared, flasks to be filled, and the general paraphernalia of beach gear to be stowed in the boot of the car, they piled into the back seat smelling strongly of tobacco and leather. Finally, they were off. Kitty sat bolt upright on the squishy leather seat, speechless with elation as the car burst into life. To think, they were setting off from their house and could go anywhere they fancied. She wanted to wave and shout at the whole world, 'Heh! Look at me, I'm in a car!' and could not stop herself smiling like an idiot as the car left the main road and took the coastal one to Lands End. She was presented with an ever-changing vista of bracken covered hills littered with huge oddly shaped boulders, as if thrown by the legendary Cornish giant to land higgledy-piggledy, one on top of the other. To the other side of her was the Aegean-blue sea beyond the small patchwork fields of stone walls. It was an ancient land and had the wildness of an impending storm and from some deep ancestral core, she connected and fell in love with it, instantly.

'Shall we stop for a moment and take in the view?' said Roy, pulling into a lay-by beside the half broken engine house and mine stack of Carn Galver Mines.

'You miss Cornwall, still, don't you Roy? Octavia observed, as he lit up a cigarette and snapped his lighter shut.

He gave a small sigh. 'You can't be born to all this,' he indicated with his cigarette, 'and not wish that you could return.'

Roy wound his window down and blew out a plume of smoke. 'Such peace,' he mused, 'after the relentless noise of a city.' He shifted and half resting his back against the door turned to face the children. 'We shall soon be passing the village of Zennor. Would you girls like to hear the story of the mermaid who is carved on the end of a pew in the church there?' Peter gave him a long suffering look and John staring out of the window, seemed oblivious to his surroundings.

Hemmed tightly in with Grace and the boys, Kitty pushed herself forward onto the edge of the seat. 'Yes, please, Uncle Roy. We love stories. Daddy is always making new ones up for us, isn't he, Grace?' turning to her and looking for confirmation. Grace nodded.

'Well, the story goes that on Sundays a beautiful lady would appear at the church. She was not dressed like ordinary folk for she wore the most beautiful dresses of silks and satins, and all who heard her singing fell under her spell. At the end of the service, she would slip away and vanish as suddenly as she had arrived and nobody knew where she came from, or where she went. Time went by and she never seemed to grow any older, and then, one day, a handsome young man called Mathy, joined the choir. He fell instantly in love with her, and was last seen following her out of the church and down towards the sea. They were never seen or heard of again, until many years later when a fisherman was anchoring his boat across a cave near Sennen. Up popped a mermaid from out of the waves. Her face seemed familiar to him, and when she asked him, most politely, if he would remove his boat so that her husband Mathy and the children could swim out to sea, he suddenly realised she was the lady from the church. And this was how the people in Zennor discovered what had happened to Mathy. He had fallen in love with a mermaid!'

'Gosh,' said Kitty, imagining it all. 'It's like a fairy tale. Do you think *we* shall see the mermaid at Sennen, Uncle Roy? asked Kitty, her face shining at the thought as she slid back against the seat.

'Cornwall has always been a magical place Kitty, and fishermen do tell tales of having seen mermaids frolicking in the sea. I'd keep my eyes peeled, if I were you. You might just see one.' Smiling broadly, he drew away from the roadside and slid a look at Octavia who shook her head in merriment at his final embellishment, and shifted the weight of Thomas from one knee to the other. He was still there, she thought, the mischievous boy she had known from childhood, if hidden by the thickening of his once boyish frame and hint of receding hair; always the storyteller who stretched credibility to the limit.

Peter rolled his eyes in disgust. 'Mermaids!' He exclaimed with a pained expression. 'You must be stupid to believe in them and all that lovey-dovey stuff. Yuk.'

'Then why do we see pictures of them in books?' asked Kitty indignantly.

'Someone made them up. It's all bunk.'

'Peter. There's no need to be rude. The legend of the mermaid has been around a lot longer than you have, so just keep your opinions to yourself.'

He scowled as Roy negotiated the twisting and turning road around right angled corners of granite farmhouses and outbuildings that seemed to have metamorphosed out of the land itself, sea green with algae and rough-edged from the elements.

John, who had been staring unblinking out of the car window, stirred into life on the steep descent into Sennen where a golden sweep of sand was fringed with a sea of Mediterranean blue blending out into dark navy. A fishing boat was making its way into the harbour.

'I like fishing,' he suddenly stated. 'I go fishing when we go into the country.'

'You're a very good fisherman, John. Do you remember when you caught that enormous perch?' asked Roy in an attempt to draw him into conversation.

'Ummm' John grunted.

'Down here, people go out on fishing trips to catch mackerel. Maybe you could . . .' Kitty's voice trailed away for John had closed back into himself.

Octavia handed Thomas to Roy and climbed stiffly out of her seat. 'My legs have gone quite numb,' she said, stretching a pair of shapely calves and ankles beneath her floral beaching skirt and cotton top tucked into the waist that emphasised her trim figure.

Roy shot her an admiring look as the children scrambled out of their seats. 'You could always turn a man's head,' he murmured, on passing Thomas to her.

She lightly frowned and shushed him with a nod at the children whose eyes and ears missed little, and he smiled in amusement as he went to open the boot of the car and handed out the buckets, spades and a blanket to eagerly waiting hands. Picking up the beach bags, he led them Indian file onto the sand where a sprinkling of people lazed beneath the grassy cliffs that undulated to the beach. Peter and Kitty sat down on the sand, yanking off their socks and sandals and hovering impatiently by Octavia who settled onto the blanket with Thomas. 'For heaven's sake you two, give me a chance,' said Octavia, as she rummaged into the beach bag and fished out the swimsuits. She knelt and held the towel around Kitty whilst she put on her knitted swimsuit, that by no stretch of her imagination could she call pretty. She hated it, for when dry it was scratchy, and once wet, it hung dripping down between her legs as if she was wetting herself. The awful embarrassment had to be endured.

With abandoned whoops, Kitty and Peter raced towards the sea, shrieking and leaping around at the water's edge.

'It's freezing,' Peter shouted.

'It always is,' Kitty shouted back. 'I'm going over to the rocks,' and she took off with Peter's wiry frame in pursuit. One-upmanship became the name of the game, out-climbing and out-jumping each other from one rock to another and peering into pools for tiddlers and crabs left behind by the tide.

Kitty discovered red sea anemones that retracted at her touch. 'They look like blobs of jelly.'

'And they feel like jelly, too,' said Peter, pushing and prodding one to dislodge it.

Kitty gave him a push. 'Don't be so cruel.'

Peter made a face at her and jumped up. 'Race you back,' he said, with a leap from the rocks onto the sand, and was gone before Kitty knew it.

'You're pretty good for a girl,' Peter gasped, flinging himself spread-eagled onto the sand.

'What cheek. I'm quicker than you,' Kitty gasped back.

'No, you're not.'

'Yes, I am because you cheated and I still caught you up,' she persisted.

'Only just,' said Peter, determined for the last word.

'I like Uncle Roy. He's fun,' Kitty said as she watched him shaping a castle and moat for Grace and Thomas.

'Yes, the old man's not too bad. Uncle Jack's pretty good, too.'

'Daddy's great. We do lots of things together,' she replied, thinking of their walks and their trips to the pictures. 'You're so lucky having a car. I wish we had one. We're always queuing for buses and trains.'

John, who had made off to see the harbour and capstan for the boats, returned and distancing himself, sat staring moodily out to sea.

Kitty glanced over at him. An aura of despondency hung around him like a sentence. Something was the matter with him. She could feel it. 'Can John swim?' she asked.

'Yes, he can. I don't know why he didn't put his swimsuit on today. He's a very good swimmer. He's been practising for the school swimming gala for weeks now.'

'But you live in a city, so where do you swim?'

'At the swimming baths, and there's a competition there each year.'

'He's very quiet, isn't he? Is he always like that?'

'Umm. Not so bad as he is now. Your Grace doesn't say much either, does she?'

'She's just shy with strangers.' They grinned in empathy at each other.

'Bet you can't walk on your hands like me,' said Peter, jumping to his feet and making a handstand. He walked unsteadily across the sand before collapsing in a heap.

Kitty was tempted to follow suit, but chose to wait until she could perform her speciality of making a handstand on a wall, and walking her legs down it, until she resembled a crab. 'I can do something much better than that,' she teased.

'Oh yeah. Like what?'

'I'll show you when we get home.' Mischievously, she picked up a handful of sand, and trickled it down over his head.

It had been the most wonderful of days; riding in a car to a new beach, and then seeing the First and Last House at Lands End where Uncle Roy had taken a photo of her and Grace beside it, wearing their first shop-bought dresses of white polka dots and piping. He promised he would send a copy of it before pointing to grey smudges on the horizon, saying they were the Scilly Isles that were once connected to the mainland. It was a land of many churches that were drowned when the sea suddenly rose, he explained, and it was said their ghostly bells could still be heard ringing beneath the sea. Kitty and Grace had turned their ears to the sea and listened, but could hearing nothing but the roar of the waves as they threw themselves against the rugged rocks beneath the cliffs and disintegrated in plumes of spray. On their return home, her favourite tea was waiting, tatie cake, emerging from the oven golden and bubbling from the creamy mix of cooked potato and suet, to be topped by a fried egg, and accompanied by the popular Moffetts skinless sausages, made in the butcher's shop in Camborne to their own special recipe. Kitty adored them.

And now, to crown the day, Uncle Roy was coming into the front room carrying a huge box of chocolates. It was decorated with a beautiful gold and white satin ribbon and bow and Kitty hoped she would be able to keep it in her box of special memories. Even before she had tasted them, the rich cocoa-sweet smell melted her mouth in anticipation as Octavia opened the box and passed them around. There were so many chocolates. Which should she choose? She finally plumped for one with a strawberry filling, sinking her teeth into the centre and letting it dissolve slowly and deliciously on her tongue. She looked across at Peter and John who declined the offer of one. Kitty was flabbergasted. 'Don't you like them? They're scrumptious.'

'I'm afraid, Kitty, with the boys it's a case of familiarity breeding contempt.'

'Oh, I see,' replied Kitty, although her face that was an open book, revealed she did not.

'I think I ought to explain Kitty why the boys are not too interested in chocolates. You see, I work for a firm that makes and sells them.'

'You mean they can have them any time, they want? Crumbs!'

'It doesn't seem fair, does it?' he sympathised.

'I would much rather have one of your pasties, Aunty,' said Peter.

'Me too,' said John unexpectedly from the depths of the arm-chair in the bay window.

'Thank you boys, I'm glad you enjoyed them. I wouldn't mind having a penny for every one I've made. I would be worth a fortune by now.'

'And what do you think of my chocolates, Grace?' Roy asked her.

'Yummy,' replied Grace, giving him a shy smile of pleasure.

Roy sitting beside her, gave her a gentle cuff with his elbow. 'Good. Would you like another?'

'Yes, please, Uncle Roy.'

'You can pass the box on to that chatterbox sister of yours,' he said, as she took one.

Kitty sitting on the tut, looked at him mournfully before scruti-nizing the chocolate labels and settled for a coffee cream.

Jack stood up from the settee. 'It's a lovely evening. Who's for a game of French cricket?'

'We are!' Kitty and Grace cried out together.

Jack chortled at Roy. 'It's the latest craze in this house. They probably play it in their sleep.'

The play was noisy and exuberant. Jack and Roy joined in, and once again, the competitive instinct in Kitty and Peter surfaced, as they did their utmost to knock each other out, much to Roy's amusement. 'She's keeping Peter on his toes. It will do him good, as he likes to think he can win at everything,' he murmured to Jack.

There was a call from Octavia at the back door. 'Anyone for a cup of tea?'

'I'm ready for one. What about you Roy?'

'I wouldn't say no. This family craze is thirsty work!' he replied. They left the children to their game, and in what remained of the evening's sun in the front room, they sat and earnestly discussed the education and hopes for the future of their children.

Growing tired of playing, Peter announced he was hungry.

'But you can't be, exclaimed Kitty in surprise. We haven't long had tea.'

'Well, I am. Let's make some tomato sauce sandwiches.'

Kitty was thrown by his remark. 'We can't do that. Mummy doesn't like us making anything in the kitchen, unless she's there,' she said.

Grace agreed. 'It's true, she won't like it.'

'Oh, go on, Kitty, it's only a sandwich.'

A tomato sauce sandwich. This was something new. She was intrigued and although uneasy at the thought, was won over by his disarming grin and led him to the kitchen. Once started, the fun of the forbidden took over as she watched him make one.

'Try it.' he said. 'It's tasty.' He cut it in half and handed one each to Kitty and Grace.

Kitty took a bite. 'It's really nice, isn't it Grace?'

He was engrossed in the making of another one when Octavia opened the connecting door from the passage. Kitty and Grace started back guiltily.

'Peter is showing me how to make a tomato sauce sandwich,' Kitty stammered, holding the half eaten sandwich and wondering quite what to do with it.

75

'So I can see,' she replied in annoyance. 'If you wanted something more to eat, why didn't you ask, Peter?'

Peter turning beetroot, looked down at the ground, and shuffled his feet.

'Well, next time, if you're still feeling hungry, tell me, and I will give you something a little more substantial than that,' she said, looking with distaste at the sandwich. Whatever next, she thought, with pursed lips as she put away the bread. 'Would you like a saffron bun, Peter? There are plenty left.'

'No, thank you, Aunty. I'll just eat this sandwich,' he replied, squirming under her look. He snatched it up and backed towards the door.

'Crikey! Your mum is fearful, isn't she?' he exclaimed in the garden.

'I told you she wouldn't like us in the kitchen.'

'Seems daft that we can make a jam sandwich but not a tomato one. Grown-ups are queer fish.'

Kitty laughed at his observation but also knew with a slight sinking feeling, it would not be the end of the matter. Peter had challenged Octavia's sense of Cornish hospitality and it would be spoken of again, but not until they had returned to Birmingham.

Chapter Ten

'I'D FORGOTTEN HOW quickly the weather changes in Cornwall,' said Roy, glancing out of the window at the scudding clouds as he spooned marmalade onto his toast.

'You've been away from the old country, too long, Roy,' replied Jack.

'You're right, there. Still, I do remember that one never waits for the weather, here. The sun can be shining on one coast and henting down rain on another,' he replied, slipping easily back into his native tongue. 'I thought, if everyone is agreeable, we could go for a round trip taking in Newlyn and Mousehole, and some magic stones on the way to Porthcurno. What do you think, young ladies? Does it sound like an interesting proposition?' asked Roy, looking quizzically across the table at Grace and Kitty whose ears pricked up at the word magic. 'What do you mean, magic rocks, Uncle Roy?'

'Ah! Well, you will have to wait and see,' he replied, pulling a face at Grace who smirked behind her hand.

Octavia looked at him from under her eyes. He could not resist embroidering an air of mystery and his eyes hid a smile as he returned her look.

'You'll love Porthcurno, girls. The beach is full of shells and I noticed you're collecting them in a jam jar in your bedroom.

They both beamed at the thought. 'When we've got enough, Uncle Roy, we're going to stick the shells over an empty cigar box that was given to us to keep our jewellery in,' said Grace shyly.

'We saw one in a shop window at St. Ives and that's what gave us the idea,' added Kitty.

'I see. Well, it seems everyone is happy with the suggestion, but you, John,' Roy said, at his morose expression. 'Do try and buck up. We don't come to Cornwall every day. Mum and I thought you would enjoy this break after the worry we've all had with Diane.'

'We should make an early start whilst the weather is reasonable,' Jack intervened brightly. 'It's forecast to come into rain by early evening although it may well stay dry. The weathermen never get it right. We're too near to the coast.'

'I think I'll give this one a miss,' said Octavia.

'Oh, darling, you must come.'

'And where would I sit? On the roof?'

The children laughed.

'And in any case, I've been to Porthcurno before.'

'Did you go on the bus, mummy?' asked Grace.

'No, on the back of a motorbike.'

'A *motorbike*!' exclaimed Kitty.

Octavia, could have cut out her tongue for Kitty's constant curiosity would want to know the who, the why and the wherefore, and Octavia, wishing the past to remain there, curtailed any impending question from Kitty by getting up from the table and lifting Thomas off his chair. 'This one misses his morning nap, and I shall be happier staying in out of this wind. You know how I hate it, Jack, and you're forgetting, I had a lovely day out yesterday with Roy.'

'Well, if you're quite sure about it, because I really don't mind staying at home with Thomas.'

Octavia was firm. 'Have you seen the Merry Maidens or Porthcurno?'

'Well, no . . .'

'I rest my case,' said Octavia as she began picking up the plates. 'Come on girls, help me to clear the table and then I'll make up a few egg sandwiches and pop some saffron buns in a bag to keep you all going until you come home. I'll have a hot meal ready for tea.'

Buttoned up warmly, for the wind was fresh, Kitty, Peter and Grace raced each other down the entry to the car, jigging around in high spirits as they waited impatiently for Roy to unlock the doors.

'Keep your eye on those two, nodded Octavia at Kitty and Peter. 'They're double trouble.'

'Don't worry, we shan't let them out of our sight,' Roy called back, as Kitty and Grace jumped into the back seat in a state of suppressed excitement and waved at Thomas standing in the doorway with Octavia. Jack slammed his door shut.

78

Roy lit a cigarette, and moved the car smoothly into gear and out of the terrace. 'I'm looking forward to seeing old haunts again. They were good times, returning to Cornwall on my Enfield. It was my pride and joy.' Roy sucked in his breath at the memory. 'You have such a sense of speed on a bike, it's exhilarating.'

'I can imagine,' murmured Jack.

'Looking back on it, we were totally irresponsible, tearing around the lanes like mad men. It's no wonder Octavia and James came off their bike. They were lucky not to be . . .' He stopped short, aware of ears on the back seat. But Kitty appeared to be deaf to everything with the thrill of watching familiar sights passing from the comfort of a car, and her young voice brimmed with eagerness to show the boys the local sights. 'Look, there's my church and in a minute you'll see my school, and the lamp-post opposite where I banged my head when we were going to the circus.'

'Don't you look where you're going?' Peter mocked.

'Yes, of course I do, silly, but I was turning to watch the circus animals and people parading down the road to the field, and when I turned back, I walked straight into it. It didn't half hurt. Luckily, Aunty Dorothy's house was nearby and we went in there to bathe my forehead in cold water but it still came up like an egg. It was huge and mummy was worried I would have a delayed reaction, like dizziness or something. But I didn't.'

Jack and Roy listened in amusement whilst she chattered on until Peter cut in over her. 'Why can't we go straight to the beach, dad?'

'As I said at breakfast, Peter, we are taking in Newlyn and Mousehole. I know you can't wait to dive in the sea, although you'll find it very cold as it's only May month, but you must understand, it's a day out for everyone. Uncle Jack and the family don't have the luxury of a car, as we do, to drive to fishing villages and isolated beaches like Porthcurno.'

'It would take us all week to get there!' Jack chortled. He settled back comfortably into his seat in the pleasant anticipation of unfamiliar sights and male conversation as they drove out of town and onto the main road to Penzance. 'This is such a pleasant change Roy, and not having to walk the hill at the end of the day will be a bonus.'

Yes, life could not be easy, thought Roy, having to walk up and down that steep hill carrying shopping and pushing pushchairs. He liked Jack immensely. Steady and reliable, he was a loving father and it was clear that he had made Kitty his own and his love for Octavia was evident. He was sensitive to her independent streak, and lightly held the reins, and above all, it was visible that she had reached calmer waters after the tide of loss and pain.

'I must ring Winnie again tonight and see how Diane is,' said Roy. 'We thought we were going to lose her, you know. It was touch and go.'

'It must have been a very anxious and worrying time for you both. How was the hospital?'

'First rate. Diane couldn't have had better treatment.' Roy cast Jack a sideways glance and chuckled. 'Now, why do I feel I'm going to be led into a discussion on Nye Bevan and the health service?'

It was inevitable that the conversation would become tinged with politics. Jack revelled in political dialogue and Roy, playing devil's advocate to Jack's socialist persuasion, equally enjoyed debating with him, for from past experience the whole tenure of political or religious conversation would always remain dispassionate and without rancour. His deeply held beliefs were his strength and with his facts, always sure, it was a formidable combination.

'Well, you can't deny Bevan's breadth of vision. No-one had ever envisaged a health service for rich and poor alike and certainly not the Tories. How they and the medical profession fought him, but he held his nerve and with the will of the people behind him, he brought it off. And this in the aftermath of a war that drained our resources dry.'

'Yes, and the health service and nationalisation schemes are costing millions, Jack. Of course, I know we're getting aid from America but the country is still in a state of flux and world trade continues to be in chaos.'

'I can't deny the task ahead to complete the welfare state programme is enormous and it will take political will-power to see it through, but what a wonderful legacy he will leave for our children. They will never have to worry about doctor's bills, as our parents did or fear illness at work.

'You're absolutely right, of course. And yet, despite the good emerging from the war, we have Americans paranoid about 'reds' under the bed and the fighting goes on with Korea.'

'And earth's proud empires pass away, like the old hymn says,' mused Jack. 'India's gone and with a fledgling commonwealth I foresee . . .'

'Dad. Quick! Stop! John says he's feeling sick.'

Roy pulled in rapidly at the sea wall by St. Michael's Mount rising like a galleon in full sail beneath the racing clouds.

John shot out of the car, his face like paste.

Roy flung open his car door and quickly followed him, putting his hands lightly around his son's stooped shoulders. 'Take deep breaths John. There's a good chap,' said Roy.

Jack and the girls looked on anxiously from the car as John gulped in a lungful of air.

Peter was irritated. 'Of all the times to be sick. I hope this doesn't mean we've got to go back. It'll spoil the whole day.'

Kitty was indignant. 'Oh, don't be so mean, Peter. He can't help feeling sick.'

'I don't care. He's been like a wet blanket for weeks. It's OK for you. You live near the sea all the time. We only have a few days here.'

Kitty was halted in her indignation, and deep inside her, she was also hoping against hope they wouldn't have to go home. And yet, she could not ignore this feeling that something was not right with John. 'I think there's a reason why he's feeling sick.'

'Big deal. They're usually is, if someone is throwing up,' he ridiculed.

Out of the blue, Grace said enigmatically, 'Kitty knows lots of things.'

Kitty looked at her in surprise.

'Kitty knows lots of things,' he mimicked. 'Like what?' He jeered.

Grace looked upset and Kitty's temper flared. 'I *told* you. Something's wrong with John, only you're too *stupid* to see it. I don't *know* what it is, but even if I did, I certainly wouldn't tell *you*! You're a selfish, nasty, horrible boy.'

Peter was flabbergasted. This fragile looking girl with whom he had felt an immediate rapport had turned on him with the speed of a spitfire. She was quite unlike the girls in his school. This one had spunk, but he was not going to give her an inch. He turned his shoulder away and stared fixedly out of the window, innocent to the fact that despite their quarrel, he would never forget the memory of this first summer's meeting, and the bond forged between them would remain strong in the years ahead.

Jack, who had only been half listening to their squabble, snapped into awareness. He twisted his head around. Kitty had a way of honing in on trouble. 'What do you mean, something's wrong with John, Kitty?'

She looked back at Jack with perplexed eyes. 'I don't know daddy.'

Troubled, he turned back and opening the car door, began walking to the sea wall where John was sitting.

'It's not like you to get carsick, John, and you've been very quiet these past few weeks. Are you worried about Diane?' Roy was asking, as Jack came up beside them, his grey flannel trousers flapping in the breeze.

'How are you feeling now, John? The sea air should help to clear your head.'

'I'm OK now, thanks, Uncle Jack.' He turned to Roy. 'I'm fine dad, really,' he said, his face slowly regaining colour. 'I suddenly came over feeling funny, I don't know why.'

'We can always turn back, you know.' said Roy, looking at him with a concerned expression.

'I'm *all right,* dad,' said John impatiently, shrugging away Roy's arm and walking rapidly towards the car.

Roy raised his hands in supplication at Jack. 'Kids!'

The car drew slowly away and Kitty knelt up to watch the fairy-like castle on the mount, until it disappeared from view out of the back car window. She slid down with a bump and let herself half-fall on top of Peter.

'Oh, I'm so sorry,' she mocked.

He pushed her back off him. 'That's not funny.'

'I thought you weren't talking to me.'

Peter pointedly turned his head away.

Roy glanced into the mirror at the four children hemmed in together. The air was simmering. 'I think we'll stop at Penzance for a cup of tea. It might help to settle John's stomach. Are there any cafés along the prom, Jack?'

'I seem to remember there's one just past the Queens Hotel.'

82

'Good, we'll do that.' His voice dropped to a murmur and he tilted a nod back at the children. 'Something's going on back there. I think a break might clear the air.'

'They were squabbling earlier, but I couldn't get to the bottom of it.'

'Hmmmm' said Roy.

As Roy predicted, the stop at the café broke the atmosphere. Peter strove to remain aloof from Kitty but her temper had died as swiftly as it had arisen and at her irrepressible spirit he grudgingly returned her overtures. She was impossible. Strolling back to the car, Kitty tried once more to discover the secret of the magic rocks, and Roy, amused at her persistence, would not be drawn. She looked up at him in exasperation. *Why* wouldn't he tell her? It was maddening, as her mother would say.

Driving through Newlyn, Roy stopped at the top of the hill for a view over the harbour and out to St. Michael's Mount, sharply outlined in the distance. Kitty looked down. She had never seen so many fishing boats. At St. Ives, there were always a few that looked colourful bobbing on a high tide, or lying beached on the sand of the harbour, but here, crammed together, they merged into one jumbled mass of nets and machinery. At the sight of the boats, John's face flickered into life.

'What fish do they catch here, Uncle Jack?'

'All sorts, John. Cod, mackerel, haddock, you name it.' Pleased that the boy had brightened and was finally showing interest in his surroundings, he continued. 'In the eighteen hundreds the main catch was pilchards. You can still see the huer's huts on cliff tops where a lookout man would keep watch for the dark shadows of the fish coming into the bay. On seeing them, he would sound the alarm by shouting, 'Hevva! Hevva!' All the men in the village would stop what they were doing and race to the seine-boats, and following the huer's hand signals, would row at full speed out to sea. When they heard the blow of his tin trumpet, they knew it was time to stop and cast their nets. The sea used to boil with millions of them struggling to escape the tuck-net, as it was called.'

'The poor fish,' said Grace.

'But tasty when mum marinates them. I love them,' said Kitty.

Grace's reply was emphatic. 'I don't.'

'That's because you hate having to pick out the pepper pods and fish bones. You're so fussy.'

Jack intervened. 'That's enough Kitty. Grace doesn't have to like them, just because you do.'

Kitty smarted at his rebuke in front of the boys.

'As I was saying John, once caught, they were scooped into waiting boats and taken ashore to the women for curing.'

Roy started up the engine, and eased away out onto the coast road to Mousehole with the sea fanning up into flutes of white from the stiff breeze. On entering the fishing village he pulled alongside the harbour wall where small fishing smacks and rowing boats lay slapping on the ripples of water. Behind them, a jigsaw of houses rose up the hillside where steep steps led to half-opened stable doors.

'It's so picturesque,' said Jack, as they continued, and wound their way through the twisting streets where pilchard cellars, long converted into sun-lit courtyards, spilt tubs of flowers.

Jack hoping to engage John's interest again, pointed one out. 'A hundred years ago, John, that's where women would stand for hours, salting, and stacking the pilchards in barrels for export to Italy. Their lives were very simple and depended wholly upon pilchards for food and fish oil for their lamps. Their houses must have stunk to high heaven.'

'Yes, life was hard in those days, especially for children of your age, so count your blessings!' Roy jested as they left the village behind and made their way inland to the Merry Maidens.

'Will all passengers wishing to see the magic stones, please leave the train,' he announced through pinched nostrils, as they came to a stop.

Peter cringed. 'Do you have to do that dad. It's not funny.'

But for Grace, who had taken a shine to Roy for he engaged with her shyness, he made her laugh. 'I think he's funny,' she giggled to Kitty, as they jumped out of the car and ran to climb over the stile into the field.

Jack, in a familiar gesture, pushed his hair back from the teasing wind as they walked to the circle of upright stones. 'I've read somewhere that water diviners have found that these ancient circles are usually over blind springs. Odd that. And, of course, they've always been associated with ancient rituals.'

'These stones were once maidens,' said Jack to the children as they stood in the centre of the ring.

'I know you're having us on, daddy,' Kitty grinned at him.

'No, it's true, Kitty. The legend says the maidens went into the fields to dance with the boys, instead of going to church, and for this they were turned to stone, along with two pipers who also stand petrified in a field down the road.'

Kitty gave him a doubtful look and began to count the stones.

'They say they can never be counted correctly, Kitty, but I tell you what,' said Roy, placing his hands on her shoulders from behind and leaning down to her ear. 'If you go over to one of the stones and place your hands on it, you'll find it tingles with warmth.'

'Dad's off again,' said Peter, laughing at her.

'Take no notice of Peter, Kitty. You go and try it.' She ran over to one and wound her arms around the rough surface. It was as cold as the wind. Disappointed, she ran to another. It felt the same. Was Uncle Roy pulling her leg? 'You come and try it Grace,' she shouted to her.

Grace ran and placed a tentative hand on one of the stones. 'I can't feel anything.'

Watching them, Roy said, 'They do say there is some force field around the stones which could account for the heat some people have felt coming from them. But who knows. I've never felt it myself,' he went on as they walked over to the girls. 'Just keep trying, Kitty, and I'm sure the stones will work their magic on you,' he said, winking at Jack.

Kitty, sighing, tried one more time. And then it happened. She was frozen to the spot with the same shiver of goose bumps that she had felt on seeing the children at Nancarrow. The circle was filled with people chanting. The women, dressed in long skirts of a coarse material and holding shawls over their heads, stood with their children in a semi-circle. The men, wearing tunics belted at the waist over thick trousers, radiated in lines to the centre where a man stood with his hands encircling a golden cup held up to the evening sun. His dark blue robe was long and flowing and decorated with golden stitching of flames, intertwined with circles and stars, and on his head was a mitred crown of polished copper. Their sing-song chanting rose and swelled in a language alien to her ears, and yet, was strangely familiar, and she felt herself responding to the invocation, the words forming on her lips.

'What is it Kitty?' asked Jack in alarm for she stood rigidly staring into space, her lips moving soundlessly. 'Kitty!' He shook her and her body relaxed and her eyes refocused upon him.

I saw people daddy, in the circle. They were dressed in clothes like you see in history books, and there was a man in a blue robe. It was beautiful and they were cha . . . n . . .ting.' Her voice faltered at his worried look. 'Didn't you *see* them?'

'No, Kitty, I didn't. I think you've let that fertile imagination of yours runaway with you,' said Jack.

'But I *did* see people . . . they were standing *here* with us, in the circle.' Kitty saw them exchange a look. Oh, what was the use. There was no point in even trying to explain. She could see they didn't believe her.

Roy called to Peter and John who were horsing about in and out of the stones. 'Come on, you two articles! We're leaving for the beach.' The boys continued to fool around, hanging onto each other and sticking feet in front of legs in an attempt to trip the other up as they walked back to the car. Kitty trailed behind them, confused and mystified at what she had seen, and hurt that Jack had thought it was her imagination. It *wasn't!* She really *had* seen those people. But how did they get there, and why was she the only one to see them?, she thought, turning to look back, again and again at the stones.

Peter's impatience for the sea was silenced. Porthcurno cove lay before them with glistening white sand sloping down to turquoise water, translucent as crystal. It was theirs alone and for the taking. Nestling between high cliffs, the beach was warm and sheltered, and throwing down a blanket, they spread out under the sun. Jack took out the sandwiches, and one by one, they fell silent under the spell of the cove. Kitty stared at the stars dancing on the water, her mind distant, thinking of the strangely dressed people in the stone circle. Perhaps she had imagined them, as her father said, but they had seemed as real to her as this magical cove with its Mediterranean blue of sea and shell-strewn sand. A movement caught her eye from the top of the cliff, a pure white bird soaring majestically over them. 'Look!' she pointed.

They all looked up. 'It's only a seagull,' said Peter.

Kitty watched the bird gliding soundless to and fro above her. It was much too beautiful to be a mere seagull. Seagulls screeched and mewed, but this one kept a silent vigil over them. Kitty wondered if it was her guardian angel, as Sandra had explained one afternoon when walking home from Sunday School. 'Everyone has an angel to keep us safe from harm,' she said. This notion appealed to Kitty, for she was forever landing herself in predicaments, like the time she and Grace were out playing in the fields with Terry and Sandra, when she pretended to be a matador, holding her coat as a cape, and taunting a field of steers by stamping her feet to and fro. Their answer was dramatic. Stirring the ground in agitation, they had charged straight at them. Grace stood frozen to the spot, until Kitty screamed at her to run for the hedge. She barely made it and in her terrified attempt to scramble over, caught her legs in the brambles and was lacerated from her thighs to her ankles. It was a horrible sight. She grimaced at the thought of the blood-red welts, even now, and fearing to take Grace home in such a state, had detoured to gran, who bathed them and dabbed on iodine at which, she cried out, over and over, and Kitty had flinched away at the sound. So where was Grace's guardian angel on that day? Maybe, she didn't have one.

Sandra's reply had been adamant. 'Yes, she has. And she escaped the steers, didn't she? She wasn't trampled to death. So there you are then.'

Their talk had led onto an earnest discussion on God.

'But how do you *know* He exists?' Sandra asked her.

'I just do,' Kitty replied. It was something she felt deep within her; a conviction that He was everywhere and knew everything, even her innermost thoughts, which wasn't always to Kitty's liking. There were times when she simply hated that spiteful Rosemary in her class who was so full of her own self-importance, and having to love and forgive her, as Jesus said she should, was just not possible.

Having eaten, the children, all but John, had changed into their swimsuits.

'You're not swimming, John?' asked Jack.

John shook his head and getting up, silently took off across the sand.

'I don't know what's the matter with him lately,' said Roy, watching his son cut a solitary figure as he walked towards the rocks. 'I wondered if Diane's illness had upset him more than we realised.'

'Who knows what goes on inside their heads. He'll get over it. Sometimes, I think children inhabit another planet,' replied Jack, leaning back on his elbows.

Roy agreed. 'It's so warm here, it's like another world from Penzance,' he said, rolling up his sleeves and lifting his face to the sun.

The rhythmic lap of the sea was hypnotic, and they fell into a companionable silence, basking in the sheltered heat under a dome of cornflower-blue. A scallop of white fringed the emerald sea on the bleached-white sand, and the cliffs were pink with tufts of thrift. How fortunate the man that captures this with a brush, thought Roy.

Jack's thoughts had led to more prosaic matters. 'It won't be long before the cricket matches between Beacon and Troon will be in full swing,' he said.

Roy, still in a contemplative mood, murmured, 'I've often thought that cricket typifies the English temperament. No outward show. Just quietly competitive. It's the perfect antidote to the pressures of work. Some evenings I go to our local cricket club and sit with the old boys and have a jar on the bench listening to the clunk of leather on willow.'

Jack gave him a roguish look. 'And how would you rate rugby for the English character?'

'Rugby, Jack, is for Cornish heathens! We always were a race apart.'

In total accord they laughed loudly at this truism, and Jack, knowing Roy would relish it, related an amusing cricket anecdote. 'You will remember, Dick,' said Jack. 'He was telling me recently, of a match between Penzance and Troon. It was all going along nicely until the umpire shouted '*Out!*' to this particular batsman, who argued that he wasn't. So the umpire said to him, "You wate 'til you read next week's *West Briton*, then!"'

Roy roared with laughter. 'It's one of the things I miss. Our Cornish humour. Nothing can touch it.'

As instructed by Octavia, they kept a watchful eye on the children as they discussed the merits of the English team, and saw the girls were oblivious to everything in their hunt for shells. Peter was jumping up and down in the sea as he waded in. It was icy cold as Roy had predicated and would take all summer to warm up. John sat away from them all on a rock and Jack wondered what ailed the sad and solitary boy.

'Look at these, Kitty,' cried Grace holding on the tips of her fingers two fan shaped shells in palest peach and pink, the size of her fingernails.

'They're everywhere,' said Kitty, running over. 'Look. I've got bigger ones,' she said, holding them out in the palm of her hands to show her. 'They're the same colour as the sienna in our paint box, aren't they? And look at these,' she said, crouching down and picking up a violet coloured topshell. 'It's like a mountain with a path going around it. They are all so pretty, I don't know which I like the best,' peering down at the coral-coloured scallop shells, and yellow periwinkles lying at the base of the bucket, before dropping her new treasure gently on top. She resumed her hunt and it was then that a pure white feather floated down and lay at her feet. There was no sign of the white bird as she looked up at the shining blue of sky, and picking it up she stroked her face with its springing edge and smiled at the sign from her guardian angel. *'I am here with you,'* a voice whispered. She looked around. 'Did you say something to me, Grace?' she called out to her sister's bowed head absorbed in following a trail of shells along a tide-line.

'No. Why?' she replied, without looking up.

'Oh, nothing,' Kitty said, puzzled, as she carefully placed the feather into her bucket. It would be her most treasured possession, but where had the voice come from? She knew she hadn't imagine it. It was soft and musical, unearthly, and suddenly, she was filled with the most indescribable feeling. She was floating on air, and so radiant with happiness her soul was singing with it. It seemed to spill from every pore in her body. If only she could speak of this sense that she was at one with all of life, but who'd believe her? They would say it's Kitty again, seeing and hearing things that no-one else could. She looked over at John. He looked forlorn

89

and lonely. Perhaps her happiness would rub off on him. She wandered over and sat beside him on the rock. 'Hi, John,' she said brightly. 'Why aren't you swimming with Peter? He told me you like swimming, and are so good, you are in your school team.'

John shifted uneasily, pushing his hands down onto the rock and kicking his foot miserably at the sand. 'I don't want to swim,' he muttered.

'But why?'

'I just don't. That's all.'

Kitty persisted, and tilted her head under his face. 'What's wrong John?'

'*Nothing*,' he replied irritably, avoiding her gaze for her eyes were persuasive and penetrating in their clarity.

Kitty shifted closer to him and their sandy legs touched. A prickle of warmth shot through him. 'Why are you so sad? Because you are, aren't you? Daddy always says, a trouble shared is a trouble halved.'

John fixed his eyes to a distant point out to sea. His fear and the need to confide fought within. What should he do? How could he tell anyone his horrible secret, and even if he tried to tell this sparky cousin, could she be trusted? His thoughts went around and around in a torment of indecision.

Kitty sat very still and waited.

'If you promise, promise on your honour not to tell anyone,' he began, finally.

'Cross my heart and hope to die.'

'There's . . . this man, my swimming instructor . . .' He swallowed nervously, and stopped.

Kitty fearing he would not continue, gently prompted. 'What about this man?'

John sighed with despair. 'He keeps me behind after school for extra swimming and diving lessons, which I don't need,' he added, quickly. 'I told dad that, but he said, I must keep on with my lessons, if Mr. Collins thinks I should.' He gave another kick of frustration. Kitty watched the damp under-layer of sand falling in a shower of dark blobs. 'He likes to muck around in the pool and comes into the changing room and . . .' He stopped at the thought of the burning shame and revulsion he felt at his touch. His face contorted with rage. 'I *hate* him! I *hate* him!'

His sudden, vehement anger took Kitty by surprise. She placed her arm around his thin shoulders and again he felt warmth shoot through his body that for one bright moment alleviated the anguish and pain. 'The same thing happens in our school, John. Miss Drew, our PT teacher comes into our changing rooms, too, and . . .'

'You don't understand Kitty. Just leave me alone,' he cried, throwing off her arm.

In that instant, a cold shudder ran through her. She felt this man's menace and John's terrified fear of him. There was something he was holding back from her. '*What* don't I understand?' she persisted.

John shook his head in exasperation.'

'Why don't you tell Uncle Roy how horrible this man is to you?'

'I can't. I just can't.'

'Have you talked to Peter about it?'

'No, he would only go and blab to mum and she's got enough on her plate with Diane.'

'Yes, mummy told us that she's been very sick.'

'They said she might die. It was awful.'

Kitty thought of Thomas ill and dying. It did not bear thinking about. Her mother would go insane.

She racked her brains for another solution. Of course, why hadn't she thought of it before? 'Just tell Mr. Collins that you don't want to be in the team.'

'I did, but he told me I was being silly and that my father wouldn't be very pleased if I threw in the towel after all these weeks of practice. I tried to tell him I didn't like being thrown into the pool' . . . he swallowed nervously, again, 'and the other things.'

What other things? Kitty wondered, as he continued.

'But he told me to stop being such a baby. It was just harmless fun and I was making a fuss about nothing.' John drew up his legs, wrapping his arms around them, 'Oh *God*. I wish I were dead,' he moaned, dropping his head on top of his knees.

Kitty was shocked and at a loss. She resorted to action. Later, the answer would come. It always did. Jumping down from the rock, she sought to allay his fears. 'You mustn't say that John. It will be all right in the end, I promise.'

He raised his head to her. The sun was firing her hair into a halo of light and her smile was luminous. Her eyes danced with a radiance that flooded his body with hope.

'Race you to the sea. Bet I can beat you! Come on daddy long legs, I dare you,' she cried, throwing down the gauntlet. Not waiting for his reply, but trusting that he would follow, she took off with the speed of a gazelle, the sand kicking up from her heels, her slim body one fluid motion of movement. Half turning, she shouted over her shoulder, as he stood there, watching her. 'You won't catch me,' Her laughter rang around the high cliffs, and with it came a sudden, uplifting release of his misery. He would catch his will-o'-the-wisp cousin, and racing after her, his long, lanky legs eating up the sand, he drew level and she saw the hunted look of an animal had gone as they stopped together at the water's edge, and waited for Peter who came out of the sea with chattering teeth and skin purple-blue with the cold.

Chapter Eleven

'JOHN SEEMS BRIGHTER, today,' said Jack to Roy over a leisurely second cup of tea at the breakfast table as the children disappeared outside.

'Yes, I noticed it too. I think that Kitty may have done some good. Yesterday, they were sitting on the rocks with their heads together. These past few weeks I haven't been able to get through to him at all, but Kitty has a winning way with her which is difficult to resist.'

'Hmmmm,' said Jack with a comic expression of doubt. 'She's certainly persistent and can be quite a handful at times, but yes, she does have her moments of sweet reasonableness.'

'So, Jack, what's the game plan today?'

'Church!'

'I see. I'm not sure that will be up the boys' street.'

'Octavia and I thought that might be the case. The service starts at two, so after dinner if you wanted to go off somewhere with the boys, we'll see you when you get back, but there's no rush. Tea will be on the table as and when you turn up. It's the Whitsun service which includes confirmation and is always well attended, and in any case, the girls won't want to miss Sunday School. It all counts towards points for the house cup.'

'House cup?'

'Yes. There are so many Sunday School children that they have been divided up into houses. Four aisles filled from front to back and named after the disciples, Matthew, Mark, Luke and John,' replied Jack. 'At the end of each year we have a prize-giving evening for those with the highest attendance.'

'It sounds like a very good system to encourage children and families to church.'

'It is, and to encourage them even more, extra points are awarded if the children bring along their parents and friends to the family service held once a month.'

'Do you and Octavia go to services every week?'

'Jack does as he's a church warden and their treasurer, so he needs to be there. I go as often as I can,' replied Octavia, as she lifted Thomas from the floor onto her lap, kissing the top of his curls and rocking as she nuzzled into his face. 'It's a very lively church and Sunday School. Kitty is the Captain of St. John's. She's terribly bossy, and orders her house to make sure they bring their bibles, because that also counts as house points towards a cup.' She laughed. 'It seems to pay off, as last year they won the cup and she won the Fisherman's prize for roping in more new children for Sunday School than anyone else. I don't know how she manages it. She probably threatens her school friends with hell and damnation if they don't come.'

'I heard that, mummy. That's not true,' said Kitty indignantly, as she returned into the sitting room with Peter. 'I told them it was fun Uncle Roy, and they could win a book for attendance like me, and they would be given a little book of empty squares to fill with a picture stamp every Sunday. But the clincher was the thought of riding on their very own train on Tea Treat day.'

'Ahhhhh, so that's how you did it. A little bit of bribery,' Octavia teased.

Kitty glared at her. 'Oh, come on Peter,' and she stomped back out of the room.

'Kitty, I was only teasing.' Octavia called after her. 'You did an excellent job recruiting so many children for our church. Oh, dear,' she laughed, 'I shall be in Kitty's bad books. I know that look.'

'Do you really have your own train?' asked Peter, on their way out of the house and onto the terrace.

'Yes we do, with a huge banner on the front, saying St. Martin's Church, Camborne. We don't stop for anyone.' She giggled. 'We thumb our noses at people waiting on the platforms and at St. Erth, we don't even have to get off the train. The engine shunts from the front to the back and carries on down the branch line to St. Ives.'

'Crikey! You lucky stinkers.'

Clambering up onto the neatly clipped hedge where neighbours would sometimes congregate and sit chatting in the long summer evenings, Kitty made her way along to the lamp-post. 'Bet you can't swing from it with your legs, like I can. Keep an eye out for mum and dad in the windows. They'll kill me if they see me!' She shinned up and turning upside down straddled the crossbars with both legs, the skirt of her dress dropping down over her head.

'You're showing your knickers,' Peter teased.

'So would you, if you had to wear a dress,' came her muffled reply, as unable to see, she struggled to bring her hands back onto the crossbars. 'I wish I was a boy and could wear short trousers all the time,' she said breathlessly, as she slipped down the post onto the hedge.

Peter, jumped to the bars, walked his feet up the post and determined to go one better, hung there on one leg.

'Show-off,' Kitty said, pulling a face at him.

'So are you,' he said, as he manoeuvred back to an upright position, swung to and fro for a moment or two, and dropped down onto the terrace. 'Where's this secret hideaway of yours? You said you'd show it to me.'

Kitty pointed to the bottom of the field. 'Down there. You see that high wall the other side of the lane? There's an old manor house behind it, called Nancarrow, which nobody lives in now. The wall goes all around the grounds, and I found a hidden door in it, in one of the fields. I squeeze through the gap into the woods and gardens where there is a big lake with a boathouse.'

'A boathouse! Has it got a boat?' he said, raring to go.

Kitty hesitated. 'I'm not allowed to play on Sundays. Usually, I do my homework, or daddy takes us for a walk before dinner and in the afternoon we go to Sunday School, and in the evenings to evensong, depending on the weather.'

'Hells Bells!'

'Don't you go to Sunday School, then?'

'No. It's too boring.'

'Ours isn't. It's fun.' Another thought struck her. 'Don't you believe in God?'

'Never thought about it. Oh, come on Kitty be a sport,' he wheedled. 'Take me to see your hideaway. We've only tomorrow left, and we won't be able to go in the morning because Uncle Jack said we'll be going to the fair, and later, some Aunty May and the family are coming up to see us. Who are they?'

'Aunty May is mummy's sister. She's a hoot and there's Uncle Ted and my cousin, Helen who likes to . . .'

95

But Peter's thoughts had already returned to his objective. His hazel eyes looked at Kitty with impatience. 'Look, are you going to take me to this place or what?'

She felt badgered, but the idea was tempting and she gave in. 'OK. We'll go there. John can come too,' she added, with the sudden thought that it might help him to forget the horrible Mr. Collins.

Peter groaned. 'Why do you want him to come? I thought this was supposed to be our secret. It would just spoil everything. He's such a misery guts.'

Unable to press the point without giving away the reason why, she agreed, and with mounting excitement at flouting the rules with a kindred spirit who was more than a match for her head-strong ways, she pushed away a tiny, niggling seed of foreboding as they ran to the hidden door of Nancarrow.

Picking up a stick and pushing aside the brambles, they squeezed their way past the flaking green paint of the door. 'We have to go down through these woods. They lead to the lake,' she said, and wondered as they followed each other down the overgrown path whether the children would be there. She hoped not and was glad that Peter was with her. The air was heavy with the scent of bluebells beneath the ancient trees and as they came to the bottom of the woods, Peter asked, 'So, where's the house then?'

'It's in a different part of the grounds. I'll show you later.'

'Have you ever been inside it?'

'No, because it's all locked up. Never mind that. In a minute, we'll come to the pets' cemetery. Look, there it is.' To the side of the path, separated by low arched railings and half hidden in the wild grasses rising up the slope, were headstones. Most had weathered into a smooth slate, but there were two distinct enough to read. Tory 1876, it said, and Tango 1916.

'I wonder what kind of dogs they were?' said Peter.

'How do you know they were dogs?' They could have been cats, or guinea pigs.'

'With names like that, they would be dogs,' said Peter decisively.

'Smarty Pants. You think you know everything, don't you?' Kitty said, giving him a push and running away before he could retaliate.

Peter chased her towards the lake, and quickly catching up, pulled at her pigtails.

'Heh! That hurts.'

'Serves you right.'

Ahead of them lay the boathouse, and Kitty was relieved to see that there was no sign of the children. Peter ran eagerly ahead towards it and down the steps and inside. 'There's no boat,' he shouted, his voice filled with disappointment.

'There was one here a few days ago, because I saw some children rowing to the island in it,' she said, joining him. 'One of the girls looked just like me.'

'S-p-o-o-k-y. You've got a double. They say everybody has one.'

'Do they? I never knew that.'

'I thought you said nobody knew of this place except you and your friends?'

'Well, I didn't think they did. I've never seen them before. They were wearing funny clothes, she mused and tugged his arm. 'Come on, I want to show you some strange faces. Continuing along the path by the side of the lake, Kitty suddenly stopped dead. 'Look over there,' she whispered, pointing across the lake to the branch of a tree dipping into the water. 'It's the heron. He's waiting to catch a fish.' There was a swift, silent flash of grey and white. A fish was taken and he was gone. 'I often see him,' said Kitty as they carried on and up steps beside the wide cascade of rushing water after a night of rain. They sat on the seat overlooking the lake, watching a mother duck and ducklings emerge from the reeds and dark shadows of low branches overhanging the lake. 'Oohhh, aren't they sweet?' said Kitty, feeling again that familiar sense of belonging as her eyes travelled over the dense covering of trees climbing sheer up the valley. Had she but known it, it was a view that one day she would see reflected in another time and place, taking her back to her magical garden. On their left, the garden rose to the house in terraces of flower beds and shrubs proliferating in wild abandon, freed from the constraint of a gardener.

'So, where are the strange faces then? he asked.

'They're over there,' she said, standing up and pointing behind her. She took him to the carved stones lying in juxtaposition with boulders around the base of two large rock formations.

'Da-dah!' she sang, with arms and hands outstretched. 'I bet you haven't seen stones like these before?' They reminded Kitty of a picture she had seen in her encyclopaedia of the stones on Easter Island. Rough cut, each face had a quirky twist as if someone had fashioned them to amuse and wonder at.

Peter crouched down and traced with his hand one of the lichen covered faces. The mouth was rounded into a pouting circle, as if ready to blow a bubble, and its eyes were off-centre. 'They're weird,' he said, standing up.

'So are you,' she teased, skipping up the steps to the top of the rockery which ran high and wide with large moss covered boulders and topped with a tall pine tree. 'I'm the king of the castle and you're the dirty rascal,' she sang as Peter chased up after her.

'You see this pine tree,' she said pointing to the top of it. 'Last year, I climbed right up and took a rook out of it's nest. I wanted it to be my pet.'

'What. Up there!' exclaimed Peter, gazing at the precariously thin lower branches. She was full of surprises.

'I put it in a cardboard box on top of the privet hedge in the garden so that when the wind blew, it would sway like the branches of the tree, and he would feel more at home. Every morning I got up very early and went digging for worms to feed it and as soon as I came home from school.'

'What happened to it? I didn't see any bird in your garden.'

'It died,' she replied wistfully. 'And I did so much want a pet. I came home from school and found it lying stiff and cold. Daddy said I shouldn't have taken it from its mother and that it would teach me a lesson. He wrapped it in newspaper and threw it into the dustbin. I wanted to give it a proper burial, but he wouldn't let me because he'd just planted Sweet William seedlings in the flower bed,' she said, reflecting on the memory, as Peter began jumping on and off the boulders. He stopped, his eye caught by a dark outline on the adjoining rockery divided from them with a path encircling both in a configuration of a figure eight.

'What's that down there? It looks like a cave.'

'That's the grotto. I don't like it. It's dark and creepy.'

Peter ran back down the steps to look. 'It's not that dark,' he called up to her, touching the crystals stones that glinted dimly where water once ran around the nooks and crannies offering small ledges for candles, and where seepage of water had collected in a basin shaped pool at the entrance.

'I'll show you the tadpoles,' said Kitty, anxious to get away from the shivery feeling it gave her from the enormous slabs of granite that comprised the roof and which she found oppressive and claustrophobic. As she waited for him on the path to the fish pond, she remembered something, and began to smile.

'What are you smiling at?'

'Shan't tell you. Wait and see!' she giggled, dancing in front of him with glee.

The statue stood in the centre of the pond, her mouth open where once water had spilled, and her coppery green tail curved around the base where water lay brown and brackish. 'See! See! I'm not the only one to believe in mermaids.' She knelt down and leaned over the low stone wall. 'Look, Peter. Look at the tadpoles. Some of them are already sprouting legs. There are thousands of them. The place will soon be crawling with frogs.'

He knelt down beside her. 'We have a small pond in our garden with goldfish and sometimes, we see the odd frog.'

'But you live in a city,' she replied, puzzled, thinking of the rows and rows of houses with courtyards and back alleys she had seen on the Pathé News in the cinema.

'We don't live right in the city. We live on the outskirts and we have a garden, like you do.'

'Oh, I *see*.' Kitty's curiosity was satisfied.

For a while they remained by the pond, absorbed in watching the teeming black commas, and trailing their fingers through the water in an attempt to catch them.

'I've got one,' cried Kitty, holding it in her cupped hands. 'It tickles,' she laughed. In fascination, they studied the protuberances that would soon become legs, before finally letting it drop back into the water. She stood up. 'I'll show you the house and rope swing and then we must get home for dinner. We always have it early on Sundays because of Sunday School.'

She led him up the steps, past the terraces of strangled and woody rose bushes, and the shrub rhododendrons ablaze in reds and purples, and her favourite, a white confectionery of large, lacy petals tinged with pink that always, for some unknown reason, made Kitty think of weddings. On the pathway to the house they passed the gardener's bothy with its small gothic shaped windows and a closed door in a very high wall.

'What's in there?' Peter asked.

'The kitchen garden and greenhouses, but we haven't time to look at them. She hurried him on.

The house stood before them, it's granite walls glinting in the May sunshine and crowned with three triangular pediments. The windows were tall and elegant to each side of a portico entrance of four ionic granite pillars.

'I'd love to get inside and explore,' said Peter, attempting to peer through the windows which were high off the ground. 'What about the back? Maybe, there's a way in there.' Before she could reply, he took off to the side of the house towards an archway leading into a courtyard with stables ranging off it.

'There's only a back door and windows of the kitchen and pantry, and they are locked,' cried Kitty, running after him to where moss covered cobblestones sprouted tall and straggly weeds through cracks of the yard. 'There's an old wooden box in the stables that I stand on to look in the windows,' she said, going over to them and pulling open the top and bottom doors of one where a lock had rusted and broken. Sunlight slid through the open door where motes danced with fine particles of grains stirred by their presence, and gave light into the gloom of high sided stalls with iron hay racks set into corners. A passageway led to the harness and tack rooms where reins, bridles and bits hung with saddles and girths, collars and traces, the leather cracked with age and begrimed with dust and cobwebs. Kitty remembered the day she had been startled by the sudden ring of hooves and clatter of wheels on the cobbles outside. There had been a terrible scream and the moaning and keening of a woman amongst the commotion of men and horses. A man's voice shouted for a stable boy. Panic-stricken, she had raced to the harness room and dived under the cleaning table. Her face screwed up at the cobwebs brushing her face and the thought of the box above her with spiders and creepy crawlies scuttling amongst the bristles of horse brushes and grooming mitts, sweat scrapers, combs and hoof picks. She had crouched there with her heart leaping out of her chest, when, just as suddenly as the clamour had begun, an eerie silence descended and straining to hear any further signs of activity, she had finally crawled out from under the table and tentatively made her way towards the door. Peeking her head around, she had found there was no-one there. It was as mystifying as seeing the people in the circle and she wondered whether to tell Peter, but instinct told her he would laugh and think she was making it up as her friends had done. It was better to keep these strange happenings to herself.

Cupping their hands, they peered through windows filmed with grime at a very large kitchen with a Cornish range and wooden cupboards with glass fronted tops filled with china. On one wall hung copper and iron saucepans whilst down the centre of the room was a long table. Peter took out his penknife and tried to slide the catch across the sash window, but corroded with weather and age, it was stuck fast and would not budge.

'All the windows are the same,' said Kitty, jumping down. 'Terry has tried them all but none of the catches will move.'

'Who's Terry?' asked Peter.

'He lives next door. We often come down here to make camps and explore.'

Peter felt an unexpected sting of resentment of her friendship with another boy that made him all the more determined to find a way in. He began to walk around the house. 'I think I've found a way in,' he yelled to Kitty who had wandered out to sit on the steps overlooking the lawn that had diversified into wild grasses and meadow flowers. He was crouching down, half hidden by a japonica that had seeded and grown comfortably in the shade of the house with a thick growth of variegated leaves hiding the lid of a coal chute and the wall that held a small grid. 'Look, Kitty, it's a coal hole,' Peter said, his voice mounting with excitement. 'This will have a chute down into a cellar. We can get in that way if we can break open the lock. What we need is a tool to lever it off. Maybe there's something in the stables I could use?'

'There's nothing there, just the horses tackle that you saw hanging on the walls' said Kitty quickly, for the thought of sliding down a chute into the unknown gave her the heebie-jeebies. 'And anyway, we don't have time to explore the house, even if we could get in. Let's go to the rope swing. It's much more fun,' said Kitty, dragging at his arm.

He shook free of her grip. 'No. I want to stay.'

'Then stay here by yourself! I'm going to the swing,' said Kitty stalking off.

With little point in remaining there alone, he moaned his way behind her to the wooded area where the rope was hanging from a knotted arm of an enormous oak, and held back to the top of a bank with string tied around a sapling. At the sight of it, Peter gave a low whistle. 'Wizard!'

'It's a bit of a jump without this string to pull the rope towards us,' said Kitty, pleased with his approval as she untied it, and holding on, swung off easily, gliding to and fro out over the bank before dropping back onto it. 'Your turn,' she said.

Peter leapt off and swung for a few minutes and as he returned, Kitty on an impulse, jumped out onto the rope with him and laughing with glee they swung together, the trees and sky a revolving mobile of colours. They did not see above them the old strands of rope tearing apart, and finally breaking in two, it plummeted them to earth where they lay sprawled at the bottom of the bank. The silence of the woods was broken by a groan from Peter. He winced with pain as he struggled to his feet and came over to Kitty who had landed on her back with the wind thumped out of her lungs and could neither breathe nor speak. He looked nervously down at her. 'Kitty, what's the matter with you? You're opening and shutting your mouth like a guppy fish.'

Kitty thought she was going to die, her punishment for playing on a Sunday. Deliverance came as the vacuum slowly released and she dragged in great draughts of air. 'I couldn't breathe. It was awful,' she whispered hoarsely with a face white as a sheet. She shakily got to her feet. 'Why are you holding your arm like that?' she said, staring at it.

'I think it's broken. It made a horrible crack as I hit the ground.'

Kitty dragged her eyes from his arm and stared up in disbelief at the frayed rope.

'You shouldn't have jumped on with me,' he said, his face turning grey with shock.'

'I know,' she replied, miserably. 'I'm sorry. Does it hurt very much?'

'Quite a lot,' he answered, unable to disguise the pain.

She felt sick at the thought of returning home. 'What are we going to tell them? We're not supposed to be here.'

Peter sat down abruptly on a fallen log, feeling weak. 'I don't know,' he said, faintly.

'Gosh Peter, you look terrible. Put your head between your legs. That's what my friend had to do in school when she felt faint.'

He tried. 'I can't. It hurts with my arm.'

She sat down beside him wracked with guilt and looked down with dismay at her grass-stained cardigan and her dress streaked with earth and dust. There was going to be the most unholy row. How could they explain Peter's arm and her filthy clothes? She mulled it over, her mind veering from one excuse to another, until there came a flash inspiration. 'I've just thought what we can say you were doing when you broke your arm,' she burst out. 'We must tell them we were on the swings in the playing fields, seeing who could jump out the furthest, and you fell on it.' Elated at having found a plausible explanation, she was immediately downcast at the sight of pain in Peter's face.

'I shall be murdered when they see your broken arm,' said Kitty tearfully.

'It's my fault. I made you come here. They'll have to murder both of us,' he said, with a ghost of a smile.

'If you're OK now, I suppose we'd better go home,' she said dismally. She held out her hand and he rose unsteadily to his feet.

'I think I can walk now, but I can't climb the hedge back into the lane. My arm won't move.'

'Don't worry. We can go through the fields to the farm gate instead,' and in that moment with his hand in hers, the pain had gone.

Octavia stood spooning fat over the roast potatoes as Roy sat at the kitchen table with Grace beside him colouring a doily. 'Merciful heaven! What's happened?' she cried, taking in at a glance Kitty's stained clothes and Peter's shocked appearance as they came through the door.

'I think I've broken my arm.' At the reassuring sight of his father, he struggled to keep a grip on his tears.

Roy came around the table to him. 'How did this happen?'

'We were, we were . . . seeing who could jump out the farthest from the swings.' His legs buckled, silencing any further questions.

Roy helped him to the armchair. 'Now calm down, Peter. It'll be alright. We'll soon sort this out and get you fixed up.'

'I'll go next door and phone for the doctor,' said Octavia, pushing the potatoes back into her pride and joy of a newly acquired gas cooker, and taking off her apron.

'No need for that Octavia. I'll take him straight to the hospital,' Roy replied, as John, on hearing the commotion appeared from the front room where he had been reading his *Biggles* book.

'What's the matter with Peter?'

'We think he's broken his arm, John.' He turned to Peter. 'Come on, son, let's get you into the car.'

Kitty was in a state of high tension and Grace, looking from one to the other, awaited the inevitable explosion, but Octavia's look was one of worry and distraction for the outcome of Peter's visit to the hospital. 'Go upstairs and wash and change Elizabeth. Put your dirty clothes in the linen basket and come down and sit in the kitchen chair where I can see you, and stay there until dinner is ready,' she said. Her voice was controlled and deadly low. Kitty's apprehension grew. There was no anger at the state of her clothes or questions asked as to how Peter had broken his arm. It was unnerving. It appeared that the storm clouds had somehow, miraculously passed her by, although she had noted she was Elizabeth, and beneath her mother's calm exterior she sensed a volcanic undercurrent that might erupt at any moment. With Grace on her heels, she escaped to the bathroom.

'What really happened, Kitty?' Grace asked, agog with curiosity.

'Like Peter said,' she replied, hiding her lie in the towel as she dried her face. 'We were seeing who could jump the furthest from the swing at Beacon and Peter landed on his arm.'

Grace looked at her incredulously. 'You went off down the field. I saw you from the window,' she accused. Kitty ran to their bedroom with Grace following her.

Kitty sat down quickly on the bed, for her legs had turned to jelly. 'If you tell mummy, I'll kill you,' she hissed.

'I won't say anything, Kitty, I promise. You look grotty,' she exclaimed, looking at Kitty's dirty clothes.

'I know,' she replied, pulling them off and changing into her white smocked dress for Whitsun, and the lacy cardigan that Octavia had knitted during the winter evenings, and before Grace could ask any awkward questions, she was out of the room and down the stairs and in an attempt to placate her mother, offered to lay the table.

With dinner over and Jack appraised of the situation on his return from morning service, Kitty kept a low profile before it was time to walk down the hill to the afternoon service. She was glad to be away from the strained atmosphere and wondered, but dared not ask, whether they would now be going to the traditional Monday Whitsun fair in Redruth. She had been looking forward to it for weeks, saving her pennies and thrupenny bits earned and given by various relatives for the rides, and to buy a stick of the wonderful fluffy candyfloss which seemed to appear by magic in the tub, and melt away just as quickly in her mouth. Octavia called them a waste of money. 'There's nothing to them Jack, just sugar and air that ends up all over their faces and clothes.'

Jack was unsympathetic to her sentiments. 'It's only once a year, Octavia. Let them have their fun.'

Kitty settled on her seat in the church with Grace and looked around. Her love for it ran deep. It did not soar and intimidate or condescend, but was comforting, and like it's people, strong as the granite that built it, braced together with a common ancestry of hardship and fellowship. Sitting in the diffused sunlight of the stained glass windows, the interior glowed mellow with age and from the shining brass eagle lectern, the cross and candleholders on the altar. On dark winter evenings, it shone soft with candle-light, when all eyes watched the sacristan light the candles on the burnished brass chandeliers hanging low from the roof of the church. The sounds of shuffling and rustling and the odd cough ceased. All were ready for worship.

The congregation stood with the organ's triumphal chords of the first hymn, and from the vestry came the sound of the choristers singing and led by the cross held high, they slowly processed their way past the pews, going up and down the aisles, until finally and quietly they filed into the choir stalls. Terry grinned at Kitty who stood obliquely to her with the choir, and she smothered a grin. The arrival of Peter and John and the excitement of going out in the car had eclipsed all other thoughts and she realised she had missed seeing him.

The Confirmation Service was simple and moving as the young men and girls in their white dresses were blessed and the hymn was sung, *Come Holy Spirit, Our Souls Inspire.* Stirred by the men's voices blending sweet and low like a prayer, and thinking of Peter's broken arm as she sang, Kitty was close to tears. Jack, sensing her emotional turmoil, looked down at his daughter, and gently laid his arm across her shoulders and with his hymn book in hand, he also drew his shy six year old close to him.

Octavia, busy washing the dishes, heard Roy and Peter's steps on the gravelled entry and wiping her hands as they came in through the doors was glad to see that Peter's face had regained his colour. His arm was held in a sling.

'How did it go?' she asked.

'Well, they x-rayed it first, and found he had broken it at the top, so he had to have the performance of a plaster put on.'

'How are you feeling, Peter?'

'A lot better, thank you, Aunty. They gave me some aspirins to take, and I've got more, if I need them.'

'Do you feel like something to eat? I've kept your dinner warm.'

'Yes, please. I'm starving,' said Peter.

'There's one thing about children, whatever happens to them, they never seem to lose their appetites for long, unless they're desperately ill,' he said, thinking of Diane.

Octavia murmured in sympathy, as she took the plates from the oven. 'You can fill me in whilst you're eating and I'll finish the pots and pans, and then I'm going upstairs to a nice hot bath. It's been quite a morning. The newspapers are in the front room Roy, and there's one or two of Kitty's books lying around if you're interested, Peter. They might help to take your mind off the pain.

Chapter Twelve

WHIT MONDAY MORNING dawned bright and clear with a light south westerly wind stirring the tree tops of Nancarrow. It had been decided the previous evening that despite Peter's arm, they would still all go to the fair. Roy said, it was an event that he too as a child had looked forward to and there really was no need to spoil the day for everyone because of the accident. In her bedroom, Kitty had done an Indian victory dance around the room. 'Sometimes, Kitty Pengelly, I think you're quite potty,' observed Grace, as Kitty giggling with elation, threw herself onto her bed.

The following morning a downcast Peter scowled as he ate his breakfast. Rides were out of the question, Roy had said. Kitty attempted to cheer him up for her complicity, which resulted in his broken arm, lay heavy on her conscience. 'There's still lots and lots of things to see and do there, Peter, apart from rides . . .'

'I *know* Kitty,' interrupted Peter, his voice edged with the sarcasm of disappointment.'

But her enthusiasm to present a brighter picture was unstoppable. 'There's the tent with the funny mirrors, and with your good hand you could play hoopla, or rolling balls into holes and pennies onto numbers. Maybe, you could win a prize like I did last year. I bought a raffle ticket from a huge stand of prizes and I won a casserole dish.'

Peter looked horrified. 'A casserole dish! Jeepers! What on earth would I do with that?'

'Mummy uses it all the time,' replied Kitty, unconcerned at his scorn. 'Shall I tell you how I won it?' Her voice dropped to a whisper. 'I watched people buying tickets and I noticed that only a green ticket won a prize. And there were hundreds of different coloured tickets in the box but only a few green ones.'

'You were just lucky,' he said.

'That's not true. I'll prove it when we get there.'

'Is she loopy or something?' said Peter, rolling his eyes as they alighted from the bus.

Kitty shrugged as her father did, and grinned at his reaction to the conductress who had clipped their tickets with the sweet sound of a nightingale. Her practice runs on the bus for the local amateur operatic society were legendary, and their jaws dropped as she continued singing up and down the aisle, and on running up the steps to the top deck could still be heard to the enjoyment of the locals. They waited for Roy and the rest of the family to arrive in the car, and could hear the punchy music of the great Gladiator organ in the fairground drifting in waves over the rooftops. Kitty's spirits rose in anticipation, eager to be there and entering up the rough step into the fair field. At last Roy's car drew in beside them. 'Have you been waiting long?' asked Octavia, as she helped Thomas out of the car. 'With so many extra buses laid on for the fair, Uncle Roy decided to come the back route around Carn Brea where there would be less traffic.'

'We've only just arrived, mummy. The bus took ages stopping and starting with so many people getting on and off,' replied Kitty.

'Well, now we're altogether again, we'll make for the town.'

The streets were shining and festive with colour from bunting and stalls lining the main street to which Octavia was immediately drawn to stop and look at the bolts of material and haberdashery, but it needed time and space to finger and inspect, and proved impossible amidst the crush of bodies and the clamour of voices. 'With so many people, I think it best if we just keep going to the fair field,' she commented, as Kitty hopped from foot to foot in a fever of impatience. Finally, they were entering the field and the noise of the clashing cymbals of the great organ and the raucous music of the fairground rides was electrifying and sent shivers of excitement through them. 'Roll Up! Roll Up! See the amazing snake lady and the smallest man in the world,' was shouted from the side tents that held wonders in dark and mysterious interiors, and above it all, the music and screams of the riders assailed their senses.

Kitty hummed and hawed as to which ride she fancied first, reluctant to spend her pocket money so soon, and yet, itching for the thrill of a ride. She finally settled for the gentle motion of the hobby horses, and as she mounted one and the ride began, her heart stopped, for there ahead of her on a horse that rose as hers fell was her double. The girl from Nancarrow wearing her quaint white apron covering her dress and her long strawberry blonde hair falling from beneath a flowered straw hat. On looking around she could see no sign of the other children, and when she came to jump off, the girl was nowhere to be seen, and she had quickly forgotten her in the thrill of flying down the helter-skelter, and chasing Jack and Grace in the dodgem cars with the sparks cracking and spitting high above her. Peter, watching them on the sidelines had turned away to one of the side stalls with Roy. His arm ached and he was resentful of John who, with Kitty beside him was whooping with laughter as he banged around. He can't drive for toffee he thought churlishly. Kitty had caught sight of Peter's doleful face and guilty at her enjoyment, ran over to Roy as the dodgems came to a stop. 'Can Peter go with me on the big wheel Uncle Roy? That won't hurt his arm, will it? Can he, please? she pleaded.

At the sight of Peter's hopeful face, Roy relented. 'He can if he rides with me. 'I'm not risking you two together on that,' he replied, gazing at the swaying movement of the seats. 'Not after yesterday's performance.'

Kitty beamed disarmingly back at him. 'That's OK, Uncle Roy. I don't mind.'

'What about you John? Would you like to ride with Kitty?' asked Jack, but John had no head for heights. 'I'd rather watch the boxing, Uncle Jack. It's due to start any minute now,' and wandered off towards the tent.

'We'll meet you there later,' Roy called after him.

'Thanks Kitty,' Peter said gratefully, as they joined the queue for the ride.

Kitty, sitting with Jack and Grace, had never been on the wheel and the swinging seat was unnerving as they lifted up into the air, but once on top with the panorama of the town and countryside spread beneath her, and with Jack pointing out the landmarks, she forgot her fear, until it started to go down and around and with the sensation of only air in front of her, her legs turned to jelly. The wheel came to a stop, and Kitty stepped unsteadily out of the chair. Peter, sitting behind them asked to stay on for another ride, but

Kitty was happy to be back on terra firma, and waved to him as it rose in the air and staying close to Octavia's inspiriting strength, she walked with her to the children's carousel and waved again at Thomas riding around in a fire engine.

On wandering the fairground, Kitty had looked everywhere for the big wonderful stand of household prizes to be won by a ticket. To win a gift seemed the perfect way to make amends to Octavia, for her look was still tense when speaking to her, but the stand was nowhere to be seen. 'Why isn't it here? It was, last year,' she said, with frustration.

'It doesn't matter, Kitty. I'm sick of looking for it. Let's find the hoopla stand,' Peter said, as they passed the chair-o-planes that whizzed out high above them and past the ghost train that had been scarily exciting with trailing cobwebs brushing her face, and hideous faces and skeletons jumping out at them. Laughing with fright, Kitty had edged closer to John, who happier than he had thought it was possible to be again, clutched her hand and shouted for her not to be frightened above the clatter of the train and the shrieks of the riders.

Peter won a goldfish and held it out to her but Kitty, piqued at his lack of interest in the tombola stand, retaliated. 'Grace won a fish last year, but it died, even though we put it into a big goldfish bowl. And you can't play with it,' she added. 'Not like a puppy or a kitten.'

'If that's the way you feel, I'll give it to Grace, then,' he replied, in a huff and walked away.

Kitty hurried after him. 'I didn't mean I didn't want it, honestly,' she said, fixing her mesmerizing green eyes upon him. 'I would love to have the goldfish. This one will probably live for ever and ever. I shall call him Percy the second. Let's ask if we can go to the tent of mirrors. He will look really funny in one of those wavy mirrors.'

Thomas was tiring and Jack suggested that it was time to leave the fairground and to remember that later, Ted, May and Helen would be joining them for tea. They made their way back to the entrance of the field where a stall sold circles of rock, toffee apples, and brittle toffee. Alongside was a stand of gaily coloured knick-knacks and the candyfloss man. Kitty looked up at Octavia. 'It's up to you Kitty, what you buy. If you want a candyfloss, then have one,' she said, as the stallholder broke the toffee and rocks with a small hammer into small pieces and scooped them into a paperbag.

She was down to her last sixpence. Should she have a candyfloss or something to take home as a reminder of the fair? She gazed at the tempting array of playthings. There were gaily decorated silver foil balls on the end of piece of elastic which were always fun to bounce around until they split and burst in a shower of sawdust. She picked up a shaker cone of colourful paper streamers that rustled in the light breeze, and eyed the bazooka whistles and windmills of primary colours spinning into a blur. She finally plumped for a bouncing ball. The boys chose bazookas. 'Anything to make a noise,' said Roy with a wry look at Jack. Grace picked up a red and blue shaker that she shook as they walked up through the town with Thomas on Jack's shoulders holding his windmill. It stirred in the breeze, and Kitty watching the vibrant colours merging one into the other, had a childish yen for one as she flung her bouncing ball at Peter's back and giggling, darted behind Octavia.

Sitting around the dining table, the mood was cheerful and filled with the talk of the fair. Kitty having finished a steaming hot bowl of vegetable soup and buttered splits was eating with a concentrated sense of enjoyment her favourite tart of blackberries and custard. 'We picked these blackberries,' she announced, remembering the scent of their sweetness as she filled her jug. 'Mummy puts them into Kilner jars so we can eat them at Christmas and at special times. When we go picking, we call out, Oil! Oil! to mummy and daddy when we find a particularly good nick.'

Jack and Octavia exchanged amused glances. 'Isn't it funny how all families seem to have their own silly words?' said Octavia to no-one in particular.

'What do you mean, you call out oil?' asked Peter.

'Oil is our code word for blackberries, and nick means a good spot for them. If anybody else is picking in the field, they won't know what we mean, will they?'

'Sounds daft to me.'

'No, it's not. We have another word, too,' said Grace, defending Kitty who looked deflated. 'A mountain. Bet you don't know what that is?'

Jack, anxious to keep the mood on an even keel, answered. 'It's the sideboard in the front room, boys. When Grace was small, she said it was as big as a mountain. With its mirrored over-mantel it must seem enormous to young children,' he addressed Roy. 'We've been thinking of getting rid of it and buying a smaller one. It takes up too much room, but it's such a beautiful and useful piece of furniture, we're reluctant to do so.'

John who had kept his customary silence, suddenly joined the conversation and in quite an unexpected way. 'Our family word is 'Pot,' he said.

'Please John, not here at the table whilst we're eating,' Roy said hastily, spooning up the remains of the tart in his dish. 'That was delicious, Octavia. It must have been a very good nick for oil,' he announced, in a vain attempt to halt the boys from silliness he knew would ensue.

'It means a fart!' said John to the girls with a sudden mischievous grin that transformed his sombre looks.

Grace's eyes widened and she clapped her hand over her mouth with a comical gasp of surprise and stifled a giggle.

Peter held his nose. 'Have you done a pot, Grace?' he whispered.

The bubble of laughter hidden behind Grace's hand erupted, and the four of them dissolved into fits of giggles that became hysterical.

'Why are they laughing, mummy?' asked Thomas as the girls doubled over, saying their stomachs hurt.

'They're having a silly five minutes, my bird,' she replied, with a smiling shake of her head and felt the remains of tension and worry over Peter's arm melting away with their laughter.

'Children! They'll hang you,' Roy said, laughing with Jack, who pushing his chair back said he was going to make a pot of tea to help calm them all down.

With dinner over, Kitty asked if she and Grace could take the boys to the chapels' annual tea treat in Nancarrow's field, and it was agreed upon with the proviso that they were not late back, for May and Ted would be joining them for tea with Helen.

'It's been a tradition for years and years,' Kitty explained, as they walked down the hill. 'The children from Wesley and Centenary chapel parade through the town, the big ones walking and the little ones in decorated lorries, and they go up the driveway of the

112

manor house even though no-one lives there any more, and branch off through a gate into a field. They have races and things and I won a sixpence last year and bought some beads from Woolworths to make a necklace. I shouldn't have entered the race really, as it's not my tea treat,' she admitted, turning into the field decorated with bunting and markers for games and races. A row of children were lined up in hessian bags for the sack race, and they stood watching them with the mothers who jumped up and down shouting encouragement in flowery print dresses and summery hats that threatened to lift with puffs of wind. The minister noticing them on the sidelines, invited them to join in a game of rounders. They stood in line with the chapel children, and Kitty's eye on the ball was unerring as she took a swing with the club and speeded around the posts. John followed suit, happy to be close to Kitty, and Peter jealously watched them as Grace took her turn. It was on her second bat that Kitty's eye was distracted, for amongst a mêlée of children in the field, she again caught sight of the girl from Nancarrow. She did not appear to be playing with them and had started to walk towards the driveway leading to the house. Kitty looked back to the thrower, but the ball was already in the air, and to her annoyance she mistimed it and waiting for the next throw she began to wonder who *was* this girl who looked like her and seemed to be everywhere she went? On completion of the circuit, Kitty checked the time with the minister's watch. They would have to be leaving.

May, Ted and Helen were already there when they arrived back. Helen who had been watching out from the window for their return, ran to them. 'I thought you were never coming.' She pulled a face. 'It's been so boring. They've been gassing on about the olden days.'

The noise of conversation and laughter died away as they entered the room and the boys were introduced to May, who beaming on them both, gave each a hug to her curvaceous figure. Blushing and embarrassed they stood unsure of what to do next, until Kitty suggested that they went out to play French cricket in the garden. Their escape was rapid.

'Jeepers! Is she always like that?' asked Peter.

'Mummy's just pleased to meet you, that's all,' said Helen, affronted.

'Well, I'm glad I don't have to meet her every day,' replied John.

Kitty's hackles rose at their criticism of her favourite aunt. 'You're both mean,' she said. 'Aunty May's really nice. I wish mummy would hug me like she does.' She glared angrily at them.

Peter mooched over to the garden seat and glowered back at her, and John, wishing he had not upset Kitty, looked sheepish and wondered whether he should join Peter for family solidarity. 'I'm sick of not being able to do anything,' Peter grumbled.

'There's nothing to stop you playing cricket with us. You can still pick up the ball with your other hand. You're not an invalid,' said Helen, who at eight years was already the same height as Kitty and equally athletic.

Peter was stung. 'How do you know what it feels like? My arm hurts a lot.'

'So what! I broke my wrist once, but I didn't go moaning around the place like you. Boys are all the same. Little babies,' Helen retorted.

Blimey, another spitfire, he thought, as he watched her placing the bat before her feet and legs. Her naturally waving black hair fell down her back as her dark brown eyes watched and waited for the ball and expertly fielded it from Kitty's throw. Just how many more pretty cousins who spat like cats and played games as good as any boy were lurking in Cornwall, he wondered.

'Don't be a spoilsport Peter. Come and play,' Kitty entreated. 'It's not much fun with only four players.'

Reluctantly he eased himself off the seat. 'Well, alright, but it won't be easy with my arm in a sling,' he muttered, shooting a look of defiance at Helen.

'Stand behind Helen then,' replied Kitty. 'She won't be able to defend and hit the ball so easily from behind her back, so you won't have to do much,' and with the game gradually dispelling any friction, they played until Jack came to the door and called that tea was ready.

No-one heard the tap on the back door with the commotion and scraping of chairs as everyone settled at the table.

'My *God!* It's Phoebe!' exclaimed May, as she entered into the sitting room. 'Where have you sprung from?'

'I was owed some time off and decided to take it. So here I am. Afternoon, one and all,' she said, sweeping her eyes around the room at the full compliment.

'You should have let us know you were coming, Phoebe,' said Octavia.

'There was no time. I caught the first train down.'

May stood up and gave her an embarrassed hug, aware of Octavia's strained look, but could not hide her delight at seeing her. 'It's lovely to see you, Pheeb. How long are you home for?'

'Just a few days. Thought I'd take a chance on staying with you and Ted. If that's alright?'

May's good will was immediate. 'Of course it is. Isn't it Ted?'

'Well . . . yes, that would be fine,' said Ted, taken aback.

'All we need now, is for Alice to suddenly jump back into our lives too, and we can all play at happy families.' Octavia's sarcasm lay heavy on the air and there was a tense silence.

Phoebe ignoring the barb, looked at the boys. 'These your boys Roy? The youngest one looks like you. Winnie and Diane not here?'

'We've had sickness in the family,' replied Roy, mentally adjusting his memory of Phoebe whom he hadn't seen since his teenage years. 'I'll fill you in, after tea.'

'Grace, you will have to move your chair up a bit and Aunt Phoebe can squeeze in beside you and Helen,' said Octavia. She motioned for Jack to get another chair from the kitchen. 'So, Phoebe. Where have you been these past two years?'

'It's a bit complicated to explain,' Phoebe began . . .

'Well, you could have at least written even if it was only a postcard. I suppose Jack and I should count ourselves lucky to have had the birth of Thomas acknowledged on our Christmas card.'

'Yes, I know I should have replied properly but events overtook me . . .' Phoebe attempted to explain again.

'That's still no excuse for not writing to dad. You know how he gets and the reason why. He's been out of his mind with worry.' Octavia's voice was clipped with emotion.

115

At the inferred implication of their mother's sudden death, Phoebe flared with quiet anger. 'Octavia, you have no idea what my life is, so please don't tell me what I should and shouldn't do.'

Jack came in with the chair. 'I'm sure there's a very good explanation why we haven't heard from Phoebe. Let's just get on with our tea,' he said quietly to Octavia.

She pursed her lips in annoyance and sat down.

'You girls have grown,' observed Phoebe, looking at them both. 'Have you been to the Whitsun fair? I used to go when I was your age.'

Grown? Kitty had no recollection of this formidable aunt, dressed in army uniform. 'Yes, we did go to the fair,' she replied, politely, with the vaguest memory of Phoebe beginning to rattle around in the back of her mind.

'And did you all have a good time?'

'Yes, thank you,' they replied in unison.

Phoebe cast her eyes on Thomas, who gazed solemnly back at her. 'So this is the long awaited son. What stunning eyes. You should cut his hair, Octavia. He looks like a girl with all those curls.'

Realizing she had gone a step too far, she retreated from Octavia's cold look of fury. 'I'm sorry, I shouldn't have said that. It's nothing to do with me,' she said quickly.

'No, it most certainly isn't,' said Octavia tightly.

Phoebe was anxious to make amends. 'Look, can we just start again,' she said, with an apologetic gesture. 'You've no idea how much I've been looking forward to seeing you all. I had a feeling that I might find you and Ted here, May, but I didn't expect to see you Roy, and the boys,' she said, turning to him. 'It's been a long time.'

'More years than I care to admit, Phoebe.'

'Yes. A lot of water has gone under the bridge.' She gave a tug of her ear lobe. 'Can't go into it here.'

Tea was a stilted affair, for Octavia said little, and the children sat in quiet awe of this strange woman who had descended upon them. Looking at her mother's tense face, Kitty felt their estrangement lay deeper than a lack of communication, something simmered beneath the surface. She studied Phoebe from across the table, taking in her guarded eyes, her angular figure, ramrod straight, and her forthright manner. She decided that she liked her, aware, instinctively, that a confidence would never be betrayed and if there was trouble, she would quickly sort it out.

If Octavia had known Kitty's thoughts, she would have been surprised at her summation. For, as she was to discover as they left the men to the offer of washing the dishes, and moved to the front room, she was right. Phoebe was an enigma, a perfect reflection of her work.

Phoebe, anxious to clear the air, apologized. 'I'm sorry Octavia that I didn't write a letter after Thomas was born, but there was a good reason. My work is highly classified and I was ordered to leave London immediately as a military attaché. I can't go into details as it's all rather hush-hush. Your letters followed me and were a lifeline.'

As Phoebe talked, Octavia had become aware of a look of strain on her face and grasped the awful possibility that she lived in the cold war of espionage.

'And I'm sorry, Pheeb, I was so teasy when you came in,' she said, with a silent plea in her look for a past forgiveness that was accepted with a softening of Phoebe's eyes.

'It's alright, Octavia, I understand . . . more than you realize.'

'It's just we were so worried,' May butted in. 'Dad was driving us crazy asking whether we'd heard any news from you,' looking at them both and relieved that good humour had been restored between them.

'Dad knows I was never a good letter writer and forgets I did add a few lines to his birthday and Christmas cards which were taken and posted for me from London,' answered Phoebe. 'It would have been difficult, under the circumstances, to write a newsy letter. He's nobody's fool and might have started to put two and two together. I'll drop by first thing tomorrow morning. I've missed seeing him. I've missed you all,' she said, with eyes that hinted at a hidden darkness and vulnerability.

'May, I think a glass of sherry would do us all good. Ask the men if they would like one as well, could you?' Octavia said, shaken by the nervous tension in Phoebe's face.

May rose from her chair and Octavia began taking out the glasses and the sherry bottle from the 'mountain'. 'I know this is silly, after all these years,' she said, when they were alone, 'but even now, I still feel a sense of guilt, Pheeb, and my defence is to bite first.'

'You always did! But there's no need to feel guilty, Octavia. We just happened to fall in love with the same man and in the end, we both lost him. Heaven knows, I've had my chances to marry since then, but I like my career and independence far too much to give it up for any man, however eligible or sexy!' She threw Octavia a sudden familiar glint from her feline eyes as she did when a teenager eyeing up the latest influx of students at the mining school. 'They've come in all shapes and sizes!' She grinned at Octavia.

'Oh Pheeb!' Octavia laughed, and was then serious for a moment. 'But we never really talked about it, did we? I'd hurt you terribly, and suddenly, you were gone.'

'Yes, I know. I just had to get away from the situation and for a while, I never wanted to see you again, but I came to realize the fault lay with James. He could never resist a pretty face. If he'd kept his sights on me whilst I was at university, instead of dancing his attention on you, it might never have happened.'

Octavia sighed. 'Well, I don't know about that,' she said, doubtfully, 'but you're right about one thing,' looking at Thomas's mass of curls. 'It's high time I bit the bullet and had his hair cut. I've just hated the thought as it marks the end of his babyhood.'

May reappeared. 'No need to ask, the men said. They're ready for a tipple, any time!' Octavia smiled and handed her a glass. 'If only Alice could be here with us as well,' May lamented. 'It would be like old times with us girls together.'

'Actually, speaking of Alice, you might be interested to hear I stopped off in Athens on my way home and took a boat over to the island of Euboea to see her,' said Phoebe, as everyone settled down in their chairs.

'Our Alice. You've seen her! Why didn't you say so before?' exclaimed May.

'Well, the atmosphere *was* a bit awkward at table,' replied Phoebe.

Octavia looked uncomfortable.

'How is she and the family?' May quickly asked.

'Considering the horrendous conditions they endured during the war, they are in good spirits and looking well.'

'Was it that bad then?' asked Octavia.

'Yes, it was grim. She said most people were starving as there was a severe food shortage, because the occupation forces were not only living off the local's food but exporting it back to Italy and Germany. Hundreds died of starvation. Alice told me she and Demetrios would barter for food; five cigarettes for a loaf of bread or twenty cigarettes for a couple of ounces of meat.'

'That's dreadful. Poor Alice. I can't bear to think of her having to do that. And there we were thinking we had it hard,' said May, shaking her head.

'It's just as well that the only communication we had was the occasional Red Cross postcards,' said Octavia. 'If we'd known how desperate things were for Alice and not being able to help her, it would have driven us all mad and dad would have been beside himself.'

'Alice said, they were the lucky ones,' continued Phoebe. 'Once, a man came knocking on the door, bearded and haggard he asked her for bread. She gave him a small piece as they barely had enough for themselves and when she later sent our cousin Micky out to buy some tomatoes and cucumbers for salad, he found the man dead a few steps down the road with the bread still in his hand. They had to contact the Town Hall and a couple of starving employees arrived, half-dead themselves, and throwing the corpse onto an old wooden cart, carried it off to the cemetery. The man was dropped into a pit together with the rest of the day's corpses, earth was shovelled on top and that was that. No priest, no funeral, no nothing, for who was going to pay for such things?'

'What exactly happened to the running of the mine once the Germans took over?' asked Jack.

'Demetrios said it was chaos. His employers, the British staff of the Anglo-Greek Magnesite Company, had to leave in a hurry, and left him in charge of everything. It was all quite unofficial, no time to put it down on paper. The Germans, efficient as always, ordered Demitrios to carry on work as usual, which was a good thing because with the famine in forty-one and forty-two, a lot of people from the nearby villages found work at the company's mine and were saved from certain death. When payday came, Demetrios used to stand quietly in the background holding a loaded revolver in his pocket, as the men filed past for their rations of blackcurrants, wheat flour, sugar, olive oil and cigarettes, in case anybody decided to snatch the sack of flour or currants and make a bolt for it. The rations were more valuable than the paper money paid out by the accountant.'

Jack stirred from his chair and refilled their glasses. 'It must have been good for her to see you, Phoebe. Someone from home to talk to about it,' he said.

'Yes, she was pretty emotional when she saw me. We talked for hours and often long into the night. She said the worst experience was when Demetrios was arrested and marched from the mine into town and was thrown into gaol as a preliminary to being executed. She said she was frantic with fear. It turned out that some 'bastard' as she called him, had told the Germans that he and other men were preparing to sabotage the installations of the mine. Luckily Demetrios was able to prove that the whole story was nonsense and they let him go. As he said, it would have been madness to sabotage his livelihood, not to mention those of the men working in the mines. Life was desperate enough as it was.'

They fell silent, reflecting on all she had told them, as the children, who had been instructed after tea to return to the tea-treat field to listen to the band, came into view on the terrace.

Grown-ups are all the same, Kitty thought looking at them sitting in the window as the four of them began walking up the entry. Whenever there was anything really interesting going on, children were speedily despatched. And there was something else that bothered her. The way Aunt Phoebe had looked at her, as if taken by surprise, as if she didn't quite fit into the picture somehow, when looking at the three of them. She sensed at once that the tense atmosphere between Octavia and Phoebe had gone, and whatever may have been the intriguing cause for it, Kitty was glad now they had gone to listen to the band, and in particular, to a solo cornet player who was good-looking and popular. As he teased the pure sweet notes into a sky melding into gold and orange with the setting sun, she wondered if the wink he gave to a bevy of girls sitting with her on the grass listening, was for her. It was hard to tell, but somehow, she didn't think so!

Kitty was despondent the next morning, as she watched Roy and the boys taking their suitcases to the car that had been her wonderful chariot to magical places. At her doleful look, Roy told her to cheer up, as they would be coming again the following summer and would be arranging to stay in a hut at Gwithian.

Gwithian! Imagine being able to spend whole days and nights at her favourite beach and going to sleep to the sound of the sea. A surge of hope ran through her. Maybe she could stay overnight with them?

'I think that would be doubtful, Kitty,' Jack cautioned her. 'You have to remember, the whole family will be down next time and the huts are not very big.'

She waved them off from the end of the terrace until she could see the car no more. She would miss Peter a lot. He had been as adventurous as herself and if he only lived here, was worthy to become a member of their Secret Service. Her thoughts turned to Terry as she walked back to the house, and her heart skipped a beat. There was so much to tell him, but in that she was to be disappointed, for on calling she discovered he had gone down with measles and was confined to barracks.

Chapter Thirteen

AN AIR OF annoyance smouldered as Octavia, exasperated with the girls who had mooned around all day, bored with themselves and bored with their surroundings, finally exploded. 'For the Lord's sake Jack, take the girls out for a walk, or something, so that I can get things back to normal.' She began banging the stiff supports of the extension leaves under the table, which jammed and Octavia cursed under her breath.

'Here, let me help,' offered Jack.

'I can manage, thanks.'

It was time to spirit away the sources of aggravation. 'Come on, girls. We'll go for a walk and stretch our legs. Mummy has been very busy these past few days and needs a bit of peace.'

'I don't *want* to stretch my legs. I want to ride in a car!' Kitty moaned, flinging herself into the armchair.

'Stop acting silly, Kitty, and get your coat on,' said Jack in exasperation.

'No,' said Kitty, defiantly.

'Is Thomas coming with us?' asked Grace.

'No, he's not. He will soon be going to bed,' replied Octavia.

'I don't want to go for a walk either,' said Grace, flinging herself in the chair opposite Kitty. Rock solid in their solidarity, they held each others eyes across the room. Neither of them moved.

'Get up, both of you. You will go for a walk with your father, and that's that,' said Octavia with a freezing look.

Kitty flirted with danger. 'I'm tired, like Thomas. He always stays here with you. It's not fair.'

'That's enough, Kitty. I wouldn't try my patience any further if I were you, after your little escapade. Heaven alone knows what Aunty Winnie thought when Peter arrived home yesterday. As if she hasn't got enough on her plate. Do I make myself clear?'

Kitty raised her eyes to the ceiling. 'Yes,' she replied with an air of resignation.

Jack shunted them out of the sitting room. 'See you later, darling,' he called out, and with a click of the door latch, they were gone.

Jack headed them in sullen mood up the hill and wondered whether to take them to see his mother in Beacon but decided a long walk would freshen their minds and tire them out.

'We're going to see Mr. Penberthy, aren't we?' Kitty asked, when they took a familiar route along the lane by the chapel in the village.

'I thought we might stop by and say hello.'

'Oh goody,' said Kitty, whose spirits immediately rose at the thought as they made their way over a stile and walked in single file along the old path to King Edward Mine.

It was a lonely wild place of gorse and blackberry brambles covering the burrows of mining waste, and punctuated for miles with haunting reminders of a time when Cornwall reverberated to the sound of men and machinery. They walked the treeless landscape with the wind blowing unhindered through the roofless engine houses and up the stacks, tall and stark against the skyline. It blew through industrial cathedrals of derelict mine buildings with their finely executed Roman-arched windows. Its backdrop of tin mines was the landscape of Kitty's world, where she played in the fields around ventilation shafts that were a dangerous and irresistible attraction. She had been warned many times of the danger and to emphasise the point, told the cautionary story of two boys playing in a field, who, when chased by the farmer, had run for their lives and mistaking the round and overgrown wall for a hedge, had jumped it and were lost down the mine shaft. This did little to deter her or her friends risking life and limb by hanging precariously to loose fencing on the top of the shafts. In a passing response to the terrible tale, they held one another's hands as they threw rocks into a black void, listening to the bangs and echoing booms as they bounced off the shaft walls, and counting the seconds they took to fall before hitting the water with a faint splash in the depths below.

The memories of its history and hardships were imprisoned in Jack's blood, for his father had worked in the oldest and deepest tin mine in the world, Dolcoath, known affectionately as The Queen. When the roar of the stamps crushing the ore and the great hearts of the mighty pumping engines stopped in the decline of the eighteen hundreds, his grandfather joined the thousands of hungry tinners seeking work in the mines in the vast continents of Australia, Africa and America where he took his young wife and her brother to work in the black hills of Dakota. Within a few short years, both had died, the brother from a falling iron cylinder and his grandfather of physical exhaustion, an old man at thirty years. His grandmother must have been a tough old bird, he said, for left alone with two small children, she somehow managed to retrace her steps over a thousand miles back to the east coast and set sail for the soft south westerly breezes of home and her family whom she thought never to see again.

'In those days,' said Jack, as they walked along, 'young women called balmaidens worked on the dressing floors of the mines, breaking the rocks and operating the round shallow vats in which the ore was washed. In my mining books at home, you will see pictures of them working, wearing long dresses and aprons, and white bonnets to protect their hair and necks.'

'I saw a little girl dressed like that when I was picking blackberries on the burrows. She walked past me carrying a basket covered with a white cloth,' said Kitty.

'She must have been going to a fancy-dress party, Kitty.'

Kitty looked doubtful. 'I don't know anyone who has fancy-dress birthday parties, do you Grace?'

'Nope. Everyone just wears their party frocks.'

'She was walking towards Dolcoath Mine, and there's no houses there, daddy. I said "Hello" to her, but she didn't answer. She looked right through me. Miserable cow!'

Jack felt a sudden twinge of anxiety.

'She must have been a ghost girl of the mines!' Grace teased, lifting her arms and whooping around.

Kitty stopped and stared at her with a thump of shock. 'Do you think I saw a ghost?' she asked Jack, with a catch in her voice.

The question was an awkward one, for he had no wish to alarm her, but it was well known that sightings and voices heard from old shafts were not uncommon, and horses had been known to stop when passing mine buildings, and dogs skirted them. It was inexplicable, but those that talked of such things were not ones for passing fancies. Of course, superstition abounded, like the 'knockers' in the mines, but were firmly believed in for warning of impending disaster. 'Well, if it was Kitty, there's nothing to worry about. Ghosts can't hurt you. There are people that say they see them, but most think it's all nonsense and imaginings, or has a rational explanation.'

'Like you, saying she was going to a party.'

'Yes, exactly.' He paused and considered. 'I think it would be wise not to talk about this girl to your mother, and this applies to you Grace as well. It would only worry her.'

'OK. We shan't say a word, will we Grace?'

'No fear! Mummy would tell us not to be so damn silly, talking about ghosts!'

Jack hid a smile at Grace's retort. Sometimes he felt that she had been here before with her old-fashioned expressions and quick riposte, remembering when she was little and had stood with her hands on her hips. 'I'm not your Cinderella, you know,' she said indignantly to Kitty, when told to pick up her toys. And although she had only joked about the ghost, she had, in her customary way, hit the nail on the head. It did seem likely that Kitty was seeing things again. As a child she had had an imaginary friend and he and Octavia had accepted it as a passing phase, but it would appear it was continuing, with her talk of seeing strangely dressed people in the Merry Maidens, and now this.

Kitty's mind was running along similar lines to Jack. Maybe she *was* seeing ghosts, thinking about the people in the stone circle as they walked down the ancient Carneymough Lane to King Edward Mine and passed the rubbled remains of tinners' earthen floor cottages. Long since worked out, the mine had been purchased by the Mining School for practical experience, and was in the vicinity of a garden that for Kitty was one of enchantment. Her footsteps quickened as they drew close to a low stone house and running ahead, she swung in through the side gate and down past sky-blue hollyhocks and delphiniums growing against the sheltering walls. She followed the winding pathway under arches of rambling roses, where she found Mr. Penberthy busy weeding the rockery. Tall and fair, he stood up, and arched his back. He smiled down at her over his pronounced hooked nose. 'Not my favourite job, weeding. And how's our Kitty today?

126

'Fine thank you, Mr. Penberthy,' Kitty beamed, her eyes dancing at him for he had a way of making her feel special. He had sensed she was a child who sought the magic in life and it had created a bond between them and although having no children of his own, he had the gift of reaching down to their level of fears and imaginings. 'Shall we go in and say "Hello" to Mrs. Penberthy,' he said, on seeing Jack and Grace walking towards the open front door.

Jack turned and raised his hand in greeting, 'Evening Dick.' Their friendship was deep-rooted and easy from a shared family history of mining and had continued with common interests in rugby and cricket. Friends from boyhood, each in his own way had continued the mining tradition. Dick working at King Edward as a mine foreman and Jack branching away into the School of Mines.

'I'll be there in one tick, Jack. Go on in. You're just in time for a cup of tea.'

Mrs. Penberthy appeared from the shadowed interior. Her hair shone silver from the sunlight stealing in through the open door and her face lifted into a warm and welcoming smile. 'Haven't seen you in a while, Jack. Come on in.'

'No, we've had family staying. They went back this morning.'

'It's lovely to see you all,' she said looking down at Kitty and Grace. 'And how are my two little maids?' she asked, pulling out the chairs from the table. 'What pretty pinafore dresses. Did mummy make them?'

Blinking at her as their eyes adjusted to the restricted light of small paned windows filtering shafts of sun onto wooden beams, they slipped onto the chairs, and smiled in greeting.

'Yes, she did,' replied Kitty. 'She's always sewing.'

'You've got a very clever mummy,' she went on as she gathered up cups and saucers from the dresser. She reminded Kitty of a little round robin as she bobbed around, and set the china down on the brown chenille table cover with a tasselled edge that Kitty fingered. 'I expect you two would rather have a glass of orange juice?'

'Yes, please,' they chorused.

She bustled away to the kitchen. There was a sound of water filling the kettle, and the opening and shutting of cupboard doors. She bobbed back in, holding a tray with two glasses of orangeade and something Kitty and Grace had been hoping for: one of her cakes. Her sponges rose as if made with air and her fruit cakes were always moist and melting, and had a very distinct aroma of something stronger than mere spices, which, on enquiry, was always vigorously denied.

Sitting restlessly with their cake and orange juice finished, Mrs. Penberthy, while pouring a second cup of tea noticed their heads turning to the open door. 'Off you go then and look for the fairies again!' She laughed at Jack as they bounded through the door like kittens. 'He's got a lot to answer for,' tilting a nod at Dick.

'There's no harm in a little drop of magic, Annie. I'm inclined to it myself,' said Dick, reaching over for another slice of cake.

The garden was warm and drowsy with the hum of droning bees as they began their hunt.

'Surely we will find them this time,' Kitty said. 'Maybe they are hiding amongst the wallflowers.' She crouched down to their honeyed scent and gently parted the stems. 'They're not here.'

'I'm going to look in the hydrangea bushes,' said Grace, running over to them. She peered under and around the woody stems that were burgeoning into small shoots from the fat buds. Looking in every nook and cranny, they finally tired, and feeling a little dispirited sat on the low wall of the fish pond beside Bill and Ben, the gnomes. They watched the goldfish lazily passing to and fro, before running over to an old Anderson shelter that faced the sun and had settled comfortably into the contours of the garden. Now turned into a garden shed with narrow side glass windows and a half paned door, it became a playhouse of endless fascination as they ran down the steps to sit on the deckchairs inside, and up again to its grass roof, to lie face down on arms that smelt of sun and summer.

Mr. Penberthy appeared from under the rose archway. 'Have you not found the fairies yet? Look, there's one on the bird bath with silver wings. She's splashing her toes in the water! And there's another, sitting on the toadstool,' he pointed.

They strained to see and with crestfallen faces looked at him. '*We* can't see them.'

He folded his long frame down beside them. 'Don't be too disappointed. They are very shy and only reveal themselves to those that truly believe in them. Maybe, they're still not quite sure that you do.'

'But we *do*,' cried Grace, lying on her elbows with her hands cupped around her face, and gazing pensively at the flowers that grew in an exuberance of colour and profusion. 'There must be lots and lots of fairies here,' she sighed.

Kitty's eyes were questioning as a seed of doubt began to form. She thought of Uncle Roy and the mermaid. Could he and Mr. Penberthy be spinning her fairy tales? 'Do you *really* believe in them, Mr. Penberthy?'

'I believe Kitty that all things that grow are part of the spirit of the universe and in my garden this manifests as fairies. Without them, nothing would flourish. I'm simply the tool to plant the flowers and vegetables. The fairies do the rest, they are the handmaidens of nature.'

He jumped up. 'Come on,' he said briskly, taking their hands and pulling them up off the grass. 'We'll leave the fairies for today. Now, tell me, what is it that two little maids always like to see when they visit me?' He winked at them both.

'The canaries!' sang out Grace.

'You've got it in one, Grace.' Their mood rising on a balloon of expectancy, they followed him to the shed at the bottom of the garden where the sound of the canaries greeted them as he opened the door. Stepping inside, the air was filled with chirping and birdsong and the soft flapping of wings. Jack appeared behind them, and watching their happiness as they pressed their faces to the netting, talking and clucking at the pale gold and saffron canaries that flitted around their cages, he had an idea. He looked at his watch. 'It's time we were making for home, girls. Run in and say cheerio to Mrs. Penberthy.'

Jack turned to Dick who was topping up the seed troughs. 'Dick, I was wondering, would it be possible to have one of the canaries for the children? They are always pleading for a pet. Kitty even took a rook out of its nest. It died and she was very upset. Octavia will not countenance a dog or cat. She said there's enough turmoil in the house with three kids as it is, but I think she might accept the idea of a canary.'

'No trouble at all Jack. When the young birds are hatched, you must bring the girls over again and they can decide which one they would like to have.'

'Capital,' said Jack.

Kitty was quiet as they walked home. For two nights she had wrestled with her conscience over John's secret. What should she do? She had promised not to tell, but soon he would be seeing that teacher again and she remembered the cold shudder of menace that ran down her spine. There had to be something she could do. But what?

As if sensing her thoughts, Jack spoke. 'You're very quiet, Kitty. What's the matter? You're not worrying about seeing that little girl, are you? I'm quite sure she wasn't a ghost.'

'No, daddy. It's not that. It's just . . . well . . . well . . .' With a sense of guilt at compromising her honour, she plunged in. 'It's about John, you see. He isn't very happy and he talked to me about Mr Collins, and he doesn't like him, and he doesn't want to swim any more,' she gabbled.

'Hold on, Kitty. Who is Mr. Collins?'

'He's John's swimming instructor.'

'I think you'd better start again, and take it slowly.'

Kitty sighed with frustration. 'John told me that he didn't like his swimming instructor because he messed around with him. He throws him in the pool and comes into his changing cubicle. He hates him, daddy. I told him that Miss Drew comes into our changing rooms too, but he said, I didn't understand. What does he mean?'

'I don't know, but rest assured Kitty, we will get to the bottom of it,' said Jack, feeling a stab of deep disquiet. If what he was thinking was true, it was little wonder that John had been so unhappy. This would have to be sorted out and quickly.

His steps unconsciously speeded up in his need to confide in Octavia.

'Why are we going so quickly, daddy?' asked Grace, half running to keep up with him.

'I'm dying for a cup of tea.'

'But you've only just had one,' said Grace.

'Yes, I know, but I'm still thirsty. What about you two? Are you ready for your cocoa and biscuits?'

'I'm too full of Mrs. Penberthy's cake,' replied Kitty.

'Mmmm, she does make lovely ones. Mummy's cakes sometimes go plonk in the middle, don't they?' and they laughed, breaking the unease that Jack could feel rising within him.

Later that evening with the children in bed, Octavia and Jack discussed Kitty's devastating revelation. 'It's a damn ticklish situation,' said Jack. 'I know you normally write to Roy, darling, but under the circumstances, it might be an idea if I wrote to him. What do you think?'

'I agree. I wouldn't know where to start. It makes me feel ill to even think about it,' she replied, as she unpicked one of Grace's summer dresses that needed letting down. 'I have no doubts that Roy will get to the bottom of it but it's not going to be easy telling the school that one of their masters is doing such a terrible thing. John must have been going through agony keeping it to himself, the poor little devil. It explains everything. His moods and silences. Of course, we don't know how far it went. Thank heavens he didn't go into details with Kitty, not that she would have understood, of course, but even so.'

'And without Kitty, we would have been none the wiser,' said Jack, as he rose from his chair and went to the sideboard drawer. 'Why is this drawer always chock-a-block?' he said, hunting around for the writing pad amongst scraps of paper, receipts and newspaper cuttings, the cheque book and old snaps. He finally located it, and went out into the passage for his fountain pen in his jacket pocket.

'And what are we going to tell Kitty? She'll pester us until she knows something has been done,' Octavia said, as he returned to the sitting room.

'We shall have to concoct something for the moment to put her mind at rest. The first thing to do is to get this letter off and we'll go from there.'

'You're right. We can do nothing, until we've had Roy's reply,' said Octavia, standing up and giving the gingham dress a hard shake away of tifflings and with it, her difficult thoughts. 'Grace is growing like a fern. I shall have to take a look at the rest of her dresses. I expect they will need letting down as well,' she said, putting away her workbasket, as Jack sat at the table and began writing the letter.

Chapter Fourteen

'CAN KITTY COME out to play?' Terry, with a lingering spot or two from the measles, stood warily at the back door after their previous 'stunt' together as Octavia had called it. It had started innocently enough in the adjacent field in front of the house where a large granite water trough and free-standing tap stood against the dividing hedge. It drew them like a magnet for water-boatmen and pond-skaters skimmed the surface, and newts and frogs were frequent visitors. Rocks flung in by children with a satisfying shower of water, lay at the bottom of its murky waters, and the ground oozed mud from the trampling of cows hooves, until high summer, when it dried into hard crusts and the trough needed constant refilling. On asking if she could take Thomas to see the tadpoles there, Octavia had, for once, agreed to Kitty's pleadings to take him out to play. She watched them from her chair in the bedroom as Kitty and Grace led Thomas carefully by the hand along the field pathway and was suddenly seized with such a transcending love it caught at her throat as she stared after them. In that instant of time, if anyone had spoken of a miracle, and it was not unknown in their house, this would be her understanding of one: the unconditional love that came as each was born and took their place within the family. She gave a soft exhalation of breath at this profundity of truth and picking up the gingham material on her lap resumed her tacking together of a dress for Grace.

'Are you going to try, Ge Ge?' asked Kitty as she and Terry clambered up the hedge and stepped across onto the lip of the trough.

'Not on your Nelly,' replied Grace, watching them tripping quickly along the edge.

'It's easy-peasy. Not like Mrs. Carveth's wall,' said Kitty. Time after time, the old lady found her, arms outstretched like a high wire artist, slowly making her way up the dividing wall which rose in steps of concrete between their houses. With her heart in her mouth and not daring to speak for fear of distracting the child, she waited until Kitty finally reached the architrave of the doorway into her courtyard, and warned her of the consequences if she fell: a broken arm or leg, or worse. Kitty listened politely and was not deterred. Danger was a challenge to be met and overcome.

'Yes, it's a doddle,' said Terry, doing a quick swivel of his feet and returning back to half collide with her and she leaped out of his way onto the ground.

'I want to see the tadpoles, Kitty,' said Thomas.

She lifted him up where he rested on his arms with his feet dangling. Squirming a little, he peered intently down at the necklace of tadpoles around the water's edge when suddenly his legs rose up beside her and in slow motion, his head vanished and he slid silently in with the tadpoles, turning turtle as he sank. Transfixed, they watched him submerge and sink to the bottom with eyes and mouth screwed tightly shut, to then gently ascend from the underworld and uncomplainingly submerge again. Bubbles rose and warning bells began to jangle.

Grace shook Kitty's arm in agitation. '*Do* something Kitty! Thomas is drowning!'

As one from a dream, Kitty leapt into action, pulling him up by his hair. 'Help me Terry,' she cried, who moving quickly slid his arms under Thomas's and together they hauled him out spluttering and sucking in great gulps of air. The dank water streamed off him, and he smelt of algae and mud. She was horrified. 'Oh Thomas. Why did you have to go and fall in? Mummy will do a fandango! Come on,' she said, despairingly. 'We must take you home.'

'You pulled my hair, Kitty. It hurt,' Thomas cried.

'I'm sorry, Thomas, but I had to get you out or you would have drowned.'

'If Thomas had drowned, mummy would have killed you,' said Grace, matter-of-factly, as they led him dripping and squelching along the field path.

'It was an accident, Grace,' she replied, irritated and upset more than she cared to admit. 'And anyway, you two just stood there watching.'

Grace was indignant. 'So did you until I made you save him!'

'Oh shut up!' said Kitty.

Terry said nothing. When these two fought it was better to keep out of it. Kitty hurried Thomas along and Octavia on seeing them leapt to her feet in dismay, her sewing dropping to the floor as she raced downstairs to the kitchen.

'For heaven's sake, Kitty. What happened? You were supposed to be looking after him. Run and fetch a towel from the airing cupboard, Grace,' said Octavia, stripping off his soaking clothes.

'He was only looking at the tadpoles and he fell in,' said Kitty miserably as Grace returned at speed to the kitchen.

'Kitty saved me,' Thomas shivered through his teeth. Octavia knelt down and pulled the towel around him. 'I closed my mouth, tight, like this,' he said, pressing his lips together, 'so I couldn't swallow the tadpoles.'

'What a clever boy to think of that.' She held him close and kissed his cheek. 'Oh my bird, you're stinking! We must get you into a bath.' She stood up to see Kitty's stricken face that was on the verge of tears. Her angry reaction over Thomas checked with the memory fresh in her mind of her epiphany at the window. 'It's all right Kitty, luckily, there's no harm done. Now, do you understand why it's best for Thomas to stay with me? He's too small for the antics you three get up to, and, as you can see, accidents happen.' Her sweeping look took in Terry who was standing with his back against the wall by the kitchen door, and watching the proceedings with interest. 'Go on, Kitty. Go back out and play with Terry.'

Grace moved to follow them. 'No, Grace, I want you here. One fright is enough for an afternoon and your dress is tacked and ready for you to try on. After Thomas has had his bath, you can play with him.'

'Why should *I* have to play with him? Why can't Kitty?' Grace moaned. 'I want to go out, as well.'

'I've just told you why . . .'

'But . . .'

'. . . and I'm not about to argue it.'

It had been a salutary experience and the fizz had gone out of her as they sat on the terrace hedge. 'So, what do we do now?' she asked, with a lack of interest.

'Let's go to Nancarrow. We haven't been there for ages,' replied Terry.

'We can't swing on the rope any more, so what's the point?'

'You know the garden always cheers you up.'

'Hmmm,' she conceded. 'I suppose I could show you what Peter found there,' she said.

'What? In the garden?'

'No, by the house but he couldn't open it.'

Terry looked at her in exasperation. 'Open what?'

'A coal chute.'

'A *coal chute!*'

'Yes, don't you see? It's a way into the house.' She shuddered. 'It gave me the heebie-jeebies.'

Flabbergasted, he gazed her. 'We've looked hundreds of times around the house, so why didn't we see it?'

'Because it's hidden behind a bush that's practically a tree.'

Fired with excitement, he rose quickly to his feet. 'Where? I want to see it. Let's go!' he said impatiently. 'You *are* coming aren't you?' he said, as she made no move.

Kitty's answer was to slide down the hedge and into the field. 'I *suppose* I'd better.' She threw a humorous stance with a hand on her hip. 'After all, what would a poor measely boy like you do without me?'

'You are a witch, sometimes, Kitty Pengelly,' he replied, jumping down beside her.

'Am I? Am I really a witch?' She spread her arms and larked around him, her equilibrium restored and her world unclouded for Thomas was safe and none the worse for his ducking.

Cutting across the woods and through the Italian garden and into the courtyard, Kitty pointed. 'It's over there,' and ran ahead to pull aside the dense foliage. 'See!'

'We need to find something to lever it open,' he said, studying the lock, 'and we shall have to clear away all these branches.'

'Peter said the same. There's that workshop off the stables. 'It's got all sorts of tools.'

In the carpenter's room, Terry ran a practised eye over the hacksaws, saws and hammers, a rack of screwdrivers and a hand drill that were hanging on the wall. Nothing suitable there. He moved to a work bench where an assembly of tools lay coated with dust and were familiar, for over the years he had learnt the rudiments of carpentry from watching and helping his father in his garden shed. 'This should do it,' said Terry, lifting up a crowbar from amongst wooden planes and mallets, and some ancient tins of fish and animal glue that had coagulated into a hardened mass.

On returning to the chute, Kitty could think of nothing but the thought of its tomb-like entry into the house, as they began tearing aside the branches. 'I must not be frightened,' she repeated to herself, like a mantra as Terry manoeuvred the wedge under the hasp. She muttered it under breath, and he looked up in surprise at her admission of fear. It was unlike her. 'There's nothing to be frightened of, Kitty. It'll be like sliding down the slide in the park,' he cheered her from beneath his dark, waving hair which Kitty envied and he despairingly combed flat, for it only to spring back. It fell forward as he struggled for purchase and using every ounce of his strength, he pulled down. The lock stayed firm.

'It's not going to move,' she said, secretly relieved.

'Yes, it will. We've just got to keep trying. We need to pull the crowbar together. If you stand beside me, and then on the count of three, pull with me as hard as you can, it will give way.' She took the handle, his blue eyes meeting hers and a spark, an awakening of awareness shot between them. She was conscious of his arms and hands warm upon hers and blushing, she dropped her eyes from his with her heart fluttering in the most funny way, as he self-consciously adjusted his hands upon the crowbar and told her to start pulling with him.

'It's coming. Keep pulling! Keep pulling!' shouted Terry.

The wood splintered as the nails flew away, and caught off balance, they fell backwards onto one another, giggling at them-selves amongst the broken branches of the bush. Terry was conscious of the nearness of her green eyes laughing into his. Her golden hair shot with copper shone like a shaft of light amongst the leaves. He scrambled to his feet, his face burning and his stomach turning flip-flops as he held out his hand and pulled her up. He turned quickly to the chute and avoided her gaze by lifting up the coal-dusty lid against the wall.

'Ugh! Creepy crawlies,' she exclaimed, looking at the underside of the lid as the spiders scuttled off into the undergrowth. She peered down into the darkness. 'There'll be even more down there.'

'No, there won't,' he said confidently to allay her fears. 'I'll go first and clear the way.' He sat down at the head of the chute and Kitty looked at him with apprehension. 'Don't be afraid Kitty.'

'But how will we get out?'

'We'll find another way, or crawl back up the chute.'

Her heart sank at the thought.

'You will follow me Kitty, won't you? Promise?'

'Yes. Alright,' she said with reluctance.

'Well, here goes.' He slid from view.

There was silence.

'Terry, are you there?' she called down, nervously.

His voice echoed back up. 'Yes. It's easy. Come on. It's your turn now.'

The fear of the enclosed space fanned through her and in an agony of indecision she hovered around the top of the chute. 'You can do it, you can do it,' she said to herself as Terry shouted up again. 'Are you coming, Kitty? You promised.' Steeling herself and gritting her teeth, she closed her eyes and slid down to land with a bump on the sharp edges of a heap of coal. She gingerly picked her way off it in the faint light from the grill on the wall, and towards Terry who was standing on steps leading to a doorway.

The door creaked open, and Kitty followed him with relief into a hallway with doors leading off. 'Golly Terry. You look like a coal man,' she exclaimed, looking at the streaks of black on his legs beneath his short trousers.

'So do you. The back of your dress is black.'

'It doesn't matter. It's only my old play one,' she replied, wiping the coal dust off her hands down the side of the dress. Come on. Let's explore!'

Finding the first door ajar, they pushed it open and entered into a kitchen.

'Gosh, isn't it big?' said Kitty, gazing at the display of painted cupboards and a dresser filled with china and glassware. A row of copper jugs stood on a shelf, above which was a clock with a large dial. She pulled open a drawer in the long, dust covered table to a neat row of odd looking utensils. 'What on earth is this?' she called, holding up a dimpled wooden mallet.

Attracted by his interest in all things mechanical, Terry had wandered over to a spit. He glanced at her outstretched hand. 'Looks like a mallet of some sort, but look at these pulleys and chains, Kitty. They worked from the iron jack when the fire was lit. Did you know, they could cook a whole pig on them?'

'Did they? I bet it worked better than your pieces of wood over our camp fires,' she grinned at him.

He pulled a face at her. 'Ha! Ha! Very funny.'

Kitty stood before the Cornish range. 'What a licker! They must have cooked for *thousands* of people!' she said, with her characteristic tendency to overstate. A door led off the kitchen and she went in. 'Nothing much in there. Just two big sinks and a draining board and plate racks on the wall,' she said, coming back out quickly and found she was talking to herself for Terry had disappeared to the room next door.

'I wonder what these are for?' he asked, looking at slate edged dishes with a hole for draining, as she came up behind him.

'I don't know. There's a marble shelf over there. Maybe it's a room to keep the milk cool or to set jellies. When mummy makes a jelly or blancmange she always puts them on our marble mantelpiece.'

They returned to the hallway and going up a few steps, pulled open a baize door, followed by a heavy panelled one, to find themselves in a large entrance hall with a wide staircase of wood-turned balustrades and a Gothic shaped window above giving light to the landing and corridors.

'Blimey!' said Terry, as they wandered in awe through rooms that were spacious with intricate plasterwork ceilings, ornate fireplaces and lavish furnishings. On the walls hung richly dark oil paintings of ladies and men in flamboyant dress.

'I've never seen such pretty things,' said Kitty, peering at porcelain vases and figurines and the blue and white of delftware in cabinets ranged around the room. She picked up a tortoiseshell box standing on a console table inlaid with parquetry, and on opening it, found inside two lead lined containers with a dusting of brown at the bottom. There was a faint smell of tea. Fancy, keeping a tea caddy in your living room, she thought, as an elegant

139

ladies escritoire, standing in the window, caught her eye. She pulled back the chair and sat running her fingers around the desk, and discovered to her surprise, a concealed drawer. 'Look, Terry!' she cried out excitedly. 'There's a little hidey-hole in this writing desk and there's something inside it.' He joined her, his eye for detail admiring the workmanship as Kitty pulled out a piece of paper. Yellowed with age, she read out the few words that were written. 'My sweet, darling Henrietta, I adore you. Say you will meet me.' It was unsigned. Kitty sucked in her breath, her eyes alight with the mystery. *'Golly!'* Do you think it was a secret lover?! I wonder if she did meet him? Maybe, she married him but we shall never know,' she said, rather sadly. He watched her carefully fold the paper and return it to the drawer with the sudden realisation he could not imagine life without Kitty. In his awakening love for her, he saw his future in one bright illuminating moment.

'One day, Kitty, I shall make you a writing desk like this for *our* house,' but she was away like a flitting butterfly, her eye caught by an octagonal sewing box that stood by a faded gold damask chair. 'Will you? Oh that's nice,' she murmured, oblivious to the intent behind his words, as she lifted the lid and fingered the array of embroidery needles and threads and ribbons. 'Mummy would love this.'

Deflated, Terry sat himself at the grand piano and lifting the polished wood lid, dulled with dust, he began tinkering with the keys. The notes were discordant, jangling his nerves and violated the privacy of the room into which they had intruded. He shut the lid.

This house is sad, Kitty thought, as they returned to the hall and walked down a long passage to a room that caused her to draw in a sharp intake of breath at the beauty of the full length Gothic window with stained glass panes at the top. She had peered many times through it from the Italian garden, but here, inside, it was breathtaking as she gazed at the library of books around it that reached from the floor to a green rib-vaulted ceiling. More books were piled on a gentleman's writing desk that held a silver inkwell and stand, and on studying a family photo of a lady in a long silk dress with two small boys and a girl sitting in a boat on the lake, Kitty's eyes widened and she recoiled with a start of recognition. They were the children in the garden. But where was the girl like herself? Terry catching her movement from the corner of his eye as he gazed down on a collection of snuff boxes in a small glass display cabinet, looked at her. 'What is it?'

'Nothing,' she answered, giving a globe map of the world a push that squeaked as it turned in its wooden stand. Her eyes roved around the room which had belonged to a man of culture, widely read and with an eye for beauty and detail. It was as if he had just slipped out and would return to his sanctuary away from the bustle of servants and demands of the estate and children. She could smell his pipe smoke around the leather armchair by the window, and imagined him, sitting there, reading one of his books and looking out occasionally onto his garden and fountain. It was rusted and dry now, but once it would have shimmered with droplets. 'Can you smell smoke?' she asked.

Terry sniffed. 'Nope, I can't smell a thing.'

'Well I can. It's like grandpa's pipe and it's coming from the chair by the window.'

'Let's go to another room,' he replied quickly as a chill ran down his spine at her words.

It was as they were returning to the brightness of the hall from the dining room with its walls of dark linen-fold panelling and a scored oak table, that Kitty saw the children again. They were dressed in party clothes, happy and excited within a circle of friends who scattered in all directions to hide from a boy holding his hands over his eyes and counting as he stood beside a Christmas tree. It reached high into the stairwell with brittles and decorations glittering with reflected light from candles on its branches, and beneath it gifts were piled. The girl resembling Kitty ran past her as on the count of a hundred, the boy began his hunt and disappeared into the drawing room.

Kitty had stopped quite still, and Terry turning around for her, saw that she was standing like a statue, her eyes wide and staring unblinking into space. He went to her. 'Kitty's what's the matter?'

She seemed not to hear him and her dancing green eyes were lifeless and gone to some far place. He waved his hand before them. 'Kitty! Look at me,' his voice was loud and urgent.

'I saw the children,' she said dully.

With mounting panic, he shook her shoulders. 'What children?'

'The ones in the garden.' She pointed. 'Over there, by the Christmas tree.'

'Christmas tree! Jeepers, Kitty, you're seeing things,' exclaimed Terry, staring over at the empty stairwell. He had never seen her like this before and was shaken. What should he do? And then, as if a light had been switched on, the awful hollow look had gone and she returned his gaze. 'Blimey! You really had me spooked, for a minute. You looked so queer.'

'I didn't mean to frighten you, but I really did see a Christmas tree and the children.' She looked at him with a plea for belief. 'You do believe me, don't you?'

'I know you wouldn't lie Kitty, but I didn't see anything and what did you mean, "you saw children in the garden?" When was this? You didn't tell me?'

'Well, I was going to and then you got the measles. It was before Peter came. I saw them getting into a boat on the lake. I was afraid they had come to live in the house.'

'Well, you can see there's no-one living here.' Her behaviour was making him jumpy. 'Look. Let's forget about this and do something else, instead.'

'No fear. After all we've done to get in here and sliding down that horrible chute,' she replied. 'We haven't even been upstairs, yet. Heh! Maybe they've got a nursery with a rocking horse,' she carolled brightly as she began walking up the grand staircase.

Terry followed her, bewildered at her quick return to normality. Together they poked their heads into bedrooms with furniture that was foreign to them both. There were gentleman's dressing chests and marble-topped washstands with small bowls and drawers, and opening a cupboard, they found a commodious chamber pot. Hugely amused they sniggered their way along the corridor to discover a vast bathroom. They stared in amazement at a shower with holes in the rounded sides and a cavernous bath with a curious long mace-like plug and an array of pipes leading to enormous antiquated taps. 'It's big enough to drown in!' exclaimed Terry. 'Sorry, Kitty, I'd forgotten about Thomas nearly drowning,' at which Kitty laughingly poked her tongue at him, and was her mischievous self and acting as if nothing unusual had happened. Terry was beginning to feel like Alice in Wonderland.

Along a separate landing, they came upon the main bedroom overlooking the terraces and lake. Despite its size, it was intimate with a woman's light touch and Kitty could smell the floral scent of roses. She picked up a small white statue of a Madonna and child that stood on the fireplace mantel alongside delicately painted porcelain birds and in wonder, gazed at the four-poster bed with faded blue and white Toile-de-Jouy drapes and coverlet. She had never seen anything so romantic but Terry, tired of bedrooms, said he was going to look for the nursery. Kitty went over to the dressing table to look at the silver dressing table set and cut glass perfume bottles. She opened one and sniffed. The smell was expensive. On the hair brush the initials of H and K were intertwined. Henrietta! A few grey hairs were caught in the bristles.

'Kitty! Come up here! I think I've found the nursery,' shouted Terry. She ran towards the electric cry of his voice, and found him struggling to open a door. 'This must have been shut for years,' he said, giving it one last push.

The room was filled with a choking mustiness, and the dust lay thick with cobwebs hanging in black trailing swags. Kitty screwed up her face. 'Ugh! Spiders, again.'

'Look. Just as you hoped, it's got a rocking horse,' Terry cried, oblivious to the state of the room, and going over to it, he swung his leg over. It creaked into life. Kitty looked around. On a long cupboard against the wall stood an Edwardian doll's house and a fort, and by the window was a blackboard and easel where a broken piece of chalk lay in the groove. A sailing boat lay at an angle against the wall and there were shelves of books and old-fashioned games. Fishing rods stood propped up in a corner. A battered armchair was drawn up to the fire surrounded by a safety guard and rail for towels, and on the nursery dining table looking incongruous and out of place was the most beautiful inlaid wooden musical box. It was so familiar that she went to it without hesitation, and lifting the lid and cranking the handle to and fro, listened to the tinkling harp-like sounds of Silver Threads Amongst The Gold. It stirred a distant memory on the edge of her consciousness, but try as she might, she was unable to recall it as she watched the metal teeth striking the pins on the brass cylinder. Mesmerised, she let it play on, haunted by its sound and although the room was hot and suffocating she felt herself becoming colder and colder. This room had breathed with the life of children and then someone had closed the door and shut the memories in. She had to get out. 'Let's go, Terry,' she said.

'Oh Kitty. Let's stay a bit longer,' Terry pleaded, jumping off the horse as his eyes alighted on a boxed Hornby train set. He blew a cloud of dust from the lid. 'What would I give for *this*. Look, it's got everything. Engines and carriages and rails and there's another box with signal boxes and stations and things.'

But Kitty had left him and was walking down a long corridor, drawn by the cries of children to a door at the end of the house. She could hear muffled thumps from behind it and as she tried to turn the handle, her skin began to crawl with fear and her body shuddered with a terror, such as she had never known. She became cold and clammy and gasping for air as the corridor closed in upon her, she crumpled to the floor.

Hearing the dull thud, Terry came running out of the room. At the sight of her face drained of colour and her body sprawled lifeless, he was sick with fear. Dropping to his knees, he put his face close to hers and felt her breath faint on his cheek. Weak with relief he patted her face. 'Kitty, wake up. Please, wake up,' he said frantically. She stirred and opening her eyes looked at him in confusion, and shakily attempted to stumble to her feet.

'No, don't move yet. Wait until you feel better.' She leaned back against him and he wrapped his arms around her to instil his warmth for she was shivering uncontrollably. 'I was so frightened. I thought you were dead. What happened?' he asked.

'I heard the cries of children from behind the door, and there was a thumping noise and then I must have fainted.'

He felt a chill run through his body as it had in the library, and he looked apprehensively at the door. 'Can you hear noises now, because I can't hear anything?'

She turned and looked at him, her eyes wide with dread in her white face. 'No, it's gone,' she replied. 'I don't like this house, Terry. Let's go home.'

Her hands were like ice as he helped her up. He rubbed them between his own, and in an attempt to cheer her, drawled in a Roy Rogers voice, 'Just stick with me kid. Me and my trusty steed, Silver, will soon get you out of here.'

She gave him a flickering smile, and holding her hand tightly, he had but one thought in mind. To get Kitty out of the house. She had been acting strangely ever since they had entered.

'Are you feeling better, now?' he asked, anxiously, as they came into the kitchen and he sat her down on one of the chairs.

'Yes, but I still feel so cold,' she replied.

He wondered how to get out of the house. It would not be easy to crawl back up the chute. He looked up at the tall sash windows above a run of low cupboards. It was worth a try. 'If I stand on those cupboards, Kitty, I could reach the catches and with something heavy, knock one of them open.'

'I hope you can, because I don't want to have to climb up the chute,' she answered in a subdued voice.

And neither do I, he thought, looking at her face still pale in the clouded light from the windows and frantically he rummaged around in the kitchen drawers. 'What we could do with is a hammer or a heavy spanner but they are more likely to be in the stables.' He frowned as he toyed with the idea of using one of the small iron cooking pots, and then saw the answer staring him in the face. He strode over and taking the key hanging from a hook by the back door, he tried the latch. It clicked. 'Eureka!' he cried, pulling it open.

'But what about the key?' she asked, outside.

'I'll put it back on the hook. We'll have to leave the house unlocked. Nobody comes here, anyway.'

She didn't want to think about it anymore, Kitty thought, as she lay in bed that night. It made her blood run cold remembering the cries of the children and the awful thumping noise. Something terrible had happened behind that door. She had felt it in her very bones. She would think about Terry instead, and the way he held her hand after she fainted. Funny, how she had never really noticed before how good-looking he was. He was kind too. He didn't laugh at her or scoff when she later told him that she thought she must be seeing and hearing ghosts. He had stared at her with a queer expression and tried to understand, but she could see it scared him half to death. In spite of that, he told her she must always tell him, for he never wanted her to feel alone and unhappy after seeing these things. It would be their secret now.

Terry was also thinking as he sat at his bedroom desk where his homework lay unfinished. He had been caught on the hop with a stir of emotions that had knocked him sideways. He was bewildered at his altered perception of the girl he had always considered to be the sister he never had, sharing his life since the first day she came to ask him out to play. The look she had given him today at Nancarrow had turned his legs to jelly and blushingly to thoughts that boys sniggered about in the school yard. Why had he never noticed how pretty she was, or realised how much he cared? He admitted, she had frightened him with her talks of ghosts, and to his shame, he'd even wondered if she were a little mad, but he had seen for himself her hollow far-away look in the hall of the house. Of one thing, he was sure, Kitty was seeing and hearing something out of the ordinary, and no matter how crazy it seemed, if anyone dare mock, or question her truthfulness, he would defend her until the day he died.

Chapter Fifteen

THE REPLY TO Jack's letter arrived early one morning three week's later. Octavia, with the dust mop half under Grace's bed, dropped it and ran down the stairs on hearing the rattle of the letterbox. The envelope was in Roy's handwriting, and apprehensive, she decided she would fortify herself with a cup of coffee before reading it, and dropping the letter onto the kitchen table, she put the milk on to heat. Stirring it into the Camp coffee syrup, she picked up the cup, sat herself down in the kitchen armchair and ripped open the envelope.

> *4 St. John's Road,*
> *Birmingham.*
> *28th June 1951*

Dear Octavia and Jack,

As you can imagine it was a terrible shock to receive the news on your letter. I immediately tackled John who after initial resistance, broke down and told me what had been going on. As you know, I'm on the board of governors, and on making an appointment with the headmaster, I hoped to have a certain amount of clout for the outcome. It transpired that this is not the first occasion the headmaster had been approached by a parent and he had been placed in a very difficult position as this man had denied all accusations. After a very lengthy discussion and a further meeting with the other boy's parents to collaborate the facts from both our sons, it was put before the governors and he was summarily dismissed and debarred from teaching.

Winnie and I are sick at heart to think this had been happening to our boy, but God willing, now that the perpetrator is no longer there, he will recover from his terrible ordeal. We shall be everlastingly grateful to Kitty for her perseverance in believing something to be wrong.

You have a very special little girl, there. Peter is progress-
ing well with his arm and will be having his plaster off soon
which needless to say, is covered in signatures from his
classmates. Diane continues to grow in strength and Winnie
benefited from a break without the boys.

It was good to see you again and thank you both for
putting us so quickly in the picture. We appreciate it could
not have been an easy letter to write.

Roy

That evening, with Kitty out of earshot having gone next door to play with Terry, Octavia showed Jack the letter.

'Thank God that bastard is no longer at the school and is barred from teaching,' said Jack with unaccustomed profanity after reading it. 'We can only hope that the memories for John will fade with time. And thank goodness for Kitty. I know she's scatterbrained, but she does seem to have a knack of sensing trouble, as well as creating it,' he added with a wry look, handing the letter back to Octavia. 'Best to get rid of this.'

'Yes, I will. Now that we know the outcome, we can tell Kitty that this Mr. Collins has moved to a different school. She has asked me several times if I'd heard if John is alright. It will put her mind at rest to know that this man is no longer there. Even now, Jack, I feel ill just thinking about it.'

His face creased with disgust. 'Yes, so do I,' he murmured.

Octavia sat in the bay of the front room, her mind busy as she began to line one of Kitty's tutus with an old liberty bodice for warmth for she had not an ounce of spare flesh on her and it could be cold backstage in the church halls when the dance troupe gave their performances. Having Roy and the boys to stay had set her to thinking how quickly the years of the children were going by. It was time, she decided, to have a professional photograph taken of them all, but as she said to Jack, 'all the best laid plans.' She glanced out over the field where cows lay in the hot sun, chewing the cud. Of all the times for Kitty to catch measles, it had to be in Jack's holiday, and as if that wasn't enough, in the hottest week of the year.

Kitty had been mortified and lay in the darkened bedroom drinking copious glasses of orange juice brought up by Jack, and bemoaning the fact that it was all her fault that they could not go to the beach and that she had spoilt his holiday. Jack told her these things happen. She looked in the mirror at the spots over her face and body and thought she had never looked so ugly in all her life. And then, just as she was beginning to take on a semblance of normality, Grace caught it, and Jack's entire holiday was finally and entirely engaged with measles.

The day dawned when on studying themselves in the mirror and finding to their immense satisfaction every sign of the poxy spots had vanished, Octavia seized her opportunity and hastily arranged a date with the photographer. The first port of call was to the barbers for Thomas to have his mop of curls tamed and cut. Phoebe's remark that he looked like a girl had hit home and when discussing it with Jack, she found that he was in agreement. 'Phoebe's right, Octavia. It's high time his hair was clipped short.' Octavia's response was decisive but she did not find it easy. On returning home, she declared around the tea table, 'he looked just like a little angel with the white cape around him and he was as good as gold as the barber cut off his beautiful curls.' With their own hair straight as sticks, Grace and Kitty exchanged a furtive look of triumph. Octavia had sadly placed a few whorls into an envelope, the last vestige of his babyhood, and dropped it into the sideboard drawer.

Kitty whispered, 'It's a pity the barber didn't cut off his eye lashes as well!'

United in sibling resentment, she and Grace gloated in gleeful mirth.

Octavia turned and looked at them both. 'I heard that. That was not very nice Kitty,' she retorted, as she pushed the drawer shut with a bang and left the room.

'Mummy's little diddums,' said Grace to Thomas who was wandering around like a shorn sheep.

He looked up at them both with eyes like saucers without his face framing curls and held up his arms to Kitty to be lifted. 'You're too heavy, Thomas. You're not a baby any more.' Thomas placidly accepted her statement and made for the chair and began to climb up onto it for his book.

'Oh, come here, Thomas,' said Kitty relenting. She sat on the chair and lifted him onto her lap. 'Shall we look at your story book?' After all, she thought, it wasn't his fault that her mother was gaga about him. At Kitty's act of betrayal, Grace scowled at her and marched out of the room.

Kitty and Grace wearing their cream shantung silk dresses that Octavia had made during the winter months, shone from head to toe. Their dresses floated around them, soft and light as vanity with puffed sleeves and yokes of embroidery. Kitty had elected to keep her hair in plaits tied with new blue satin ribbons, for she could not face a torturous night tossing and turning on a head of rag curls, while Grace's washed and held in pinwheels when drying, brushed out into soft curls around her face. Wreathed in smiles she raced upstairs with Kitty where they spun around before Octavia's dressing table mirror. They now sat waiting for Octavia who came into the sitting room with Thomas dressed in red shorts buttoned to a matching checked shirt. Their mother's eyes passed over them for a final inspection. 'You're both looking lovely,' she said. Grace and Kitty exchanged an amazed look of delight. Octavia glanced in the mirror at her short and sleek nineteen twenties hairstyle, waved to one side with Amami setting lotion, and which she had found no reason to change, until a persuasive friend egged her on to try out the new craze of a perm. 'I look like a damn gollywog!' she'd fumed, when she emerged from her cubicle with her thick hair frizzed around her face. It had taken weeks to cut it out, since when, the merest suggestion of changing her hair to the latest new style brought a sharp response. 'Nothing but a pair of scissors will ever be coming near my head again!' Finally, the family were off, out of the back door and down the hill like a flock of chirping birds. There was no stopping at the corner shop with their ration book, and agonizing over glass jars of sweets, and they did not dare risk a hopscotch or two on the flagstone pavement as they walked along. They were on a mission and dressed to the nines.

Standing next to the photographer's simple smart frontage with large portrait photos against a black backdrop, was the ironmonger's with a window that was an Aladdin's cave. It was crammed with every conceivable household item. Sunlight soap, Zebo blackening for the range, Oxydol soap power and Lux flakes stood cheek by jowl with galvanised pails, mousetraps, enamelled

150

bowls, Dolly blueing bags, rolls of chicken netting, a clothes line and centre stage, the star turn, a magnificent paraffin heater. The decorative brass gleamed, and Kitty thought it the most wonderful thing. She had asked why they couldn't have one, like Sandra's mother because her kitchen was always warm and had a comforting smell from the heater which Kitty loved. 'I'm very wary of them,' Octavia replied. 'Houses have been known to catch fire when one has fallen over and I'm not taking that risk. We have the gas cooker now and it quickly warms up the kitchen when I leave the oven door open.'

'Yes, but what if the flames went out? We could be gassed before I can dance my solo again in the autumn concert. Only kidding,' she said quickly, at the look of rebuke on Octavia's face.'

With no time to linger, they were hurried into the photographer's shop to a jangle of the overhead doorbell. Stepping into a darkened room their voices dropped into silence as they stood looking around a rather bare room with two spot lamps, a battered stool in front of a midnight-blue velvet curtain and a strange looking camera standing on a tripod from which hung a large black cloth. The photographer, a man with the face of a mournful basset hound sat them in a row on the long, wide stool, and placing their arms and legs this way and that until he was satisfied, then told them to watch for a rabbit. Mystified, they waited as he moved back into the shadows. With a sudden swirl of movement, he vanished. A disembodied hand materialised holding a bulb on the end of a tube. Another hand appeared wildly waving a toy rabbit in the air. Thomas sat mesmerised.

'He's a magician,' Kitty whispered into his ear.'

Thomas turning to Octavia, pointed to the black box. 'Magician, mummy!' Simultaneously, the room was lit by a blinding flash. Up sprang the photographer's head like a jack-in-the-box.

'We'll take it again,' he said, and fussed around them, rearranging their arms and legs. One leg a fraction more to the side, one arm to rest on their laps, and planting Thomas's hands firmly behind him. 'Now, you must sit *still* and smile at the rabbit,' he said in barely disguised annoyance as he slid another glass square into the camera. Kitty grinned glassily at the demented rabbit and there was another eye-popping flash.

There was muttering. Grace had pulled a face.

A nervous air permeated through them and Thomas's eyes widened with apprehension. Kitty and Grace dared not move and sat like slabs of marble and were blinded when the room flared again. There was more muttering as he emerged from under the cloth with his striped bow tie slewed sideways, and his hair, stiff with Brylcreme, was standing on end.

'He looks like Dennis the Menace,' Grace hissed through barred teeth.

In vain, they struggled to stifle the fits of giggles that oozed out of them and the photographer in one last despairing attempt, lit up the room and prayed.

A week later the photographs were ready to be collected. 'It really is quite surprising how well they have turned out, after the performances our children put on,' commented Octavia to Jack, as she sat looking at them. 'Dennis the Menace has surpassed himself. Even the one with Grace biting her lip is perfectly acceptable as she has a smile with it. It's difficult deciding which one to keep. Which do you like Jack?'

'They are all very good,' said Jack, looking at them in turn. 'I leave the decision entirely to you, darling, then I can't be accused of picking the wrong one.'

'Oh Jack, don't be so daft,' laughed Octavia. 'I think this one. It's the most natural looking of the three of them,' she said, holding it up to Jack, who agreed. 'Now, all I have to do is buy a photo frame when I next go into town.'

Chapter Sixteen

KITTY SAT ON the grass savouring the last of a steaming hot pasty, encased in a brown paper bag and sprinkled after the first bite of the corner, with vinegar. A custom, she discovered not everyone shared. No-one could make a pasty like Octavia, she thought, not even Aunty May, and eating them in the fresh air in the garden on a summer's day, they tasted even better as she took the final bite of the meat and juices hiding in the corner. She remembered Grace and herself telling Octavia that she was the 'pasty queen' thinking it would please her, but for some unknown reason, it had quite the opposite effect, and she looked irritated. 'There's just no pleasing some people,' Grace remarked and Kitty grinned at her. She did come out with the quaintest of expressions. Kitty lay studying a grasshopper and wondering whether she should get a jam jar and catch it. The trouble was, they seemed to lose their legs so easily if caught beneath the rim of the glass, it was horrible. She turned over onto her back and gazed up into the sky. Through the open door of the kitchen she could hear the slap-slapping of Octavia's knife beating an egg white on a plate. There was a pause, whilst she briefly rested her arm, and then it continued, the slapping of the viscous bubbles until they grew into a mass to be spread over the lemon pie mixture and baked. The tartness of the lemon combined with the sweetness of the meringue was a mouth watering thought as she idly watched the changing shapes of clouds, fluffy and white as Octavia's meringue. The sky was a constant wonder. On slow sunset evenings it spread before her other worlds suspended in the sky; shimmering deserts of bruised orange and gold, and misty amethyst mountains with lakes of pearled pistachio. On clear frosty nights, she stared until her neck ached at the zillions of stars sprinkled over the black velvety canopy and wondered at their flashing mystery, as she studied them through her grandfather's binoculars.

It was on one such evening that she and Sandra arranged to meet. With innocent faces, the fibs were told: they would be star gazing in each others gardens, but had something quite different and far more exciting in mind. It had been inspired from the latest war film and would be a great new adventure for the Secret Service. Under cover of darkness they would creep up the gardens to the double-fronted houses of the neighbouring terrace across the hill and make secret observations on the latest technical innovation. The television! A luxury few possessed. Their hearts thumped from the fear of discovery as they crept up the first garden looking around the house for a chink of light. There was none. They were out. They tried another, and were in luck. A window was flooded with light and the family within were watching a flickering screen, but it was difficult to see for chairs were gathered around it in front of a blazing fire that reinforced the creeping numbness of their feet and hands. A woman came to the window and began to pull the curtains shut. Had she seen them? In a panic they fled in the inky blackness, giggling with fright as they stumbled into bushes and flowerbeds, and arrived weak-kneed with relief at the sight of the garden gate. Their breaths rose in quick bursts of vapour. On a high of excitement, they decided to continue, keeping well away from the pathways that could be lit by the sudden opening of a door. To their disappointment, curtains were drawn against the cold, until they came to the last imposing house. Kitty, straining on tip-toe to look through the window, heard the frantic barking of a dog and the entrance door burst open, fanning light out into the darkness. A man appeared. 'Who's there?' he shouted. His dog bounded over, trapping her against the window sill where she stood terrified. The man's face black and featureless from the backdrop of light loomed up at her. 'What are you doing here creeping around my house?' His annoyance at being disturbed from his meal changed to one of surprise as he brought his dog to heel. 'It's Kitty!' he exclaimed to his wife who had tentatively followed him out. 'Are you alright, child?'

'I . . . I . . . um . . .' Her brain had turned to cotton wool and excuses that normally came so easily to her lips floated away on the night air, and she stood dumbly, her mind racing as to how he knew her for his face was not familiar. She looked around for Sandra who was nowhere to be seen.

At the sight of the man and his dog, Sandra had fled as if the hound of the Baskervilles was snapping at her heels, and arrived home incoherent with fright, her fear communicating itself between breathless gulps of air. 'There's a man . . . and he's got . . . hold of Kitty!'

'Oh my God!' cried her father, leaping out of his chair and taking no heed of a coat for the cold, frantically stuffed on his shoes and ran and banged on his neighbour's door. 'Come with me, Bert! Some man or other's got hold of Kitty!' Ready and prepared to do murder, they charged up the garden path of the house Sandra pointed to, and found Dr. Lewis who had attended Kitty as an infant, calmly warning her not to do such a silly thing again. The outcome could have been a lot worse, he was saying, if she had disturbed someone less sympathetic than himself. Fuming with embarrassment and feeling extremely foolish, Sandra's father explained and apologised for their intrusion, and was put immediately at ease as the doctor said he quite understood his daughter's misunderstanding of the situation. He had teenage sons of his own with crazy ideas, and it was easy to get hold of the wrong end of the stick. As the men relaxed and chatted briefly for a few minutes before leaving, his two sons brought to the door with the commotion, grinned aggravating at them and Kitty felt sick at the thought that Octavia and Jack would come to hear of it. On the way home, she begged Sandra's father not to tell her parents saying it would only worry them. He eyed her in irritation. He had been caught on a fool's errand and this was not the first time Kitty had dragged his Sandra into one of her madcap ideas. She created more pandemonium than anyone he knew. Kitty stared up at him with her odd quality of innocence and perception and relenting in spite of himself, he agreed this one time to say no more about it. Even now, Kitty felt uncomfortable at the memory of the doctor's dressing down and later, of Sandra's mother's caustic observations. 'You haven't got a brain between you, you nincompoops. From now on, your clandestine night-time meetings in other people's gardens are over. 'I'll give you star gazing! You can put those ever fertile imaginations of yours to your school work instead!'

Kitty had retreated from her wrath and continued to star-gaze alone, following the constellations as they moved through the seasons and once, when the stars were so bright she felt she could reach out and touch them, she had an awesome thought. What if the millions of stars were the souls of people? After her prayers with Jack, she had delivered him the notion. 'Do you think when people die daddy, that they become stars? The bible says that heaven is God's kingdom, and although you can't see the stars in daytime, they are always there, aren't they? Looking down, keeping watch over us, like God.'

'Well, Kitty,' he replied, after due consideration. 'It is an interesting concept. Jesus said, that in his Father's house were many mansions and perhaps the stars are one of them, but I fear we shall never know the answer until our time comes, and that is a very long way off for one little girl.' He gave her a kiss. 'Time for sleep, and you too, Grace,' as he went over to her. 'Mummy will be up in a minute to say goodnight.' Jack had descended the stairs with a smile. 'That child,' he said later to Octavia, 'never ceases to amaze me. She comes out with the most extraordinary ideas and questions. This time it was about the stars and if we become one when we die! Whatever will she ask me next?'

'Kitty has always had a vivid imagination,' replied Octavia, absent-mindedly, engrossed in her library book, *How Green Was My Valley*.

It was true that Kitty had a colourful imagination, Jack thought, as he sat down and picked up his book, but remembering the day at the Merry Maidens and Kitty's sightings of the little girl that walked to Dolcoath, who was to say they were not real? They had been real enough to Kitty for her reaction at the circle had been spontaneous and genuine. There were, after all, many things in life that were inexplicable, as were the miracles of Jesus. People attempted to extenuate them, or to find a scientific explanation. Was it not better to simply have faith and accept there were people who had extraordinary gifts, who could heal, sense and see things that the average mortal could not? Perhaps, Kitty was one of them. She appeared to know intuitively when things were wrong, and seemed to possess that sixth sense that man was acknowledged to have had, and lost. He had attempted once to talk of such things to Octavia, to discuss the phenomenon of ghosts materialising to rational and intelligent people, and the concept of life after death. Pragmatic and down to earth, she had laughed at the idea of ghosts and as for an afterlife, it was nonsensical. How could the millions who have died possibly exist in heaven? They would hardly have the room of a pinhead! The possibility that heaven might exist as another dimension would invite her derision. She believed Christ had existed, his teachings profound, and if we all could live as he taught us to do, the world would be a better place, and that was what mattered. Not the manner of his death which was commonplace in those days, or the belief in the resurrection. And yet, thought Jack, his resurrection was pivotal. In the recently discovered Gnostic gospels, it was said, He appeared after His crucifixion to bear witness that the soul survived death, and on his reading of a scientific journal demonstrating that all things were made from the same core elements, from the smallest flower to the highest mountain, it struck him that all of life *was* God, an embodiment of the divine. Nothing separate from Him, but one infinitesimal part, making the whole. It was breathtaking in its simplicity. And if that were the case, then man could not point a finger at God and ask why he did not stop wars and the evils of the world, for that power lay within ourselves. We had been given freedom of choice but to whom could he talk and discuss such a concept. He gave a small sigh at which Octavia looked up, but Jack's eyes had returned to his book.

Kitty sat up from the grass, impatiently waiting for Octavia to go into town. The letter had arrived in the morning, postmarked Canada. She had handed it to Octavia, and on asking her who it was from, was told it was an old school friend who now lived out there. There was an expression and an evasive look in her eyes, as she quickly pushed the letter into her apron pocket and continued her chores. Kitty stared after her, her curiosity instantly aroused. The minds of adults were a perpetual mystery, their manoeuvres and manipulations to be shrugged off, but on this occasion, some compelling instinct to discover why her mother had not read the letter, as she would normally do, zinged away inside her. She had made an excuse not to go into town, saying she would rather stay at home and sort out the stamps that Jack had collected for her from the numerous overseas letters sent to the Mining School. At last, they came out of the back door, and Kitty waving them off, dashed into the house and watched the two chestnut heads on each side of Octavia, until they turned the corner from the terrace. The coast was clear.

With a certain amount of misgiving for it was simply not done to read others people's letters, she rifled through the letter rack on the sideboard that held Aunt Alice's letters from Greece and bills that arrived with monotonous regularity, as her mother would say. It was not there. How odd. Letters were placed in the rack until answered. Where on earth was it? She yanked open the sideboard drawer with its annoying tendency to stick, and rummaged around. It was not there either. Driven by a compulsion that something momentous lay in that letter, she hunted the house for it. The kitchen cabinet was occupied with everyday cutlery and cooking utensils, and looking in the 'mountain' drawers she found only the table linen. That left only one place - her parent's bedroom. She ran upstairs to the dressing table that stood alongside the window, and pulling open the drawers on each side of the kneehole, found it with Octavia's folded silk scarves. Her heart thumped as she sat down in her mother's small moquette armchair and easing it from the envelope with shaking hands, she began reading it. It was short and poignant and gripped her attention.

Thank you so much Octavia for the lovely photo of the children. Prue was so pleased to receive it. They are all growing away, so quickly, aren't they? Kitty is quite a young lady now and the likeness to James as a child is striking. I had hopes that one day we should meet Kitty, but for my darling Prue the dream will not be coming true. I am desperately sad to tell you, she is fading fast and the doctor says it's only a matter of time. I hope you and the children keep well, and please give our very best wishes to Jack.

With fond wishes,
Henry

Again and again, she read the paragraph. Octavia had said the letter was written by a school friend so how could she, Kitty, resemble this James? She frowned in puzzlement. Unless of course, he was a long-lost cousin like Peter and John, but if that were the case, where was the need for Octavia to lie and hide the letter? And why would they wish to meet her, and not mention Grace or Thomas? She had the strongest feeling, that in some particular way, this letter was connected only to herself. She was mystified as she stared unseeing out of the window, mulling it over and over. The name James was vaguely familiar. Where had she heard it before? With a jolt, she remembered a snatch of conversation in the car when Uncle Roy had spoken of James and a motorbike, and stopped abruptly in mid-sentence, and now, she wondered why. The answer, she knew, lay with her mother but to ask would mean admitting to reading the letter. She dare not. There was only one person she could talk to about it. Terry. She jumped up and hastily replacing the letter amongst the scarves, ran next door. Mrs. Retallack opened it to a troubled looking Kitty. 'Can Terry come out to play?'

'I'm sorry Kitty, Terry has gone to play cricket with the boys,' she replied, and on closing the door, the boy's mother was thoughtful. Something was up, and it was then that something else struck her. The child had a feyness about her. Why had she never noticed it before? It was as clear as those crystal green eyes of hers.

'Drat! Drat! Drat!' Kitty exploded under her breath as she came up the entry of Greenview. Of all days, why did it have to be this one for Terry to go and play cricket?!'

Chapter Seventeen

AT DINNER THE following morning, Octavia told them not to disappear out to play for she would be taking them to the church-yard. It was time to attend to her mother's headstone, to cut the grass and arrange fresh flowers, and on the way home, they would drop by to see her father. With the scrubbing brush and shears in her shopping bag, and with 'pinks' from the garden wrapped in a newspaper and held by Grace, they set forth with Kitty swinging an empty jam jar on a string handle.

The churchyard was a haven of peace and warmth; as familiar to Kitty as her own garden and holding no fears. Returning home from school, she and her friends often wandered around reading the old headstones, and hunting through the fallen leaves for conkers beneath the massive horse chestnut tree as the boys threw up sticks to knock them down. Squealing with delight at finding the green spiny cases and breaking them open to reveal the fat and burnished brown conkers, scuffles would break out with the boys who endeavoured to snatch their finds for conker fights, but the girls had run away, laughing and weaving amongst the graves.

At the graveside, Octavia busied herself emptying the dead flowers from the holder and began to cut the grass around the curb stones. 'Grace, take Thomas with you,' she called, to Grace who had headed off with the jam jar towards the tortoiseshell and peacock butterflies that flitted amongst the wildflowers growing on the fringes of the churchyard. She returned and taking his hand, Octavia smiled as she heard her telling him she wanted to catch a butterfly and that he would have to be very still and quiet. Two more quiet souls, would be difficult to find, she thought: Thomas, passive in temperament and already showing signs of a love for books, and Grace shy and 'deeper than Dolcoath,' as Jack had often observed.

'Run and fetch a can of water, Kitty,' Octavia murmured, as she cut the grass and pulled the weeds. Kitty returned with the water slurping over the top of the can, and dropping it down with a thud, began scooping up the grass and weeds and placed them on a sheet of newspaper. Octavia knelt at the curb stone and dipping the brush into the can, began scrubbing away the blown earth and dust.

Kitty stood watching her. It would be scrubbed until the granite shone. There were times, Kitty thought, when a modicum of restraint in cleaning and tidying would be appreciated, like when she was sick in the winter, and Octavia had stripped and remade her bed, as she did each day, and all the residual warmth of her body on the sheets was gone. Shivering, she had clambered back in, hugging her stone hot-water bottle to her as Octavia gave the underside of her bed a sweep with the mop on the linoleum. Now finishing the surrounding curb stone, Octavia started on the headstone and Kitty on reading the familiar words, 'In loving memory of Elizabeth, beloved wife of William Henry Tremayne,' found the question without conscious thought popping out of her, 'What happened to granny? Daddy told me she died in an accident.'

The water pouring down over the keystone, stopped and trickled away over the granite chippings, and with a studied action, Octavia placed the watering can down. Her body that had been vigorous and alive in the quietude of the churchyard, collapsed a little, and her face changed to the saddest expression that Kitty had ever seen, and she wished she had never asked. Octavia sat down. 'We'll have a rest for a minute or two,' she said, and patted the grass for Kitty to join her. Her grey-blue eyes were shadowed as she looked at Kitty.

'You were named after her, you know.' With a sigh, Octavia gazed away to some distant memory. 'She was a wonderful mother to us four girls and was taken from us far too early in life.' She turned her head back to a levelled look at her daughter. 'I wish you could have known her, Kitty. She was always ready to help others and was loved for her kindness by all who knew her. I remember on one occasion she gave her best silk blouse to the lady who came each week to help her with the washing. Flora, she was called. It was her daughter's wedding in a few weeks time, and she was worried that she had nothing new to wear to the service. My mother quietly disappeared upstairs when we were all sitting in the kitchen having a break with a cup of tea, and she returned with this exquisite blouse. Pale coffee it was, with a high lace neckline.

Flora was overwhelmed and protested that she couldn't possibly take it, but mother insisted. She was like that, she would give away her last penny. Your grandfather would often grumble he was the saviour of Redruth!' She smiled wistfully. 'For all his apparent sternness, he can be very funny at times. And then one day, mother, May and I had gone to the picture house in Redruth, to see our very first talkie. Jessie Matthews was in it, and we were on our way up through the town to catch the bus home . . .' Octavia stumbled for a moment, fighting the image, and Kitty feeling guilty that she had upset her mother, looked away as she recovered her composure.

'We were so happy, Aunty May and I, one each side of mother chatting about the thrill of seeing the first talking picture when we heard shouts from the policeman conducting the traffic by the town clock and we saw a car running backwards down the hill. People were scattering out of its way as it bounced off a sweet stall and mounting a pavement, it gathered speed. Your granny tripped as she pushed us out of the way from each side of her, and was caught under the wheels. Our mother took the impact through the shop window. It was horrific,' she whispered, her eyes glistening with tears. 'She died later in hospital. Every detail of her terrible injuries was reported in the local newspapers. It even reached the Nationals, and to see it there, in print, the way she was ripped from us . . .' Octavia's face contorted with remembered grief. 'Aunty May who was fifteen at the time,' she continued, wiping the tears with her hankie, 'lost the use of her speech for a while, and your grandfather was like one demented. He was murderous towards the old man who lost control of the car. And Aunty Alice, who had just married Uncle Demetrios and gone with him to Greece, returned home again in total disbelief, as did Phoebe. It nearly killed us all and took us years to recover. In fact, we never did, really.'

Kitty was shocked and silent. A fearful feeling washed over her. She could not imagine life without her mother. 'What a horrible way to die, mummy,' she said, in a small voice, unsure of what else to say or do.

'Yes, it was, and when you lose your mother, no-one can replace her.'

'Not even daddy?'

'That is a different sort of love which you will understand more when you grow up. Without him, I wouldn't have had you three. And then, where would I be? Enjoying some peace and quiet, I dare say!'

Kitty looked at her balefully, and Octavia gave her a quick hug. At this uncharacteristic gesture of affection, Kitty longed to ask about the letter, and was about to pluck up courage when Octavia jumped to her feet to look for Grace and Thomas, and the moment had passed.

Grace came running over to show her a red admiral resting on a leaf in the jam jar.

Octavia barely looked, 'Where's Thomas, Grace? He should be with you.'

The pleasure of showing her the butterfly died on Grace's face. 'He's coming. Don't worry mummy. You're always fussing about him.'

Octavia stared at her. 'And with good reason Grace. He's just two year's old.'

'He's nearly three.' Grace retorted, looking at Octavia with defiance.

As one, Octavia and Kitty eyed her in amazement as Thomas veered into view.

It was a reflective walk to William's house. If thoughts could be read, Grace was not a little surprised at herself for her outburst at Octavia, and Kitty was thinking of her grandmother's death and of the letter. She glanced up out of the corner of her eye at Octavia. Her face was impassive. There was no sign of the tearful emotion she had shown to Kitty. It was if it had never happened.

'H-e-l-l-o. Is anyone at home?' Octavia called out, as they entered from the back lane and up the garden path. The kitchen clock sounded loud in the silence of the house. 'Gramp is probably taking a nap. Have a look in his bedroom, Kitty.'

She skipped ahead down the passage and poked her head around the sitting room door which had been converted into a bedroom. William was lying under the coverlet. His habitual look and bearing of an old soldier that Kitty found forbidding had softened with sleep in a triangle of sunlight that fell across his face. She shook him. 'Wake up gramp. Mummy's here. We've come to see you,' and then stopped very still staring in horror at something she had never seen before that rested at the side of the bed. It gave her the shivers. He stirred sleepily and heaving himself up, sat back against the headrest, his eyes focusing into awareness as the others came in behind her.

'Hello, dad. Thought we'd drop by on our way home.'

'I must have nodded off. It's warm in this room with the sun. I see the troops are here,' looking at the three of them.

'Yes, We've had a busy afternoon. I'll make us a cup of tea.'

'So, what have you three been up to?' he asked, as Octavia disappeared to the kitchen. 'Come and sit beside me, Thomas, and you two girls can sit on the edge of the bed.

Kitty was still staring uneasily at the artificial leg, long and pink and attached to a harness. She touched it and quickly withdrew her hand. It felt cold and smooth.

William saw her look of apprehension. 'You didn't realise my artificial leg looked like that, did you, Kitty?'

She shook her head.

'Why have you taken it off, gramp?' Grace asked, staring at it with interest.

'Because it chaffs the stump, Grace. It gets a bit sore sometimes.'

Kitty's eyes slid over to it again. 'But what happened to your own leg, gramp?

'It's a sorry tale Kitty, and one, that you in particular should take note of, because if you're not careful, my girl, you are going to end up like me with only one leg! Mummy tells me that you are forever scraping your knees, and picking off the scabs. I used to do the same thing, and because I never gave the skin a chance to heal, in the end, my leg became poisoned and had to be sawn off!'

She eyed him looking for a hint of amusement that he was pulling her leg. There was none.

'Kitty's always hurting herself and digging off the scabs and making them all bloody and horrible,' Grace announced.

Kitty glowered at her. 'That's not true.'

Grace raised her eyebrows over accusatory eyes, 'It is, so,' and snapped her head down in confirmation of her words. Crossing her legs on the bed, she gave William an old-fashioned look. 'Grown-ups don't do things like that.'

'You're too smart for me, young lady,' replied William. His eyes appraised her. 'No, you're right, Grace. The reason I lost my leg was because of the war.' He shifted his gaze onto Thomas who was resting in the crook of his arm, and tickled his neck with his moustache. Thomas squirmed and twisted away to look up at him. 'And don't ever let them tell you, my little soldier, that there's glory in war, because there's not. Only men getting killed.'

At his mention of the word killed, Kitty was reminded of her grandmother's death. 'Granny was killed because of a car, wasn't she?' she blurted out. 'Mummy told me in the churchyard. That must have been awful for you, gramp,' she said, looking at him with concern.

Taken by surprise, William's face fell into a shocked silence. Instantly, Kitty knew she should not have said it. Grace looked from one to the other at the charged atmosphere as Octavia came through the door with two cups of tea. 'Yours are out on the kitchen table girls with a biscuit. Take Thomas with you and drink your tea out there, whilst I chat to gramp. After you've finished, you can go and play out in the garden for a while.'

Looking sheepish, Kitty slid off the bed.

Octavia gave her a sharp look. 'What's up with you?'

'Nothing.' She gave William a conscience stricken look as the others went out through the door. 'I'm sorry gramp. I didn't mean to upset you,' she said and went rapidly down the passage before Octavia could make any comment.

'What on earth has she been saying, dad?'

'She told me you had spoken to her about your mother's death.'

'Yes, I did. She asked me point blank about her as I was doing the grave.' She sighed. 'Kitty shouldn't have said anything to you. She never thinks before she speaks or acts.'

'Children rarely do. She caught me unawares, that's all, and I think my reaction upset her a little. Sometimes, Octavia, I think you are too hard on her.'

'Maybe, but she has to be reined in. Grace and Thomas look at her in awe at the antics she gets up to. Grace is such a timid child,' and then, remembering the unexpected ticking off she had received in the churchyard, she smiled. 'She's getting better though. I'm discovering there's a fire in her belly. It's just better hidden than Kitty's.'

'Good, I'm glad to hear it. I can't stand namby-pamby kids.'

'So I remember!'

'How's Jack?'

'Oh, busy as always. You know what the school office is like. Getting ready for the next influx of students and sorting out digs for them. I heard from Henry, the other day. Seems Prue is pretty ill and hasn't long to live.'

'I'm sorry to hear that. Cancer is such a ghastly thing. Henry has taken some very hard knocks over the years, and this looks to be another.'

'My marriage to James seems like a dream, now. We hardly knew one another. His work and the war put paid to that, but there's one thing I do know. I couldn't have had a better husband or father for Kitty, in Jack.'

'Yes, he mused. 'He's a good man. You chose well. Have you spoken to Kitty, yet, about James? You should Octavia, before someone else lets the cat out of the bag. People talk.'

'I suppose I've been waiting for an opportune moment, but you're right, it's time I told her. It's going to be a bit of a bombshell.'

'Kitty will take it in her stride, you'll see, and be out with anything she wants to know.'

'Don't I know it. She never stops asking Jack questions. Thankfully, she's wise enough to know I just haven't got the time or the energy with three of them to look after, not to mention walking that hill every day, humping the shopping, to start delving into the whys and wherefores of every living thing.'

William, dropping his cup on the bedside table, heaved himself over to the edge of the bed, 'Which is the point I was making a minute ago. In her way, she understands more than you realise. Just try and give her a little of your time, though I do appreciate how busy you are.' He began putting on his leg and adjusting the harness and supporting straps over his shoulders. 'She was quite nervous of this you know,' he said, tapping it. I hadn't really thought before that they've never seen it. I told them my leg was poisoned from picking off scabs!'

'What on earth made you say that?'

'I thought it might halt Kitty. She won't leave those scabs alone. It did make her stop and think for a moment. She wasn't quite sure what to make of it. Grace saw through me in a minute. No flies on that one. Help me on with my trousers Octavia. What a performance this always is,' he said, as she knelt, 'and I'm weary of it. I never imagined I would end up a cripple, dependant on others. There have been times when all I have wished is to join your mother. Life has never been the same without her,' he said, reaching for his crutches. 'And that doesn't mean that I'm not grateful for all that you and May do for me. You have kept me going, and watching the grandchildren growing away has been a delight, but you've all got your own lives to lead.' Caught unawares by Kitty, his guard had dropped and this admission of his continuing grief, rarely expressed or seen by Octavia, filled her with immeasurable sadness. She was about to say that she understood, for even now to think of her mother brought tears, when the children came running into the room.

'I'm starving mummy. Is it teatime, yet?' asked Kitty.

'It won't be long, and it's time we were making a move,' Octavia replied, as she pushed William's armchair back to its light and sunny position in front of the window for his reading. His library books and the latest *Picture Post* with its up-to-date spreads and reportage on the world scene lay on the small table by the chair where he passed his days, content with the passive pursuits of reading or listening to his wireless. His passion for marksmanship had died with the cessation of war and the scenes of carnage seared into his mind and body, and he now took simple pleasure in visiting the library at the end of the road and chatting to the librarian who kept him up-to-date on the latest publications. On days when his leg pained him as if it were still attached, Joan would drop in to exchange his books along with her own.

Chapter Eighteen

'ARE YOU GIRLS ready, or not?' Octavia shouted up the stairs. 'If you don't hurry up, the carnival will be over before we've even got there!'

'C-o-m-i-n-g.' There was a galloping of feet down the stairs.

'What took you so long?' Octavia asked, as they tore the coats off the pegs in the passage and thrust their arms into them. 'And those are not the dresses I told you to wear. Well, there's no time to change them,' she muttered. 'If you're cold, it's your own fault.'

Mission accomplished. Kitty and Grace exchanged under-eye glances at their successful late manoeuvre, as they buttoned up and Jack pushed Thomas in his pushchair out of the back door.

The town had been buzzing for weeks and all were caught up in the excitement of the forthcoming joint celebrations of Holman Brothers and Camborne shopping week. Bunting festooned the streets and shop windows were transformed. Post-war drabness was replaced with festive floral decorations, ribbons and spotlights as the town's traders vied with each other to win the rosettes for the best dressed windows. They walked down the hill intermingling with people from Beacon and those decanted at the station, laughing and grizzling at the sight of Trevithick's statue bathed in pale gold from floodlights, his head sporting a traffic cone and his face draped with a pair of men's drawers. His prominent nose poked through the strategic opening which drew some disapproving looks and the children's laughter. Jack said it was probably the students getting up to their usual daft pranks.

People poured in from the neighbouring towns by the bus load and Camborne streets were jam-packed and filled to bursting point. Struggling to find a good viewing position, the children were pushed by a good natured crowd to the front allowing them a grandstand view. Anticipation was hammering away inside of Kitty, and shivers ran up and down her spine as she heard the first stirring music of Camborne Town Band. Winning championships since the year nineteen twelve, they had teased William that it was much better than Redruth's band, the best in the west, in fact, and he had ragged them back, as they knew he would. 'Ah, but Redruth has the best rugby team, girls.' Resplendent in their uniforms, the band marched past, drums beating and brasses gleaming as they led the first float, and there she was, the carnival queen, sitting high, high above in a long, silky blue dress, her crown sparkling like diamonds as she waved under a canopy of flowers.

The day was overcast and cold from a lack of sun, and Kitty was glad it was not she that was sitting up there. She had been summarily dismissed from the platform at the recreation ground, when, some weeks previously, she had watched the judging for the fairy queen. Imagining the thrill of smiling down and waving to envious friends, she had, on an impulse, dived into a horde of best dresses and ribboned hair surging up the steps to be judged. She anxiously scanned the spectators for any familiar faces that might report back to base. Dancing on the stage in her ballet class was one thing, but this would be viewed as making an exhibition of herself. No shrinking violets, her competitors paraded and twirled with flouncing curls, no pigtails for them. Their shark smiles of even pearly white teeth mocked hers that would soon be requiring braces, and she wished she could die. She stepped forward and was dismissed with an airy wave of an arm. Sharp disappointment mingled with relief as she jumped down and walked quickly out of the grounds. Huh! Who cared about being a fairy queen stuck up on a lorry!

A tableau drew alongside them drawing enthusiastic applause for winning the Holman directors' trophy as the premier tableau of queen and attendants against strong competition. It had beaten them all, even the Malpas queen sitting on her magnificent seagull with outstretched wings and Gwithian's beautifully dressed horse-drawn vehicle with arches of flowers.

'Fancy, a little village like Beacon, winning the cup,' said a man standing a row back in a flat cap and black donkey jacket. 'They heathens in Redruth went like that. They thought they's all set to win,' he said, in a voice loud enough to be heard by the heathens behind him.

'No, and you didn win'n either, my luvver!' came a Redruth voice from the back.

There was a wave of tittering amusement.

Kitty turned to grin up at Jack and Octavia at the ribbing between the two towns that was long-standing, as into view came a man dressed as a woman pushing an enormous pram. Inside a young man sat in a short dress and bonnet, sucking a large dummy, his bony knees splayed skywards. 'Some pretty looking 'lil maid, misses. Who she b'long to?' the man in the flat cap bantered, getting into his stride.

The mother stopped and hitching up her skirts and patting her tumbling mass of curling wig, hollered back with a saucy grin, 'I can tell 'ee wan thing, she eaden mine. I got plenty of me awn!'

There was a further ripple of laughter.

'She d' look like wan of they gypsies parked up Brea way.'

Mother's over-rouged face and cupid's bow of bright red lipstick, leaned over the pram with a rapt, amusing expression and with a hairy hand tutted the baby's face with its nine o'clock shadow from side to side. 'Es she do, don't she, but then, her mother was a very popular lady!' The baby poked out her tongue and received a bonk on the head with mother's handbag, and Kitty laughing along with the crowd, stopped abruptly. On the opposite pavement were women wearing long skirts and hats, and men in high-winged collars and waistcoats under jackets. There amongst them was the lady in the photograph on the desk in Nancarrow with her two sons and her daughter. Her auburn hair was swept up under a wide-brimmed hat that framed her delicately boned face and she was laughing with the children at six men sitting squashed together on an enormous fake horse. Wearing smocks and long leather boots, they sported bushy beards beneath an assortment of squashed farmers hats, a stove top hat and a trilby. The clay pipes clamped between their teeth were removed with a flourish as they roared out, Bill Brewer, Peter Gurney, Harry Hawk . . .

A giggling Grace threw a penny at a cowboy float. It chinked into a charity bucket held out on the hoof of a horse whose rear end had collapsed onto a bale of straw, and cocking his head to one side, he fluttered his long spiky lashes at her. 'Aren't you going to throw your penny in?' Grace asked, looking up at Kitty who was humming the tune, Uncle Tom Cobbly and whose eyes were frozen into an unblinking stare. Grace gave her a dig. 'Quick Kitty. Throw yours in, too.' Kitty ignored her and stood woodenly and unresponsive. Grace was put out. 'Why won't you speak to me?' Receiving no answer, she turned to Octavia. 'Mummy, what's the matter with Kitty? She won't speak to me and she's looking funny.'

Octavia leaned forward and pulled Kitty's rigid shoulders around to face her. 'Are you alright, Kitty?' she asked. 'You're not feeling sick, are you?' studying Kitty's dazed look.

'No,' Kitty shook her head at Octavia. The music of *Ghost Riders in the Sky* came blaring out from an approaching tableau. Kitty gloomily watched the spectres dressed in unearthly shades of green and riding imaginary horses in front of a painted stormy sky. My ghosts are real, and I wish they'd go away and leave me alone, she thought, as the Malpas Lifeboat crew passed by, dressed like villainous pirates and making villainous noises at the man walking the plank, and grinning like Cheshire cats. Kitty could barely raise a smile at them.

With the last of local business lorries bringing up the rear, the crowd surged onto the road as the riot of colour and noise finally came to an end, and the family was carried along with the heaving mass of people to the recreation ground. There, they eagerly awaited the thrills of the high wire acts of The Diavolos that had been depicted in colourful posters around the town. With bated breaths they watched them ride motorcycles across the wire, seventy feet above them, and the crowd went deathly quiet as they walked with long bending poles and carefully manoeuvred to stand on each others shoulders in a pyramid. The safety net looked small and flimsy below them.

'What a way to earn a livin", a voice said, as the Diavolos finished their act. It was the man in the flat cap, again. Kitty craned her head around but the tightly packed people hid him from view.

'There's more to come yet, boy. How do ee fancy goin round on that thing?' asked his friend, indicating The Marcellos climbing a tower that swayed alarmingly with a rising wind.

'No, bleddy fear! You went catch me goin up there. I just as soon jump off the North cliffs!' he replied, as the plane began to revolve around.

Kitty bit back a grin under a bowed head. It was a death defying display as the plane flew further and further out from the tower with the men standing on their heads on the wings against a darkening sky. Clapping their appreciation, the men returned to terra firma with a sweeping flourish of acknowledgment to the spectators, and there was a sudden barrage of cracking stars that made Kitty and Grace jump and Thomas's head to jerk up from a nodding sleep. The grand fireworks finale was exciting and magical, watching silver fountains and Roman candles, and cascades of crimson aerolites shooting up into the sky with bursts of sapphire stars and hissing snakes. Oooos and Aaaahs rose in waves from the crowd whose faces flared briefly in the bright magnesium light. Grace clapped her hands over Thomas's ears at the deafening explosion of a volcano streaming molten lava, and they watched in wonder at a skeleton dancing jerkily across the skyline. All too soon, it was over with 'Goodnight' fizzing in rainbow colours high above them and with happy sighs of regret, they streamed out through the gates with Thomas already falling back asleep in his chair and Grace's quiet voice chattering about the sights they had seen.

Kitty was thinking about the evening's carnival dance. 'I can't wait until I can go to the Old Tyme dance after the fireworks,' she said.

'That day will come sooner than you think, Kitty,' Jack said, and sensed her childhood was already beginning to slip imperceptibly from his grasp. All too soon, his children would be blossoming into young men and women eager to taste life. He understood Kitty's wish, for dance seemed to be in her bones, and she took part in all its forms, in folk dance displays and the maypole at the local summer fêtes. With two left feet, he had never craved the dance floor, and as a young man was content with the talkies, or a pint in the local with his friends, discussing the cricket and rugby and the political wranglings in the newspapers.

'I remember the balls before the war,' Octavia was saying. 'There was no shortage of fabrics then, and the dresses were beautiful. I wore a long champagne coloured satin dress that was the height of fashion.' She chuckled. 'The women didn't miss a beat as they waltzed past each other noting every detail of a new design. You could see them wondering if a new boutique had opened. I never had that worry. I would cut out a pattern and make it myself.'

'And your mother would have looked beautiful,' said Jack, to the girls.

'Those days of wine and roses are long gone,' she replied, with a nodding wry smile.

His reply was soft and for her alone. 'But not for me.'

As Octavia and Jack quietly murmured to each other, Kitty's thoughts had returned to the family from Nancarrow, the mother looking elegant and beautiful as she watched with the children a carnival in a distant time and place. These glimpses into the past with the children were becoming more frequent, although the girl who was her double, was not there today. Kitty wondered if she was simply a friend of theirs who came to play, for she remembered she was not in the photograph on the desk, either. When on that day in Nancarrow house she had finally realized they were ghosts, she was glad Terry was there, for now, she had someone to confide in, who accepted her mystifying experiences, the fact that she was different from everyone else, and with that acceptance, the burden of questioning had been lifted.

Kitty scrutinised the shop windows as they took the longer way home and walked up the main street after the evening service where they had come out from the church into the soft glow of floodlights. Armed with her entry form for the window competition of Holman's Week, she had spent afternoons seeking out the odd item in windows that were not normally associated with the shop and had ticked off all but two stores. She peered hard and long through the double-fronted window of Rices. She felt sure that the misplaced object would catch her eye exposed by the window's spotlights, but the array of items in the window was considerable, for the shop sold all manner of ladies and men's clothing, haberdashery and undergarments down to the last sock and nylon stocking. It had an intriguing payment system that Kitty would watch with fascination from behind the scuffed wooden counter top as the money was placed into a screw-top container and a chain pulled to propel it along an overhead system to the cashier sitting in her glass fronted room overlooking the shop. Shops had some funny ways of taking your money, she thought, as it disappeared and the change came whizzing back along the little rail. The Co-op's system was even stranger. It simply vanished into a tube and shot up to the top floor on a vacuum system. At Home and Colonial, try as she might, she still could not spot the odd item for the window was crammed with tins of tea and biscuits, jars of jams and pickles, and groceries of every description and disappointed she resigned herself to handing her form in with the vain hope that others would find even less objects than herself.

In the evenings, with a week of rugby, cricket and soccer games and various sports competitions at the recreation ground, Jack slipped away after his tea to watch, but tonight, he sat with Kitty near the front of Holman's canteen hall, awaiting the singers, recitations, and instrumentalists for the talent spotting contest. The hall was filling quickly and there was a hum of voices and expectancy in the air. Grace was not with them for it had been decided that one late night out was enough for her, and Kitty was secretly pleased to have Jack to herself. She smiled up at him and moved closer, when a pretty woman with dark hair, sat herself next to Kitty.

Jack leaned around. 'Hello, Mrs. Bowden. Come to join in the scrum?'

'Oh, hello Mr. Pengelly.' She flushed a little. 'Yes, I thought I'd join in the local celebrations.'

Jack laughed, 'It gets very noisy, so be warned. Gerald not with you?'

'No, I'm afraid it's not his scene,' she replied, as the lights went down and the first contestant came onto the stage.

Kitty and Jack clapped until their hands stung, and drummed their feet with the cheering audience to register their favourite with the most noise they could muster, to be registered on an electrical applause meter, from which the winners would be chosen. Laughing together at the rumpus, Jack gave Kitty his familiar 'isn't this fun?' grin with a quick shrugging up and down of his shoulders as they joined in the proceedings with the enthusiasm of knowing they were as much a participant as those on stage. She gave Jack's ribs a dig as the barbershop singers came on, faces with which she was familiar, for they often entertained in the church and chapel halls. Listening to them harmonising to a popular love song, her attention was drawn to Mr. Curnow, the milkman, who came whistling into their house each morning with his heavy can of milk and measuring jug. His handsome looks were dark and swarthy from the Spanish influence of early invaders that had settled and married local girls, and he was always ready for a laugh and a joke in the kitchen. Kitty watched as he sang, 'I only have eyes for you, dear,' with the barbershop singers, his eyes twinkling away at her. She returned him a beaming smile. On the second verse came the realisation he was not looking at her at all, but was gazing at the young and pretty lady sitting beside her. Feeling rather silly, Kitty looked around for Mrs. Curnow, a pleasant and rather mousy looking woman who helped with the cricket teas. She was nowhere to be seen. Kitty sneaked a sideways look at Mrs. Bowden. A secret smile played around her lips, as she gazed back at the milkman. Kitty's eyes went from one to the other, and it occurred to her, she had the same moony expression as the couple that she and Sandra saw smooching in the lane one summer's evening, when sitting, hardly daring to breathe, high up in the branches of a tree. When the couple moved off, they had giggled their way back down, but later that night, Kitty wondered what it would be like to be kissed. Someone in school had said that the proper way was touching tongues like the French did and she persuaded a reluctant Grace to stick her tongue out and they had touched at the tips. Ugh! It was awful and they had both fallen about laughing and feeling foolish. I wouldn't mind being kissed by Terry, though, as long as it wasn't a French one. I wonder where the noses go?

'Who was that lady?' Kitty asked on their way home.

'You mean Mrs. Bowden? I met her at a cricket match. She and her husband, Gerald have just moved to the area and he has joined the cricket team. He is a very good batsman and she has a very good singing voice. She has joined the chapel choir.'

'Mr. Curnow is in the choir, too, isn't he?'

'Yes, he is. Why do you ask?

'Oh, nothing. I just wondered,' she replied, and quickly switched to asking him who he thought was the best contestant.

Jack was not fooled by Kitty's rapid change of subject, but did not press her, and was left with the intriguing possibility of clandestine goings-on with his milkman, for it had not escaped his notice, either, that the milkman as he sang the words, had only eyes for the pretty Mrs. Bowden.

Chapter Nineteen

KITTY SAT AT the kitchen table cleaning the vinegar-stained cutlery with Vim before cutting the remains of old wallpaper into strips to line the drawers. It was a chore she loved, for it gave her immense satisfaction to see the knives, forks and spoons shining again on a bed of clean paper. She took the cutlery to the sink to rinse as Octavia picked up the saffron dough that had been covered and standing overnight in the warmth of the kitchen where it had slowly risen as if by magic to fill the enamel bowl. Setting it down on the table she began singing the old song, *Daisy, Daisy, give me your answer do*, and Kitty joined her, in a clear sweet voice as Octavia made the buns. It was a rare moment having Octavia to herself, and as they sang together in a shared sense of purpose, Kitty felt as happy as a bird. 'Your grandfather used to sing this song to my mother,' Octavia said, 'as it took her quite a while to make up her mind to marry him!' Kitty grinned at this nugget of information. It was funny how singing induced a feeling of happiness and often she would catch herself singing under her breath, as she went down the hill into town or out to play, stopping with a blush if caught by a passer-by.

Any moment now, she will tell me we are going to Gwithian. The two go hand in hand, she thought.

'If this nice weather continues tomorrow, we could go to Gwithian,' said Octavia, as she pulled up handfuls of elastic yellow dough and rolled it into balls, gently patting the tops before placing them on the floured cooking sheath.

Bingo! thought Kitty.

'Could Terry come too?'

'No, I don't think so, Kitty.'

'But why not? Terry and I do everything together.'

'Yes, it has been noted,' said Octavia with a quick slide of the buns into the oven.

'He's much more fun than girls. Girls are such cissies, apart from Sandra. Always afraid of hurting themselves. I bet daddy wouldn't mind him coming. You know how they like playing cricket on the beach.'

'Well, we'll see.'

The reply was encouraging.

'What you can do, now that you've finished the drawers, is go down to Aunty May's and see if they would like to join us tomorrow.'

'Yippee!'

'I thought that might liven you up.'

Kitty turned to go out of the door, 'Oh, and tell Aunty May, we'll be catching the eleven o'clock morning bus, instead of the two o'clock. It'll give us a nice long day on the beach.'

'What about Uncle Ted, mummy?'

'It's up to them. Uncle Ted can always join us later after the bank closes.' Kitty skipped out of the house and walked rapidly down the hill, her humour rising by the minute at the thought of a day at her favourite beach, and high in hopes that Terry would be able to join them.

May was cleaning her oven as Kitty entered the back door. 'You're just the excuse I need to stop and put the kettle on,' she smiled warmly. 'Helen is out playing with her friend Ann, so you and I shall have a natter over a cup of tea together.' She took out the tablecloth and began singing, *'If I knew you were coming I'd have baked a cake,'* a song she invariably sang when Kitty called, and together they sang, laughing and jigging to the words. 'Everyone is happy today, Aunty May,' she said. 'Mummy was singing too this morning.'

'There must be something in the air,' May replied, putting the cups and saucers on the table and bringing out a jar of home-made jam. She buttered a couple of splits. 'You always did sing, even as a little girl, you know. Your mother and I would hear you piping away, *'Jesus wants me for a sunbeam,'* in your bed. Your voice was like a little bell.' She poured a cup of tea. 'Now, you know what to do,' she said. 'Eat up, there's nothing to you.'

'Mummy said to ask if you and Uncle Ted and Helen can join us for a day at Gwithian tomorrow? She said we would be catching the eleven o'clock bus.'

'I don't see why not. The good weather seems set for a day or two.'

'Oh, goody.' Kitty smiled at her, her eyes bright with affection. Aunty May always made her feel warm inside.

May chuckled at a sudden memory. 'Did I ever tell you about the time you entertained some soldiers?! It was during the war when mummy and I were living together. Aunty Vi and I were coming home off night shift from Holmans and bumped into some young soldiers, just off the train. They asked us if there was anywhere they could grab a cup of tea. Well, of course, at that time in the morning, the cafés were shut, so I invited them up to the house. It was quite a surprise for your mother to find these young men on her doorstep, so early in the morning. Anyway, on hearing the commotion, you came down the stairs in your nightie, and into the sitting room like a little doll. They were making a fuss of you and then you did such a funny thing. You quickly lifted up your nightie to show them your knees and then dropped it again. It caused some fun, I can tell you. The more they laughed, the more you did it. I shall always remember it, and those young soldiers going off to war,' she sighed. 'You were such a dear little thing. I don't know what we would have done without you. You kept us going through those awful days.'

'I don't think mummy thinks I'm such a dear little thing, now! How old was I then, Aunty May?'

'About two, I should think.' There was the noise of the back door opening and Helen and her friend, Ann came in. 'I think they smelt the tea pot, Kitty.'

'Hi Helen. I was sent down to ask if you would like to come with us to Gwithian tomorrow and Aunty May said, yes.'

Helen's face lit up. 'Super! We haven't been to the beach for ages. We're just getting the long skipping rope. The rest of the gang is down the road, do you want to come with us?'

'Yes, but I musn't be late back. Mummy said she's cooking a hot tea.'

The following morning found them all in the long Saturday queue as it snaked away from the town square, past the book shop and around the corner. 'Ted will be down on the one o'clock bus and I told him we'd be sitting on the beach near Sheep's Pool,' providing the tide's out,' May informed Octavia and Jack. The queue began to move and a bus quickly filled as another drew into the square. They were now at the head of the queue and the children were poised and ready to race upstairs to the front of the top deck. Swaying and bumping along, the bus took off out of town and the children playfully swayed and jostled each other as they passed farms and fields bursting with ripened corn and others already harvested standing in wigwam sheaves. It was hot in the bus and Kitty jumped up to open the front spring windows, only to quickly shut them again as passengers at the back complained of a draught, but she was irrepressible, for Terry was sitting beside her, and a whole day lay ahead on her favourite beach.

Alighting in Gwithian village, they began what seemed like an endless trek to the sea. They passed the old chapel and thatched cottages with roses around doorways and gardens bright with flowers, that reminded Kitty of the picture on the biscuit tin where she kept her collection of stamps from around the world that Jack brought home from the mining school, before sticking them into her album. On walking past the small thirteenth century church of St. Gothian, Octavia said she remembered a magnificent old fig tree that had once stood by the lych-gate and bore fruit for many years.

'What's a fig like, mummy?' Kitty asked.

'Chewy and sweet,' she replied. 'They are traditional at Christmas time, like dates and nuts. They are slowly beginning to come back into the shops again after the war stopped all imports of foreign fruits.'

They turned towards the sea on an ancient sandy track where the breeze was cut with the shelter of the dunes. The air was still with a feeling of timelessness, and Kitty was aware of the old ones, their whisperings through the pores of the sand, as the path led them over a medieval village, long buried by sand blowing across the fields for centuries from a break in the cliffs on the southern half of Gwithian beach. The marran grass zinged as they trudged with buckets and spades swinging, and any complaints of tiredness were swiftly curtailed with reminders of how Octavia and May when children, walked from Camborne to Portreath. 'Think how tired you would be after having to walk to the beach and back.' There really was no answer to that one as they steadily plodded on. Finally, they came to neat rows of huts, each with its own garden enclosed by white picket fencing and their spirits lifted. A happy jump over a stile and before them, in the distance, the vista of Godrevy Lighthouse, gleaming white amidst the azure sea. They could smell the heady-scented mixture of sea and sand, clover flowers and seapinks, and with a whoop of expectation, they chased down the slope of springing grass, Kitty racing Terry, and Helen laughing with Grace, as they hurtled down, the one with her dark hair streaming and Grace's shorter, sun-browned legs running hard to keep up.

'Just look at them,' laughed May, as she clambered over the stile. 'Full of boundless energy.'

'I wouldn't mind some of it, would you?' said Octavia, handing Thomas over to May and the heavy beach bags to Jack. The savoury smell of pasties, baked that morning and kept warm in greaseproof paper and teacloths, wafted to him as he picked them up, and mingled with the saffron buns whose sweet aroma had greeted him the previous evening through the open kitchen door.

The golden sand gleamed and stretched as far as the eye could see to the Hayle estuary, for the tide was well out and scrambling down the cleft in the cliffs, they made their way through a sandy break in an outcrop of rocks dividing the beach in two, and forming Sheep's Pool. The origin of its name was lost beyond living memory, but it was thought that maybe the farmers driving their sheep across from the dunes on the south beach, used it for dipping their sheep which grazed on the cliff tops that had been common land. The children ran ahead, bagging a spot close to the pool which filled with the movement of the tide. In the summer it was deep with rocks below the surface on either side that caught many an unwary diver, and in winter with the wild winds and sea dragging the sand to and fro, it became shallow enough to wade through.

Dresses were hastily shed to reveal swimsuits beneath, and as Jack, Octavia and May dropped their bags and settled, Terry and Kitty raced to the pool, leaving the others to play on the sand. Scrambling up the rocks, they sat on the top overlooking the pool, and Kitty was conscious of his arms touching hers, and looking at him, she felt oddly shy and looked quickly away with her heart thumping as they watched some boys leaping off in front of them.

Terry could resist it, no longer. He stood up. 'Come on, Kitty. Let's do a honey-pot.' She shook her head. She had attempted to dive once, and had belly flopped with water shooting up her nose, and her stomach hitting the surface like a stone. It had been the end to any further attempts. Kitty followed him to the brink of the rocks. He held his nose and jumped. She watched the water fountain up around him as he disappeared for a minute, and surfaced blowing like a porpoise. She grinned and waved down at him swimming to the pool's edge where he was hidden by the overhanging rocks, and waited until his head suddenly appeared over the top with the person she least wanted or expected to see. Rosemary! She was looking as pretty as a picture in a beautiful yellow and blue ruched swimsuit. No scratchy knitted one for her. They were laughing together and Kitty could scarcely believe it as she took his hand and with a sly glance at her of triumph, suggested they jumped together. Opened mouthed, she watched them leap from view and on surfacing they played around, Rosemary splashing him and squealing as he splashed her back, before swimming to the edge of the pool when she raced off to the sea with Terry in pursuit.

Kitty was stunned and stared after them. Hurt and anger welled up, and jumping recklessly down from the rocks, she ran and ran until she could run no more, and flung herself onto the sand. Breathing heavily, she glanced back. The rocks of the pool were a smudge in the distance. She had outrun and outdistanced the few people that had sought solitude further along the beach. She was quite alone. Good. He won't be able to find me, she thought and with it the realisation he probably wouldn't want to anyway, now that he was with *her*. There was a hard lump in her throat at his betrayal. Against her will, the tears came hot and treacherously down her face. Angrily she pushed them away. 'I hate her! I hate her!' she hissed through clenched teeth. 'And I hate him, too,' but even as she said it, a little voice inside denied the untruth. She stared miserably out to sea and wished she were dead. She would drown herself. No-one would miss her for trouble followed her around like a black cloud – Peter breaking his arm, Thomas falling in the trough, and Grace scratching her arms and legs most horribly after running for their lives from the steers. Wallowing in self-pity and melodrama, she imagined her funeral with flowers over her coffin and the family weeping, and Terry remorseful for swimming with Rosemary, after all their years together, sharing *everything*, even the ghosts. The thought struck her that if she drowned, she would become one, and could haunt him for evermore. It would serve him right. But the thought of never seeing him again, sent her into a fresh floods of tears, and finally drained of emotion, she flopped back onto the sand, pushing it into aimless semicircles from her outstretched arms. She could hear the distant roar of the sea and immersed in its sound and the warmth of soft sand, she fell into a dreamlike state under the glare of the sun, until her fair skin began prickling and was tight with heat. She quickly sat up. She would cool off in the sea before her skin burnt any more. The air was fresh and invigorating as she ran to the water's edge, and jumping up and down with the shock of the cold she waded in, pushing forward against the waves until her feet bottomed out and all warnings from Jack not to swim alone were forgotten.

The sea was smooth and deceptively easy, and turning on her back, she floated with the gentle movement of the swell that blocked sound to her ears and creating a dreamy out-of-the-world sensation as she gazed up at a dome of blue with puffs of feathery clouds. Turning lazily over to swim back, she saw she had drifted far from shore. A needle of fear coursed through her as she began swimming and found with the ebbing tide she was making no headway and a strong cross current like a twisting serpent was threatening to pull her down under the sea. She struggled on fighting the pull of those treacherous tentacles, her arms and legs tiring, as she gulped air and swallowed choking mouthfuls of sea. Panic stricken, she cried out for help, her reedy voice faint and snatched away with the wind. Again, and again, she struck for the shore, but her young body was no match for the power of the undertow now dragging her down into the ocean's cold embrace. Her foolish wish was coming true. But I didn't mean it, I don't want to die! her mind screamed. With lungs bursting, she gave one last feeble attempt to kick and propel herself upwards to the light of the sun, but her limbs were as lead, and her last thought as the darkness of death closed around her, would she become a star?

Chatting companionably to Octavia of a programme they'd heard on the wireless, May had seen Kitty hurriedly descend from the rocks and vanish amongst the children milling around the pool. She waited for a while, looking for sight of her. There was none and she stood up.

'What is it, May?' asked Octavia.

'Kitty seems to have disappeared from the pool, but Terry's still there larking around with one of Kitty's classmates. I think it's Rosemary.'

Octavia was puzzled. 'I'm surprised at that. Rosemary is not one of Kitty's favourite people and Terry knows it. The girl has a spiteful streak, for all her butter-won't-melt-in-her-mouth looks.'

'Perhaps Kitty and Terry have had a tiff. You know kids. They switch on and off each other like light bulbs!'

Octavia laughed. 'You do come out with some beauties, May!'

'It runs in the family, or hadn't you noticed?'

'Hmmm,' Octavia smiled in answer. 'Kitty has probably gone hunting for shells. She and Grace have been collecting them to cover their jewellery box.'

'Can't see her anywhere,' replied May, shielding her eyes from the glare of the sand as she looked along the beach.

'Jack, have you seen Kitty?' Octavia called to him kneeling on the sand and making a sandcastle for Thomas.

'The last time I saw her, she was running towards Helen and Grace by the rock pools.'

'I'll go over and take a look. She might like to have a dip in the sea with her old Aunty May,' said May, pulling on her bathing cap and looking down at Octavia tanning her legs with her dress half-pulled up. 'You know, if it wasn't for me, she wouldn't be able to swim at all. Jack can't and you won't.'

'I know, I never did like the water, either in it or on it. A bath is my limit.'

They both chuckled. May began walking across the beach, and Octavia watched with affection her sister's curvaceous figure lilting along in her floral swimsuit, and giving a twitch of her tail and a small hand wave behind her, knowing full well that Octavia's eyes were upon her.

'Have you seen Kitty?' asked May, at two heads gazing intently down at the rock pool as Grace pulled up seaweed from the underside of the rocks.

They looked up. 'She ran that way, along the beach,' replied Helen, pointing in the direction of Hayle with her shrimping net. 'She was going like stink! I called to her but she wouldn't stop.'

Grace held out her bucket to May. 'Look what I've caught. A crab.'

May gazed down into Grace's bucket. 'He's very small, isn't he? If you find a nice big one, we could take him home for tea.'

Grace's amber eyes opened wide with horror. 'Oh no, Aunty May! I would never do that. You have to boil them, and that's cruel.'

May quickly retracted her remark. 'You're quite right, Grace. That was not a good idea at all,' and leaving them to their hunt for minnows, returned to Jack and Octavia. 'She's not with the girls. Apparently she ran off along the beach. I'll go and look for her.'

Jack felt a stab of unease. 'I'm coming with you, May,' he said.

'Yes, go with her, Jack,' said Octavia as she stood up, her eyes searching the beach. 'She's nowhere in sight.' Her face creased with worry. 'Dear Lord. Why will she never do as she's told, and stay near to us?'

'It's my fault, I should have kept a closer eye on her,' said Jack by now, thoroughly alarmed, 'but I thought she was with Terry in the pool. I hope to goodness she hasn't gone to swim in the sea. I've told her, time after time not to go too far out in it, but she's so venturesome and has no idea of danger.'

'Now, look, you two, stop worrying. I'm sure she's OK. We will probably find her playing with a child further along the beach. You know how quickly she makes friends with people.'

'That's the problem,' replied Octavia. 'She's too trusting. She'd go off with any Tom, Dick or Harry.'

Jack and May began walking rapidly across the beach, their eyes scouring the sea and sand. In the distance they could see a couple sitting half hidden by rocks. As they drew nearer to them, Jack saw it was Stan Curnow and Joy Bowden believing themselves to be safe from prying eyes. This was going to be awkward. 'May,

I'll carry on across the beach whilst you ask that couple if they've seen Kitty,' he said.

He looked distinctly uncomfortable and May raised enquiring eyebrows but did as he asked, as Jack, seeing there was no-one else in the vicinity of the cliffs, headed smartly down the beach to the sea.

May approached the couple who looked warily at her. 'I don't suppose you've seen a little girl have you, running this way with fair hair in plaits.'

'You mean, Kitty?' said Stan.

May was taken aback. 'Yes, that's right.'

'She went running past us, a while back. Is everything alright?'

'I hope so. We can't find her for the moment.' She thanked him and ran after Jack.

Stan swore. 'Damn! That's put the cat among the pigeons. That was Jack Pengelly walking down to the sea.'

'I thought I'd recognized him,' said Joy. I met him briefly at a cricket match and again at the Holman's talent contest.'

'Well, it's no good crying over spilt milk. We can only hope that Jack doesn't talk.'

'I think we can count on his discretion. He struck me as a very nice man,' said Joy. 'Who was that with him?'

'I believe it was his sister-in-law.'

'Hmm.' Joy Bowden looked thoughtful as she stared out to sea. Villages were notorious for talk. It was time to bring this little chapter to an end, before it was too late, and anyway, she was growing weary of him.

'Those two looked as if they'd been stung by a bee,' May said breathlessly, as she caught up with Jack.

'I'm not surprised. It's our milkman caught in flagrante delicto as it were with a newcomer to the village, Joy Bowden. I suspected something at the Holman's talent contest, looking sheep's eyes at each other, and so did our Kitty. She picks up on things, very quickly.'

May smirked. 'That explains everything and how he knew Kitty.'

'It's none of my business, but it will make for awkwardness at the cricket matches now I know what's going on. Joy's husband, Gerald, is such a decent chap, and Mr. Curnow's wife, is a nice little soul.' As they walked further and further along the beach, Jack's thoughts were far from dalliances and he became despairing and filled with dread. 'Where *is* she, May? Where on earth could she have got to? She must have run for miles.'

May agreed, speaking far more positively than she felt. 'We've just got to keep going Jack. We know she went this way and we'll keep looking until we find her,' but doubts for her safety were gnawing away. It was always more dangerous on the Hayle side of Gwithian with rip currents from the tidal estuary and if Kitty had taken it into her head to go for a swim, it would be very easy for her to get into trouble. The thought of losing Kitty whom she had known and loved from birth, hit her with a thump in the solar plexus. They must find her. The alternative was too terrible to contemplate. She stopped, suddenly.

'Jack did you hear anything? I could have sworn I heard a cry.' She stared out over the waves. 'There's someone in the sea. 'It's Kitty! I'm sure of it. Yes, it is. Thank God!'

Jack looked out over the expanse of water but could see nothing through the thick lens of his glasses. 'What's happening to her? Is she alright, May?'

May did not reply, for to her alarm, Kitty had disappeared from view. 'I'm going in Jack. You stay here. I'll bring her back.'

'Dear God, she's drowning, isn't she?' he cried in anguish, and began wading into the tide behind May, and realising it was futile for he could do nothing to help, stood with the sea swirling around his trouser legs, frantic with fear and the frustration of being unable to save his daughter and he did the only thing that he could. He prayed to his maker as he had never prayed before.

May swam strongly and could feel the undertow as her strokes cut through the water with the speed and strength of one possessed towards the spot where she had last seen Kitty. 'Please Lord, help me to find her. I cannot return to Octavia and Jack without her,' she prayed, as she tread water and gazed in every direction. There was no sign of her. She plunged beneath the swell, searching until her lungs cried for air, and coming up and taking a deep breath, plunged below once more. She would not and could not leave Kitty here, alone, to die. Desperately, she hunted, again and again, until she knew there was no hope of finding her, and she must make for the shore or drown as surely as Kitty had. Exhausted and distraught she swam like an automation towards Jack who was standing drenched in waves that swept around his legs and as she did so, a head shot out of the water beside her. Taken utterly by surprise, May choked on a mouthful of sea and stared at her as if at a ghost. 'Kitty!' she spluttered. 'I've been looking everywhere for you. I thought you'd drowned.' Her distraught face at the thought of losing Kitty was white with the shock of seeing her.

'So did I, Aunty May.'

'Are you able to swim to shore?'

'Yes, I can,' for Kitty had found the leaden weights on her limbs had miraculously gone. Her body felt as light as thistledown.

'Then stay close to me. We'll swim parallel to the shore and gradually aim towards the sand. The tide is turning, so it will be easier,' she said, her heart suddenly buoyant, and as they swam to Jack, she wondered at Kitty's odd remark, that she herself thought she had drowned.

The strain of waiting was etched deeply on Jack's face, and his legs half buckled as they came towards him. In the curling waves he held her small body tightly, as an exhausted May, staggered onto the sand and collapsed. Kitty clung to him. 'What were you thinking of running away like that?' his voice sharp with relief and rebuke.

'I don't know,' her teeth chattered against his chest. 'I was angry with Terry.' She began to shiver violently.

Jack took off his shirt and wrapped it around her. 'What on earth for? This morning, you couldn't wait for him to come with us to the beach.'

Regaining her breath, May shakily stood up, as Jack and Kitty waded towards her. Release of tension exploded into anger. 'You could have drowned Kitty. We both could have done. The undertow was very strong.'

Kitty had never seen May so angry and could not bear it, and burst into tears of remorse. 'I'm so sorry, Aunty May,' looking to Jack for comfort, and finding him wanting.

'Aunty May is right, Kitty. How many times have I told you not to go into the sea without telling us? But the main thing is, you're safe,' his face visibly relaxing with the knowledge that it was actually true, for he was sure he had lost her. 'Now, come on. Let's get you back to your mother. She'll be frantic with worry.'

Grace and Helen ran towards them as they approached, 'What happened Kitty? Where did you go?' asked Helen.

'You've been in the sea, haven't you?' accused Grace. 'You're not supposed to without telling anyone. And you didn't wear your bathing cap,' she said, looking at Kitty's bedraggled hair.

'That's enough, you two. Just leave her be,' said May.

Kitty sat down shivering with cold and shock on the towel beside Octavia, who had paced the beach with Thomas, and on hearing she had got into difficulties in the sea, remonstrated from angry relief. 'From now on, my lady, you stay in my sight. If you so much as disappear, even for a second, we shall all go home. How many times more times do you have to be told not to go into the sea without telling us? Perhaps you've learnt your lesson, now.'

Kitty's eyes welled with tears and she stared down at the towel to avoid her mother's irate stare. It would have been better if she *had* drowned because everyone was angry with her and Terry didn't seem to care if she lived or died for he was nowhere to be seen.

'What exactly happened, May?' Octavia asked, and telling Kitty to put her clothes on, she poured a hot cup of tea to warm her for she was shivering like a winnard.

'I'll explain later,' May replied mysteriously.

It was hunger that finally drove Terry from the pool and he came running up and sat down beside Kitty who looked away from him. 'Where did you go? I looked for you, everywhere.'

She made no reply.

'What's the matter, Kitty?'

Eliciting still no response, he looked from one to the other, sensing something had happened for their faces were tense.

Taking pity on him, Jack briefly explained. Octavia handed Kitty a hot pasty. 'You'll feel better after you've eaten,' she said more calmly and curious as to why she must wait for the full story.

Kitty slid Terry a glance. He looked downcast.

'I wasn't with Rosemary long. I'm sorry,' he whispered.

Kitty continued to ignore him and Octavia and May made a distracting fuss of unwrapping their warm pasties and handing them around, as Ted appeared through the dividing rocks of Sheep's Pool.

'Right on cue,' May said. 'Ted can smell my pasties a mile off.'

His arrival broke the strained atmosphere and after eating, Jack felt everyone needed to take their minds off the near tragedy, his, not least of all, and he suggested a game of cricket. Terry attempted to join Kitty and Helen as they walked along the sweep of beach away from the crowds where only their footprints followed them on the firm golden sand, but she pointedly turned away and began running ahead, leaving him to stare despondently after her as the men came up to him.

'Just give her time, Terry. She'll soon come around,' said Jack sympathetically.

'Yes, women are like plants. They thrive on love and attention,' agreed Ted, whose garden was his passion and May had long believed it to be his analogy for life. What you sowed, so you reaped.'

Jack pointed. 'Look, if you could set up the stumps over there, Terry, Mr. Curtis can pace out the run.'

'The agonies of young love,' said Jack, as Terry ran off with the stumps.

'I wouldn't want to go back there, would you?' said Ted.

'Not for all the tea in China,' replied Jack as they walked over to join Terry. 'You can go first Grace,' he said, handing her the bat, and waited for the women busy talking as they brought up the rear.

'I don't know, Octavia, I can't explain it,' May was saying. 'I heard her call and then she disappeared beneath the waves. I swam out to find her and I was looking for a long time. The next thing I knew was when she suddenly popped up beside me. It was the strangest thing,' she half-spoke to herself with a shake of the head. 'All I can say is, someone upstairs must have been keeping her safe.'

Octavia felt as if the life had been sucked out of her. 'What you're trying to say is, you expected to find her drowned.'

'Yes,' she admitted, quietly.

Octavia stopped and gazed incredulously at her as the rest of the family took their places to field the ball.

Teatime found them all on the cliff top and Kitty nestling down in the springing grass was deep in thought. She could not explain to them, or even to herself how she was saved from drowning. She

190

could only remember being very tired and sinking beneath the water, and after that, things were hazy and fragmented like a dream: a light came around her as bright as the sun and a voice spoke in her ear, and she felt the touch of gentle hands. She had told Jack, as they made their way up the cliffs, that she was sure her guardian angel had saved her, and he had said, it could well be true for it was a miracle she was still alive. She did not confess to him the voice saying, *'I am here. I am always with you'*, but she knew she *had* heard it, soft and silvery, like the voice at Porth-curno, she thought, squinting up at a lark rising in the sky to become a speck in the blue, and leaving his notes cascading down to earth. Her near drowning now seemed as if it had happened to someone else, like when you came out of the pictures and were not sure if it was real or make-believe.

Octavia's voice broke in on her thoughts, as her mother handed her some money. 'Kitty, run with Helen to the Jam Pot and fetch some Dandelion and Burdock and Lemonade.'

Leaping to their feet, they raced off over the dunes to the old coast guard hut with its conical roof, that had been converted into a shop selling snacks and the paraphernalia of summer. They waited as people in front of them were served. Kitty studied the taller of the two women who ran the shop as she lifted the crates of bottles and spoke in her husky voice. With shingled hair and wearing trousers, she was a constant source of fascination. Kitty could not imagine Octavia sporting trousers or the mothers of any of her friends. What a funny way to dress! Octavia had explained that women wore them in the war, and some had continued to do so, but even so, there was something odd about her, and Kitty couldn't quite put her finger on it. Running back, they flopped down on the turf, pushing off the spring top of the lemonade bottle which exploded and fizzed yellow liquid over their fingers as they poured it into enamel cups that May held out. 'You shouldn't have run with them, you know it always makes them fizzy,' she remarked, as they laughingly licked their fingers. Octavia passed tea around and opened the bag of saffron buns. Kitty settled down again into the cushiony grass that was heavy with the scent of clover and sea pinks. The murmur of the incoming tide mingled with that of the skylark and his song would be a defining reminder of this day when she was saved by an angel.

'I'm sick of saffron buns!' The admission burst forth from Grace. 'Can't we have something else, for a change?'

Octavia looked at her in surprise. What on earth was happening to her shy little maid? Grace's quietly stubborn streak which Octavia had experienced on numerous occasions was now finding a voice and was, apparently, not in the least bothered at any adverse reaction it might create.

'We do have them rather a lot, mummy,' championed Kitty.

Octavia's hackles rose. 'Really? Well, if that's the way you both feel, we shall have to do something about it, won't we?'

Jack inwardly sighed. The signs were ominous.

'Oh, take no notice, Octavia,' May interrupted quickly, delving into her food bag. 'Kids say all sorts that they don't mean. You know what they're like.' She took out some slices of Victoria sponge. Anyone interested? What about you, Terry?'

'Yes, please Mrs. Curtis.' He took a large bite and the jam spurted onto his chin. Kitty laughed and handed him her hankie. 'Thanks Kitty.' He took it with a grateful look, after her freezing rebuffs. Mr. Pengelly was right. It was just a case of biding your time.

'I made the blackberry jam, last year. It won't be long before we're all picking them again, will it?' continued May, anxious to steer the conversation from saffron buns into safer waters.

'No, it won't, May,' replied Jack, taking up her cue. 'We must have a family day out looking for good nicks of oil,' and the girls were immediately reminded of John and his family word, and they giggled and whispered it to Helen and Terry who shouted with laughter.

''Let's not start that again,' said Jack. He looked at his watch. 'We have an hour before we must catch the bus. Shall we have a ball game of piggy in the middle in that flat area behind the dunes?'

'Sounds a very good idea Jack,' said Ted as he polished off his slice of sponge. Thomas gazed up at Ted's face which had caught the sun beneath his gingery fair hair, and showed him his wind-up boat. 'That's a grand boat, Thomas. Shall we have a ball game with the girls and Terry?' who, with Jack, had already made off into the dunes. Taking Thomas's hand, Ted left Octavia and May to lie back in the grass with thoughts and questions lying between them like tense wire and having no answers.

All too soon, it was time to pack up for the trek back to the bus stop. At the tail-end of the dunes, Grace and Kitty filled their buckets with sand. They had heard that sand killed weeds and there was plenty of them in the grass at home, but as they walked through the hamlet, the buckets grew heavier and heavier, until they felt as if they weighed a ton. Their good intentions evaporated. Little by little as they emptied them, until there was only a small layer in their buckets that was hardly worth the taking home, and tipping it out, left behind them a trail of small golden heaps. The weeds would just have to multiply!

It was not until a few weeks later that it gradually dawned. There was no more smell of baking saffron. On asking Octavia one afternoon if she would make some buns, she had said, that as the bakers were now making them, she would buy them instead when she next went into town.

'It's your fault, you shouldn't have said you were fed up with them,' moaned Kitty, as she returned to making daisy chains with Grace.

'You said you were sick of them, too.'

'I was sticking up for you.'

'Nobody asked you, to.'

'Right. I shan't then, in future.' Scowling, she jumped up. 'You can stay here and make these silly daisy chains on your own. I'm going to the recreation ground on the American swing with the boys.'

'Your welcome! I don't want to risk my life and limbs with *silly* boys, anyway!' Grace yelled at Kitty's retreating back, for from past experience, she knew the boys were reckless, standing one each end, pushing the long seat to and fro until it was practically level with the bars. It was terrifying.

'You're just a big baby,' Kitty taunted over her shoulder as she walked down the entry.

Chapter Twenty

OCTAVIA'S THOUGHTS RAN as quickly as the needle in her hand, as she sat in the window tacking together a dress for herself for the coming autumn. The realisation that she had nearly lost Kitty had shaken her to the core and left her with an undercurrent of fear as inexplicable as May's explanation of the near drowning. Whichever way she looked at it, something out of the ordinary had happened. Jack had said Kitty was convinced her guardian angel had saved her but she had pooh-poohed and laughed it off. She didn't believe in latter-day miracles, coincidences maybe. A rational explanation she believed could always be found, but, she had to admit, May would not have lied, and although as bewildered as herself, had thought it to be divine intervention. Octavia sighed. Life had dealt her too many blows to accept the miraculous, and it rattled her sense for the order of things and her ridicule, she admitted to herself, came from self-conscious embarrassment. Kitty was an enigma with her strange talk and intuition or sixth sense, call it what you will, that set her apart from Grace and Thomas. John's problem was a case in point. Kitty had instinctively known some-thing was deeply wrong, and her dog-like persistence had finally wormed it out of him. Octavia's thoughts turned to her conversation with her father William. The old man was right, it was high time to tell Kitty about James. She had shied away from it for too long, and with everyone else out of the house, this was as good a moment as any. She put her sewing down decisively on top of her work basket, and as if reading her thoughts, a hot and dishevelled Kitty appeared around the door. 'Terry's gone in for tea. Can we have ours in the garden and can we have ice cream? It's boiling out! I could put the chairs in the shady part of the garden.'

Octavia, for a moment nonplussed at her opportune appearance, automatically corrected her. 'It's may we have ice-cream, Kitty.'

'*May* we have ice-cream in the garden?' she repeated with a pleading grin.

'Come and sit by me, Kitty, I've something to tell you.' Her face was grave and Kitty's smile faded as she walked apprehensively towards her and sat down in the chair opposite, looking at Octavia with a frisson of alarm.

Octavia's face relaxed. 'It's alright, Kitty. You haven't done anything wrong. I have something to tell you. It's about your father . . .' she hesitated.

Kitty gave a puzzled frown, 'What about daddy?'

'No, I mean your *real* father. You see . . . I was married before, to your own father, who was killed in the war. You were only two years old when he died and he never saw you. Later, I met daddy and we married and had Grace and Thomas.' It was finally said and the tension dropped from her body.

'Oh!' Kitty sat in stunned silence and Octavia giving her time to digest the bombshell, sat quietly, looking back at her shocked face with love and concern. William had been confident that she would take this news in her stride, but nevertheless, it was a momentous revelation.

'You must have been very sad, mummy,' she said, finally.

'Yes, I was. But you just have to pick up the pieces and carry on.'

'So, if daddy, isn't my daddy,' her voice faltered, 'then . . . who is?'

'His name was James. James Treneer.'

James! The same name as in the letter!

'His parents, who are your grandparents, live in Canada.'

Kitty stared out of the window. She felt as if a gauze curtain had been drawn back and her world was suddenly bright and clear. 'That letter you had from Canada was from them, wasn't it?' she burst out, and immediately realised she had given herself away. She coloured up.

'Yes it was.' Her outburst confirmed a suspicion that Octavia had harboured for some time, after finding her scarves around the letter had been disturbed.

'Did you read it, Kitty?'

'Yes, I did. Please don't be angry with me.' Her confession spilled in a rush of pent-up confusion. 'You said the letter was from a friend, but I just knew it wasn't, and I looked everywhere until I found it. I didn't understand what it said, why I looked like

196

James and why they wanted to meet me and I was afraid to ask you because I knew I shouldn't have read the letter.'

'No, you shouldn't have, for the reason you discovered for yourself. Letters may well say things that only the person receiving it, understands.'

'I know. I'm sorry . . .' The guilty tears welled and rolled down her cheeks.

Sitting forward in her chair, Octavia half gestured towards her. Why did she find it so difficult to show her love for Kitty? It was as if the umbilical cord when cut, had severed all the bonds, and yet, with each needing the other for survival, the tie had been strong, but now, she seemed unable to find within herself a way of drawing her close. 'It's all right Kitty. There's no need to be upset. I understand why you were so puzzled. It's my fault. I should have told you sooner about your father.'

Kitty pushed away the tears with the palms of her hands, and was struck with a thought. 'If I have another father, does that mean that Grace and Thomas are not my brother and sister because I've always felt different from them.'

'Of course they are. They are your half-brother and sister because you have the same mother but different fathers.'

'Oh, I see.'

'The only way you differ from them, is in temperament. They are quieter than you.'

'And they don't have my colour hair, or eyes.'

'No. That's true.'

'But why am I called Pengelly? You said my father's name was Treneer.'

'It was decided that as it was daddy who would be bringing you up, it was easier all round, if we gave you his name. You would not have to explain to everyone why your name was different from ours. Do you mind Kitty?'

She thought for a minute. 'No, I don't. I'm glad.'

'And I'm glad we've had this talk. It was time that you knew. Is there anything else you would like to know about your father?' she asked gently.

With her mind still reeling at the discovery, Kitty for the moment, could think of nothing.

'The fact that you are not daddy's, hasn't made an iota of difference to him. He loves you exactly the same as Grace and Thomas. You know that don't you?'

'Yes, I do.'

Octavia laughed a little. 'You two have always been as thick as thieves.'

Kitty gave a watery smile.

'Now, when Thomas and Grace return from town with daddy, you can fetch the ice-cream. We shall have tea in the garden as you suggested. It will make a nice change.'

Kitty rose from the chair wishing to share with her some physical expression of this bewildering news that had been imparted, but although Octavia's eyes were loving, her body remained composed in the chair. As Kitty left the room, Octavia hoped with the barriers of secrecy gone, it would herald a bond of understanding, if not closeness, for Kitty's ways were as incomprehensible to her as Jack's talk of life after death.

Kitty felt strangely liberated and quite unique as she walked to Beacon for the ice-cream. None of her friends, that she knew of, had the distinction of having two fathers. She wondered what her father had looked like. Was he tall, or short like daddy? The letter said, she was like him. Perhaps they had the same colour hair or eyes. She would ask Octavia if she had a photo of him. She felt sorry he died in the war of which she had no memory except sticking a Union Jack out of the window on VE day. He was merely a shadow from the past and beyond her imagination.

As she waited in the queue to be served the block of ice cream wrapped in layers of newspapers to prevent it melting on her way home, there came a shocked and sobering knowledge. If her own grandparents were in Canada, then Gran, like daddy, wasn't hers, either. The thought stung Kitty, for she loved her dearly, although she didn't see her as often as she might for the days had filled with school friends and the activities of church and her dancing class. The early memories of time spent together were happy ones – tipping out her button box and laying them out in patterns of glass and jet, mother of pearl and cloth – sitting on her lap as she read Sunny Stories, smelling of lavender soap and baking, her wrinkled face soft and downy when she kissed her - the joy of toasting bread on the fire, something they never did at home, and spreading it with her thick home-made jam from strawberries they had picked together in her garden – the wintry days of infants school when she hoped it would rain and rain, so that she could run next door to her for dinner, as arranged with Octavia when the weather was bad. There, lulled with the warmth of the fire in the sitting room and the ticking of the tall grandfather clock, she ate her meals, and talked of her new school friends in class, and how they made a miniature garden from moss and daises and used a pocket mirror for the pond – the thrill she had felt when she had been chosen to be the fairy in a poem read out in class to 'sit under a toadstool out of the rain to shelter herself' and gran had laughed when she said, the toadstool was a table! She had told her about her imaginary friend and said mummy and daddy didn't understand it at all, but Gran did, and nodding sagely to the rhythm of the clock, had murmured, 'I see' and 'Well, I never,' and thought to herself what an odd but sweet child she was with her wide smile in her thin face and eyes with a percipience that unsettled her.

At home, Octavia quickly warned Jack that she had had a talk with Kitty who now knew about her father.

'How did she take it?' he asked with concern.

'As William said, she would. In her stride. She was shocked naturally, but she was more upset at being found out that she had read Henry's letter.'

'The little monkey!'

'I remember her asking me who the letter was from after seeing the Canadian postmark. I spun some yarn that it was from an old school friend who emigrated to Canada. Obviously, she didn't believe it. As you have often said, she does seem to have an uncanny instinct for sussing out the truth. I had expected a lot of questions, like how did I meet her father, or what did he look like, but no doubt that will come when she's had time to mull things over.'

Jack looked anxious.

'There's no need to worry about her, Jack. It will add an air of mystery about herself when she tells her friends. You may be sure they will be told!'

She was conscious of the fact she was different from her friends in class, and they, at times, would look at her warily, as if she were wise to their meanest intentions. Now, they were agog to discover that her father had lived in Canada and died in the war. *Canada!* They crowded around like chattering sparrows. 'Why did he live there and not in Cornwall as their fathers did? How did he die? What did he look like? Did she have a photo of him?' A boy whooped around her, his arms outstretched. 'Have you seen his ghost?' he taunted, and she had freaked out and fled to the toilets of the play yard and stayed there until break time was over. After school, a subdued and uncertain Kitty walked the hill home. They had asked so many questions for which she had no answers. Octavia said to ask her anything she wanted about James, but she worried that Jack would be hurt and think her disloyal. It was all so confusing. And so what, if her father had lived in Canada. It was no big deal. Her friend Janet's father worked abroad, and when he came home he brought her the most exotic presents like the beautiful China doll with real hair that she plaited and brushed. It was nearly as tall as Kitty, and dressed in taffeta and lace and could walk and say, Mama. She had been pea-green with envy, but quickly discovered, the doll was only brought out on special occasions from her cellophane box, and was not a comforting playmate like Teddy and Rose with her painted hair and knitted dress. It occurred to her then, that Janet hardly ever saw her father. She had her father every day, and even when he was cross with her, no walking talking China doll could ever make up for that!

Chapter Twenty-One

KITTY AWOKE WITH a start with her heart pounding and her mouth dry with fear. It was that dream again. It haunted her days and nights. It began happily with her playing hide and seek with the children in the garden, laughing and laughing when they found her until her laughter turned into screams of terror as they began pushing her down into the musical box against the sharp pins on the cylinder, and shrieking with delight as she went around and around with the music. Her breath rasping, she lay until her thudding heart had quietened, and feeling thirsty, she slipped out of bed and on reaching for the landing light was surprised to find she couldn't connect with it, and was floating down the stairs in a soft milky light that emanated around her. She stopped outside the sitting room door where she could hear the murmur of Octavia and Jack talking, and stood listening above the cool Victorian tiled floor.

'With Kitty telling her friends about her father,' Octavia was saying, 'it occurred to me that it might set people thinking and talking, and there's one yap in particular, who needs no stirring up, and you know who I mean. She never could keep her tongue quiet.'

'I don't think we need to worry, darling. It happened a long time ago and the tragedy will have receded in people's minds. Even today's news is soon forgotten and wrapping up tomorrow's fish and chips.'

Kitty strained her ear to the door. *A tragedy? What tragedy?*

Octavia was still to be convinced. 'I hope you're right Jack. It would give Kitty nightmares if she found out, and she suffers from them enough, as it is.'

Found out what?

'Have you noticed that she's been worse lately, crying out and murmuring in her sleep?' she went on.

'Yes, I've noticed that, too.'

Kitty hoping to hear more, found to her annoyance she was suddenly back in her bedroom and could see herself lying in bed.

How bizarre. She looked down at a sleeping Grace, her hair lying thick and tousled on the pillow and simultaneously, was snapped back into her own bed. She fought to stay awake for there was something she had to remember, something Jack had said, but the opium of sleep was heavy and dragging her down into a pit of blackness.

'Hurry up, you girls! Get weaving!' called out Jack, the following day. 'We're not going to waste this lovely weather, indoors,' he said, as he picked up a paper bag of bananas and the sweet rations, and stuffed them down beside Thomas in his pushchair.

'Where are we going?' asked Kitty.

'Treslothan church,' replied Jack.

'But that's miles!' Kitty moaned.

'Which is why I have a few sweeteners to keep those spirits up,' Jack consoled. 'Really, Kitty, it's not that far. You go much further than that when you race around playing.'

It was hot with the faintest dancing breeze as they walked down the hill and into the lane between the hawthorn hedge and the high walls of Nancarrow, and as they continued along and left the walls of the estate behind, the lane became stone hedges with fields on either side. Kitty glanced at a gnarled and twisted hawthorn tree, her imagined ship with the wind blowing through its sails. She loitered behind, climbing the hedge and half resting across the top lay listening to the peaceful, mulching sounds of the cows. A dog barked in the distant farmyard and a blackbird sang high in a tree accompanied by sparrows hidden in the dense leaves of the hawthorn shrubs. The countryside pulsated and resonated within her. She could not imagine living in a city like Peter, away from fields with their earthy scent after rain and spider's webs left glittering like jewels in the hedgerows and the stream rushing over rocks in the woods. Did he have trees to climb? Up there, swaying with the branches it was like inhabiting another world where the squabbles of home and school seemed far away and pointless. Below the tree, life thrummed unseen, in a smaller, darker world of fungus and insects and small creatures scurrying around in the undergrowth. In the meadows, she found pellets of owls and on occasion, the shed paper skin coil of a grass snake that she nervously hunted but never saw, for they slithered away quickly at the vibrations of her feet. She felt sorry for Peter and John who had probably never seen such things, although John did say they went into the countryside for fishing. But that wasn't quite the same as living all the time in the country like she did. Even so, she had to admit, nature was not all sweetness and light. There were unforeseen dangers, too.

It could catch her unawares as it did last week as she and Grace swished their way through the grasses of a meadow sending up puffs of seeds amongst the meadowsweet and scabious. They were making for the stream, and out of the corner of her eye, Kitty noticed a carthorse appear from the far side of the field. She hoped Grace had not seen it, for she was fearful of farm animals, but she had caught her glance and saw the reason for the sudden quickening of Kitty's steps. She stopped. 'I want to go back, Kitty,' she cried.

'No, we've got to keep going. We're nearly there, now.'

'I don't want to see the stream, any more,' said Grace stubbornly. 'I want to go home.'

Telling her not to be such a baby, and pulling at her arm, Kitty saw, to her horror, the horse was now powering towards them. 'Run, Grace!' she screamed.

They ran for their lives, swarming up the bank with an ease born of fear. Kitty landed with a thump on the opposite side and turned with dismay to see Grace struggling to pull herself from the stream. The horse slewed by them, pounding his massive body alongside the bank and in terror, Grace frantically grabbed handfuls of grass in an attempt to drag herself up the bank where she had slipped back. Having seen them off his territory, the horse slowed and paced restlessly for a while and wandered away into the next field and resumed grazing. A cloud of gnats rose, as Kitty, ashen faced, scrambled back down the bank and began tugging at Grace's outstretched hand to pull her from the thick oozing mud into which her feet had sunk. With a slight plopping of release, she dragged her free, and saw one of her sandals was missing. Kitty's heart sank with the shoe.

Grace sat shaking and gazing in sheer panic at the mud. '*Now*, what do we do? I've lost my new sandal. It's all your fault. I *told* you we should have gone back.'

'Don't start! We're just going to have to find it,' said Kitty, hunting for a stick. 'You look for one, too, and we'll use them to comb the mud for it.'

'We're never going to find it,' Kitty said in a state of despair after pulling the sticks to and fro all afternoon. 'We've been looking for hours. We might as well go home.'

'What about the horse?' said Grace, with fear in her voice.

'He's in the next field and can't see us. Come on. We can't stay here for ever.'

'I wouldn't mind,' muttered Grace under her breath.

As they drew closer to home with Grace upping and downing beside her, Kitty's anxiety grew. Although money was never discussed in front of them, she was aware, 'that it didn't grow on trees,' and having to buy yet another pair of new sandals, would create the problem of an unexpected expenditure.

'Why don't you take the other sandal off?' she suggested. 'It will be easier for you to walk without it.'

'No! I don't want to.'

'You're like Hoppalong Cassidy,'

'So what?'

They lapsed into a silence of apprehension and on reaching the back door, Kitty in a ferment of fear pushed Grace through it and ran. Making for the hawthorn tree, she sat there in a blue funk and staring wide-eyed into space, until, unable to deny the hunger pains any longer, she dragged her footsteps home. The atmosphere was surprisingly calm when she entered the kitchen where everyone was sitting around the table quietly getting on with their tea. Grace cast her an injured look as she slid onto her seat, and Jack's voice was casual as he said he'd heard all about the run-in with the horse and Grace losing her sandal. Kitty, reluctant to stir the seemingly quiet mood, mumbled she was scared to death and they were lucky to escape from the horse.

'You should know by now, you can never trust a carthorse,' was all Octavia said, rising from her seat to prepare a plate of toast and baked beans, and Kitty, having psyched herself up for a hauling over the coals, was left in a stew of guilt and relief.

Parents! You just never knew where you were with them, she thought, as she slid back down the hedge, and ran to catch the family up where they crossed the road and into another lane that led to the quaintly named hamlet of Knave-go-by.

The granite terraced houses in the hamlet were doll-like with long, narrow gardens where one was ablaze with dahlias. Giant yellow cactus dahlias with petals rolling downwards like curved quills competed with the tangerines and pinks in every shape and hue. Kitty's favourites were the show ones, the size of cricket balls with lilac-pink petals and shaped like honeycombs, and the smaller pompons in royal purples and reds. They stood admiring the array of colours as Percy, who was never far from his flowers, turned from them and came over to the garden gate. A fairhaired man with a thin face and prominent cheek bones, he grinned at them. 'Afternoon, everybody. Lovely day for a walk.'

'Yes, that's what I told them,' replied Jack. 'How are things?'

'Can't complain, Jack. And what have you girls been up to, lately?' he asked, resting his elbows on the gate and looking down at them from his deep set eyes.

'We've been picking blackberries in the field in front of our house, and my friend Sandra, and I, took water over to the men building the houses at Pengegon,' replied Kitty.

'Really?' he replied, throwing Jack and Octavia a quizzical look.

'Yes. They were sweating boiling! We used pop bottles. Sandra went home and collected her bottles, too, because they drank an awful lot and we had to keep refilling them. It was quite tiring actually,' she added as an afterthought:

'I expect it was. They must have been grateful.'

'Yes, they were. Some of the men were so hot they took their shirts off and poured the water all over themselves.' The talk of water reminded Kitty of the nearby spring. 'Can we go on down to the shute for a drink?'

Octavia nodded. 'Yes, alright. We'll be with you in a minute,' she said, as they ran off. She gave a 'tut' with a small up-tilt of the head. 'You have to be like lightning to keep up with her train of thought, Percy. I don't know what it is about water, but it attracts Kitty like a magnet and has led her into more scrapes than I care to talk about. I think half the reason the men asked for a drink was to keep them out of their hair. Kitty let it slip, they were warned it was dangerous to play amongst the half-built houses. Fetching water kept them occupied for hours.'

'It's looking like a big housing development,' Jack remarked. 'The blackberry fields around us are rapidly disappearing,' he said with a tone of regret.

'There's nothing as constant as change, Jack, and that's a fact. Look how Beacon has expanded over the years.'

Jack agreed, and slipped the brake off the pushchair. 'Well, Percy, we'd best be getting on.'

Percy picked up his hoe. 'Stop by on the way back and I'll have a bunch of dahlias ready for you,' he called out.

'That would be lovely. Thank you,' replied Octavia with a small grimace at Jack, as they walked off down the road towards the shute where Grace and Kitty were laughing and squealing as they dodged around flicking droplets of water at each other. The water had run there for as long as people could remember: a bubbling spring that never dried up, arched with rough stone and enclosing the clear, pure water: a place for women to congregate with their pails resting on its lip, and gossip during the long hot days of summer and to hurry from when the snow lay deep, before taps came into homes to isolate them one from the other. Cupping his hands, Jack offered Thomas a sip of water before sipping some himself and let it run like silk through his fingers.

Leaving the hamlet, they continued down the old winding road towards John Wesley's tree between hedges embroidered with the bright yellows of cinquefoil and creeping jenny amongst the blues of vetch and speedwells, the purply-pinks of knapweed and herb roberts. The cow parsley that brushed their faces earlier in the summer, had died back to be replaced by a phalanx of pink soldiers guarding the lane, standing high and proud of the hedge. They picked the foxglove's petals, popping one over each finger and stroking Thomas's cheeks with their velvety softness, as he determinedly pushed his own pushchair.

'These are foxgloves,' said Kitty.

He looked up at her. 'You push me, Kitty. Thomas is tired, now.'

Octavia and Jack's eyes shone with indulgent love, smiling in tender amusement at his words, and saying what a good, good boy he was, as he clambered into his chair. Kitty raised her eyes to the heavens at Grace as she took the handlebars.

Soon, into view came John Wesley's tree, a large spreading chestnut at the junction of the road. Beneath it, like a circular pedestal was a grassy mound, and Kitty hastily relinquishing the handles of the pushchair to Octavia, ran to it and scrambled on top with Grace. They knew well the story of John Wesley the great Methodist preacher. 'It seems to me that truly good men, like John, are often persecuted,' Jack observed on one occasion, as they sat beneath its branches, and he retold the story of him preaching there to a hushed and attentive crowd until some rough and drunken men began hurling abuse and throwing stones at him. A noisy scuffle had ensued with his followers attempting to restrain one of the culprits. Above the commotion, John was heard to call out, 'Let the knave go by!' and from this, Jack said, the hamlet was named, although of course, he added, nobody knew for certain if the legend was true.

He handed each of them a sweet and Kitty, resting her back against the trunk, stared up into the leaves, turning over and over in her mind what had happened the previous night, and slowly sucking her coffee cream sweet to make it last, until it disintegrated and melted over her tongue. Was it a dream, her sensation of floating down the stairs? The more she thought about it, the more she knew it was not, for dreams were ephemeral and faded soon after she opened her eyes. But how was it possible to float down the stairs and to see herself in bed? It defied explanation. And something else was jiggling around. Something that Jack and Octavia had said, but no matter how hard she tried to remember, it slithered away out of her reach. She sighed with frustration.

'Time to be moving on,' Jack said, brushing off the yellowed grass where he had been resting. Kitty and Grace jumped down after him, and stealthily picking long strands of sticky goose grass from the hedge, lightly placed them on the back of his tweed jacket. They giggled together behind him as they took the left fork and walked the road to Treslothan Church.

Jack turned around. 'What's up with you, two?'

'Nothing,' they chorused, innocent of eye and struggling to keep a straight face.

'Hmmm. Something is tickling your funny bones.' His face was a question mark as he smiled with a suspicion forming as to their merriment.

'Honestly, daddy, we're not laughing at anything,' Grace said, stifling her amusement.

'Oh, put your father out of his misery!' Octavia laughed with them.

Grinning, they pulled the long sticky stems dangling from his back and held them up and well away from contact with their dresses.

'You monkeys! I thought as much,' he chortled.

'I wish the bluebells were still out. We could have picked them and taken them home,' said Kitty, as they came to the woods of Pendarves Estate that met in a cathedral arch of dappled sunlight from either side of the road. In May, a sweeping haze of pow-dered-blue rolled and undulated away under the fresh lime-green leaves of the trees, enticing them over the hedge to pick armfuls amidst the feathery ferns.

'They are better off left in the woods where everyone can enjoy them and you know how quickly they wilt, once picked,' Octavia said.

'You don't like taking home Percy's flowers, either, mummy,' Kitty flashed back at her.

'Liking has nothing to do with it, and it's Mr. Kitto to you. You know full well they overrun with earwigs, Kitty.'

It was undeniable. She had heard horror stories of earwigs that crawled into your ears when you were asleep, and burrowed into your brain, turning you stark, staring mad! It had put the fear of God into her and despite Octavia standing them head first in a bucket of water until the livestock had quite dispersed, Kitty was uneasy and forever peering under cushions and chairs.

Ahead, the road divided and bore them right to Treslothan. The church, at first hidden by the curve of the lane, slowly came into view with the war memorial standing in the centre of the road which had widened out into a circle. It was encompassed by the vicarage with a row of tiny cottages behind it, a tenancy house, the church itself and a well enclosed in an elaborate weathered arch. Built on Gothic lines by the Pendarves family as a model village in the Victorian period, the buildings pivoted around the church that was thought to stand on ancient chapel ruins from the eleventh century. Secluded and hidden by trees and rhododendrons, it was time caught in a capsule and never failed to induce a feeling of stumbling into the past. If ladies wearing long silk dresses and carrying lacy parasols alighted from carriages, to join the simply clothed worshippers from the cottages and neighbouring farms, it would not have surprised Kitty in the least. She felt they were the interlopers, the visitors from a future time and place.

There was no-one around, and pushing open the squeaking wrought-iron gate, they made for the seat under the trees in the churchyard where Octavia and Jack sat down as Grace and Kitty spread themselves alongside on the short clipped grass. The stillness was broken only by the rustle of the treetops whose sound to Kitty was reminiscent of the sea and reminded her of Gwithian. 'Can we go to Gwithian soon?' she asked.

'Yes, if the weather stays nice and warm like it is now, I expect we shall go again,' replied Octavia. She opened the paper bag with the bananas. 'I would hate to think of the number of times I've queued for these when they came back into the shops,' she said, as she peeled one for Thomas.

'I remember there was quite a fanfare when the first boatload of them came into Bristol after the war,' said Jack. 'Nineteen forty six, it was,' his memory as faultless as ever.

'And I can remember my first taste of them,' said Kitty.

'Can you really?' said Octavia in mild surprise, handing a banana to Grace.

'Yes, you came home one afternoon looking very pleased with yourself, and told us to go into the sitting room because you had something special to give us. "These are a fruit called bananas," you said. Do you remember, Grace?'

'No, I don't,' Grace replied as she peeled down the skin.

'You've forgotten, Kitty, that Grace was hardly more than a baby,' remarked Octavia.

'Yes, I suppose so. I remember thinking what a queer shape they were. All the other fruits we eat, are round. It was the most delicious thing I'd ever tasted. Margaret in school said, she didn't like them at all. How could she not like them? They are sweet and lovely. Much better than oranges. They can be awfully sour.'

Octavia chuckled lightly at a sudden memory. 'One day during the war, when you were a baby, I left you behind in town, Kitty.'

'You *left* me in town. What, on my own?' Kitty asked, incredulously.

'Yes, I'm afraid, I did.'

'Crumbs!' she exclaimed at the thought.

'I bet she wouldn't have forgotten Thomas!' said Grace under her breath.

'What was that, Grace?'

'Nothing! She replied, turning away from Octavia's questioning stare.

'Yes, well, as I was saying. I'd been queuing for hours in the cold and couldn't wait to get home by the fire. I took off like a stream train up the hill, went to open the door and suddenly remembered I'd started out with a pram and a baby! I didn't even stop to think and drop my heavy shopping bags inside the door. I raced back down the hill and tore along the streets to Home and Colonial as if my *ass* was on fire! How *could* I have forgotten my baby! And the *relief* when I found you! You lay looking up at me like a little winnard.'

This was a side of Octavia seldom seen by the children and was quite deliciously funny. Jack shared with the girls a puckish, isn't she a naughty girl, look, and a whisper of mirth passed between them.

'I must have seemed like someone demented, and I wouldn't be the first in Camborne,' Octavia went on, with the memory of odd characters over the years walking the streets. 'There was one who used to direct traffic in his wife's wedding dress and another going around the streets collecting boxes and old clothing and wheeling them endlessly around the town. Poor *sawls*,' she said, her voice dropping into a low Cornish intonation.

'What's a winnard, mummy?' asked Kitty, squeezing back the laughter and locking eyes with Grace.

'It's a bird that looks sad and dejected in winter,' replied Octavia. At this, the girls unable to hold back any longer, dissolved into peals of laughter.

'Well, I don't know what's so funny about that, I'm sure.' She pulled a comical, 'what have I said?' expression at Jack, that sent them into further paroxysms of giggles infecting them all. And their family laughter rippled through the peace of the churchyard.

'Honestly, Jack, you're as bad as the children,' she chided, as they all calmed down.

Jack stood up and said, 'I want to show you girls something.' They followed him over to a lichen covered headstone. 'This is the grave of the poet, John Harris. He was distantly related to my family through marriage, on my granny's side. He's largely forgotten these days for what he achieved with his poetry as a poor miner working at Dolcoath in the eighteen hundreds. He was only ten when he started work in the mines, and with little schooling, John educated himself and began writing verse. As he had no ink of his own, he used blackberry juice and any scrap of paper he could find. Imagine that. Just think how easy it is for us to write. We have all the necessary tools, even typewriters. I think John would have appreciated one, just like you do, Kitty. In time, he became quite famous and gained first prize in a national competition. That was no mean feat in those days for an uneducated man . . .'

'I wish I didn't have to go back to school,' interrupted Kitty who was thinking of the eleven-plus that was looming.

'That's a silly thing to say, Kitty after what I've just told you, isn't it? I thought you would be old enough to understand and appreciate how lucky you are. What made you say that?'

'Because Miss Kneebone said, I will have to work even harder at my arithmetic next year, because of the eleven-plus, and you know how I hate sums, especially mental arithmetic.'

'I know you do but you're forgetting that not so long ago, you were singled out for getting all your sums right.'

Kitty wasn't sure who had been the more surprised, herself or her maths teacher. Miss Kneebone had come striding into the classroom from next door and planted herself in front of the class and stared at Kitty for several seconds. She felt certain she must have done something unspeakable, but instead, found herself praised to the skies for knuckling down and working hard at her arithmetic. She'd come top in the weekly test. It had been the sweetest moment of her life, for praise rarely came her way, and she had basked in its sweetness for days and days.

'So, I don't think you need to worry too much about your eleven-plus, do you? Jack was saying. 'And you know, I'm always ready to help you.'

'I know daddy,' Kitty said, as she looked across at the open fronted and gated Gothic structure of the mausoleum, that stood alongside John Harris's grave. A shiver ran up and down her back. It gave her the creeps. She wandered over to the old headstones and began reading them before returning to sit on the grass and recalling again every detail of herself floating down the stairs. It was as vivid as sitting here in the churchyard. What *was* it, Jack said last night? It was dancing at the back of her mind. Annoyed and frustrated, she frowned and looked away to where a movement had caught her eye. She watched a young woman wearing an ankle length red coat with a rounded fur collar and cuffs and hands encased in a fur muff, passing in front of the war memorial. Her dark hair fell straight to her shoulders and her face was pensive in a pretty heart shaped face. She must be awfully hot in that coat, Kitty thought.

From a long way off, she could hear Octavia's voice. 'Kitty, I'm speaking to you.'

Startled, she looked at her. 'Sorry, mummy. What did you say?'

'I was asking if you'd like another sweet. You were away with the fairies.'

'I was just thinking, that's all.'

Jack too had noticed her looking intently through the churchyard gates. 'What were you staring at, Kitty?'

Only a ghost! Kitty's eyes shied away from Jack. 'Uhmm, nothing really' she replied lamely, and he was left with the distinct feeling that once again, she had seen something else from the past, as he suggested it was time to return home for tea.

They were half-way home when Kitty stopped dead, thunderstruck.

'Watch your step, Kitty. I nearly tripped over you,' said Jack, behind her.

Kitty looked at him uncomprehendingly with her mind racing. She remembered! Jack had spoken of a tragedy. As they walked on, the jigsaw was beginning to fall into place - the flicker of fear on Octavia's face when forbidding her to play at Nancarrow, the sadness that pervaded the house and the terror and panic she felt as she turned the handle of the locked door where the children were crying. The tragedy had happened in the manor house, and it had seeped and enveloped it like a shroud.

Kitty could barely wait to share her revelation with Terry and changed at breakneck speed into her play clothes, reasoning, as she dashed next door, that his parents would be sure to know what tragedy had happened at Nancarrow for they had lived on the terrace for ever! She would enlist Terry, for asking his mother herself, might prompt a discussion between Mrs. Retallack and Octavia and invite awkward questions.

Terry, bided his time and after watching his father disappear into the garden shed, seized the moment and cornered his mother. 'My friend in school said, something terrible happened at Nancarrow. Is it true, mum?' Mrs. Retallack gazing back at the studied innocence of her son's face, and acquainted with far more of his boyhood shenanigans than he ever imagined, was immediately on her guard at this out of the blue and leading question. She professed to knowing nothing and was left with a feeling of unease that the past was threatening to emerge for Octavia, and not knowing quite what to do about it. They were good neighbours, respecting each others privacy, and she had always known that Octavia wished for the past to remain there. Nancarrow was never spoken of, but now she wondered if she should mention Terry's sudden interest. After mulling it over, she decided to wait and see, for children's minds were like grasshoppers. In all probability the interest would soon die a natural death.

On returning to school, and pressing her friends, Kitty discovered most parents were ignorant of Nancarrow's history and those that remembered were surprised to be asked for it was mostly forgotten and looking suspiciously at their offspring, asked how they had heard of it. On learning it was Kitty, they clammed up as tight as the limpets on the rocks at Gwithian and the yap to whom Octavia had alluded was in no mood to risk the wrath of Octavia which Kitty would have understood, for it could be considerable. The answer to the mystery remained as tightly locked as the door in Nancarrow.

Chapter Twenty-Two

THE CELEBRATION OF Easter was upon them and Kitty was caught off balance and in a state of emotional guilt-ridden confusion. If only she had not allowed herself to be persuaded by Terry to continue to go to the Old Tyme dances without him. Why oh why had she listened to him.

The intervening years had slipped by, folding Kitty's memories one into the other like snapshots in an album. Her escapes into the tranquillity of Nancarrow's estate ceased after the children's appearance in the garden and under the Christmas tree, for it had had a disturbing effect upon her, and within a year from that fateful day when they had broken into the house, it was sold for conversion into a convalescent home. Terry was now returning home each month to see her from Exeter, where he was apprenticed to a firm of cabinet makers. He had fulfilled his promise to her that day in Nancarrow house and was now in his second year making fine furniture and working towards their future together. He had shared and accepted that side of her that was inexplicable; the strange intuitions and flashbacks, and she was secure in the knowledge of his love for her. Marriage to the keeper of her secrets was the accepted culmination of that childhood and waited quietly in the wings, until Terry had said, 'You know how you love dancing, and you'd miss seeing the gang on Saturday nights. Don't be so silly, go!'

It was there, in the village hall, just after her twenty-first birthday, that her long golden red hair caught Lawrence's eye as her circular pinafore skirt, the colour of a daffodil, spun around her and came to settle in deep folds with the weight of the sailcloth material. It had an innocence of style that suited the wearer who herself, he was quite sure, was unaware of its sensuous movement, or of her sensuality. He moved quickly to appear in front of her as she sat in animated laughter with Sandra, and looking down into the most arresting eyes he had ever encountered, asked her for the dance.

Kitty was instantly attracted to this man that stood before her and with an intake of breath, rose to her feet and self-consciously walked ahead of him onto the dance floor. She turned to face him, and placing his arms confidently around her, he guided her into the impassioned strains of a tango.

'Is this the first time you've come to the dance?' Kitty asked, easing back from his self-assured hold.

'Yes, it is.'

'I thought I hadn't seen you here, before.'

'Our family has only recently moved into the area. Dad's in insurance and he was transferred from the Bristol office to head up the Camborne branch.'

'I see,' Kitty replied, tilting her head back in order to see his face. He was tall, taller than Terry and altogether different with sandy hair shaped neatly to his head and his eyes in an angular face were a deep-set grey. Looking up into them, she was conscious of a fluttering in the pit of her stomach.

Lawrence was shaken at her direct look. It was unexpected. He was not unaware of his attraction to girls that provoked the bolder to become flirtatious and teasing and others to become flustered and tongue-tied with shyness. This one did neither, but simply appraised him. Her eyes held a fire and strength that would not succumb to easy charm or persuasion, he thought with a frisson of excitement at the challenge they presented. He recovered himself with an easy smile. 'How long have you been coming to the dances?'

'Oh, forever!' Kitty enthused. 'I love dancing.'

'Yes. I can see that. I've been watching you.'

'Is that so!' Kitty's eyes mocked him.

Careful Scott-Thomas. Easy does it, he warned himself.

'Are you at the technical college?' she asked him.

'No, I'm in my first year at the School of Mines.'

'Really! What a coincidence. My father is the Registrar, there.'

'Mr. Pengelly?'

'Yes, that's right.'

'Well, I'll be damned.'

'Life is full of surprises,' she replied, with irony in her voice.

'You can say that again,' he replied, with undisguised appreciation as he took in her high cheek bones and generous mouth that invited intimacy. She was quite extraordinary.

'I'm Elizabeth, by the way.' The tone did not invite familiarity.

'And I'm Lawrence Scott-Thomas,' he replied.

And cocky with it, Kitty thought, sensing the danger of him. She looked quickly away and in her confusion missed a step and stumbled over his feet.

'Oh God! I'm sorry! I'm a bit out of practice,' he apologised, and to Kitty's surprise, his face reddened.

So, there was an underbelly to his brashness, Kitty thought, as she replied, 'No, no, it was my fault.' To her intense relief, the music came to an end, and cursing herself for practically falling at his feet, she hastened him to her seat to regain her composure.

'Who was *that?*' asked Sandra as she sat down beside Kitty, and eyed Lawrence's athletic body rejoining the other students. 'He's a nice bit of stuff, isn't he!?'

'Mmmm! He think he's the bees knees.' But her cheeks had a tell-tale flush that was revealing to her friend, and he was showing more than a passing interest, judging by the way he continuously glanced over to them.

Sandra's brown eyes were teasing. 'Whoever he is, he keeps looking at you.'

'I know,' Kitty replied, studiously avoiding to look in his direction. 'He's called Lawrence Scott-Thomas.'

'My Gar! What a mouthful,' exclaimed Sandra.

Kitty gave a self-conscious chortle. 'You won't believe this, but he's a student at the School.'

'Is he? Where's he been hiding himself? ' Sandra asked, with a casual sweep of the eye around the room for another interested look at him.

'In Bristol. His family have only just moved here,' replied Kitty as the master of ceremonies called out for everyone to take to the floor for the progressive waltz, the Valeta.

'Oh-my-Lor! He's coming over, again,' Sandra mouthed at Kitty, smothering a grin.

Kitty stood up quickly for flight to the tea and soft drinks bar but he quickly sidestepped her intention, and catching her hand with a smile that melted her resistance, allowed herself to be led onto the dance floor. Acutely conscious of his eyes upon her, she kept hers low, for his touch affected her as Terry's had never done, and her instincts were to flee, and yet, as she was spun away from his hold to the next partner, she longed to remain in his arms. As she danced from partner to partner, she surreptitiously checked the room for him, and Lawrence catching her watchful look, smiled. It was warm and intimate and as she came full circle and he was holding her again, Kitty had the strongest feeling that destiny lay with this man she had barely met. He escorted her back to Sandra, and sat himself beside them, engaging both in light-hearted talk but his eyes were for Kitty, alone.

'Kitty, I'm just going to get myself a cup of tea.' said Sandra, feeling like a gooseberry. 'Shall I get a drink for you?'

Kitty shook her head. 'I'm OK thanks.'

'Did you want one, Lawrence?' Sandra asked, with a piqued raise of her eyebrows.

'No, I'm fine thanks, Sandra,' he replied, with barely a fleeting glance. A drink was the last thing on his mind, Sandra thought and on getting up from her chair, flashed Kitty a warning signal that said, 'watch it,' and excusing herself, they were left alone.

'So, it's Kitty, is it?' he murmured.

'To my close friends, yes.'

'In that case, I shall do my utmost to become one. Do you think I shall succeed?' he asked, brushing his lips against her ear.

His touch was like an electric shock and her heart lurched. Kismet had thrown his dice and she knew there was not a thing she could do about it.

'Happy Easter! It's cold but glorious out,' Phoebe announced, as she strode in through the sitting room door as Octavia and Kitty were laying the table. Kitty thought she looked incredibly striking in a long black coat whose severe lines were softened with grey astrakhan cuffs with an encircling mandarin collar, and a red crocheted hat framing her face and giving light to her pale blue eyes.

'Dinner won't be long,' said Octavia. 'Easter lamb and all the trimmings to be followed by Jack's favourite, sherry trifle, a nice piece of cheese and the last of Roy's petit fours,' she dashed off with a flourish.

Phoebe was amused at her high spirits and thought of their mother, as she took off her coat. Octavia had inherited their mother's instinct to lay a good table. 'Sounds great, Octavia,' and handed her a bottle of wine.

'Oh, that looks good. I'll get Jack to open it up. It will oil the wheels.' She chuckled to herself as she took it out to the kitchen.

Phoebe laughed. 'I don't think it will take a lot to oil the wheels, do you?'

'No, she's already well on her way! Must be the weather. You've brought the sun with you. We've had nothing but weeks of wind and rain,' and smiling back at her, she thought of the time when Phoebe had unexpectedly called, and found Uncle Roy and all the family around their table. Even then, as a child, Kitty had instinctively known Phoebe was someone in whom she could trust, and she was seized with the sudden urge to confide in her about Lawrence.

The Easter meal, aided and abetted by wine, was one of uproarious laughter, and a shared looking back on memories of old school friends who had married and left town, and recalling with hilarity the antics of William. He had died suddenly with a stroke, three years previously, taking them all by surprise, but although the shock of his death had saddened them greatly, they were relieved at his quick release, for they knew he would have found it intolerable with a further disability.

'Do you remember him Phoebe, coming home that Christmas night from the local?' said Octavia.

'Who could forget it. It went down in family history,' laughed Phoebe.

Octavia chortled to the others. 'He'd had a skinful, and feeling peckish, spied mother's 'specially prepared joint of ham in the pantry. He gathered it up and hacked himself several generous slices, shook the sauce bottle over his meat and settled down to enjoy it. His face . . . his face . . .' Octavia, rosy with Phoebe's wine, dissolved into snorting laughter. 'I shall never forget it. He took a bite or two, and gazed in bewilderment at his plate. "What the hell's the matter with this meat?" he said, when our mother came into the kitchen. Well . . . her face was a study as she stared at the massacred remains of her ham that had taken *days* to prepare, soaking, boiling and roasting with cloves and sugar, for her visitors the next day. If she'd had the meat cleaver in her hand, I doubt he would have survived!' Octavia said, struggling to contain her merriment.' "You silly old fool," mother said. "You've covered my ham in Camp coffee!" Shamefaced, he looked up at her and then back at the meat. He didn't know what to be at. "You'd better eat it, William Tremayne, every last bit," she said. "And I hope it chokes you. It would serve you damn well right!"' Octavia broke into further peals of laughter.

Grace and Thomas eyed their mother's inebriated mirth. This was a decided change of tempo.

Phoebe, grinning at her, helped herself to a petit four and nibbling it, said, 'And then, there was that time when the fish man came to the door. Father fancied a nice piece of haddock and went out to his cart ahead of mother. He eyed the freshly caught and beautifully laid out fish, and said, "Is that fish fresh?!" The fish man gazed at him in wonder. "No! Tis stinkin!" he said.

Octavia held her hankie to her face, helpless with laughter at the memory. 'Mother wanted to *die* of shame,' she snorted, wiping her tears.

'Your father was a one-off,' said Jack, recalling amusing anecdotes of him in the office, with a gift of mimicry that kept the laughter circling the table, and rounding up his repertoire with a childhood memory of the local minister of his village. 'This is going back a few years, now,' he said, looking at Octavia with a wine-merry grin, 'before I thought it politic to change from chapel to church! Our minister was rather theatrical, and on this particular evening, he was standing in the pulpit expounding on the wonders of creation. His chest was puffed out like an amorous rooster, and expanding his arms to the heavens, he boomed at us, "And God said, let there be light!" and leaning forward to the lamp, he was plunged into darkness. The silly twerp had turned the pulpit gas light off instead of up. Well, the chapel was rocking. He had some job to stop them laughing and grizzling. He never lived it down and didn't dare show his face around the door of the local. The cry would go up! Switch off the lights! It kept the village going for *years.*'

As their laughter died away, Kitty said, 'I'll make us some coffee, shall I?' and went out to put the milk on. Their happiness enveloped her in a cloud that floated with her to the kitchen, and she felt a surge of love for them all. This was where she belonged, rooted to her family, to Terry, and to Cornwall. But on some deep unconscious level, she had already left, for every part of her being yearned to be with Lawrence. Her thoughts encircled him, her heart leapt at hearing his voice, she was made weak with his touch. Her mind went over and over it as the milk heated. The consequences if she stayed with Lawrence would be life changing, for it was unlikely they would remain in England, and the thought of the hurt she would inflict on Terry was more than she could endure. The weight of decision balled her stomach into knots, as she picked up the tray with the coffee.

'Shall I tell my nieces and nephew of that time when our granny was laid out in the best room?' Phoebe was saying to Octavia, as Kitty entered the room.

'I don't see why not. We were only children,' she replied, with laughter still playing around her eyes.

'Well,' Phoebe said, looking at the three of them. 'We were very naughty. We'd never seen a dead body before, and Alice and I were fascinated. We started lifting up granny's arms and legs and letting them drop back into the coffin with a thump, it was great fun, and then, your mother came in. She couldn't have been much more than four, and she started fiddling with granny's hair and it came off in her hands! It frightened the life out of her and she became hysterical. We were too busy trying to get the wig back on, to take a lot of notice, and then our mother appeared to see what the uproar was about. You can imagine her reaction. She was horrified. William wasn't the only one who could feel the end of our mother's tongue.'

'And I thought it was only me that got into mischief,' said Kitty, with a wry raise of her eyebrows at Octavia.

'Oh, I could tell you a lot, Kitty,' said Phoebe. 'Your mother was the worst of us all. She was a little monkey!'

'Dear me!' Octavia pulled a face and stuck out her tongue at Phoebe.

It was an unexpected glimpse of a child. All three gazed at their mother in amazement. Their mother? Acting like a monkey? Perhaps, it wasn't so difficult to imagine, after all.

Later, as they washed the dishes, Kitty, anxious to have time alone with Phoebe, suggested going out for a breath of air before the afternoon drew in. 'I'd love to come,' she said, hanging up the tea towel. 'It's a long time since I've surveyed the metropolis of Camborne. You don't mind, Octavia, do you, if we take off for an hour?'

'No, of course not, Phoebe. It'll be nice for Kitty to have time with you on her own. She can tell you about her new job.'

Leaving the others to their books in front of the fire, and to Thomas sorting out his John Bull printing outfit, Kitty pulled on her brown woollen coat and a hooded cream scarf, turning with an uncertain smile to Phoebe. Something was afoot, Phoebe thought, as they set off down the hill towards the recreation ground and out across lanes to the quiet and pretty village of Penponds. It was a favourite walk of Kitty's and the nearby woods were carpeted with primroses which were picked, as was the tradition, by the children of the Sunday School to decorate the church for Easter.

'So, what's this about a new job, Kitty? I thought you were working at Holmans?'

'Yes, I was, but it was so boring just typing time sheets. I wanted something more interesting, so I applied for Assistant Secretary at Barncoose Hospital. I work for a couple of consultants, typing up case notes, arranging for admissions and discharges of patients, that sort of thing.'

'Do you like it?' Phoebe asked, as they walked briskly across the lanes and down between a row of terraced houses in the village and on into a winding and sheltered lane that led to an old mill.

'I love it, Aunt Phoebe. Once I left the grammar school and took my secretarial exams I never looked back. I was a bit of a rebel against school's rules and regulations. College was freedom and I was treated as an adult. I liked that, and working in a geriatric hospital has opened my eyes to many things, not least our mortality. Gran died there, you know. She'd fallen and broken her hip, and went downhill rapidly after that.' Kitty gave her an apologetic look. 'No offence, but I would hate having my life ordered for me as they do in The Forces, or are you so far up the professional ladder that it doesn't apply?'

'To a certain extent, Kitty. Working as a military attaché gives me a certain amount of autonomy. It's quite different from the run-of-the-mill services.'

'I see.' Kitty's face that was normally open and expressive was distracted. Phoebe looking at her sharply, asked without any preamble, 'What's the matter, Kitty? There *is* something the matter, isn't there?'

'Actually, Aunt Phoebe, to tell you the truth, life has become complicated and I'm in an awful pickle.'

Phoebe wondered. Kitty had been courting Terry for a long time. There was no delicate way of putting this. 'You're not pregnant, are you?'

'Noooo! Aunt Phoebe,' she chuckled out loud. 'Nothing like that. It's just that I've met someone else, and I really don't know what to do.'

'Ah! That old chestnut.'

''Fraid, so. He's called Lawrence. We met on the dance floor just after my twenty-first birthday.' Kitty's face became animated and her eyes shone. 'He's gorgeous! He's tall and fair with deep set grey eyes and I've fallen head over heels for him. Before Lawrence, Terry and I flirted around, a little, but nothing serious, and we always ended up coming back to each other. When he went to Exeter, we came to an understanding that once he was working and earning, we would get married. But then I met Lawrence and I've never felt this way before. I love him so much that when I see him, my legs turn to jelly, and it's hard to keep the brakes on.' She blushed. She could hardly believe she had said that. 'I can't bear the thought of ever losing him.'

'If he loves you, you won't lose him, Kitty. He will wait.'

'I know I should tell Terry about Lawrence, but I haven't been able to bring myself to do it, yet. I couldn't write a 'Dear Johnny, letter,' that would be too cruel, so I thought I'd wait until he was home for Easter. Oh Lord. What a mess. He's going to be terribly hurt. If only he hadn't gone away, Lawrence would never have happened.'

'Your mother told me Terry is training to be a carpenter?'

'Yes, he's apprenticed to a firm of cabinetmakers in Exeter and comes home once a month, and, of course, for bank holidays and two weeks in the summer. He'll be around later for tea. I'm dreading it.' She sighed. 'The thing is, no-one knows me better than him and he has always accepted . . .' she hesitated with a small intake of breath . . . 'my problem.'

'Your problem?'

'It's difficult to explain, Aunt Phoebe. You'll think I'm mad. I know mum does.'

'Shall we sit for a moment on the wall by the clapper bridge,' Phoebe said, as they rounded the final corner of the winding lane.

Kitty looked back at her in surprise. 'I know this walk like the back of my hand, Kitty. It's always been a favourite of courting couples, even for your mother in the dark evenings after the church services. All those grassy hedges to canoodle in.'

Who would have thought it, Kitty smiled to herself, as they passed the old mill and the clapper bridge came into view. The water ran high beneath it, and standing on the old granite clapper bridge, they broke off small pieces of dead wood from a hawthorn tree hanging over the stream, and for a moment or two, played pooh sticks, laughing like children, before sitting down on the stone wall and watching the flow of water over the bright green reeds beneath.

Phoebe gazed at her niece, slender and attractive in her well cut coat and high boots. 'Now, what's this problem you have?'

'Well, you see, it seemed to start when I was about ten and just coming into puberty, when I think about it. I began seeing things that no-one else could. People, places as they were years ago. I tried to tell dad once, but he said it was my imagination, although, I have a suspicion that he's inclined to believe me. Mum, definitely doesn't. She has always thought ghosts and such things are a load of nonsense. The only one who I could confide in, was Terry. He didn't understand it, any more than I did, but he was always there for me. I used to wish that I could be normal like everybody else, but in the end, I grew to accept it. And there's something else. Terry told me once, after he hurt himself, that when I touched him, the pain went away.'

'I see,' said Phoebe thoughtfully. 'It sounds like you have the gift of healing, Kitty. I have only met one other like yourself, and although I'm practical and down-to-earth, as is your mother, unlike her, I believe there is a fundamental truth hidden there somewhere, although what it is, I've yet to discover.'

'I'm so glad you don't scoff at it, Aunt Phoebe. Perhaps these ghosts that I see are imprints held in the ether or in the walls of houses, and recorded like a snapshot, and I tune into the vibrations. It's the only way I can explain it to myself. I just don't know. The first time it happened, was at Nancarrow. I saw some children getting into a boat. I had no idea they were ghosts, they looked so solid and real. One of the girls looked awfully like me, she had the same colour hair.'

The hairs on the back of Phoebe's arms rose.

'It wasn't until Terry and I broke into the house and I saw the children again under a Christmas tree, that I knew I was seeing ghosts, because Terry said he couldn't see them. We wandered all over Nancarrow that day, and everywhere we went, I felt this melancholy. We finished up in the nursery where there was a musical box. When I played it, the tunes were familiar, as if I've always known them, and then, I began to feel queer, and I wanted to get out of the nursery. In the corridor, I heard children's voices behind a door. I tried to open it, but it was locked, and there was a strange thumping noise and I felt this terror and panic. I knew something awful had happened and probably behind that door. After that, I fainted which frightened the life out of Terry. He thought I'd died! Anyway, I didn't dare ask mum or dad about the house, as any talk of Nancarrow is taboo. Do you know if anything bad happened there, Aunt Phoebe?'

As Phoebe listened, pins and needles shot down her spine. If ever she needed confirmation of second sight, she had now heard it. 'Yes, as a matter of fact, I do, Kitty. Two little girls died there and one of them was your father's sister, Mary.'

Kitty's eyes widened in astonishment. 'My father's *sister?!* Mum never said anything to me about him having a sister.'

'No, well, after what happened to Mary, I'm not surprised. She was five at the time, and there was a Christmas party at Nancarrow which was the home of the Killigrew family. They were playing hide and seek and Victoria, the daughter of the house who was the same age as Mary, took your father's sister up to the storeroom to hide in a trunk. They shut and locked the door of the room, jumped into the trunk and closed the lid. It had one of those brass locks that you have to slide and lift up to open, so of course, they couldn't get out, and by the time they were found, they had suffocated.'

Kitty felt her blood run cold with gooseflesh of horror crawling over her body. The flush of colour from walking drained away to an ivory pallor.

'Oh my God, Aunt Phoebe. I saw them on the day they died. They were running up the stairs as a little boy was counting to a hundred under a Christmas tree.' Kitty's body became cold and clammy as she spoke and her voice seemed not to belong to her.

Phoebe saw her sway, and quickly put her arms around her shoulders. 'It's OK Kitty. Now head down between your knees and take deep breaths.'

As Kitty breathed deeply and the waves of nausea and faintness died away, she began to understand it all. It was the children's terror and panic she had felt outside that door. 'Oh, Aunt Phoebe. Those poor little girls. I know what they suffered. I felt it.' She closed her eyes against the memory. 'It's too horrible for words. No wonder there's such an air of sadness about the house.' She stared down blindly at the reeds lying horizontal under the weight of running water. 'So that little girl who looked like me was Mary. She would have been my aunt had she lived . . .' Her voice died away.

'I'm sorry you've had to find out in this way,' Phoebe replied gently. 'Your mother should have told you these things, but I know how difficult it is for her to talk about the past. I remember seeing Mary's photo in the newspapers. You do bear a strong resemblance. As you can imagine, it was the talk of the town for weeks.'

'But what I don't understand is, what was Mary doing in Nancarrow? I thought my father's family lived in Canada?'

'Your grandfather was head gardener there and he and your grandmother lived in a cottage on the estate. After Mary died, your grandmother couldn't accept living on the estate any longer and soon after, your grandfather packed up his job at Nancarrow and they emigrated to Canada for a fresh start away from the memories. It was there that your father was born.'

Kitty was rendered speechless. So that's why she had always felt so at home in the garden; her grandfather had lived and worked there. 'Incredible as it seems, I know where the cottage is,' Kitty said, finally. 'We discovered it one day, down the end of an overgrown path. It was semi-derelict. I remember walking across the open roof beams. If I'd fallen I would have broken my neck. We even made a fire there once, in the remains of the grate. Sandra brought her mother's frying pan, Michael the bacon, and me, the eggs. Terry brought butter because he couldn't find any fat. Can you imagine the sacrilege of using food that was on ration. We were so young and silly we didn't give it a thought, or remember to bring plates and cutlery. Not that we needed them, the butter caught fire, and the bacon and eggs burnt to a frazzle and stuck fast to the pan. The fall-out lasted for days when our parents discovered their weekly rations had vanished. Sandra was banned from seeing me for a week because her mother's frying pan was ruined. I remember how afraid she was to take it home.'

They chuckled together in light relief at the foolishness of children, before Kitty continued. 'When mum told me about my father, she didn't say anything about his parents living on the estate.'

'No, she wouldn't have. Your mother has a horror of the place. She feels it's jinxed. It was said that another child of the previous owners died running out under the wheels of a carriage. This was years before the Killigrews came to live there.'

Kitty stared at Phoebe, her whole body alive again with goose flesh. 'So that's what I heard,' she said under breath. 'I was hiding in the stables one afternoon. There was this clattering of horses and carriage wheels in the courtyard and men shouting, and then, the terrible screams of a woman. I can hear it now. It was like an animal in pain. When I came to look, there was no-one there. I thought about it for days afterwards and wondered whether I was going mad.'

Phoebe felt a rush of compassion for the child who had had to keep to herself so many inexplicable happenings. 'There has been a great deal of unhappiness in that house, Kitty, and it doesn't end with Mary. The children you saw in the garden were Oliver and Simon Killigrew who lived there, with their sister, Victoria. I'm not surprised you picked up on the sadness of Nancarrow, Kitty, because both boys died in the Second World War. Several years later, their father, Ralph Killigrew, who was a very cultured man and well liked, also died, in a tragic riding accident on the estate. They believe a pheasant must have flown out from a hedge and startled his horse. He fell and was crushed beneath its hooves. Henrietta, his wife, had now lost all her family. It was said, her mind was turned with grief, for she locked up and left the house, as it stood, and went to live with her sister in Surrey. That would have been around nineteen forty nine.'

'I think I was about eight at the time when I first went there to play. So that date would be about right.'

'We eventually heard that Henrietta died of a sudden heart attack. Some would say, it was from a broken heart. After that, of

227

course, the house was sold.'

'The whole story is like some terrible fairy tale,' said Kitty. 'It's no wonder mum forbid me to go anywhere near the place, but of course, we did,' she admitted. 'It's a posh nursing home, now. With its history, I don't rate the chances of those who enter its portals, do you?' she said, with gallows humour and then she fell silent, thinking over all that Phoebe had told her. 'I loved the garden. It always felt familiar to me, although I could never understand why.'

'Inherited memory, perhaps?' suggested Phoebe.

'Could be.' Kitty shivered. 'Gosh, I don't know about you, but I'm beginning to feel cold. Shall we go home?' She jumped down from the wall.

'Are you quite sure you're OK Kitty? This has been a shock for you.' Phoebe's face was concerned.

'Yes, I'm feeling fine, now, thanks. I'm so glad that you've told me, Aunt Phoebe. At last I have an explanation for so many things that have puzzled me. I wonder why, though, I felt I knew the tunes from that musical box?'

'Inherited memory, again? Mary would have listened to it with Victoria. It's the sort of thing that would have entranced two little girls. On the other hand, I've met people who believe in reincarnation and there would be no question with the Buddhists. They would say that you were Mary reincarnated.'

'Oh my sainted aunt! I'm not sure I like that idea.' She was thoughtful for a moment. 'Reincarnation does have a mad sort of logic and it would explain my extreme claustrophobia.' She laughed suddenly.

Phoebe gave her a questioning look.

'I was just imagining having this conversation with mum.'

Phoebe chuckled with her. 'She would think we were both off our heads.'

'That's for certain,' Kitty agreed. 'Well, whatever the answer is to the familiarity of the music, it was a beautiful box. I took quite a fancy to it.'

'Shall we finish our walk by going the full circle, or take the same route back?' asked Phoebe.

'Oh, I think, we should complete our walk, Aunt Phoebe. The hedges are looking so pretty with the primroses and the cherry blossoms are already out in some peoples gardens. Spring is my favourite time of the year. Some like the autumn colours. Me, I love the freshness of Spring. The new greens, the daffodils, and primroses, the bluebells. It makes me feel so alive,' replied Kitty.

Phoebe linked her arm through Kitty's. 'For heaven's sake just call me Phoebe. Aunt makes me feel old.'

Kitty squeezed her arm, conscious of a shared closeness, rarely given. 'You sounded like mum, then. I don't know how she will react to the idea of calling you, Phoebe.'

'Why shouldn't you? You're not a child any longer. *I'll* deal with your mother,' she smiled, and then was serious, again. 'You know, we didn't finish our conversation about Terry and Lawrence. What does your mother say about it? Have you discussed it with her?'

'She knows there's someone else, and has told me to think very carefully. She thinks I'm too young to make any hasty decision and doesn't want me to throw away substance for what might be a shadow. Mum likes Terry and feels he is steady and reliable. Rather like dad, really. And, if I'm honest, even I am a little doubtful as to how Lawrence will react when I tell him about my episodes, and it's important to me that he does understand, although lately, I've noticed they've become less frequent, so, as yet, I haven't felt the need to tell him.'

'Well, your mother does have a point. Terry knows you, like no other and that can count for a great deal, but I also know, you have to follow your heart, Kitty. It won't be easy telling him, and of course, he's going to be very hurt, but you really don't have any choice. At least warn him that you are unsure of your feelings.' She was quiet for a moment, with an odd pensive look before she spoke again. 'When I was about your age, I fell very much in love, but I had ambitions for a career and went to university. I believed in the independence of women. There was plenty of time for marriage, I told myself and then the war came, and the services took me away from Cornwall.'

'And did this man love you?'

'Yes, he did, but his eyes came to rest upon another and it's very difficult to fight competition when you are out of their orbit.'

Kitty winced. 'Like Terry is for me?'

'The circumstances are a little similar. However, I was in the right territory to meet other men. Hundreds of them, in fact!' She chuckled. 'And I've had my chances of marriage. It's all water under the bridge and you can't turn the clock back,' she added briskly.

But if I could, and your mother had not stepped into my shoes, you my dear, might even have been my daughter with your father, James.

Chapter Twenty-Three

THE AFTERMATH HAD left Kitty shaken and miserable and it had affected the whole family.

'How could you do that to Terry? He doesn't deserve it,' Grace had accused her.

Octavia and Jack who were looking forward to having him as a son-in-law were concerned that she was making a choice she would later regret. 'He loves you a great deal, Kitty,' said Jack.

'Yes, I hope you know what you're doing. You will have to go a long way to find someone as steady and kind as Terry,' said Octavia who had feared this might happen for there had been an unmistakeable glow to Kitty when speaking of a new mining student at the Saturday dance.

Telling Terry had torn her apart. The following day, after her talk with Phoebe, Kitty had suggested to him they went for a walk. From the moment they set out, Terry sensed something was wrong for she was unusually quiet as they walked down the hill. It had been the same at tea the previous day when Kitty was not herself, but he put it down to the revelations she had heard from Phoebe about James's family. He expressed his gladness that she now had the answers she sought as a child, and said it was the last of their secrets to share. Her face had crumpled at his words, and pleading she felt unwell, he kissed her goodnight and left early.

On reaching the gardens of the recreation ground, Kitty suggested they sat in the Victorian shelter. He looked at her in surprise for they had barely begun their walk, but she avoided his gaze as she led him towards the seat.

'What's the matter Kitty? You're very quiet today,' and attempted to hug her. She resisted and he felt a sudden pit of fear in his stomach, for her face and body seemed devoid of life.

Kitty forced herself to look into his eyes, taking in the intense blue of them, his lock of waving hair that he hated so much, falling down over his brow. Her heart was swept with memories. He was so dear to her, and the tension inside was making her light-headed and her mouth dry. Oh God. How can I do this, she thought.

His eyes were questioning.

'I have something to tell you, and there's no easy way of saying it.' She could feel the emotion rising and constricting her throat. 'I've met someone else.'

It was said so quietly, Terry thought he must be mistaken. It wasn't possible what he had heard. 'Did you just say to me, you've met someone else?'

'Yes, I met him at the Saturday dance.'

He felt the breath sucked out of his body and the blood thumped in his ears. 'When was this?' he forced himself to ask.

'In January, just after my birthday.'

'Is he someone I know?'

'No, he only moved here recently.'

Terry was silent, reeling from the import of what she was saying. 'Are you trying to tell me it's over between us?' he finally said.

'Yes, she whispered.

Terry's face dropped into a stricken mask. 'You can't mean that, Kitty. We're going to be married.'

'I know, I know. I'm so sorry, Terry.'

'And you love him?'

'Yes, I do.'

'But you say you've only just met him. How can you be so sure? Does he feel the same? Does he . . . love you?' he stumbled over the words.

'Yes, he does,' she answered, crushed at the sadness she was inflicting on Terry. The agony was in his face.

He sat as if turned to stone. 'I should never have gone away. I must have been mad to leave you.'

'Don't say that, Terry. Oh God!' she cried, 'I've never wanted to hurt you like this.'

He caught her hands, and sought her eyes, his voice broken with emotion. 'Don't do this Kitty. I love you so much. I can't believe this is happening to us.' He began to weep.

His tears affected her more than any anger might have done at her betrayal. It cut her to ribbons. She could not stand to see his distress and tentatively placed her arms around him. Please don't cry, Terry. I can't bear it.'

At her sympathetic touch, a spark of bitterness flared and he flinched away from her.

'Does he know about us?'

'Yes, I've told Lawrence.'

'So, that's his name. The man who's willing to take what isn't his, and hasn't the guts to tell me himself.'

Lawrence had, in fact, wished to see him, and offered to be with Kitty, but she had said, 'No, you must leave me to explain,' and at Terry's accusation said in the pain of rejection, knew she had been right. She had to face this guilt and anguish at his terrible humiliation, this utter destruction of them both, alone.

With an effort of will, Terry pulled himself together. 'And what about your visions?' he asked, 'Does he know about them?'

'Not at this moment, no.'

'I wonder how he will react when he does. I know you better than anyone else, Kitty, and how you are when you have these time-slips. He may not understand and accept that side of you that has always been kept between us.'

'There is that chance, yes, but it's one I'm willing to take.'

So, her love for him ran that deep, he thought. To keep her, he must fight. 'I won't accept this, I can't, Kitty.' He cupped his hands around her face, willing her to feel the intensity of his feelings. 'I love you with all my being. I can't imagine my life without you.'

Kitty's eyes that were bright with unshed tears, fell away from his gaze.

In despair, his hands dropped. 'How can you throw away all that we've meant to each other? We've been together since children, and have always returned to each other. I shall wait for you, however long it takes.'

Kitty took his hands into hers, forced him to look at her. She had to make him see that this time, it was different. 'I love Lawrence, Terry, and I'm going to marry him. You must not wait for me,' she said, through tears she could no longer control.

'Oh Kitty, come here.' He put his arms around her and she rested into them, as she had done all her life, and in a silent misery of grief they watched some children who had arrived to play on the swings, before they began to slowly walk home.

The invitation for him to join Kitty and their mutual friends for a get-together a few days before her wedding, came in the summer of sixty four. It was to be held in Tyack's Hotel bar in Camborne, where past and present mining students gathered at the local watering hole. Terry was torn. Could he bear to see Kitty on the arm of this man? It would seem churlish and unkind not to attend, but he would not find it easy. He finally decided he would go, and consoled himself with the thought it would also be an opportunity to meet and catch up on the news of old friends whom he had not seen since that Easter visit.

Kitty looked radiant in a figure hugging short dress of royal blue silk as she came over to him with Lawrence, where he stood with Peter reminiscing on his boyhood holidays in Cornwall. On introduction, Lawrence and Terry were ill at ease, and acknowledged each other with the briefest nod of the head. Kitty, acutely aware of the tension between the men, sought to defuse the atmosphere and turned to Peter.

'This is my cousin Peter, Lawrence. He and his older brother John, who unfortunately is unable to be here for our wedding, came to stay with us one summer, and after that, the family came down to stay every year in a hut at Gwithian. We three were inseparable, and managed to frighten the wits out of the neighbourhood with our crazy ideas.

'She was an awful tomboy, Lawrence,' said Peter, relaxed and expansive from a glass or two of beer, and oblivious to the hostility between the two men. 'I shall never forget her walking across the beams of a derelict cottage at Nancarrow where the ceiling had collapsed onto the floor. On that particular occasion, we had more sense than to follow her. Mind you, when I think of the things we got up to, it's a wonder any of us survived childhood.'

'Peter was always breaking things,' she teased, laughing at him.

'That's because you were always leading me into trouble! My arm has never been the same since.'

'I shall clarify that last remark or it could be open to misinterpretation,' Kitty bantered back. 'We were swinging over a bank on a rope, Lawrence, that had probably hung for years from this old oak tree, and it snapped in two and we crashed to the ground. Peter broke his arm and the breath was knocked right out of me. The first time in my life, I was rendered speechless!'

'I can vouch for that. She was a chatterbox but lovely with it,' Peter laughed.

234

'Oh! Be quiet you!' Kitty retaliated in jest. 'I think it was an omen because every year after that, he was always scatting something up. First it was the safety bar of a bunk bed in a hut at Gwithian, and then with a cricket ball, he broke a pane in Mr. Thomas's greenhouse that overlooks the playing field. Finally, he crashed our Dandy.'

Terry gave him a playful punch on the arm. 'It took me weeks of foraging for old pram wheels and pieces of wood to make it, and within five minutes of putting your grand derriere on the seat, it was a mangled wreck.'

Peter raised an eyebrow at Lawrence. 'The steering was all cock-eyed. The fact that I could have been killed was neither here nor there to them. They were far more concerned for their Dandy.'

Terry snorted. 'Rubbish! My Dandy was a masterpiece of engineering. It was your lousy sense of direction.'

Kitty, amused at their repartee that had continued since child-hood when they had vied for her approval of their crazy schemes looked at Lawrence. His face held a false smile, and with surprise, realised that jealousy lurked beneath the surface.

A light frown that had crossed Lawrence's face at their banter, had not gone unnoticed by Terry. Charm he might have in abundance, and a sensuality that attracted women, but he suspected a shallowness at the core and was troubled with misgivings for Kitty. He had hoped to speak to her, to ask if she had seen any more ghosts from the past, and if she had spoken of them to Lawrence, but Lawrence had possessively stayed at Kitty's side and there had been no opportunity. He glanced around the room, and said he must mingle and catch up with old friends, and kissing her on the cheek and wishing them both every happiness, quickly excused himself before the anguish that he still felt at losing her would be reflected in his eyes.

Her happiness on her wedding day shone encompassing them all as Terry watched her marry Lawrence at the altar where he would have stood. She looked exquisite in a creation of white lace, and with the sun lighting her hair, and teased into a tumble of curls, she was as beautiful to him as a Titian painting. Mrs. Retallack sitting beside Terry in the church pew, was grieved for her son's pain, still plain to see, and the whole distressing

235

outcome had left both families and their good neighbourly relationship on an awkward footing.

On their way home on the train from their honeymoon in London, where Kitty had revelled in the architecture and sights, and the quick tempo of life after the slow and easy pace of Cornwall, her thoughts meandered with the rhythm of the wheels, to light hearted girlish chats before the wedding. Half-jokingly, they warned that men changed, once married, but, thus far, she had not found it to be so. She had discovered soon after meeting him that Lawrence had an edge of impatience and did not suffer fools gladly, but to her, he was attentive and affectionate, and the intensity of their love had not palled. Their lovemaking transported her to an almost mystical sense of oneness, and later lying in Lawrence's arms felt it must be the nearest thing to God's love transformed into human understanding, and although she longed to share with him this unexpected sense of wonder, she kept it to herself, unsure of what his response would be.

In the interim period before flying, they rented a bungalow, close to the family on the crest of the hill to Beacon, where, in the kitchen, they laughed at Kitty's attempts at cooking from a large practical cookery book that Octavia had given to her. She had followed the recipes to the letter for rationing and Octavia's preference for having the kitchen to herself, had precluded any chance of her experimenting before marriage. Lawrence told her that soon it would not matter in the slightest, if she could cook or not, as her every wish would be catered for by amahs. Kitty was not at all sure that she liked the idea. Caring for Lawrence fulfilled an unconscious need to demonstrate her love.

They hired a car and explored places inaccessible by bus or train, and clambering down to the seclusion of a hidden cove of virgin sand with the cry of the wheeling sea birds above them, they made love in a world that was theirs alone. And later, with Lawrence's élan burning brightly within and boundless, he sprang to his feet. 'Let's go skinny dipping!'

Kitty laughingly protested as he tugged her to her feet. 'Oh no. We can't, Lawrence.'

'Why ever not? There's no-one here. It's great fun. The sensation of water around you without clothes on is wonderful!'

His eagerness was infectious and catching him unawares, she took to her heels, and raced ahead, her body achingly beautiful to him, as she splashed into the cove's clear ultramarine waters and began swimming with the sheer joy of water embracing her whole body freed from the self-effacement of clothing. In the recess of her mind lay that day at Gwithian, but any prick of residual fear of the sea was stifled with the knowledge of a voice that promised, *'she would always be with her'*.

The following day, they took the road to St. Just and walked the rugged mine-worn cliffs to Botallack Mine, marvelling at the ingenuity of miners who built engine houses perched at the edge of the land, and at the courage it took for them to win the ore, in candlelight and claustrophobic darkness, a seam of tin that ran for miles under the sea. It was said that the men could hear the boulders rolling and groaning on the ocean floor above them, and Kitty expressed to Lawrence how relieved she was that he would be working on an open-cast mine and not down in the bowels of the earth. Just the thought of it made her shudder with fear.

With the freedom of the car to take them where they will, the moors had lured them away from the coast, and they roamed through the heather and over rocks and streams, before stretching out on a grassy knoll beneath Roughtor. There they breathed in air as fresh and intense as a bottle of wine and in the potent silence of its wild tranquillity, Kitty suddenly sensed they were not alone and sat up. A girl was walking beneath the slopes of Roughtor. She wore a long gown of muted colours, and held a red shawl around her shoulders. On her head was a silk bonnet. She stopped every now and then, shading her eyes from the sun and Kitty realised she was looking for someone. She watched her picking her way across the moor to fade into the brightness of the sun. Lawrence noticing her fixed and unblinking eyes, pushed himself up. 'What are you looking at?'

Kitty shook off the familiar dreamlike sensation and standing up, suggested they climbed to the top of the tor. 'I thought I saw someone, but I was mistaken,' she replied.

Lawrence was not persuaded by her answer. There had been the strangest expression on her face, he thought, as he caught her up, and marvelled at the rock formations on the summit. 'Are you sure you're up for this? It's quite a climb.'

'Of course, I am. They say the view from the top is fantastic.' She took his hand and together they climbed.

They arrived, breathless at the top, and surveyed its reaches. Lawrence wrapped his arms around her body with her head nestling beneath his chin as they watched a glint of water meandering through the rough terrain. It was a place alive to her with the voices of the ancient ones, and of the miners and men who had lived and worked amongst the wind and rain sculpted rocks, stacked like giant plates one upon the other and moving with a life of their own, as light and shadow chased across the immense sky. Kitty, once again, connected with its untamed beauty, as she had as a child on the ancient road to Land's End. On their way home, they stopped for a meal at the Jamaica Inn, and Lawrence on ordering at the bar, looked back at her and smiled, but Kitty did not respond. The room had taken on the patina of an oil painting, dark and smoky, and sitting by the fire was a man dressed in clothes from another century and smoking a clay pipe. Lawrence returned with the drinks and the man vanished, leaving the room lit by low sunlight and the grate empty. 'You were miles away, when I looked at you.'

'Was I? Sorry darling.' She sipped her ginger beer, her thoughts troubled that she would not always be able to disguise or deny her ghosts and apprehensive that it could be a bone of contention between them.

Chapter Twenty-Four

Malaya 1964

KITTY GAZED DOWN as they dropped in ever decreasing height over the North Western tip of Malaya to a sight of impenetrable jungle, moving out to kampongs and paddy fields and carpets of palm trees, and later, she would discover, the tops of thousands of rubber trees that formed a vital part of the economy of Malaya. She could see little sign of habitation until they came into land over pockets of housing on the fringes of Kuala Lumpur. She thought of her mother, and how strange it was that she was starting her married life here, as her mother would have done, had her father lived. Raised in tropical sunshine, she would never have known the bracing sea winds, the solitude of swirling wraiths of mists that descended without warning, and the ever changing moods of an ancient land of Celtic cross and cromlech that was deep in her psyche. She felt a mixture of excitement and apprehension, as the plane came to a whistle fading stop and Lawrence squeezed her hand. 'Well, we've arrived, Kitty. Another continent and all in one very long day.'

Kitty agreed, and smiled, giving him a kiss on his cheek that still held the lingering scent of his aftershave, as she rose stiffly to her feet from the long flight. Moving from the air-conditioned comfort of the cabin to the open aircraft door, she was met with a blast of furnace heat that took her breath away as she clattered down the aircraft steps. Her clothes began to cling to her like a wet blanket as they cleared customs and were met by a company car. Kitty tired beyond thought from the nineteen hour flight, barely took in the kaleidoscope of noise and colour as they drove through the streets to their hotel where they collapsed between the bliss of freshly laundered sheets and fell instantly asleep with a creaking fan above them stirring the humid air.

She awoke the following morning hung-over with jetlag and sleepily lurched into a bathroom that transported her back to

Nancarrow. No matter how far she roamed, there seemed no escape from the memories of the manor. The roll-top bath was cavernous with huge taps and tortuous piping which clanked into life gushing water, as she sank down and was lost in its depths. This bath is big enough for three, she thought with amusement, as she lifted a sponge of water and trickled it over her face, and lay there, lazily swishing it through her fingers.

Her thoughts were of home and of her mother and Phoebe who had arrived for her wedding carrying an oblong gift wrapped most beautifully. It was heavy and carefully unwrapping it, Kitty had been overwhelmed, and to the amazement of Octavia, had burst into tears. Feeling foolish, she said, it must be her wedding that was making her more emotional than usual, and explained that she had always craved a musical box, and stroking the top whose inlaid rosewood shone with the patina of years, she looked at Phoebe with wondering eyes as she wound the handle and set it to play tunes that had never ceased to haunt her.

Was it Mary's spirit that had led her to the musical box that Kitty had played at Nancarrow, thought Phoebe as she listened to the music with a cup of tea in her hand. Or was it simply one of life's many coincidences? Kitty would say it was the spirit within us that guided our thoughts and actions. Octavia would think it utter nonsense. She had found it when browsing in an antique shop in Surrey and on asking the proprietor if he knew of its origins, he had told her it had originated from a manor house in Cornwall. An elderly lady had brought it in and said, that it held too many sad memories and the little girl who had loved to hear it, had died in tragic circumstances. Phoebe felt the hairs on her arms stand up as he spoke and with fate playing so opportunely into her hands, she told Kitty she would have bought it, if it had cost a king's ransom, and Kitty was conscious it was a measure of her love and understanding.

It was when she had begun packing their trunk to be shipped to Malaya and preparing for the wrench of leaving their families behind for a long stretch of two years, that she had asked for her birth certificate and discovered from Octavia that she was one of a twin.

Kitty looked at her in utter amazement. 'A twin!'

'Yes. You had an identical twin sister. She died at birth.'

'For goodness sake, mum. Why haven't you told me this before?'

'There didn't seem to be any need. It was all such a long time ago,' replied Octavia with a tone of finality.

Kitty exploded. 'So why even bother to tell me now. My God! I've never known anyone practice the maxim of keeping their own counsel, as you do. You seem to find it impossible to speak of the past. I had to find out about my father's sister, Mary, and the fact that my grandfather worked at Nancarrow from Phoebe.'

Octavia frowned and her eyes narrowed. 'Phoebe *told* you? She had no right.'

'Well, someone had to, and it certainly wasn't going to be you, was it?'

'How long have you known this?'

'Years. Phoebe told me when she came down for Easter, that time. We had gone for a walk, if you remember, and I was telling her that Terry and I had broken into Nancarrow house and I felt . . .'

'Just a minute, Kitty. You're telling me that you and Terry actually broke into the house, after all my warnings about it?'

'Yes, we did.'

'Well, that does surprise me. Terry struck me as having more common sense.'

'Mum. We were children. What did you expect? If children are told not to do something, that's the very time they do, unless they are given an explanation as to why they shouldn't. Believe it or not, it was Peter that discovered the way in. It was down a coal chute. And whilst I'm on the subject, I might as well confess that he did not break his arm on the playground swings. That was also in Nancarrow on a rope swing that snapped in two.'

Octavia gazed at her. 'I always did have my suspicions about that. So, Peter's been with you to Nancarrow, as well.'

'Yes, and you haven't heard the half of it.'

'And I don't want to.'

'I think you'd better as it's pretty relevant to us both. When I was ten, I saw Mary and Victoria in the garden with two boys. At the time, I didn't realise they were ghosts. They seemed so real. The next time I saw them was with Terry. They were gathered around a Christmas tree.'

Octavia could scarce believe what she was hearing. Her ears heard it, but her mind refused to accept the words Kitty was speaking.

'That was when I knew the children were ghosts because Terry told me he couldn't see them. All the time we were there, I had this awful feeling something bad had happened. I asked Phoebe if she knew anything about the people who had lived there and she told me about Mary and Victoria who died in a trunk, and about her brothers, Oliver and Simon who were killed in the war, and their father Ralph, dying in a horse riding accident. So many people have died there, mum, no wonder you had such a horror of the place. You should have told me. You've no idea how frightening it was to have had those glimpses into the past and to find that no-one else could see them. Oh, yes, I almost forgot about the little girl who ran out under the wheels of a carriage. I didn't see that accident. I heard it from the stables where I was hiding, but when I came to look, there was no-one there. Just think how weird that was for me. Once Phoebe explained all that had happened at Nancarrow, I understood the reasons why you tried to keep me away.'

'Well, be that as it may, all this talk of ghosts, is foolish Kitty. It would be wise to keep it to yourself. I don't think Lawrence would understand or appreciate it, any more than I do and it could well do damage to your relationship. And even if you did see these things, what good does it do and don't you think, under the circumstances, I made the right decision to try and keep you away from the place? Supposing I had told you. You would have suffered even more from nightmares.'

The very same words Octavia had spoken the night she had floated down the stairs, but she certainly wouldn't be telling Octavia that! It would be the final confirmation that her daughter was indeed in the realms of fantasy or madness.

'Maybe, but you could have done so, later. You keep things so close to your chest, mum. And whilst we're on the subject of keeping things to oneself, do you realise that all my life, I've only ever seen you show affection for Thomas?' The ache held in for so long had sprung with words from the pent-up longing of years, unleashed by her love of Lawrence.

If Octavia had been shot, she could not have looked more astounded at this sudden and unexpected quarter of attack. She acknowledged, she should have spoken of Mary, but this . . . 'That's simply not true, Kitty.'

'Yes, it is. I can't ever remember you giving me a hug or saying you love me. Or Grace and dad for that matter.'

Octavia's ire rose and she bridled. 'Now, that is quite enough. I won't hear another word. What nonsense. Of course, I care for you.'

'You see, you can't even say the word, love, can you?'

Octavia sighed in exasperation. 'It wasn't easy to get close to you. You were a strange child, living in a world of your own, seeing things that no-one else could. When you were small, you would spend hours playing with an imaginary friend and talking in a little language all of your own.'

Kitty's anger stopped in its tracks. 'Did I?'

'Dad and I used to laugh about it. We couldn't understand a word you were saying. It was all gobbledegook to us. You even told gran about her. Don't you remember?'

'No, not really.'

'As for implying that I don't love your father. How could you even begin to think such a thing? You really have no idea what you're talking about. You are about to discover for yourself that marriage is, for the most part, a private one. And that's how it should be. I couldn't have married a kinder or better man if I had looked the length and breadth of England. Whatever next, Kitty.'

'Well, that's how I've always felt,' said Kitty, her voice low and resigned.

'I'm going to show you something, which might help you to understand why I find it difficult to speak of the past. She rummaged through the sideboard drawer and drew out a dog-eared scrap of paper. 'I saw these words in a poem and they struck a particular chord with me at the time, so I wrote them down and kept them. She handed the paper to her. "There are dreams of which I cannot speak, there are thoughts that will not die. Your leaving left my strong heart weak and with tears to fill the sky."

On reading it, Kitty was instantly remorseful. 'I'm sorry, mum. I shouldn't have said those things,' she said handing the scrap back to her. 'And I know the reason you told me so little about my father's family, was partly my fault. I should have asked more questions. It's just that . . . when you first told me, it seemed so remote. The only father I'd ever known was dad, and I know it sounds silly, but I felt it would have been disloyal to him. And later, after Prue, my grandmother died and Henry remarried, there seemed little point in raking up the past.' Kitty sighed. 'I don't want to fall out, mum, especially now I'm going away. It's just that every whip and flip a bombshell drops in my lap. First discovering that James was my father, then learning about Mary his sister, and that my grandfather lived at Nancarrow, and now, I find, I had a twin sister.'

'Put like that, I can see I should have told you these things, a long time ago.'

'Is there anything else lurking in the past that I should know about?' Kitty asked, half-jokingly.

'No, unless you count the fact that our father, William also knew the Killigrew family. Did Phoebe tell you that?'

It was Kitty's turn to look surprised. 'No, she didn't.'

Octavia's reply was caustic. 'That was something she managed to keep to herself, then. It was when William and Ralph Killigrew were young men. They met at a rifle club and became good friends which was unusual in those days for the classes didn't mix. As a family, we have often said how strange it was, the connections we had with the Killigrews. William was a crack shot as you know, and he and Ralph entered competitions that William invariably won. I remember William telling me once, that Ralph had jokingly asked him if, just for once, William would not enter the local competition to give him a chance at winning the cup. Despite that, they would often go shooting together on the estate, and William used to see Henry, your grandfather, working in the garden. What is also extraordinary, is that both Ralph and William fell in love with our mother, who was quite a beauty in her day. It was the beginning of the end of their friendship, for Ralph must have felt where William was involved, Ralph ran a poor second, despite the fact, that he had a lot more to offer her than our father. Then, the first world war came, by which time, your grandfather Henry had emigrated to Canada, and the rest, as they say, is history.'

Kitty was astounded. 'You couldn't make it up, it's so incredible.'

'No, that's true. To anyone else, it would sound too far-fetched. Life is very strange. It throws people together, they part, and the link continues where you least expect it.'

'So it would seem. I think I'll make us both a cup of tea. I need time to digest it all!' said Kitty.

As they sat in the sitting room, Octavia talked of her birth, and how difficult it had been to pull her through. For the first time, Kitty realised that her mother's strength and detachment came from loss and adversity, and any heartache had been firmly locked away within her whilst she got on with the business of life. Since that conversation with her mother, Kitty had wondered who the imaginary child was that she had played with. Could it have been Mary? For try as she might, she had no recollection of it.

Lawrence came brightly into the bathroom and sat on the edge of the bath. 'Good morning, Mrs. Scott-Thomas,' he smiled down on her.

She grinned back up at him. 'Good morning Mr. Scott-Thomas. Sandra said, my new name is a mouthful, but I think it has a certain ring to it,' Kitty enthused.

He looked at her indulgently. His wife. As foreseen by her ballet teacher, her thin face had blossomed with the filling out of maturity into looks that were striking, but it was her eyes that held him, and he admitted to himself, at times could rattle his self-possession with their insight, as if she could read his very thoughts. They made an arresting couple. Tall and lithe with unconventional good looks Lawrence was attractive to women, but nevertheless, was resentful of anyone Kitty knew and favoured with a particular intimate look from an upward sweep of lash. He had known, of course, of her love for Terry and of her distress at telling him it was over. Terry had pleaded his love and strength of their relationship, saying he knew her as Lawrence did not, which he knew to be true, and despite her every word and action to the contrary, Lawrence wondered if she held a lingering regret for rejecting him. As she lay there, her golden hair dark with wetness, and the swell of her breasts rising and falling from her slim body, he felt the quickening of desire as she stepped out of the bath and wrapped a towel around herself. He reached out to catch and hold her close, but with teasing laughter at his arousal, declared that she was starving and deftly ducked away into the bedroom.

'You, Mrs. Scott-Thomas are nothing but a little minx,' he called after her, and grinning to himself as he peered at his two days stubble in the mirror, filled the wash basin, and soaping up, began to shave.

Later, venturing forth into the city by taxi arranged by the hotel, they found a world far removed from anything they could have imagined. Kuala Lumpur was looking to the future. A polyglot of Chinese, Indians, and Malays, it teemed with life and the stability of a self-governing democracy that had survived the armed revolt of communists, the upheaval of two worlds wars and the fluctuating prosperity of rubber and tin. It was now on an ambitious burst of modern development. As their stay would be a short one of two days before travelling by rail to Ipoh, they asked their Sikh driver to point out sights of interest. He began by driving them around the Padang, the focal point of colonial Kuala Lumpur and British administration with imposing Moorish-style buildings of arches and domes that housed the Government Offices, and beside it the Post Office with its wide arcaded verandas of pointed horseshoe arches. On the west side of the Padang they were shown the Royal Selangor Club, built as a social and cricket club and looking incongruous amongst the Islamic style buildings, for it was designed as a mock Tudor house. The Sikh, dressed in a pristine white shirt and his head covered with a navy turban, informed them it was affectionately known as The Spotted Dog. Kitty stared at the immaculately wound turban. She had never seen one before. How on earth did they do it? she wondered, as he explained the many origins of the sobriquet for the Spotted Dog. His favourite being the one of a memsahib who strode imperiously into the club with her black and white Dalmatian dogs. He chuckled. 'Animals are strictly forbidden in the club, but no-one dared to complain as she was the Police Commissioner's wife! It's a very popular club Tuan with the planters and miners who come down from up North.'

'In that case, I expect we shall be paying it a visit in the future,' replied Lawrence. 'We are soon off to the mines in Ipoh.

'I should tell you, Tuan, that you have to be a member.'

Lawrence thanked him for the tip as he drove them through the streets bearing the stamp of the Portuguese, Dutch and British who came for the spices, rubber and tin, and were reflected in the style of buildings that were an exotic mixture of Islamic, Neo-classical and Art Deco, and engaged Kitty's curiosity in its sheer diversity. Their driver whisked them out over newly constructed flyovers to see Parliament House and University, the Mosque and Museum and the National Monument, each spectacularly modern and beautiful, yet reflecting Islamic refinement, and set out in spacious grounds with wide roads. It was clear that KL, as the locals called it, had its sights set firmly on expansion for its multi-racial citizens.

246

On returning to the centre of the town, he dropped them off in Chinatown where they wandered the crowded streets under the cover of arcaded walkways that gave shelter from the sun and rain. The shops burst their wares out onto the pavement, baskets of ikan bilis, a dried fish the size of a small finger, dried meat and spices, exotic fruits - melons and paw-paws, rambutans, and the evil smelling fruit Durian that tasted delicious, they were told, if you could get past the smell. At goldsmith's shops, an array of rich gold jewellery was guarded by a sikh at the open-fronted entrances and everywhere was a cacophony of hooting cars and bicycle bells. They stopped for a cup of tea in a café with marble topped tables and old Bentwood chairs, where orders were shouted from one end of the building to the other. The city was a culture shock of noise and of sights that assaulted their senses, as appetising smells of unfamiliar food wafted by them to tables where the Chinese ate rapidly, holding bowls to their mouths and spooning rice with chop sticks. The Chinese, they were to discover were fond of eating at the roadside stalls, where cheap and delicious bowls of soup and Hokkien Mee could be bought. The latter became a firm favourite when learning to master chopsticks, sitting and eating above mon-soon drains with the Chinese from the towns. They saw few Europeans, preferring to eat in the restaurants, but Kitty and Lawrence took the way of the Chinese, as ducks to water, and, as they ate, watched the dishes and chopsticks being washed by women hunkering down and dipping them in and out along a line of bowls of soap and boiling water, to emerge gleaming at the other end.

That evening, sitting at a table set with a snowy white damask tablecloth and heavy silver service cutlery and condiments with fans whirling above them, Kitty looked around. The room exuded an air of genteel decline. Square cut pillars rose to a high ceiling, between which hung dust-faded glass chandeliers. Exquisitely embroidered pictures in Chinese silk hung on the walls. The black rosewood tables and fan-backed chairs were well worn, and ranged along the wall was a matching service cupboard with reeded panels upon which were a row of Chinese bowls and serving dishes. In the corner stood a threadbare blue velvet dais beside which two large potted palms stood one each side. The waiter having given them the menu, disappeared, and alone in the silence of the big empty room, the atmosphere was heavy with old Colonial days and motes dancing in shafts of sunlight from the fan's lazy stirring of the languid air. From somewhere in the hotel Kitty could hear faint strains of music.

'I wonder where the music is coming from?' she asked Lawrence.

He looked puzzled. 'Music? I can't hear anything.'

'It's that old Glen Miller tune, *In The Mood.*' She began to hum along, clicking her fingers and dancing to the rhythm with her head and shoulders. 'It must be coming from the lounge next door.'

Lawrence shushed her as he listened. 'The only thing I can hear is the ticking of the long case clock in the hallway,' he said, as he watched her jigging in time to the imaginary tune in her head. 'For goodness sake, stop, Kitty. It's embarrassing. You're like a bouncing puppet.' His voice was sharp.

Startled, Kitty abruptly stopped and stared at him. 'For heaven's sake, Lawrence, we are the only ones here, and if you can't hear the music, then you must be deaf!' She looked away in anger across to the dais as the strains grew stronger, and saw that a small band was playing. The room was crowded and smoke filled, and people were laughing and talking at a small bar, whilst others sat at tables around the parquet dance floor with drinks clinking with ice. She could smell the pungent aroma of curry and rice as in the heat and humidity, the men in their tuxedos popped beads of perspiration as they quickstepped their partners in elegant slipper satin dresses around the floor. The dance came to an end with a ripple of polite clapping, and the tempo changed with a man crooning, *'Love Is The Sweetest Thing'* into a large microphone. One couple came close to her chair, the woman's silver dress brushing her leg as the man held her close and murmured in her ear. They were oblivious to all in the room, and with a cold, terrible shock Kitty realised she was looking at her James, her father. There was no mistaking the red gold hair, the aquiline nose and the green-grey eyes. He was identical to the man she had seen one Christmas night in her bedroom and in the photo her mother had shown her. She watched them moving around the room with the easy intimacy of a couple who knew each other well. This was no casual encounter. The woman was quite beautiful laughing up at him with her head thrown back and her tawny hair falling in a mass of waves and curls. The other women wore the hairstyle of the day, a sausage curl on top and around the napes of their necks, but hers invited touch to the watchful male eyes following them around the room. Kitty could almost read their thoughts imagining the sensual sensation of twining their fingers through it.

'Kitty! Kitty!' Lawrence snapped his fingers in front of her eyes. 'Kitty look at me.'

Kitty blinked at his summons, and in desperation, picked up the large menu and disappeared behind it. Lawrence must not see her state of shock, for how could she explain it? She stared unseeing at the dishes on the list, her thoughts in a turmoil. Who was the woman? She could not deny the sexual chemistry between the two dancers. It was there for all to see. Did her mother know about her? With her mother's penchant for keeping her own counsel, it was possible, but she had been pretty convincing when assuring her there were no more secrets from the past. On the other hand, if she had had an inkling or even known, it would be something her mother would never divulge. She would take it to her grave.

Lawrence annoyed at her dismissal of him, was also shaken. Kitty's look had been the same fixed and far away look he had seen on the moors and in the Jamaica Inn and something in the back of his mind began to resonate. He had seen it before, when a boy, on the face of one of his mother's friends. It was the classic symptom of Petit Mal, and the thought that Kitty might be ill, unnerved him, but before speaking of it, he would have a quiet word with the company doctor at the mine. Concealing his worry at his suspicion, Lawrence's approach was conciliatory. He gently pulled the menu down from her face. 'Are you alright, darling?'

Kitty stared coldly over the menu. 'I've never felt better, Lawrence.' Her voice smarted from his disapproval. 'And don't ever call me a puppet again.'

'I know, I'm sorry. I shouldn't have said that. You were happy and I spoilt it.'

'Yes, you did and I *know* what I heard, Lawrence.' She gave him an arched look.

'Please, don't let's argue Kitty. Not on our first day in Malaya.' Her lovely face, always so open to him was now veiled and secretive. He had hurt her deeply for something that was no fault of her own. Perhaps hearing music was a symptom of the disease. He had no way of knowing and he felt remorse when, with a small sigh, she asked him what he fancied for dinner.

As he studied his menu, Kitty was filled with a conflict of emotions. Curiosity for the father she never knew mingled with anger and dismay at seeing him in such a compromising situation. How dared he do this to her mother. If only, she were able to share the sight she had seen, with Lawrence. She needed to talk about it and found herself wishing for the safe assurance of Terry.

A cry of surprise came from behind them. 'Madeline!' and Kitty felt a tap on her shoulder. 'What are you doing back in KL? You should have let me know you were coming. I . . .'

Turning around, Kitty looked up into the face of a woman in her early fifties. Her light brown hair touched with grey was tucked neatly back into a bun and her eyes of pale blue changed from one of surprise to embarrassment. 'I'm so sorry, my dear. I thought you were someone else.' She stared at Kitty. 'You are so like her. It's uncanny.'

Lawrence stood. 'This is my wife, Kitty, and I'm Lawrence. We've just arrived from England and are on our way up to Ipoh.'

She shook his outstretched hand and then Kitty's. 'I'm Mrs. Nicholls. How do you do.' She smiled courteously. 'I don't often see Europeans staying in the hotel. They seem to have migrated to the newly built, Merlin Hotel.'

'Please won't you join us? That is, if you're free. We were just about to order our meal,' said Lawrence with a worried look at Kitty's white face.

'Thank you, I'd love to.' She settled herself and looked across at Kitty. 'Are you alright, my dear? You look a little pale,' she said.

'I just felt a little faint for a minute. I think it must be the heat.'

'Yes, it is rather overpowering when you first arrive in the country. You will find that your body will adjust as the blood gets thinner.'

'Do you live in KL?' Lawrence asked.

'As a matter of fact, I live here in the hotel.'

She smiled at their look of surprise. 'Strange but true. A wistful look flitted across her face. 'It used to buzz with life. Planters and miners, and the men and their wives from the Administration Offices at the Padang. And the dinner dances in this room . . . well, they were quite wonderful.' She softly sighed at the memory.

Kitty felt a familiar prickle run down her spine.

'My husband worked for the civil service in KL until he died in nineteen fifty nine, shortly after Malaya gained its independence. It was very sudden, a heart attack. The war and the emergency had taken a terrible toll on his health.'

'Oh, I'm so sorry.' Kitty replied sympathetically.

'Yes, it was a ghastly shock. We were looking forward to retirement after living here all our married lives. We loved the country and its people and apart from holidays in Cornwall, we felt KL to be very much our home.'

'Cornwall!' they both exclaimed together. 'We've just arrived from there,' said Lawrence.

'What a coincidence,' she smiled.

There's no such thing as coincidences – only the reasons why, Kitty thought.

'Which part are you from?' Mrs. Nicholls asked.

'The South West. I was born and bred in Camborne, and this one,' Kitty pulled a face at Lawrence, 'is a foreigner, and hails from across the Tamar!'

'Bristol, actually,' said Lawrence ruefully.

'Yes, I know how you feel, Lawrence. I discovered you have to live a very long time in Cornwall to be accepted, although I personally found the natives friendly.'

'And where did you stay in Cornwall, Mrs. Nicholls?' Kitty asked.

'Penzance. And please, do call me Verity. Maurice and I had a holiday house on the seafront, not far from the Morrab Gardens which, as you know, are sub-tropical, though the weather is hardly tropical when the wind and the sea joined forces.'

Kitty nodded with amused understanding. 'Our weather can be very wild and unpredictable.'

'If it isn't a rude question. Why did you decide to stay on in KL?' enquired Lawrence.

'Well, after my parents died, I had to make a decision. We were not blessed with children and as I have no other relatives, I decided to spend my remaining days in KL although I still go to our holiday home for a break and the bracing Cornish air. My rooms here are comfortable, if a little old-fashioned, and I have made a great number of friends both European and Asian over the years. Of course, most of the expats have left now, but those that remain link up with me for a game of Mahjong or bridge and they take tea with me in my rooms or in the gardens of the hotel. We also love to visit the Merlin for its superb food and evening shows from around the world. Life is so much easier here. I have many interests and I'm well looked after by Cassim,' she continued, smiling up at a white linen-clad waiter wearing a songkok who appeared at their table.

'Good evening, Mem.' His smile took in her companions. 'You have company, tonight, Mem.'

'Yes, Cassim, and I couldn't be more delighted to be sharing my evening meal. Usually, I eat in my room,' she informed them. She picked up the menu. 'If you haven't already decided, may I suggest Pulau Ayam. It's delicious. It's chicken cooked in the Malay style and flavoured with coconut.'

Giving him their orders, he soft-footed away. 'You will find the manners of the waiters here impeccable and they are always so obliging. I have a particular soft spot for Cassim,' she confided. 'Don't be afraid to ask for anything you need.'

The rest of the evening passed quickly and pleasantly, as Mrs. Nicholls regaled them with amusing anecdotes of the people she had known and of her life in Malaya, and how the city was changing fast. There was a spirit of optimism with the gaining of independence, and the ending of the communist revolt. Before the meal was over, Kitty sensed a friendship had been forged with a mutual empathy and liking on both sides, and Mrs. Nicholls was eager to keep in touch. 'You must come and have a meal with me when you next visit KL. I do so enjoy hearing the latest gossip from out station,' she said as she took her leave.

'What a lovely lady,' said Lawrence.

'Yes, she is,' replied Kitty, with the oddest feeling of presentiment tingling away inside of her.

The journey up to Ipoh by train had been stifling despite the open windows and although Kitty was now dressed in cool cotton, she was still bathed in perspiration, as she watched the countryside go by punctuated with glimpses of kampongs of houses on stilts and Chinese villages of low attap houses where buffalows pulled laden carts. The rubber trees were a dense darkness from the train, and as they travelled further north, the landscape became a moonscape of mine workings with the glint of dredging pools. Arriving at

Ipoh station, they were met by the manager, introducing himself as Jock Henderson and driving them to the mine camp. A Sikh jaga saluted smartly as they entered the gates. Kitty threw a half-stifled glance of amused embarrassment at Lawrence as they came to houses on stilts with neat, open gardens of grass and bushes of bright red hibiscus flowers. Getting out of the car, a Chinese amah came to greet them at the door, and behind her stood two small boys and a young girl of teenage years. 'Good afternoon, Tuan, Mem.'

'This is Ah How. Your amah,' Henderson introduced her.

'I hope you had a good journey?' she said, with an engaging smile of uneven teeth.

'Yes, we did, thank you,' replied Lawrence, and Kitty smiled, unsure of her next move. She was longing for a cup of tea. Should she ask her to make one, but the thought had been anticipated.

'I will make you tea,' Ah How said, softly disappearing in her bare feet into a long corridor shaped kitchen that ran along the back of the house, with the youngest hanging shyly onto her cotton trousers.

'Ah How's children,' said Henderson. 'She was widowed a couple of years ago. You will find her a good worker, and her daughter Mei Ling will be your wash amah. They live in the village just outside the camp, but Ah How will spend most of her time here with you, apart from her day off on Sunday.'

'Where does she sleep when she's here, Mr. Henderson?' asked Kitty.

'Please. My friends call me, Jock. There's separate accommodation for amahs at the back of the house, and it's where the washing is done,' he said, as the driver dropped their suitcases on the tiled floor.

The room was large and light and airy with bare cushions on rattan chairs, in front of which were glass topped rattan coffee and occasional tables. At the other end of the room was the dining table and chairs and a sideboard and their trunk which had arrived ahead of them. Home lay wrapped inside: their wedding gifts and linen, pictures, books and records, and souvenirs of places they had visited that would personalise the bareness of the house.

'No curtains?' she asked, looking from the windows that were covered with a fine mesh to deter mosquitoes, to Henderson.

'Soft furnishings you provide for yourselves,' he explained. 'We found that everyone has their own taste in colour and style, and for the same reason, we have painted the rooms a neutral colour to blend with your choice of furnishings. When you've settled in, you will find most things you need in Kampar a mile or two down the road. The Indian shops there have a large choice of materials and haberdashery and will run up curtains and cushion covers for you. And if you want a pretty frock, there is a Chinese dressmaker who can cut a pattern to any style you wish and make it within a matter of hours. The Chinese can turn their hands to anything.'

Ah How came in with a tray of tea and a sponge cake which she placed onto the coffee table.

'Did you make this Ah How?' asked Kitty.

'Yes, Mem.'

'See what I mean?' smiled Henderson.

'It looks delicious,' said Kitty, taking the knife and slicing it as Ah How poured and handed Jock and Lawrence a cup of tea.

'For your food provisions there is Chop Lee Sin in Kampar. It's an amazing place, not much bigger than a shack, but it stocks everything from French cheeses to tinned peas,' Henderson continued, as he took a slice of the cake that Kitty offered. 'The driver can take you there in the morning. The larger town of Ipoh has a Cold Storage, and Jamnadas, a good men's outfitters run by the Indians. There's also a shop called Shitpeng, a rather unfortunate name,' he chuckled, 'where expats go to have their work-shorts made. And I'd advise a hat. The midday sun is a killer. Further afield, there's Robinsons, a departmental store in KL that sells Europeans goods and gifts, if you're looking for something special. It's a favourite of the mems, especially at Christmas time.' He continued to chat for a while of life in Malaya before announcing he must be off, and squashing a battered hat back onto his head, he stood up. 'It's time I was getting back to the mine. Ah How will make up your beds, and there are a few basics in the fridge for supper and your breakfast. Your milk is the powdered variety. No milk man here. It has to be made up each day with boiled and filtered water, and incidentally, all food must be kept in airtight containers and in the cupboard standing in tins of oil to deter the cockroaches and ants. Oh, and don't leave a sugar bowl lying around after you've used it, or it will be black with them!'

Kitty grimaced and he grinned. 'You'll soon get used to it. Ah How will show you the ropes. On Monday, I will pick you up at seven, Lawrence to take you around the mine and introduce you to the staff and workforce.' He turned to Kitty with a lopsided smile. 'I hope you will be happy here. You must come over for a meal. I'd introduce you to my wife, but she's in the UK with the children and won't be out until the summer holidays. I'm what is commonly known as a married bachelor. You will come across one or two of us here and at the club where families gravitate from outstation for a swim and a curry tiffin at weekends.'

'Club?' Kitty gave him an enquiring look.

'Sorry. I forgot to mention it. It's a few miles from the mine.' He turned to Lawrence. 'If you would like I'll take you there on Sunday. The road takes in the most archaic ferry you are ever likely to set eyes on, and I'll introduce you to Wong, the barman, the guardian of many a lonely man's drinking secrets.'

'What do you think, Kitty?' asked Lawrence.

'A swim sounds wonderful.'

'Done. I will pick you up at midday.'

Walking with him to the car, Henderson said. 'You'll be fine once you find your feet, Kitty,' looking at the young woman's slightly anxious face before him, and remembering his wife's disorientation on first arriving in the country. He jumped into his mini-moke. 'See you both on Sunday,' he said with a nod, and throwing it into gear, drove off in a cloud of dust.

'I can't get over how quickly night drops upon us,' observed Kitty. 'One minute, it's daylight and the next, we're standing in the dark. No twilight hours or the long sunsets of home,' she continued, as she began hanging up their clothes in the bedroom to a cacophony of cicadas and croaking bullfrogs that came with the blackness along with the bark of a feral dog and other bewildering night sounds. Lawrence agreed as he switched on the air-conditioner set low into the wall and which rattled into a steady roar.

'I don't know which is the worst, the noises of the night or the air-conditioner,' said Kitty as she finished unpacking. 'Either way, trying to get to sleep is going to be fun. And I hate the idea of these,' she announced, gazing at the two military-precision-made beds pushed together. She sat down on one. 'Gosh, it's firm,' peering underneath to discover a Dunlow pillow mattress on a slatted base. 'It's not like having a lovely sprung mattress to bounce up and down on, is it?' she giggled suggestively.

Lawrence, playfully pushed her back and they romped across the beds to collapse onto their backs, laughing and breathless. 'I guess sleeping apart, is something we're going to have to get used to,' Lawrence admitted, staring up at the fan, 'but we can always start off in mine.' He rolled over onto his side, grinning at her in devilment, 'and having had my wicked way with you, I shall kick you out into your own bed!'

'So what's stopping you?' teased Kitty slipping off her clothes. Lawrence's laughter faded as she came to lie beside him aroused by the line of his neck against his white open-necked shirt. She closed his eyes and brushed them with light kisses, and covering his face with them continued along his neck and shoulder. With a moan of pleasure, he drew her down and made love, the touch of his fingertips awakening her skin and senses to fire, and tears came from the wondrous sense of oneness and belonging. Lawrence on seeing them was perplexed. Had he hurt or upset her in some way? Shaking her head and wanting to melt into his body, held him tightly to her. 'I'm just so happy, that's all,' and together they drifted to sleep with the temperature dropping as they slept. They awoke in the night feeling chilled and crawling apart, slipped into their separate beds. Lawrence fell immediately back into a deep slumber but Kitty lay thinking of the apparition of her father dancing with the woman at the hotel. Had he loved her as she loved Lawrence? Or was it the simple sexual attraction of a man alone for too many nights? She would probably never know, she thought, turning to sleep to the steady roar of the air-conditioner.

Chapter Twenty-Five

KITTY SAT AT the poolside under a long purpose-built shaded area in a state of unhappiness thinking of the row the night before with Lawrence. She had been enjoying one of her favourite meals of Ah How's Nasi Goreng with Chinese vegetables and chicken when he dropped his bombshell. 'I've had a chat with our company doctor, Kitty.'

She was immediately alarmed. 'Why? Are you ill? Why haven't you told me, Lawrence?'

'I'm fine. It was about you, actually.'

'*Me!* What on earth for? I'm fit as a fiddle.'

He hesitated. This was not going to be easy. 'You remember our meal at the hotel in KL just before Verity joined us?'

'Yes. What about it?'

'You had a funny turn. Do you remember? I asked you if you were OK as you looked miles away.'

Oh fishhooks! The childhood exclamation at being caught out sprang from the recesses of her mind. She had hoped he had forgotten that.

'When I was a boy I had a friend whose mother suffered from Petit Mal. Do you know what that is, Kitty?'

'Of course I do. I typed up a case note on it when I worked in the hospital.'

'Well, I think you have it. And I would like you to see the doctor.'

Kitty was incredulous. Her eyes widened and her voice rose. '*What!* Don't be so ridiculous Lawrence. I do *not* have Petit Mal or anything else, for that matter and that includes a baby.'

'Don't let's get onto that, again.'

'No. You're right. I must never talk about anything as normal as having a baby. It's Vorboten! No. The best you can do is come up with the mad idea that I've got *Petit Mal*.' She glared at him.

'That's simply not true, Kitty. All I've ever said, is that we wait awhile and enjoy each other before we have a child. Look, we're getting off the subject.' He sought to pacify. 'Kitty, I'm really worried about you. Every now and then you go off into a trance. It is a classic symptom of it, unless, of course, you have some other explanation for your peculiar turns?'

She did not reply.

'Well? Do you?' he asked in exasperation.

'Yes, I do. But you wouldn't believe me, if I told you.'

'Try me.'

She sighed. 'All right, I will. Ever since I was a child, I've heard and seen things from the past. I can't explain it, it just happens and it can be anywhere. For instance, I saw my father's sister who died when she was a little girl, playing with some children in the garden at Nancarrow. And when we were on the moors that day, you asked what I was looking at. Well, it was a young woman that I later discovered had been killed at Roughtor in the eighteen hundreds and I also saw an old man by the fire in Jamaica Inn. Does that answer your question? Oh, and there's something else you might as well know. I sense when people are unhappy or in pain and when I touch them, they tell me they feel better. Some call it, the gift of healing.'

It was more bizarre than he could ever have imagined. 'And was this what happened when we were in the hotel in KL?'

'Yes, it is. That's why I was singing along to the music *'In The Mood'* which at first seemed to be coming from another room, and then, I saw the band on the dais and the dining room was full of people, including James, my father who was dancing very intimately with a woman who most certainly wasn't my mother!'

Lawrence exploded. 'My God, Kitty! You've got to stop this nonsense. People will think you're barking mad.'

'You see. I'm right. This is exactly what I feared, and why I've never talked about it. I knew it would be a waste of time. You will never understand.'

'Unlike Terry, no doubt. He, of course, would believe your every word.'

Momentarily, Kitty was taken aback and then her eyes blazed and angrily she pushed her chair back and stood up. 'Why are you bringing Terry into this? But since you have, I know one thing. He has more perception and patience in his little finger than you'll ever have,' she hissed across the table.

'Now, we're getting to it.' Lawrence's voice was heavy

with sarcasm.

'What is *that* supposed to mean?'

'I think you know.'

'I have no idea what you're talking about. Look, this is getting us nowhere.' She got up. 'I'm going to bed to read my book.'

Lawrence leaped from his chair and caught her wrist 'You will not go to bed until we've talked this thing through.'

'Don't speak to me like a child and let go of me, Lawrence.' She struggled from his grip. 'You're hurting me, please let me go.'

His eyes were cold. 'You still love him, don't you?'

'No. Of course, I don't. How could you think that? You know how much I love you.'

Lawrence dropped her hand and backed away from her wounded look. What on earth had come over him to behave in this way? He was making a pig's ear of it. Petit Mal was a delicate subject, he should have been more tactful, led into it gently.

'I can't believe you're harbouring the crazy notion that I still love Terry.' She moved to put her arms around him, but some stubborn and deeply feared suspicion childishly resisted her embrace. She slipped her arms away from him and flung herself down into the rattan chair. 'You know it's not true. For heaven's sake Lawrence, grow up. And don't be so stupid.'

His voice was like ice. 'I'm not so stupid as to believe in ghosts, and until I see one for myself I never will.'

'In that case, there's no more to be said about it. And I'm not going to see any doctor, and that's final.'

It had ended on a total impasse, retiring to their separate beds in silence with a forced 'Goodnight' between them, and the atmosphere was cool at breakfast the following morning. Somehow, Kitty thought, we have to get around this. But how could she deny the gift she had been born with? The inexplicable materialization of the past and her healing touch? It would be to deny her very self. But equally, she could not bear this estrangement. To please him she would go to the doctor. It would heal the rift between them, fruitless though she knew the outcome would prove to be.

She rose and walked to the wooden clubhouse for another glass of freshly squeezed orange juice, a delight she had discovered in every clubhouse and restaurant. It was empty apart from Wong behind the bar. A large picture of the Queen hung on the wall above scattered chintzy-covered rattan chairs and tables.

'Another glass of orange juice, please, Wong' she said, as she sat herself on the bar stool.

'Your friend, not arrived yet, mem?' he asked, as he began cutting and squeezing the oranges.

'She should be here soon. I came early, today,' she replied, and wondered as she watched Wong, if her father had met the woman in this very same club, for her mother had said he did exploration work in Northern Perak. A place like this would have been buzzing with life, a magnet for married bachelors, and crowded with mine workers, planters and their wives and children. It would be easy for a man to strike up a liaison in that sort of environment. Could she, in all honesty, condemn him? The responsibility lay with the unrealistic conditions of employment. Three years was a long time for a man to be apart from his wife. How fortunate she was that the terms of contract had changed. What chance they had of happiness was beset with obstacles not of her father's making, and then, as if that wasn't enough, came the war. She was saddened for her mother as she wandered back to the poolside, and as she waited for Maggie she realised all that mattered was her love for Lawrence. She had the sudden memory of herself high in the branches of the oak tree, and, as then, recognized that quarrelling was pointless. But once the doctor had confirmed that she did not suffer from Petit Mal, how could she ever convince him that what she saw were not delusions of the mind? She would confide in Maggie. Maggie of the lilting Irish voice and a sense of humour that always had her laughing. She had fallen upon her with the thirst of man in the desert, for she had found the women from neighbouring tin mines had not sought to invite her to join them as she sat alone by the pool, and fearing a rebuff, she had kept her distance. On meeting her, Maggie had expressed with ironic amusement that having married a Chinese dredge-master she was persona non grata on both sides of the cultural divide.

'How did you meet your husband?' Kitty had asked.

'Cheng Moi was sent to Ireland for his education. I met him at a Technical College where he was studying engineering. It wasn't long before we realised we wanted to spend the rest of our lives together but for Cheng Moi to have fallen in love out of his race was a huge stumbling block. Like should marry like. It's the same in the Malay and Indian communities here. We had no choice but to tie the knot over there.' There was a sparkle of defiance in her eye. 'You can imagine the furore it caused when he returned to his home with a wife on tow. I was treated, more or less, as an unpaid servant, as is the way of Chinese matriarchs. Mother rules the roost. Things became easier when Cheng Moi found work on the mine and we moved to our own house on the camp, and having children broke down the final barriers. Times are changing too, and with the education of so many of the indigenous races overseas, the easy going ways of the western world are beginning to influence them, and perhaps not always for the better,' she observed shrewdly.

What she would have done without Maggie's friendship, Kitty could not imagine. Time was broken into segments by Lawrence's return for breakfast and lunch, but with no other company apart from the amah whose English was basic, and whose time was taken with cooking and housework, the days were long. She was left with little to do but read and write letters home. There was the sound of voices, and Kitty looked around to see a young woman who waved and whooped a greeting of surprise as she walked towards the pool with her two small children. 'What on earth are you doing here, Madeline?'

'Before you go any further,' Kitty interrupted. 'I'm afraid you've mistaken me for someone else.'

'Oh my giddy aunt! You're right!' She stared at Kitty. 'Yes, I can see the difference, now, but you are awfully like her. It's the hair,' she continued, studying Kitty. 'It's the same colour as hers.'

'I think I must have a double,' smiled Kitty. 'You are the second person since I've arrived in Malaya to have made the same mistake. I'm Kitty Scott-Thomas from Tronoh Mines,' she said, holding out her hand, as she caught sight of Maggie coming over to join her with her brood of children. They ran up with the enviable good looks of all Eurasians, and shrieking with the exuberance of youth, jumped in the pool and swam up and down underwater with the agility of porpoises.

'Hi! Jean,' said Maggie as she dropped a huge bag of towels beside her and sat down. 'I see you've met Kitty.'

'Yes, and I've just made the mistake of thinking she was Madeline. I'm feeling such an idiot.'

'I barely remember her as I'd only just arrived in Malaya, but I do remember her strawberry-blonde hair. It was so striking,' said Maggie.

Listening to their exchange, Kitty could not helping asking. 'I'm intrigued. Who, exactly, is this double of mine?'

'She used to live outstation, like I did,' Jean explained. 'Her father was the manager of a rubber plantation, and she came to the club with her parents which is where I met her. We became best friends and used to stop over at each others houses. I think she was rather lonely without any brothers or sisters. That were official! Her father had an eye for the Indian ladies,' she chuckled, rolling her eyes and thrusting her head from side to side in an Indian head dance.

It was impossible not to laugh. 'Oh Jean! Honestly. You're incorrigible,' said Maggie.

'I know, I know,' said Jean laughing with them, 'but it was well known he had a roving eye even before Madeline's mother divorced him. After they left Malaya I used to stay with Madeline on my exeats from boarding school. We still keep in touch although I don't write as often as I should. You know how it is, life goes on it's merry way, husbands, kids. You are so like her,' she said, staring again at Kitty in between blowing up wings and pushing them onto her children's arms before leading them to the pool's edge for a swim.

Maggie grinned at Kitty as they watched her slip into the pool. 'She's great fun but don't ever trust her with a secret.'

For one wild moment as Jean was talking, Kitty had the irrational idea that this Madeline was her twin who hadn't died at all, and was another of her mother's secrets. Oh, for goodness sake, you're beginning to lose your marbles, she said to herself.

'Isn't it odd,' she mused to Maggie as they watched the children diving off the swimming board with the abandon and fearlessness of the young, 'the other person who mistook me for Madeline lives in KL.'

'Was she called Verity Nicholls, by any chance?'

'Yes, she was, as a matter of fact. Why, do you know her?'

'Only by name. She was a friend of Madeline's mother during the war.'

At her words, Kitty felt a shiver of presentiment run through her. It had been no coincidence meeting Verity in the hotel. It was predestined. 'Actually, I've been thinking of having her to stay. We met at our hotel on our first day in KL and Lawrence and I liked her very much. I think I'll give her a ring and invite her up.'

Chapter Twenty-Six

'I HOPE YOU slept well,' said Kitty over breakfast the following morning after Verity had arrived.

'Like a top, my dear, once I switched off the air-conditioner. I found I could never get on with them. I'm too accustomed to the slow rhythm of a fan turning. It never fails to lull me off.'

'I tried the fan, but the room was still so hot, I couldn't sleep,' said Kitty. 'If only the temperature dropped at night like it does in the desert.'

'I'm fortunate that the humidity doesn't affect me as much as it does Kitty,' said Lawrence, as he stood up from the table and kissed her before returning to work. 'It's lovely to see you again, Verity. It will do Kitty a power of good to have some company. I know it can get very lonely for her,' he said, as he walked out of the veranda door and jumping straight into his seat of the roofless mini-moke, with a wave of the hand, he was gone.

Verity was thoughtful. On arrival, she had the distinct impression that all was not well between them. There was an edginess to Lawrence that was not previously there. 'He's a good looking man, your husband,' murmured Verity as she watched him drive away.

Kitty's reply was cryptic. 'Handsome is, as handsome does. Sorry. I didn't mean to sound churlish. Just a lover's tiff. We're getting over it,' she smiled as she passed the marmalade.

Her engaging honesty was refreshing. 'It seems a lifetime ago that Maurice and I fell in love, but I can still remember those ecstatic highs and desperate lows if we were offside with one another. We were soul mates and never lost that spark between us and as the years rolled by, our love settled down to a wonderful warmth and companionship. I feel I was a very lucky woman to have known Maurice,' said Verity as she buttered another piece of toast and chatted across the table. They discovered they had much in common and the disparity in age did not preclude confidences, and, in a curious way, was to bond them to an enduring friendship.

It was as if they had known one another all their lives.

'I thought we might go to the club later this morning, have a swim and a spot of lunch if that's OK with you, and there's a couple of friends I'd like you to meet, Maggie and Jean. When I met them, I found it a very strange coincidence, that they, like you, thought I had a strong resemblance to a girl they once knew, called Madeline.'

Verity's cup stopped on the way to her mouth.

'By your expression, I take it, she must be the same person you mistook me for in KL?'

'Yes, she is. Well, I never. I do remember Madeline talking about a friend called Jean, when she came to stay with me.'

Kitty felt a dart of expectation. 'If you've finished, perhaps you'd like to sit on the veranda,' Kitty suggested.

'How pretty it looks with your pots of bougainvillea,' said Verity as they moved outside and stretched out on the lounging chairs.

'Yes, they do make a lovely splash of colour,' said Kitty.

'I used to grow orchids in my garden in KL.'

'I'm afraid I leave all my gardening to the kabun. I don't have green fingers. The nearest I've come to having orchids is when Lawrence brings me home an arranged basket of them. I was thrilled, they are so beautiful. You just don't see them at home like that. Even a small spray costs a fortune. So, who is this Madeline who apparently looks so much like me?' she asked, continuing the thread of conversation from breakfast.

'She's the daughter of a friend of mine, Faith. We met on board ship in November nineteen forty one. She was going home to see her parents and introduce them to their granddaughter, Madeline. I was on my way home to see my mother who had not been very well and suddenly became worse and died within a short time of my arrival.'

'I'm so sorry. That must have been very upsetting for you.'

'Yes, it was. After the funeral, I wrote and asked Faith if she would like to come and visit me in Penzance. I liked her. She was intelligent and amusing and on board ship, we had fallen into an easygoing friendship. Whilst staying with me, we said it must have been providence for us both to have left for England when we did, as within a month of us leaving, the Japs had invaded Malaya. For those left there, it was a scramble for any troop ship which was arriving with reinforcements for the defence of Malaya. There was one family I knew well. The husband was a plant pathologist at the rubber research institute in KL, who only just succeeded in getting his wife and children to Singapore by car. He watched them embark on the Empress of Japan with bombs dropping all around them. Deidre, his wife, said the journey was an absolute nightmare. The ship was terribly overcrowded with people sleeping on mattresses on the deck and for those below it was stifling with the portholes closed as part of the blackout. It took them seven weeks to get home. Other friends of mine managed to get a boat to India. We counted our blessings to be in Penzance and with Faith's parents living in London, we decided it was safer for her and Madeline to remain with me during the war, however long that turned out to be.'

'Did you go back together to Malaya after the war?'

Verity suddenly looked discomfited. 'No, as a matter of fact we didn't. It's rather a long story.'

'I'm sorry. I didn't mean to pry.'

'No need to apologise, my dear. You see, I was put into a rather difficult situation with her and promised I would keep her confidence but it did put our friendship under a strain.'

'I see,' replied Kitty. 'These things do happen.'

'Yes, they do. Unlike Faith, I've been so fortunate. I've always had the support of a good husband, and after the war, we had some wonderful years together before he died. It took me a long time to get over losing him, but in the end, you just have to pick up the pieces and get on with life.

'That's what mum said after my father died in the war, somewhere here in Malaya just before my second birthday.'

Verity looked at her in surprise. 'So, your father was in Malaya, too?'

'Yes, he was a mining engineer. Mum never lived here. The war came before she was able to join him.'

'And here you are following in your father's footsteps. How curious life is.'

'Yes, it is. Mum married again and had my sister Grace and Thomas, my brother.'

'That must have been a great comfort for her.'

'It was and I couldn't have wished for a better step-father.' The warmth in her voice was plain. 'He's a dear. In many ways I feel closer to him than my mother. Our temperaments clash. I was far too adventurous as a child and landed myself in all sorts of scrapes. Looking back on it, I must have been quite a handful.'

'I would call it having spirit.'

'I'm not sure my mother would see it that way,' replied Kitty with a wry grin as Ah How appeared silently at their sides. 'Coffee mem?'

'Yes, that would be lovely, Ah How. Oh, and some biscuits. You know, I still can't get over being waited on,' said Kitty as she withdrew.

'You will. The humidity can be very enervating.'

'Yes, I'm missing the bracing seawinds of home.'

'You must do. Maurice and I always found the sea air invigorating as we walked across the Penzance prom. It worked up an appetite,' she said as Ah How reappeared with a tray and setting it down, poured each of them a cup.

'After our coffee, would you like to have a quick wander around the camp before we go to the club? There's not a lot to see but the gardens are looking lovely with the red and yellows of canna and hibiscus and we have two magnificent flame of the forest trees.'

'I'd be delighted to,' replied Verity.

'Everything here seems to grow with such an abundance of foliage and intensity of colour,' Kitty said, as they walked along and she pointed out the empty houses on either side of the road. 'Most of the junior ex-patriots have gone, and it's rather spooky at night with not a light in any of the windows. There are Asian staff on the other side of the camp but they keep very much to themselves. We have one or two married bachelors who have, shall we say, lady friends, until their wives and families come out for the holidays. I was green as sticks when I arrived and it was quite an eye-opener.'

'It is quite common here, I'm afraid when men are outstation and alone,' said Verity. Kitty thought of James.

'Still, I can't help feeling a little awkward when the wives come out. I feel part of the conspiracy.'

'I wouldn't worry about it too much. In all probability the wives know and have an 'understanding' with their husbands, which they're hardly likely to admit to a lovely young newly-wed,' she said, smiling at Kitty's innocence.

'You're probably right. Talking of families, the manager has told me that we shall soon be having a replacement electrician and his wife and young family to live next door. It will be lovely to have the company of another woman and to hear children's voices around the garden.'

'I can imagine it will,' Verity replied, sympathetic to Kitty's isolation. Someone who was as vital as she was, needed the contact of young people and she was glad that she had made friends at the club and looked forward to meeting them.

'I said we'd meet Maggie and Jean at about eleven,' said Kitty as they completed the circuit of the camp. 'We'll just pick up our swimsuits and be off. It takes about twenty minutes to get there in the car and we have to cross the river by ferry, if one could call it that. It's not much more than a raft and is hauled over by hand with a chain. When Lawrence first taught me to drive on the camp, I was very nervous of driving onto it.' Kitty suddenly chortled. 'There's a well known character around here, very dapper and well spoken, who is not adverse to rather a lot of drink, and on one famously recorded evening, drove his beautiful new car, his pride and joy, down to the ferry, and, merry as a fish, didn't happen to notice that the ferry was on the other side, and quietly trundled into the river! He managed to scramble out and up the bank and as his car started to gently drift downstream, he suddenly called out he had forgotten something, and waded back in again, to emerge from the car holding up his cigars and lighter! The Chinese laugh and talk about it, even now. It's already gone down into folklore of 'mad dogs and Englishmen.'

'I can imagine it has,' laughed Verity.

'I did enjoy your friends' company today, Kitty,' said Verity as they sat down with Lawrence for the evening meal. 'How strange that Jean and I both knew Faith and Madeline, and yet, we ourselves, never met.'

'Yes, it is,' replied Kitty as Ah How placed a pasty before Verity.

'What a treat! A Cornish pasty,' she exclaimed. 'I do so miss them and that wonderful savoury smell as they come out of the oven.'

'I thought I'd make it a Cornish evening with Russian Cream for dessert. I've always thought it an odd name for a Cornish dish but it's ideal after a pasty. It's so light it just slips down. I hope you'll like it.'

'You've no doubt heard the saying, Verity, wherever you go in the world at the bottom of a hole you will find a Cornish man,' said Lawrence. 'What they don't tell you is, the pasty goes with them!'

Kitty laughed. 'Yes, it was the first thing I taught Ah How to make and she picked up the knack of crimping very quickly. In fact, she's better at making them than I am.'

'Well, I for one, am pleased it has travelled to Malaya with you, Kitty,' she smiled, as she tucked into it. 'How do you find working on the mine with Jock Henderson, Lawrence?'

Lawrence looked up in surprise. 'You know him?'

'Maurice and I met him one evening at the Spotted Dog. It's a popular watering hole for those that come in from outstation. He was quite a character, Jock. The last time I saw him he was knocking back stengahs and regaling the men with rather risque stories. That was many years ago before he moved to this district and his wife joined him. I should imagine, by now, he has been well and truly tamed,' she laughed.

'Almost,' he acknowledged. 'He still spins the most amazing yarns but is careful to tone down his language in front of the ladies.'

'His anecdotes are hilarious. He's a real tonic,' said Kitty.

'Kitty gathers him up with the other bachelors from time to time for a meal. She thinks they need the civilising company of women to prevent them going bush.'

'One or two already have from what I can gather,' said Kitty with an expressive raise of her eyebrows.

'Well, ladies,' said Lawrence, as he finished his cup of coffee, 'If you'll forgive me, I shall disappear to my desk upstairs, I've paperwork to catch up on.'

'I've something to show you,' Kitty said, as they relaxed with their coffee. She jumped up and went to the sideboard and bringing out a photo album began flicking through it. 'I thought you might like to meet the family. This is mum and dad in our garden, and that one is Grace sitting in the window studying for her university exams. Thomas wants to go to university as well and I'm sure he will have no trouble at all. He's awfully bright. His head's in a book most of the time. Unlike me. I was a tomboy and much preferred climbing trees.' They browsed together over the photos, with Kitty pointing out beaches familiar to them both. 'I nearly drowned at Gwithian. Not doing as I was told, again, and all over a boy.' Her smile was impish. 'That's him there, sitting on the beach with me. He was called Terry and lived next door. We were inseparable.'

As she turned the pages, a photo slipped out from the back of the album and dropped to the floor. Verity picked it up. She peered at it closely, frowned, and looked again. 'Who is this?'

'It's James, my father.'

'Your *father?!*'

'Verity. Whatever is it?' said Kitty, startled at her look of shock.

'I can hardly believe this,' Verity murmured to herself.

'Hardly believe what?'

She hesitated. 'That your father was James. Maurice knew him during the war.'

'He *knew* my father! He actually knew my father?' Kitty was stunned.

'Maurice spoke of him often, and I have a photograph . . .'

Kitty jumped up before she could finish. 'Forgive me, Verity, but I must call Lawrence down to hear this.' Her voice had the nervously rising ring of something amiss as she called up the stairs. Lawrence shot out of his seat and came bounding down.

'Whatever is it, Kitty?'

'I've just discovered something from Verity. Maurice knew my father. Apparently they met during the war . . . it's incredible.' Overcome with emotion, she sat down, abruptly.

Lawrence took over. 'Did Maurice know him well?'

'Yes, they were together throughout the war. Kitty was showing me photographs of her family, and there was James. I recognized him immediately from the photo I have of them together. They were in the same unit and worked closely together in intelligence deep in the interior behind enemy lines. Maurice was fluent in Chinese and Malay and with James's knowledge from exploration work in the jungle, they were responsible for setting up a network of men for guerrilla warfare against the Japs.'

'Good God!' exclaimed Lawrence. 'I think we could all do with a drink,' he announced, seeing Kitty's dazed face. He went to the sideboard and took out bottles of Cinzano and gin, and then walked quickly to the kitchen and returned with small bottles of tonic and lemonade from the fridge. 'Drink Verity? Kitty?' he asked as he unscrewed the bottle tops.

'Cinzano and lemonade would be lovely,' said Verity.

'And I'll have one, too,' said Kitty, finding her voice.

Lawrence handed them both a drink and came and sat close to Kitty. He placed a reassuring arm around her as she took several long sips. 'Did Maurice say what my father was like?'

'He used to say he was exceptionally bright, full of determination and with a dry sense of humour that relieved some tense situations. He also said, he was very brave. Maurice didn't speak a great deal of his time during the war as the work was classified and the tactics later used against the communists during the emergency. He did say that communication was dangerous and difficult, and living conditions were primitive. There was always a shortage of food, but the worst of it, Maurice said, were the insects that drove them mad. The midges apparently, were far worse than the mosquitoes. In the mornings, their faces were so swollen with bites, they could barely open their eyes. On top of that, they both had bouts of malaria which left them weak. Your father, I'm sorry to say Kitty, was killed during a raid on a Japanese encampment and his courageous action saved many of his comrades lives.' She did not go into detail for it had made her weep. 'Maurice always said, he should have received a medal for his bravery.'

Lawrence pulled Kitty close and kissed her. 'Are you OK sweetheart? Hearing this can't be easy for you.'

'No, but at least I now know what happened to him,' she replied, thinking to herself that she also knew more about her father than any daughter should. A question was beginning to coalesce. If Maurice knew James, in all probability, he would have known of the woman who was dancing with him, and there was something else Verity had said that echoed tantalisingly at the back of her mind, and with a bolt of certainty, the truth stared her in the face. She gulped down the last of her drink.

'What did your friend Faith look like?'

The unexpectedness of the question took Verity by surprise. '*Faith?* . . . Well . . . she was very beautiful and had a mass of reddish brown hair. Why do you ask?'

'I believe that Faith and my father knew each other very well. In fact, they were in love, weren't they?'

'What on earth are you saying, Kitty?' Lawrence asked, as Verity's face paled and she nervously fingered the strand of pearls at her neck. She stared at Kitty in disbelief. 'How could you possibly know that,' she half-whispered.

'There's something I should tell you, Verity. You see, I have these psychic experiences. Have done since I was a child. I see things from the past.'

Lawrence shifted in his seat with irritation and dropping his arm away from her, his voice was tense, 'Please, Kitty. Don't start banging that drum again.'

'Unfortunately, Lawrence doesn't believe in them and we had a row about it.'

So that was the reason for the change in him, thought Verity.

'You will remember when we met that evening in the hotel, I appeared to have a funny turn because of the heat?' she continued.

'Yes, I remember it, well.'

'The reason I was faint was that I had just had one of my visions. I saw James dancing with a woman in the hotel dining room. There were tables and chairs set around a parquet floor, and it had a bar in the corner and a band that played Glen Miller music. I'm right, aren't I?'

'Yes, you are,' Verity replied, the amazement plain upon her face.

'They danced very close to my chair, and I now know from your description of her, that it was your friend, Faith. She was wearing a silver slipper-satin dress, ruched in at the waist.'

Verity gaped at Kitty.

It was Lawrence that broke the pregnant silence. 'For goodness sake, Kitty. This has got to stop! It's doing you no good at all,' he snapped, and appealed to Verity. 'Please tell her I'm right. I'm so worried about her.'

Assembling her shaken thoughts, Verity rose to Kitty's defence. 'What Kitty has told us, is absolutely true, and exactly as it happened, Lawrence,' she said quietly. 'Faith told me herself, that she and James spent their last night together in the hotel before she sailed home from Singapore. She showed me a photo of them together, and the dress is exactly as Kitty described it. There's no possible way Kitty could have known this, so how do you explain it?'

Lawrence's shrug was dismissive. 'I have no idea.'

'No, and neither do I, having never experienced such things for myself, but I know these time-slips, call them what you will, do happen. And the reason I do, is that Maurice talked of premonitions and witnessed many things during the war that could not be explained rationally. A more down-to-earth person, you couldn't wish to meet, but he came to believe in them. I believe too, that James had a premonition, for he wrote a letter to Faith which he made Maurice promise to give to her if anything should happen to him.'

Hope rose in Kitty. Perhaps now, with Verity's confirmation, Lawrence would accept her paranormal abilities over which she had no control. Verity was not a woman to dissemble or speak lightly of such matters.

'There's something else that I have to tell you,' said Verity. 'It's about Faith's daughter, Madeline.'

'I think I already know. Madeline is my half-sister, isn't she?'

With the words taken out of her mouth, Verity looked at her in astonishment.

'At the back of my mind, I remembered you saying that Faith's little girl had a cloud of golden red hair and with you and Jean both mistaking me for Madeline, and now, your description of Faith, it was obvious.'

Lawrence looked dumbfounded. 'Is this true, Verity?' he asked in disbelief.

'Yes, it is. Faith confessed of her affair with James shortly after she came to stay with me in Penzance. I was shocked, and told her she was playing with fire. What she didn't tell me, was that Madeline was not her husband's child. I discovered that when Maurice returned home to recuperate after the war. He had given her James's letter, and she became utterly distraught and in a flood of tears, admitted it to us both. Maurice who was a stickler for proprieties was astounded that Roger, her husband, hadn't been told. Faith replied, she wasn't going to tell him, either, as he was a philandering bastard. A great deal of anger and bitterness spilt out of her that day, and there was no doubting that Roger had treated her badly. Whilst having sympathy, I ventured that Roger did have a right to know that Madeline was not his, and eventually, she would also have to tell Madeline. We had quite an argument about it, but when she had calmed down, she agreed, but for the time being, begged me to keep her confidence. With James gone, she was at a complete loss as to what to do, but eventually decided to return to Malaya. She hoped with the aftermath of a pretty bloody war, that Roger had come to his senses and perhaps they should try and make a fresh start. Personally, I wasn't optimistic. She was still very much in love with James.'

Verity paused, sipping her drink, her countenance pensive with thoughts of Maurice's weakened state on his return to Cornwall. 'We stayed on in Penzance for Maurice to recover his strength and Faith went on up to London to say goodbye to her parents before returning to Malaya. On our return there, we kept in touch by phone and letter, and it was obvious, even then, the marriage was not working, and then one day, she rang to say she was leaving Roger and was returning to live with her parents until she could find a place of her own. She stayed with me for a few days in KL before sailing home and told me that Roger was up to his old ways. They had a monumental row about it, and she had flung the fact that Madeline wasn't his daughter in his face. She said, revenge was sweet seeing the dawning realisation that his wife had had an affair and he was devastated to discover that Madeline was not his.'

Kitty, listening intently was thinking of her half-sister. 'Does Madeline know that James is her father?'

'Yes, she does. And that was strange in its telling, as well. She came to stay with me in Penzance, one year when she was in her early teens, and brought up the subject of Roger, herself. Strong intuitions seem to run in both of you. We were walking along the seafront and chatting about this and that, when she suddenly said, she'd often wondered why she was so different from her father in colouring and looks, and that she had never felt part of her father's family. 'It's as if I don't belong with them,' were her words. I hardly knew what to say, and was angry with Faith for not keeping her promise in telling her the truth. I had no choice but to say she must have a talk with her mother on her return home which, of course, she did. After that, Madeline's contact with Roger dwindled away. She had been seeing him on his leaves home, for he was still very fond of her which is understandable, after all, he had thought she was his for those first few years, but even he could see with Madeline's striking looks, that she never had been and never could be his daughter. Faith said it cut him to pieces and it was ironic, that in the end he had become the loser. What surprises me, is that neither Faith nor Madeline have ever mentioned you to me, Kitty, which makes me pretty certain they have no idea you exist.

Perhaps with the war upon them, James felt unable to write and tell Faith that his wife was expecting his baby for it would only complicate an already complicated situation. We shall never know.'

Kitty, who had been sitting away from Lawrence as glacial as a statue, stirred in the chair. 'It gives me a very odd feeling knowing that my half-sister was growing up only a few miles from me. What was she like?'

'She was delightful, very lively and inquisitive, and like you, Kitty, she loved the sea which of course was right on her doorstep. She must have been about three when there was a terrific storm and the waves came crashing over the prom. We were terrified that it would come washing into the house but she ran upstairs to watch laughing and clapping her hands with excitement at the waves. She was quite self-contained in many ways, perhaps because she spent so much time with just the two of us and we were pleased when she started school. She needed friends of her own age and she settled in and was a quick learner. She was just turning six when she returned to Malaya, and eight when Faith divorced Roger. Within a couple of years, she was remarried to a policeman. Madeline always said to me, she loved and respected her step-father, Edward a lot. On leaving school, she took up nursing and is now working in the Great Ormond Street Hospital.'

Lawrence rose from his chair. 'Well, I don't know about you, but after hearing all I have tonight, I think I could do with another drink. Anyone for a top-up?' Replenishing their drinks, he admitted to Verity. 'I have to confess, I still find the idea of Kitty seeing ghosts from the past hard to accept, but I have been at fault too for not trying to be more sympathetic and her dreamlike states are clearly not Petit Mal. Two women singing from the same song sheet is too much for any one man. I graciously concede defeat,' he said with a dry smile.

Kitty thawing at his words wound her arms around him. 'I've hated the upset between us, Lawrence, and it means such a lot to hear you say that. I appreciate it hasn't been easy for you, either. Not everyone is into ghosts!' she half-chuckled with an embarrassed wince. 'And it's all thanks to you, Verity,' her face suddenly bright with happiness. It was an evening Lawrence and Kitty would long remember, for each had discovered unpalatable truths, but for Kitty, a glimmer of hope was beginning to burn brightly.

Chapter Twenty-Seven

WITH THE ARRIVAL of the electrician Robert, and his wife Wendy and their two young boys, the mining camp became alive with shouts and laughter. A large inflatable pool had been set up in the garden in which they all sat to cool off, and watching the children splashing around, Kitty yearned for a child of her own. It was the one thing that marred her happiness with Lawrence, but she could not help but notice his disinterest in Robert's children and those of her friends. The children, in turn, did not appear to warm to him and eyed him warily. She told herself, this would change with a child of their own, and she must have patience. As he had said, they had all the time in the world for children.

Slowly, Kitty began to settle into the languorous rhythm of life in the tropics for mems. Early breakfast with Lawrence was usually followed by Wendy or herself wandering across the open gardens to each others homes for coffee, after which they occasionally took a trip to the club and met up with Maggie and Jean for a swim and lunch, and returned to rest in their air-conditioned bedrooms. Robert taught them to play bridge. It was challenging but once having mastered the Acol system of bidding and the rules for leads of play, she and Lawrence became proficient partners. The quickly falling dark of the evenings were pleasantly passed playing a rubber of bridge over a drink, and Kitty had accepted Robert's offer of a cigarette, at which, Lawrence had frowned, as they later sat chatting about the game before walking home across the garden. She coughed a little, remembering her first cigarette with Sandra in the cinema, and giggling together at their daring, as Robert related the story of a man, so incensed at his wife inadvertently trumping his trick, he left the room, fetched his gun and shot her! 'People do get very heated over mistakes at bridge but you two love birds must never let it get to that stage. It's easily done. Wendy and I have had a few choice words across the table from time to time. She just won't accept that I'm always right!' He grinned back at his wife's sardonic look.

Gradually, there gathered around Kitty a small circle of friends. Maggie would take her into the town of Ipoh, where they meandered in and out of the open-fronted shops and the market. Maggie taught her to barter and haggle, and was amused that the price wound up exactly where the vendor and purchaser intended. It was a game each side expected to be played out, and Kitty herself, came to relish the good humoured sparring as each purchase became a bargain to be won. Lunches with Maggie were a gastronomic delight of Chinese dishes; steamed wontons that melted in the mouth, pork, prawns, chicken, soups, rice and noodle dishes with exotic oriental flavours, black bean, sweet and sour, lemon grass, chilli, and garlic. 'Quite a change from pasties, pies and roasts!' she said to Maggie, who ordered the dishes in fluent Chinese amidst the energetic nasal cadence of other Chinese diners. It was an assault on all her senses, and so far removed from life at home, she told Maggie, 'Sometimes, I can hardly believe I'm here.' On other days, Kitty took the long and lonely road to visit Gill, the wife of Bryan, a rubber planter, whom they had met at a game of duplicate bridge. The denseness of the rubber trees, row upon row, threw dark sinister shadows over the road, and Kitty was always glad to be out again and up into the sunshine where Gill's house stood high on a hill. Kitty envied its position, for the house caught the slightest breath of air, and was large and open on all sides with patio doors leading out to their swimming pool. She and Gill would spend hours, slipping in and out of the water, and lazing in the shade, chatting about their families at home in England, and of Gill's children who had recently started boarding school. She said how quiet the house now was, and how much she missed them. It was the downside to living in the sticks. Lunch was served by her Malay amah who appeared with delicious curries of chicken and beef with the most amazing selection of side dishes; peanuts, bananas, cucumber, tomatoes, ikan bilis, coconut, chutneys and pineapple. To cool their palates from the hot curry came a pudding of Gula Malacca; a mould of sago with a jug of sweet toffee tasting syrup made from sugar cane slowly dissolved over the fire and strained through a muslin, and with it, a jug of cool coconut milk. Kitty had laughed and said, she could eat it every day, and Gill told her the clubs always served it with curry tiffin on Sundays. She could stuff herself silly!

Christmas came and was spent with Robert and Wendy who invited them for Christmas lunch and the women had played games with the children as the men sipped Tiger beers and chatted on the veranda. It had seemed very strange celebrating Christmas with only a branch of a tree to decorate, and with the finishing touches of tinsel completed, it looked odd and out of place in their sun-flooded living room. Kitty thought of the wonderfully scented pine trees that would now be standing outside of the grocers at home, and sitting down in the chair, her thoughts drifted back to the Christmases of her childhood. The memories stood out like beacons of light. The picking of holly from the woods with Jack, to decorate the mirror over the fireplace and the top of the 'mountain' in the freezing cold of the front room. Somehow, they never seemed to feel it with the excitement of Christmas upon them as Jack struggled in with the tree in its bucket of earth and stood it in the window. The fresh scent of pine permeated the room and mingled with the musty smell of the old hatbox as it was opened and revealed the big paper bell lying on top. On opening it and folding it around to form its shape, Kitty passed it up to Jack standing on a chair in the centre of the room below the ceiling rose where he pinned it, to hang in honeycombed sections of bright red and yellow before moving his chair across to each corner and linking it to the homemade chains, until Chinese lanterns became the rage. The bell always heralded the nearness of Christmas for Kitty and she had sucked in her breath with expectation as she took out from the tissue paper the tree decorations – old favourites of glass birds with stranded silky tails, bells that tinkled prettily, and brittles of a house and Father Christmas and multi-hued balls. Octavia placed the gold star on the top of the tree as Kitty and Grace began to hang the decorations on the lower branches. Finally dressed and sparkling with silver tinsel, they stood back to admire their handiwork, as Thomas gazed up at it with his face alight and ran in sheer joy around the room. 'Santa Claus is coming with presents for Thomas,' he cried, his eyes shining with expectation.

'And what are we going to leave for Santa?' Grace asked him.

'A mince pie and a *very* small glass of sherry!'

'And why's that, Thomas?' asked Kitty.

'Because we don't want to make Santa tiddly!' he cried out, and they all laughed.

'Clever boy,' Jack beamed at him.

Octavia gazed on him with adoration, as if he were the baby

Jesus himself thought Kitty, as she took in the tree, the room decorations and the fireplace where, annually, Octavia painted the old tiles silver, and laid the grate, to await Christmas morning.

'I can't stand this cold any longer, Jack. Let's get back to the sitting room fire,' said Octavia, shivering.

'And, I'll make us all a steaming hot cup of cocoa. That'll soon warm us up,' replied Jack.

With the room and tree decorated, the season was well and truly upon them, and she and Grace were eager to go carol singing to raise money towards gifts for Octavia and Jack. With the white globe of the moon hanging like a bauble amidst the stars, they joined with Sandra and Terry, going from door to door around the neighbourhood. It had gone well, and elated, they decided to carry on the following evening, despite the gloom, for the moon was misted out with a soup of foggy drizzle. Their torches cast a halo of light as they sang in high spirits on the doorstep of 'ole mother Moore.' Kitty grinned to herself at the memory, for the season of good will vanished in a trice upon her seeing them, as she gave them the length of her tongue for begging from old people. Kitty could hardly blame her, as she remembered the years of playing knick-knock, and flying pieces of newspapers over her wall on windy days. One unforgettable afternoon, the poor woman had finally snapped. With the idea gleaned from a recent cowboy film of making Red Indian smoke signals, they filled the dustbin in Sandra's courtyard with newspapers and setting it alight, sent up glorious clouds of smoke signals as they lifted the lid up and down. It was a magnificent success and they had dispersed for tea reeking in smoke and buoyed with euphoria, until Kitty saw the alarming sight of ole mother Moore storming into the terrace, her face working with fury. Kitty sagged like a pricked balloon as the door knocker banged with the staccato of gunfire and on opening the door, Jack had barely time to greet her before in a very loud and agitated voice, she launched forth.

'I've come about your daughter, Kitty, Mr. Pengelly. She's a li'l pest. I've ad her knocking on m'door till I'm nearly crazy, an throwing bits of paper over m'wall makin m'garden an awful mess. Now she's ruined m'washing with smoke and smuts. You got stop her Mr. Pengelly. You give her a good talking to, but don't 'ee beat her mind – she ed'n very big!' Her voice rose an octave. 'Ted'n only she, mind, te's that maid Sandra as well. I've already ad words with her mother. They're like a couple of lunatics when they get together, leading each other on makin people's lives a misery.'

There was an abrupt silence. The family listening spellbound in the front room awaited his reaction to her voluble indignation. In sotto voce, he offered his apologies assuring her that he would not be beating Kitty, as he had never done such a thing in his life, but he would be making sure there would be no more trouble from his daughter. Intent on battle, the wind was taken out of her sails, and she stared at him with a comical look of perplexity. She harrumphed, 'Well, I'm glad to hear it, Mr. Pengelly,' and muttering under her breath, she turned away and the door was shut quietly behind her.

'She's an old bat! Nobody likes her, you know,' said Kitty defensively, as he came into the front room. 'And she never let us pick blackberries in her field and there's millions of them!'

'There are other fields you can pick in, Kitty. What on earth were you doing to make her washing dirty?'

Kitty opened her mouth to explain and was stopped. 'No, it doesn't matter. I don't want to hear the ins and outs of it. You must stop aggravating the woman. We all know she's cantankerous enough as it is,' replied Jack.

'Your father's right. Just keep away from her,' warned Octavia. 'I don't want that woman ranting and raving on my doorstep, ever again. What a thing!' And Kitty chuckled to herself remembering when the old woman died a few years later, Octavia's cryptic observation, 'There was no-one left for her to fight!'

In the town, the rare sight of chickens hung in the butchers windows, and the grocers shops smelt of exotic spices and dried fruit, and were stacked with boxes of dates and nuts. The greengrocers were bright with oranges and apples, and shop windows were decked in festive colours as she and Grace walked the streets with their carol-singing money and a little extra from Octavia, burning holes in their pockets. Kitty stood with Grace on the creaking floorboards of Woolworths gazing at the array of gifts and stocking fillers laid out on the broad display counters. Kitty picked up and pressed the button of a funny little dog who stood stiffly on a small stand. His legs collapsed, and laughing, her eyes were taken with a rainbow of satin ribbons and novelty hair slides, colourful wooden beads and brooches on cards. Should she buy a brooch? No, Octavia had a number of them in her jewellery box. Jack had been easy. White hankies, for he went through them, like nobody's business, mummy said. Perhaps she should get a pretty hanky for her as well, or maybe one of the square boxes of bath salts, or a small bottle of California Poppy or Devon Violets perfume? Which should she choose? She hummed and hawed and finally plumped for the California Poppy. Grace decided on the bath salts, and a comb in a case for Jack.

On her return home, she and Grace made demands for wrapping paper and scissors, and with secret whisperings disappeared upstairs and returned to the sitting room pleased as Punch with themselves, and shielding the gifts protectively from everyone's gaze.

'We're going to put them under the tree and you mustn't feel or try to guess what they are until Christmas Day,' said Grace.

'Don't worry, we shan't,' replied Jack. He and Octavia exchanged amused looks as the girls went next door.

Octavia had liked and used Grace's box of bath salts, but Kitty remembered wryly, had never worn the perfume, which she had to admit now, was pretty revolting, but couldn't she have done so for just one day? Why had it always been so difficult for her to please Octavia?

As was their tradition, Christmas Eve afternoon was spent at the pictures, leaving Octavia to last minute preparations, and, no doubt, thought Kitty, to the wrapping of their gifts for their pillow cases that night. They stopped at the sweet shop for their quarter ration of sweets, gazing at the array of jars of acid drops that sucked the roof out of your mouth, sherbert lemons, and humbugs and the bull's eye gob-stoppers, dolly mixtures and packets of sweet cigarettes that made you feel grown up when you puffed them, but what she really wanted to buy were the love hearts and give one to Terry, with a little saying on the sweet, 'I love you.' In the end, a family decision was reached for jelly babies, and taking their places in the long queue, they ate their first one as they waited in restless anticipation for the film and thought of Christmas Day ahead. Kitty glanced over at the Post Office where a man, a casualty of the war, stood in the dampness of the afternoon, holding a tray of matches and a tin. She felt sorry for him as he stood there on one leg with a crutch under his arm and the trousers leg of his missing limb folded up. He reminded her of another old man, her mother had talked about, who would sing Onward Christian Soldiers around Camborne and dance with his tin cup and white stick. 'Poor, dear souls,' her mother had said, 'War is so cruel, and reduces people.'

'Can we buy a box of matches, daddy?' Kitty begged.

'We've got plenty, Kitty,' Jack replied, puzzled at her request and then saw her look across the road. 'Yes, alright,' and giving her a few pence, she ran across and with her brightest smile wished him happy Christmas as she took the matches and on returning to the queue which had slowly begun to move forward, she concentrated on the billboard advertising the swashbuckling film of the week. *Scaramouch.*

That evening, after tea with Thomas staying up longer than his normal bedtime, they eagerly awaited their traditional drink to greet the season as Jack fetched the bottle of port and ginger cordial from the lead-lined bottle drawer in the 'mountain' and Octavia brought in a tray of cut glasses. With a flourish, Jack presented them with the golden wine, and sipping it from the beautiful glasses that were normally the preserve of adults, lent an added spice of excitement.

'Happy Christmas, everyone,' said Octavia, raising her glass to them all.

'Happy Christmas, mummy,' they replied, and sipping the fiery liquid, Kitty immediately began to cough.

'It always does this to me,' she spluttered.

'You don't have to drink it, Kitty. I can give you some orange juice instead,' said Octavia.

'No, it wouldn't be Christmas without ginger wine!' she said, with a joyous smile.

'And now I've got something for you all,' announced Octavia, with a mystifying look. 'It arrived by special parcel post a few days ago.'

'A parcel! We never have parcels,' exclaimed Kitty.

'What is it, mummy?' asked Grace, her amber eyes lighting with curiosity.

'Wait and see,' replied Octavia, smiling mysteriously, as Jack disappeared out of the sitting room.

There was the sound of careful footsteps coming down the stairs and Jack entered into the room with his arms wrapped around a box.

'Crumbs!' exclaimed Kitty, as Jack laid it down on the mat in front of the fire. 'It's huge.'

'It's from your Uncle Roy. Fetch me the scissors from the kitchen drawer, Kitty,' said Octavia as she knelt in front of the box.

In what seemed to be one movement, Kitty had gone and returned and watched as Octavia prised open the lid and scooped out a heap of packing straw. Thomas clutched the top of the opened box and peered in.

'Now, what have we here, Thomas,' she said, as she drew out a large flat box, smoothing away small pieces of straw to reveal a snowy Christmas scene. The girls faces lit up. 'Chocolates!' they shouted out in glee. Thomas's lower lip quivered with a look of alarm and he drew closer to Octavia.

'It's like those lucky dips at the fêtes, only they use sawdust,' Kitty said, as Octavia continued to pull out box after box hidden within the packing straw. Kunzel cakes appeared with chocolate sides and rich cream fillings. There were chocolate shell show-boats filled with sponge cake piped and decorated with butter cream, fondant fancies, after dinner mints and petit fours, and nestling at the bottom were two surprises.

'Crackers!' Kitty's face was one of sheer delight as Octavia passed the box to her. She peered down at the gold and red shiny paper through the cellophane window. 'I've always wanted these. Look, Grace. There's a pretty decoration on the top of each one. There's a hunting horn, and a golden bell and a silver star, holly and all sorts of things. Can we keep them, mummy?'

'Yes, of course, you can Kitty,' said Octavia, smiling. The children were so easily pleased and she felt a momentary stab of guilt at not buying them herself, but luxuries such as these were beyond her pocket. Gifts for the three children had taken months of careful budgeting and laying a good table was far more important than pretty pieces of paper to dress it. And, if she was honest with herself, she felt the true meaning of Christmas was lost in too many such fripperies and in an over-indulgence of food that one could ill afford, but did, nevertheless, as had her dear mother, stirring and baking for weeks in the old range for hordes of family and friends that called, knowing a feast of hospitality would be spread upon her table. 'I must seem like old Scrooge when I talk like this,' she admitted to Jack, 'but we had such abundance in comparison to so many, and now it's gone full circle, as everyone struggles with rationing and shortages. There never seems to be a happy medium.'

Kitty beamed and beamed. Oh, she could hardly wait for tomorrow to see the crackers on the table and to discover what was inside. 'This is going to be the best Christmas, *ever!*' she announced in a voice high with happiness, as Octavia pulled out the final deep sided box. Lifting off the lid revealed the most magnificent cake that Kitty had ever seen with elaborate iced lattice work and scrolls and decorated with holly, silver bells and small red bows.

'What a beautiful cake. It certainly puts mine into the shade,' observed Octavia, holding it up amidst the piles of packing straw. 'Even when icing sugar was plentiful, I never learnt the knack of fancy piping.'

'I like your cakes mummy with Santa standing on the path to the house with the little fir tree in the snow,' said Grace.

'Yes, your cakes always look Christmassy, darling, and it's what's inside that matters and they taste lovely. What with rationing, and one thing and another, I don't know how you manage it.'

'Thank you Jack,' she smiled as she stood up. 'Well, wasn't that a wonderful start to Christmas? Roy always was the most generous of men,' she said as she began pushing the straw back into the box leaving stray bits scattered over the mat as she placed the Christmas fayre onto the sideboard.

'Yes, it certainly was, wasn't it, girls? I think we should round the evening off with a game of Ludo and when we've finished that, it will be time for bed.' Grace and Kitty looked at him in dismay.

'Can't we stay up a bit longer, like Thomas?' they pleaded.

'The sooner you go to bed, the sooner it will be Christmas,' he answered, as he pulled out the Ludo box from the cupboard by the fire.

'Do you fancy a game with us, darling?'

'Not at the moment, Jack. I must Ewbank up the shavings, before they get carried around the house and I have a few things left to do in the kitchen for tomorrow, so I'll leave you three to it. Bed for a little boy, I think,' said Octavia taking Thomas's hand, as Jack picked up the packing box and took it out to the wash-house.

Christmas morning, Kitty had found in her pillowslip, all that she had hoped for: her favourite School Friend Annual, a jigsaw puzzle, a writing set, a small, wooden weaving loom and there was a game she had not seen before, called, Tell Me. She opened the box and spun the wheel. Beside it was a stack of cards with questions. She picked up one or two and read them. 'This is super! Can we play it after our Christmas dinner?'

'That's the general idea, Kitty.'

'Oh goody!' and was then struck by an idea. 'Instead of Capitals and Countries, you could ask us these questions instead, daddy. There's *hundreds* of them,' she said, flipping through the cards.

'A slight exaggeration, Kitty, but it is an idea.'

It had been a game devised by Jack, and had become a tradition for the long summer evenings when the children found it difficult to sleep. He and Octavia had taken to retiring early on Sundays with the wireless on for all the family to listen to the light orchestral music of Grand Hotel from their beds, and more in hope than expectation that the music would help them to sleep. And when it was finished, they played their family game of Capitals and Countries. It tested their general knowledge and was a game they loved, as Jack called out the questions and chuckled with amusement when their answers were off course. 'Booos,' issued forth from their room. 'You can do better than that. Try again!' They could hear Octavia's laughter, and giggling themselves at their mistakes, they kept score until the light faded.

'You would have made a wonderful teacher, Jack,' said Octavia as she placed her book on the bedside table and slid down onto her pillow.

He kissed her goodnight. 'Well, the opportunity never material-ised, so the next best thing is to teach our children. I want to give them a head start in their lessons, and in particular to tickle up Kitty's general knowledge. Her eleven-plus is fast coming up.'

'I do love you Jack Pengelly,' she murmured from deep in her pillow.

It *had* been one of the best Christmases, for downstairs something that she had hoped against hope for, but not really expected, was waiting; a scooter propped up against the wall of the bay window.

Kitty rose from her reverie to make herself a cup of tea and as she poured the boiled and filtered water into the kettle and stood waiting for it to boil, she gazed out of the window, lost in the memory of the Christmas Eve that had stood out above all the rest. She had awoken with a sigh of annoyance in the middle of the night for she had not meant to fall asleep. She crawled down to the end of her bed and felt for her pillowcase that crackled with exciting shapes and sizes. Darn! She had missed Octavia and Jack sneaking into their bedroom with the sacks. She slipped back under the sheets, and tossed and turned, and finally lay on her back and imagined decorating the bedroom with colourful streamers. She was on the point of drifting off when a man appeared at the foot of her bed. It was not Jack. Her heart thumped. Was she dream-ing? She blinked hard. No, he was still there, tall and slim as in the photo Octavia had shown her. It was James. She lay rigid with fright until after a moment or two of looking at her and giving her the deepest smile that she had ever seen, he faded away. Kitty who had sucked in a cold breath of fear, exhaled slowly. She was covered in goose bumps and hunted around under the sheets for her stone hot-water bottle and hugged its remaining warmth to her. It was comforting as the sounds of her heart jumping out of her chest gradually subsided. For a long time, she lay thinking of what she had seen, and an image came to her of the oak tree she liked to climb when the spring-green leaves uncurled and changed in colour with the seasons, until they dropped to earth in burnished reds and gold and were reborn again in the spring. God must be like an oak tree and we are the leaves, she thought, and with it a feeling of the most wonderful peace and happiness washed over her from her head to her toes. Never again would she be frightened of these people she saw, whom others could not, for now with a blinding clarity, she understood. Life never died but constantly renewed itself.

That same Christmas, she had happened to glance at herself in the mirror that was glowing in the darkness from the flames of the fire. The room had changed. The furniture and furnishings were dark and heavy, and decorated with swags of holly and red ribbons. A tree glimmered with candlelight and a lady dressed in fine silks and lace sat at a piano. The flicker of light fell soft on her face as her hands rippled the keys, and she smiled at a man who sat with a baby upon his knee clapping together its tiny hands. A little girl played with a china doll and toy tea service, and a boy with his train set on the carpet. It was a scene depicted thousands of times on Christmas cards, and Kitty, caught up in the love and joy that shone between them in the candlelight, watched, entranced. It was another scene for her store of cinematic pictures from the past, as she called them, and as it faded, she had wondered who they were and the kind of life they had lived in their house. Kitty sighed quietly, and thought how good it would be to share with Lawrence such memories, but although he had seemed more understanding after Verity had left, she sensed, it was more to please and pacify her than in any belief of all she told him.

She returned to her chair and sat drinking her tea with a sudden longing to hear the Cornish chatter of the family at home, to walk in through the back door, and to sit with them in the sun of the front room, talking about incidents in the church and town, and laughing at her father's anecdotes of the goings-on with the students in the mining school. It was a need that immersed her in a well of homesickness, for Lawrence, she was discovering, was controlling and possessive with a jealous streak that had shown itself at the club's Christmas party. She had been dancing with Graham, an amiable man who lived on the neighbouring rubber plantation from Bryan and Gill. At the end of the dance, Graham led her to her seat and sat beside her, continuing to regale her with amusing tales of characters who had lived in Malaya and laughing together, at once, they caught sight of Lawrence's face. It was dark with anger, and Graham hastily rose, excused himself and left her side. Lawrence came and sat with her, and on her asking what the matter was, he replied they would talk about it later. After the buffet supper was over, Lawrence offered their excuses and they left early. Kitty had seen the looks exchanged on their friends' faces and felt acutely embarrassed as he walked her quickly from the hall.

'What did you think you were doing, embarrassing me, like that?' he said, as soon as they were in their car.

Kitty was startled. 'What are you talking about?'

'Oh don't act as if you didn't know, Kitty.'

'I've no idea what you mean.'

'You were flirting with Graham I know that particular look you give to men.'

'Oh for goodness sake Lawrence. He was telling me some very funny anecdotes of people he had known in Malaya. One of them was about an unfortunate incidence that a lady had with a thunder-box. Shall I tell you?' she said, grinning with the recollection.

'I'm not interested, Kitty. The point is, I don't want to see you dancing that way with anyone again.'

Bewildered, Kitty stared at him. 'Dancing what way?'

'You know exactly what I'm talking about. It was close and intimate.'

'What! That's ridiculous. Yes, I enjoyed dancing with Graham, he's a good dancer, but it certainly wasn't in the way you're suggesting. I resent that,' Kitty snapped back as Lawrence slammed the car into gear and roared out onto the road.

Lawrence's face was set as he drove home in silence. Kitty stared ahead, terrified at his reckless speed, and in disbelief at his accusation. Later, as they lay in bed, Kitty attempted to speak of it in a calm way without the heat of temper, for she hated the hostile atmosphere and to fall asleep on bad feeling between them. 'Look Lawrence, if that's how it seemed, I'm sorry. It certainly wasn't intended. The only one I want to dance closely with, is you. You know that. And I can hardly be rude and turn friends down when I'm asked to dance, or ignore their conversation. You must see that, surely?'

Lawrence leaned over to his bedside lamp. 'I've said how I feel. If you don't understand, there's no more to be said,' and he switched off his light, leaving Kitty feeling in despair.

The incident had blighted their Christmas, and a few days later, at the club poolside, Maggie saw Kitty's bubbling exuberance had gone. She was sitting staring disconsolately at the pool as she sat down beside her.

'Wendy not here, today?'

'No, she's gone shopping in Ipoh.'

'What's the matter, Kitty? You look as if you've been shot.'

'I feel as though I have. It's Lawrence.' Her eyes were bright with unshed tears.

'Do you want to tell me about it?' Maggie asked.

Kitty hesitated. Loyalty to Lawrence conflicted with her need to talk. At times, as well as being her closest friend, she looked upon Maggie, who was several years older than herself, as a surrogate mother, someone she felt she could always confide in. Kitty took the bull by the horns and told her everything.

As Maggie listened, she saw in Kitty's eyes, the deep worry and despair. This had evidently been going on for some time. 'Look, Kitty,' she said in her soft sing-song Irish. 'Lawrence knows full well you're not the type of woman to flirt or mess around. He sounds insecure.'

'I don't know why. He's an only child and has been loved and indulged in, all his life.'

'That sounds like half the problem. He's inclined to throw a wobbly if he doesn't get his own way. I hope you don't mind me mentioning this Kitty, but I noticed he drank rather a lot at the party. That could have been the reason for his behaviour. Drink affects people in different ways.'

'Yes, I've noticed too, drink does affect him. His whole mood changes, and he becomes quite nasty.'

'It might be an idea, Kitty, to talk it out with him before it gets out of hand. It's so easy to slip into the way of having a drink to relax in the evenings. One drink leads to another. I've seen it happen to women as well as men. It's all too common out here, drinking becomes a way of life. If it affects Lawrence as you say it does, then you have to try and nip it in the bud.' She looked at Kitty apologetically. 'Sorry, I must sound like an old mother hen.'

'No. You're right. I know I must speak to Lawrence about it. I felt so embarrassed at the party and I know everyone was looking at us when he hurried me out of the hall. I don't want that to happen again,' and as she spoke, unbidden, came the thought of Terry. He would never have behaved in such a way.

The rainy season was over with storms that were unlike any Kitty had experienced at home. She would slip out of bed, charged and exhilarated as she watched the forces of the storm; the sky lit with sheet lightening that illuminated everything in a stark, eerie brilliance, the deafening overhead thunder reverberating throughout the house, the sudden savage wind bearing down the trees, the first large plops of rain that became torrential and poured down with such ferocity it bounced back off the ground and gave cool relief from the humidity, the final loud drippings of water from the trees and veranda. Today, the air was oppressive and Lawrence eyed Kitty as they sat eating their salad lunch. She was looking pale and listless. 'How do you fancy a trip to the Cameron Highlands for our anniversary darling? Bryan's company has a bungalow we could use. I think the fresh air would do you good.'

Kitty's face lit with pleasure. 'That sounds wonderful, Lawrence. I've heard a lot about it from friends. They say, it's quite like home with an Elizabethan style hotel called the Smoke House and the gardens are like our English ones.'

'Right. I'll sort out my days off with head office, and you will have to dig out our woollens and slacks. It's cold enough up there to wear them.'

'What a glorious thought!' replied Kitty, brightening at the prospect. 'It will be like a second honeymoon,' she smiled up at him as he came over and nuzzling into her neck, kissed her. 'I love you, Kitty. You know that, don't you? I hate the thought that I sometimes make you unhappy. I know I do. Forgive me.'

Kitty stood up and wound her arms around him, returning his kiss. 'As long as we love each other, Lawrence, that's all that matters.' Her heart had lifted with his words, as she watched him walk out through the veranda doors and jump into the mini-moke. This break away from home for their first anniversary would be a perfect time to speak of his drinking and bring back the closeness they seemed to have lost.

On the winding and twisting road up to the Camerons, impenetrable trees rose up above her, and Kitty was instantly reminded of the garden of Nancarrow. It seemed as if she could never quite escape the ties and memories that bound her to it. The air was becoming cooler and already Kitty was beginning to feel energised. They stopped at the roadside where a stall sold beautiful exotic butterflies from the forest, impaled in glass-fronted boxes. Kitty bought one, and immediately regretted it, thinking of the creature that had once flitted free as a bird, and was caught simply for her gratification.

Kitty shivered with the delight of stepping into the cold atmosphere of the bungalow. 'It feels just like home,' she said. That evening they lit the fire and after a simple meal, sat before the flames, with the remains of the wine, reminiscing on their wedding and honeymoon. 'One dead bottle,' said Lawrence, holding up the wine bottle. He rose to his feet. 'I'll just have a nightcap, before we go to bed.'

'No, please darling, don't have a whisky tonight.'

'Why ever not?'

'Because it always affects you so badly.'

Lawrence looked perplexed. 'I don't know what you mean.'

'You must know Lawrence that your drinking is causing problems between us. I thought that's what you meant when you asked me to forgive you.'

He frowned. 'No. I was thinking of the night we fell out over Graham.'

'That would never have happened if you hadn't had too much to drink.'

'You're talking nonsense, Kitty,' he said irritable at her criticism.

'No, I'm not. It's been noticed.' *Damn! She shouldn't have said that.*

His eyes flashed with anger. 'So, now you're talking about

me to other people?'

'No, well yes, but only with Maggie, because I was so worried about you.'

His voice rose. 'I don't expect my wife to go blabbing out our private life to all and sundry.'

Kitty kept her voice steady. 'Please Lawrence, please listen to me. I have to say this. With a glass or two of wine, you're fine, but once you mix it with spirits, your personality changes, and you say the most hurtful things, and the next day, when I try to talk about it, you've no recollection at all of what you've said. The worry is making me sick.'

He glared away from her, his breathing heavy with temper.

'I'm not saying these things to upset you. I just want us to be happy, again, and we're not, are we? Look at me, and tell me if you think we are.'

He met her gaze and was reminded of their first meeting, when her eyes held a fire that excited him. But now, he realised, the light had gone out of them, and in its place, a sadness and apprehension lurked. Is this what he was doing to Kitty? It was true, these past few months they had not been happy, and to be told that drink was the cause of it, was shattering. Kitty was the most honest person he knew, and it was clear his actions were beginning to threaten the love she had for him. He must assure her that it would never happen again. He went and held her close. 'I'm so sorry Kitty for hurting you. I promise it won't happen again, and I want you to stop me, if I start to drink more than I should.'

His admission was the calm after the storms, and as they held one another, the friction between them was gone, and that night, freed of emotional restraint, their lovemaking was abandoned and all forgiving, their love needing no words, but the balm of sleep until the morning.

Lawrence lay watching her as the sun came up, the curve of her cheek, her hair upon the pillow like a cloth of burnished gold. Her loveliness was heart catching, and she was strong, stronger in spirit than he, and, unwillingly, he acknowledged a self-indulgent weakness lay within him.

Later that day, he took her to a tea plantation where they watched the picking and drying process and the amazing speed of the Tamil women forming a packet of tea with skilful fingers folding the jacket into shape with the finishing tap of a piece of wood. 'Even a machine would have a job to keep up with those women!' said Kitty, as they came out of the shed and bought from the shop, packets of loose Cameronian tea to take back to England on their leave. 'Mum will love it. She likes her tea as strong as bark!' grinned Kitty.

He hugged her to him, laughing at the happiness that shone in her eyes, and resolved to never let that light die again. On the evening of their anniversary, they took their meal seated in a beamed nook of the Smoke House beside an open fire, and for a while, Kitty could imagine they were back in the old pub on Bodmin moor, but unlike their honeymoon, no ghosts or scenes from the past materialised. There was nothing to mar their intimacy.

The days passed quickly with walks through the woods, and sitting in a small park where young children were playing, Kitty ran to pick up a little boy who had tripped and fallen as he ran towards the slide and had begun to cry. Kitty chatted for a few minutes to his mother who came up and thanked her. Lawrence watched. Was there something wrong with him that he had no desire for squalling and messy progeny? It would give happiness to Kitty to have a child of her own, and fulfil her deepest need, and, it occurred to him, with his child, she would be wholly his.

Kitty watched the change in him as drinks were pressed upon them at the round of Christmas and New Year parties. He brushed her off when she tried to stop him – 'it was Christmas, it was New Year,' and now it was any excuse. It was beginning all over again.

Jock Henderson came to the door as Lawrence was spitting his drink-ridden venom at her. Jock saw the flush of anger in his face, as Lawrence quickly recovered himself and invited him in. Kitty on hearing the knock ran upstairs, unable to face any caller. 'It's a telegram for Kitty, Lawrence. I hope it's not bad news,' and realizing he had called at a bad moment, made his excuses and quickly left. Lawrence went upstairs to the bedroom and handed Kitty the telegram. Her body seemed to collapse within itself as she passed it to Lawrence to read.

Dad gravely ill and asking to see you. Ted will meet you at the airport. Let us know your arrangements. Mum.

Chapter Twenty-Eight

THE DAY HAD come as she had known it would with a pale brittle sun on the scattered daffodils. It held no warmth – hollow as the grief held within her. Kitty stood at the door of the church where Jack had worshipped, barely aware of the murmured voices of condolence and conscious only of the daffodils: bright beacons of light that lit up and then dimmed as the sun travelled in and out of the clouds. There was a touch at her elbow. Eyes of intense blue that were as familiar as her own, looked steadily at her. 'Hello, Kitty,' he said.

She sat with him on the long stretch of golden sand, filling her lungs with the sweet invigorating air from the sea. They talked over old times, and laughed at their escapades as children, and remembered the day she had run from him there at Gwithian, and nearly drowned.

'And do you still think your guardian angel saved you, Kitty?' he asked.

'Yes, more than ever,' she replied. 'I believe it was my twin sister. I feel she is always watching over me.'

'You had a twin *sister?*! When did you discover that?'

'When I was getting ready to leave for Malaya, mum told me. Rather late in the day, but you know how she always liked to keep things to herself. Apparently, my twin died at birth.'

'It must have been quite a shock for you.'

'You can say that again! Poor mum, she's had more than her fair share of losing people she loved, and now, dad.' Kitty swallowed hard against the painful memory.

Terry looked saddened. "I couldn't believe it, when I heard the news. I'm so dreadfully sorry this has happened. I was very fond of your dad. I used to think he understood more than he let on about you seeing ghosts. Do you still see things from the past, Kitty?'

'Yes, and the last time was pretty devastating.' Kitty revealed to him the secret of James and his daughter, Madeline, and how she had discovered the truth from Verity, and how paradoxical it was, that she, who had accused Octavia of keeping the past from her, was concealing the biggest skeleton of them all.

Terry sat in shocked silence. 'I hardly know what to say.'

'You can imagine how I felt. Before he died, I told dad about James, and he said, mum must never know, and to let sleeping dogs lie. He's right of course, but time and again, I've longed to write or ring Madeline, but out of loyalty to mum, I let it go. I can't go behind her back, it would seem like condoning James's deceit.'

'Perhaps, it's for the best Kitty, but only you can decide.'

'Yes, that's what Lawrence said.'

'He knows about everything, then?'

'It was a baptism of fire,' she said, with a wry smile, 'and even now, I think he still finds it far-fetched. He wished he could have been here to see dad before he died, but the Manager, Jock Henderson is on leave and it's against company policy to have two senior staff away over the same period, but with luck, he will be home in time for the birth. We are looking forward so much to having our baby.'

'You always wanted children. You must be very happy.'

'Yes, we are both overjoyed,' she lied, avoiding his eyes, for how could she admit the thrill of discovering she was expecting a baby was overshadowed by Lawrence's drinking. It had not stopped, and he had turned a deaf ear to her pleadings. With the arrival of the telegram of Jack's illness, the decision had crystallized in her mind, and Kitty played her one and only card. On the eve of her departure for home, she warned him, she would not be returning to Malaya, if his drinking continued. She did not intend their child to be brought up in the hostile atmosphere of his drink-ridden abuse and it was up to him now, if they were to make a fresh start. Lawrence had recognized it was no idle threat, for her honesty in their relationship would not accept less than his total commitment to herself and their child. Kitty hoped it would be the spur that he needed but was conscious that something precious had been lost, that innocence of love, and knew she would never quite recapture it again, and inside her, was a sadness she could never repair the whispered loss of Terry.

Her tears of unhappiness ran unheeded down her face. 'I can't believe dad is gone, Terry. The thought of never seeing him again, hurts so much. He would have made a wonderful granddad. Children were his life.'

'My mother said, when he knew he was going to be a grandfather, he was tickled pink.'

'Yes, I can imagine dad saying that.'

When Jack had died, it had affected Terry with the same intensity as the family, and seeing his sorrow, words sprang from her love and remorse.

'You are very dear to me, Terry. No-one can take away the love we had, and you will always be a special part of me. I regret, terribly, the hurt I caused you.'

'If you're happy with Lawrence Kitty, then I'm content.'

'I know.'

His eyes were dark and unreadable against the sun's low rays. He had been shaken when seeing her at the funeral. He had anticipated she would be distraught at the loss of Jack, but this went deeper, for her eyes were shadowed and secretive, and her spirit seemed crushed. He felt sure Lawrence was the reason, but for now, he could do nothing, but wait, as he had waited, as a boy and man. There was only Kitty.

She gave him a soft kiss on the cheek and leaned back against that same protective shoulder as she had on that day in Nancarrow when they had awakened to the first tender flowering of love. Kitty gazed out to the deceptively innocent sea beneath the blue of a celestial sky and felt the quickening of her baby inside her, like the gentle rolling of a wave. She suddenly remembered the night when she had pictured the oak and the new leaves forming — the circle of life, ever-new and everlasting. Intuitively, she knew it would be a daughter, the spirit of her twin, of Mary, living on through the continuing circle that bound Kitty to them. A dancing breeze began stroking her face with the softness of wings, playing with her golden hair aflame with the sun, and the silvered voice was in her ear.

'I am here. I am always with you.'

ABOUT THE AUTHOR

KATIE-LOUISE MERRITT was born and raised in Camborne, Cornwall. On her marriage, she lived for several years in West Africa and Malaysia, and returned to England in 1972. She now lives in Cornwall near her family and grandchildren.

Her memories of childhood, when her maiden name was Kathryn Andrews have featured in local publications, and her poems winning recognition in competitions, have been widely published. A collection of her poetry, *The Voice That Calls*, came out in 2001.